SAND DOOM

AND OTHER TALES OF ADVENTURE

SAND DOOM

AND OTHER TALES OF ADVENTURE

MURRAY LEINSTER

INTRODUCTION BY
JOHN GREGORY BETANCOURT

WILDSIDE PRESS

SAND DOOM AND OTHER TALES OF ADVENTURE

CONTENTS

INTRODUCTION

MURRAY LEINSTER.

I have always had a great fondness for this man's work. As a teenager in the 1970s, I sought out used copies of his old science fiction books, discovering such tales as *The Wailing Asteroid* (contained in this volume), *War with the Gizmos, The Mutant Weapon, The Pirates of Zan*, and many, many others. He wrote the book that became *The Time Tunnel*. According to the web site maintained by his daughter, he published 56 novels in all. Plus more than a dozen collections of his short stories.

But that was only the tip of the iceberg.

When I began collecting pulp magazines, I began seeing stories under the Leinster volume in non-science fiction pulp magazines. And the farther back in time I went, I *still* saw them. Dozens of them. In every genre imaginable. Back before there *were* science fiction pulps, Leinster was a capable author, turning out scores of stories . . . mysteries, western, detective stories, and (before it had a name as such) even science fiction.

"MURRAY LEINSTER" was the pen name of William Fitzgerald Jenkins (1896–1975) — a writer whose career spanned the first six decades of the 20th century. From mystery and adventure stories in the earliest years to science fiction in his later years, he worked steadily and at a highly professional level of craftsmanship longer than most writers of his generation.

Leinster won a Science Fiction Achievement Award — better known as the Hugo — in 1956 for his novelet "Exploration Team," and in 1995 the Sidewise Award for Alternate History took its name from his classic story, "Sidewise in Time." His last original work appeared in 1967.

Here, then, are four rare Murray Leinster stories and a complete novel, celebrating a writer whose work has definitely withstood the test of time. Four are science fiction; only "Atmosphere" — originally published in *Argosy* magazine in 1918 — is horror. And it's as creepy as they come, the product of a master storyteller at home in any genre.

Enjoy!

— John Gregory Betancourt

SAND DOOM

Bordman knew there was something wrong when the throbbing, acutely uncomfortable vibration of rocket blasts shook the ship. Rockets were strictly emergency devices, these days, so when they were used there was obviously an emergency.

He sat still. He had been reading, in the passenger lounge of the *Warlock* — a very small lounge indeed — but as a senior Colonial Survey officer he was well-traveled enough to know when things did not go right. He looked up from the bookscreen, waiting. Nobody came to explain the eccentricity of a spaceship using rockets. It would have been immediate, on a regular liner, but the *Warlock* was practically a tramp. This trip it carried just two passengers. Passenger service was not yet authorized to the planet ahead, and would not be until Bordman had made the report he was on his way to compile. At the moment, though, the rockets blasted, and stopped, and blasted again. There was something definitely wrong.

The *Warlock's* other passenger came out of her cabin. She looked surprised. She was Aletha Redfeather, an unusually lovely Amerind. It was extraordinary that a girl could be so self-sufficient on a tedious space-voyage, and Bordman approved of her. She was making the journey to Xosa II as a representative of the Amerind Historical Society, but she'd brought her own bookreels and some elaborate fancywork which — woman-fashion — she used to occupy her hands. She hadn't been at all a nuisance. Now she tilted her head on one side as she looked inquiringly at Bordman.

"I'm wondering, too," he told her, just as an especially sustained and violent shuddering of rocket-impulsion made his chair legs thutter on the floor.

There was a long period of stillness. Then another violent but much shorter blast. A shorter one still. Presently there was a half-second blast which must have been from a single rocket tube because of the mild shaking it produced. After that there was nothing at all.

Bordman frowned to himself. He'd been anticipating groundfall within a matter of hours, certainly. He'd just gone through his spec-book carefully and re-familiarized himself with the work he was to survey on Xosa II. It was a perfectly commonplace minerals-planet development, and he'd expected to clear it FE — fully established — and probably TP and NQ ratings as well, indicating that tourists were permitted and no quarantine was necessary. Considering the aridity of the planet, no bacteriological dangers could be expected to exist, and if tourists wanted to view its monstrous deserts and infernolike wind sculptures — why they should be welcome.

But the ship had used rocket drive in the planet's near vicinity. Emergency. Which was ridiculous. This was a perfectly routine sort of voyage. Its purpose was the delivery of heavy equipment — specifically a smelter — and a senior Colonial Survey officer to report the completion of primary development.

Aletha waited, as if for more rocket blasts. Presently she smiled at some thought that had occurred to her.

"If this were an adventure tape," she said humorously, "the loudspeaker would now announce that the ship had established itself in an orbit around the strange, uncharted planet first sighted three days ago, and that volunteers were wanted for a boat landing."

Bordman demanded impatiently:

"Do you bother with adventure tapes? They're nonsense! A pure waste of time!"

Aletha smiled again.

"My ancestors," she told him, "used to hold tribal dances and make medicine and boast about how many scalps they'd taken and how they did it. It was satisfying — and educational for the young. Adolescents became familiar with the idea of what we nowadays call adventure. They were partly ready for it when it came. I suspect your ancestors used to tell each other stories about hunting mammoths and such. So I think it would be fun to hear that we were in orbit and that a boat landing was in order."

Bordman grunted. There were no longer adventures. The universe was settled; civilized. Of course there were still frontier planets — Xosa II was one — but pioneers had only hardships. Not adventures.

The ship-phone speaker clicked. It said curtly:

"Notice. We have arrived at Xosa II and have established an orbit about it. A landing will be made by boat."

Bordman's mouth dropped open.

"What the devil's this?" he demanded.

"Adventure, maybe," said Aletha. Her eyes crinkled very pleasantly when she smiled. She wore the modern Amerind dress — a sign of pride in the ancestry which now implied such diverse occupations as interstellar steel construction and animal husbandry and llano-planet colonization. "If it were adventure, as the only girl on this ship I'd have to be in the landing party, lest the tedium of orbital waiting make the" — her smile widened to a grin — "the pent-up restlessness of trouble-makers in the crew —"

The ship-phone clicked again.

"Mr. Bordman. Miss Redfeather. According to advices from the ground, the ship may have to stay in orbit for a considerable time. You will accordingly be landed by boat. Will you make yourselves ready, please, and report to the boat-blister?" The voice paused and added, "Hand luggage only, please."

Aletha's eyes brightened. Bordman felt the shocked incredulity of a man accustomed to routine when routine is impossibly broken. Of course survey ships made boat landings from orbit, and colony ships let down robot hulls by rocket when there was as yet no landing grid for the handling of a ship. But never before in his experience had an ordinary freighter, on a routine voyage to a colony ready for its final degree-of-completion survey, ever landed anybody by boat.

"This is ridiculous!" said Bordman, fuming.

"Maybe it's adventure," said Aletha. "I'll pack."

She disappeared into her cabin. Bordman hesitated. Then he went into his own. The colony on Xosa II had been established two years ago. Minimum comfort conditions had been realized within six months. A temporary landing grid for light supply ships was up within a year. It had permitted stock-piling, and it had been taken down to be rebuilt as a permanent grid with every possible contingency provided for. The eight months since the last ship landing was more than enough for the building of the gigantic, spidery, half-mile-high structure which would handle this planet's interstellar commerce. There was no excuse for an emergency! A boat landing was nonsensical!

But he surveyed the contents of his cabin. Most of the cargo of the *Warlock* was smelter equipment which was to complete the outfitting of the colony. It was to be unloaded first. By the time the ship's holds were wholly empty, the smelter would be operating. The ship would wait for a full cargo of pig metal. Bordman had expected to live in this cabin while he worked on the survey he'd come to make, and to leave again with the ship.

Now he was to go aground by boat. He fretted. The only emergency equipment he could possibly need was a heat-suit. He doubted the urgency of that. But he packed some clothing for indoors, and then defiantly included his specbook and the volumes of definitive data to which specifications for structures and colonial establishments always referred. He'd get to work on his report immediately he landed.

He went out of the passenger's lounge to the boat-blister. An engineer's legs projected from the boat port. The engineer withdrew, with a strip of tape from the boat's computer. He compared it dourly with a similar strip from the ship's figurebox. Bordman consciously acted according to the best traditions of passengers.

"What's the trouble?" he asked.

"We can't land," said the engineer shortly.

He went away — according to the tradition by which ships' crews are always scornful of passengers.

Bordman scowled. Then Aletha came, carrying a not-too-heavy bag. Bordman put it in the boat, disapproving of the crampedness of the craft. But this wasn't a lifeboat. It was a landing boat. A lifeboat had Lawlor drive and could travel light-years, but in the place of rockets and rocket fuel it had air-purifiers and water-recovery units and food-stores. It couldn't land without a landing grid aground, but it could get to a civilized planet. This landing boat could land without a grid, but its air wouldn't last long.

"Whatever's the matter," said Bordman darkly, "it's incompetence somewhere!"

But he couldn't figure it out. This was a cargo ship. Cargo ships neither took off nor landed under their own power. It was too costly of fuel they would have to carry. So landing grids used local power — which did not have to be lifted — to heave ships out into space, and again used local power to draw them to ground again. Therefore ships carried fuel only for actual space-flight, which was economy. Yet landing grids had no moving parts, and while they did have to be monstrous structures they actually drew power from planetary ionospheres. So with no moving parts to break down and no possibility of the failure of a power source — landing grids couldn't fail! So there couldn't be an emergency to make a ship ride orbit around a planet which had a landing grid!

The engineer came back. He carried a mail sack full of letter-reels. He waved his hand. Aletha crawled into the landing-boat port. Bordman followed. Four people, with a little crowding, could have gotten into the little ship. Three pretty well filled it. The engineer followed them and sealed the port.

"Sealed off," he said into the microphone before him.

The exterior-pressure needle moved halfway across the dial. The interior-pressure needle stayed steady.

"All tight," said the engineer.

The exterior-pressure needle flicked to zero. There were clanking sounds. The long halves of the boat-blister stirred and opened, and abruptly the landing boat was in an elongated cup in the hull-plating, and above them there were many, many stars. The enormous disk of a nearby planet floated into view around the hull. It was monstrous and blindingly bright. It was of a tawny color, with great, irregular areas of yellow and patches of bluishness. But most of it was the color of sand. And all its colors varied in shade — some places were lighter and some darker — and over at one edge there was blinding whiteness which could not be anything but an ice cap. But Bordman knew that there was no ocean or sea or lake on all this whole planet, and the ice cap was more nearly hoarfrost than such mile-deep glaciation as would be found at the poles of a maximum-comfort world.

"Strap in," said the engineer over his shoulder. "No-gravity coming, and then rocket-push. Settle your heads."

Bordman irritably strapped himself in. He saw Aletha busy at the same task, her eyes shining. Without warning, there came a sensation of acute discomfort. It was the landing boat detaching itself from the ship and the diminishment of the ship's closely-confined artificial-gravity field. That field suddenly dropped to nothingness, and Bordman had the momentary sickish dizziness that flicked-off gravity always produces. At the same time his heart pounded unbearably in the instinctive, racial-memory reaction to the feel of falling.

Then roarings. He was thrust savagely back against his seat. His tongue tried to slide back into his throat. There was an enormous oppression on his chest. He found himself thinking panicky profanity.

Simultaneously the vision ports went black, because they were out of the shadow of the ship. The landing boat turned — but there was no sensation of centrifugal force — and they were in a vast obscurity with merely a dim phantom of the planetary surface to be seen. But behind them a blue-white sun shone terribly. Its light was warm — hot — even though it came through the polarized shielding ports.

"Did . . . did you say," panted Aletha happily — breathless because of the acceleration — "that there weren't any adventures?"

Bordman did not answer. But he did not count discomfort as an adventure.

The engineer did not look out the ports at all. He watched the screen before him. There was a vertical line across the side of the lighted disk. A blip moved downward across it, showing their height in thousands of miles. After a long time the blip reached the bottom, and the vertical line became double and another blip began to descend. It measured height in hundreds of miles. A bright spot — a square — appeared at one side of the screen. A voice muttered metallically, and suddenly seemed to shout, and then muttered again. Bordman looked out one of the black ports and saw the planet as if through smoked glass. It was a ghostly reddish thing which filled half the cosmos. It had mottlings. Its edge was curved. That would be the horizon.

The engineer moved controls and the white square moved. It went across the screen. He moved more controls. It came back to the center. The height-in-hundreds blip was at the bottom, now, and the vertical line tripled and a tens-of-miles-height blip crawled downward.

There were sudden, monstrous plungings of the landing boat. It had hit the outermost fringes of atmosphere. The engineer said words it was not appropriate for Aletha to hear. The plungings became more violent. Bordman held on — to keep from being shaken to pieces despite the straps — and stared at the murky surface of the planet. It seemed to be fleeing from them and they to be trying to overtake it. Gradually, very gradually, its flight appeared to slow. They were down to twenty miles, then.

Quite abruptly the landing boat steadied. The square spot bobbed about in the center of the astrogation screen. The engineer worked controls to steady it.

The ports cleared a little. Bordman could see the ground below more distinctly. There were patches of every tint that mineral coloring could produce. There were vast stretches of tawny sand. A little while more, and he could see the shadows of mountains. He made out mountain flanks which should have had valleys between them and other mountain flanks beyond, but they had tawny flatnesses between, instead. These, he knew, would be the sand plateaus which had been observed on this planet and which had only a still-disputed explanation. But he could see areas of glistening yellow and dirty white, and splashes of pink and streaks of ultramarine and gray and violet, and the incredible red of iron oxide covering square miles — too much to be believed.

The landing-boat's rockets cut off. It coasted. Presently the horizon tilted and all the dazzling ground below turned sedately beneath them. There came staccato instructions from a voice-speaker, which the engineer obeyed. The landing boat swung low — below the tips of giant mauve mountains with a sand plateau beyond them — and its nose went up. It stalled.

Then the rockets roared again — and now, with air about them and after a momentary pause, they were horribly loud — and the boat settled down and down upon its own tail of fire.

There was a completely blinding mass of dust and rocket fumes which cut off all sight of everything else. Then there was a crunching crash, and the engineer swore peevishly to himself. He cut the rockets again. Finally.

Bordman found himself staring straight up, still strapped in his chair. The boat had settled on its own tail fins, and his feet were higher than his head, and he felt ridiculous. He saw the engineer at work unstrapping himself. He duplicated the action, but it was absurdly difficult to get out of the chair.

Aletha managed more gracefully. She didn't need help.

"Wait," said the engineer ungraciously, "till somebody comes."

So they waited, using what had been chair backs for seats.

The engineer moved a control and the windows cleared further. They saw the surface of Xosa II. There was no living thing in sight. The ground itself was pebbles and small rocks and minor boulders — all apparently tumbled from the starkly magnificent mountains to one side. There were monstrous, many-colored cliffs and mesas, every one eaten at in the unmistakable fashion of wind-erosion. Through a notch in the mountain wall before them a strange, fan-shaped, frozen formation appeared. If such a thing had been credible, Bordman would have said that it was a flow of sand simulating a waterfall. And everywhere there was blinding brightness and the look and feel of blistering sunshine. But there was not one single leaf or twig or blade of grass. This was pure desert. This was Xosa II.

Aletha regarded it with bright eyes.

"Beautiful!" she said happily. "Isn't it?"

"Personally," said Bordman, "I never saw a place that looked less homelike or attractive."

Aletha laughed.

"My eyes see it differently."

Which was true. It was accepted, nowadays, that humankind might be one species but was many races, and each saw the cosmos in its own fashion. On Kalmet III there was a dense, predominantly Asiatic population which terraced its mountainsides for agriculture and deftly mingled modern techniques with social customs not to be found on — say — Demeter I, where there were many red-tiled stucco towns and very many olive groves. In the llano planets of the Equis cluster, Amerinds — Aletha's kin — zestfully rode over plains dotted with the descendants of buffalo and antelope and cattle brought from ancient Earth. On the oases of Rustam IV there were date palms and riding camels and much argument about what should be substituted for the direction of Mecca at the times for prayer, while wheat fields spanned provinces on Canna I and highly civilized emigrants from the continent of Africa on Earth stored jungle gums and lustrous gems in the warehouses of their spaceport city of Timbuk.

So it was natural for Aletha to look at this wind-carved wilderness otherwise than as Bordman did. Her racial kindred were the pioneers of the stars, these days. Their heritage made them less than appreciative of urban life. Their inborn indifference to heights made them the steel-construction men of the cosmos, and more than two-thirds of the landing grids in the whole galaxy had their coup-feather symbols on the key posts. But the planet government on Algonka V was housed in a three-thousand-foot white stone tepee, and the best horses known to men were raised by ranchers with bronze skins and high cheekbones on the llano planet Chagan.

Now, here, in the *Warlock's* landing boat, the engineer snorted. A vehicle came around a cliff wall, clanking its way on those eccentric caterwheels that new-founded colonies find so useful. The vehicle glittered. It crawled over tumbled boulders, and flowed over fallen scree. It came briskly toward them. The engineer snorted again.

"That's my cousin Ralph!" said Aletha in pleased surprise.

Bordman blinked and looked again. He did not quite believe his eyes. But they told the truth. The figure controlling the ground car was Indian — Amerind — wearing a breechcloth and thick-soled sandals and three streamlined feathers in a band about his head. Moreover, he did not ride in a seat. He sat astride a semi-cylindrical part of the ground car, over which a gaily-colored blanket had been thrown.

The ship's engineer rumbled disgustedly. But then Bordman saw how sane this method of riding was — here. The ground vehicle lurched and swayed and rolled and pitched and tossed as it came over the uneven ground. To sit in anything like a chair would have been foolish. A back rest would throw one forward in a frontward lurch, and give no support in case of a backward one. A sidewise tilt would tend to throw one out. Riding a ground car as if in a saddle was sense!

But Bordman was not so sure about the costume. The engineer opened the port and spoke hostilely out of it:

"D'you know there's a lady in this thing?"

The young Indian grinned. He waved his hand to Aletha, who pressed her nose against a viewport. And just then Bordman did understand the costume or lack of it. Air came in the open exit port. It was hot and desiccated. It was furnace-like!

"How, 'Letha," called the rider on the caterwheel steed. "Either dress for the climate or put on a heat-suit before you come out of there!"

Aletha chuckled. Bordman heard a stirring behind him. Then Aletha climbed to the exit port and swung out. Bordman heard a dour muttering from the engineer. Then he saw her greeting her cousin. She had slipped out of the conventionalized Amerind outfit to which Bordman was accustomed. Now she was clad as Anglo-Saxon girls dressed for beaches on the cool-temperature planets.

For a moment Bordman thought of sunstroke, with his own eyes dazzled by the still-partly-filtered sunlight. But Aletha's Amerind coloring was perfectly suited to sunshine even of this intensity. Wind blowing upon her body would cool her skin. Her thick, straight black hair was at least as good protection against sunstroke as a heat-helmet. She might feel hot, but she would be perfectly safe. She wouldn't even sunburn. But he, Bordman

He grimly stripped to underwear and put on the heat-suit from his bag. He filled its canteens from the boat's water tank. He turned on the tiny, battery-powered motors. The suit ballooned out. It was intended for short periods of intolerable heat. The motors kept it inflated — away from his skin — and cooled its interior by the evaporation of sweat plus water from its canteen tanks. It was a miniature air-conditioning system for one man, and it should enable him to endure temperatures otherwise lethal to someone with his skin and coloring. But it would use a lot of water.

He climbed to the exit port and went clumsily down the exterior ladder to the tail fin. He adjusted his goggles. He went over to the chattering young Indians, young man and girl. He held out his gloved hand.

"I'm Bordman," he said painfully. "Here to make a degree-of-completion survey. What's wrong that we had to land by boat?"

Aletha's cousin shook hands cordially.

"I'm Ralph Redfeather," he said, introducing himself. "Project engineer. About everything's wrong. Our landing grid's gone. We couldn't contact your ship in time to warn it off. It was in our gravity field before it answered, and its Lawlor drive couldn't take it away — not working because of the field. Our power, of course, went with the landing grid. The ship you came in can't get back, and we can't send a distress message anywhere, and our best estimate is that the colony will be wiped out — thirst and starvation — in six months. I'm sorry you and Aletha have to be included."

Then he turned to Aletha and said amiably:

"How's Mike Thundercloud and Sally Whitehorse and the gang in general, 'Letha?"

The *Warlock* rolled on in her newly-established orbit about Xosa II. The landing boat was aground, having removed the two passengers. It would come back. Nobody on the ship wanted to stay aground, because they knew the conditions and the situation below — unbearable heat and the complete absence of hope. But nobody had anything to do! The ship had been maintained in standard operating condition during its two-months' voyage from Trent to here. No repairs or overhaulings were needed. There was no maintenance-work to speak of. There would be only stand-by watches until something happened. There would be nothing to do on those watches. There would be off-watch time for twenty-one out of every twenty-four hours, and no purposeful activity to fill even half an hour of it. In a matter of — probably — years, the *Warlock* should receive aid. She might be towed out of her orbit to space in which the Lawlor drive could function, or the crew might simply be taken off. But meanwhile, those on board were as completely frustrated as the colony. They could not do anything at all to help themselves.

In one fashion the crewmen were worse off than the colonists. The colonists had at least the colorful prospect of death before them. They could prepare for it in their several ways. But the members of the *Warlock*'s crew had nothing ahead but tedium.

The skipper faced the future with extreme, grim distaste.

The ride to the colony was torment. Aletha rode behind her cousin on the saddle-blanket, and apparently suffered little if at all. But Bordman could only ride in the ground-car's cargo space, along with the sack of mail from the ship. The ground was unbelievably rough and the jolting intolerable. The heat was literally murderous. In the metal cargo space, the temperature reached a hundred and sixty degrees in the sunshine — and given enough time, food will cook in no more heat than that. Of course a man has been known to enter an oven and stay there while a roast was cooked, and to come out alive. But the oven wasn't throwing him violently about or bringing sun-heated — blue-white-sun heated — metal to press his heat-suit against him.

The suit did make survival possible, but that was all. The contents of its canteens gave out just before arrival, and for a short time Bordman had only sweat for his suit to work with. It kept him alive by forced ventilation, but he arrived in a state of collapse. He drank the iced salt water they gave him and went to bed. He'd get back his strength with a proper sodium level in his blood. But he slept for twelve hours straight.

When he got up, he was physically normal again, but abysmally ashamed. It did no good to remind himself that Xosa II was rated minimum-comfort class D — a blue-white sun and a mean temperature of one hundred and ten degrees. Africans could take such a climate — with night-relief quarters. Amerinds could do steel construction work in the open, protected only by insulated shoes and gloves. But Bordman could not venture out-of-doors except in a heat-suit. He couldn't stay long then. It was not a weakness. It was a matter of genetics. But he was ashamed.

Aletha nodded to him when he found the Project Engineer's office. It occupied one of the hulls in which colony-establishment materials had been lowered by rocket power. There were forty of the hulls, and they had been emptied and arranged for inter-communication in three separate communities, so that an individual could change his quarters and ordinary associates from time to time and colony fever — frantic irritation with one's companions — was minimized.

Aletha sat at a desk, busily making notes from a loose leaf volume before her. The wall behind the desk was fairly lined with similar volumes.

"I made a spectacle of myself!" said Bordman, bitterly.

"Not at all!" Aletha assured him. "It could happen to anybody. I wouldn't do too well on Timbuk."

There was no answer to that. Timbuk was essentially a jungle planet, barely emerging from the carboniferous stage. Its colonists thrived because their ancestors had lived on the shores of the Gulf of Guinea, on Earth. But Anglos did not find its climate healthful, nor would many other races. Amerinds died there quicker than most.

"Ralph's on the way here now," added Aletha. "He and Dr. Chuka were out picking a place to leave the records. The sand dunes here are terrible, you know. When an explorer-ship does come to find out what's happened to us, these buildings could be covered up completely. Any place could be. It isn't easy to pick a record-cache that's quite sure to be found."

"When," said Bordman skeptically, "there's nobody left alive to point it out. Is that it?"

"That's it," agreed Aletha. "It's pretty bad all around. I didn't plan to die just yet."

Her voice was perfectly normal. Bordman snorted. As a senior Colonial Survey officer, he'd been around. But he'd never yet known a human colony to be extinguished when it was properly equipped and after a proper pre-settlement survey. He'd seen panic, but never real cause for a matter-of-fact acceptance of doom.

There was a clanking noise outside the hulk which was the Project Engineer's headquarters. Bordman couldn't see clearly through the filtered ports. He reached over and opened a door. The brightness outside struck his eyes like a blow. He blinked them shut instantly and turned away. But he'd seen a glistening, caterwheel ground car stopping not far from the doorway.

He stood wiping tears from his light-dazzled eyes as footsteps sounded outside. Aletha's cousin came in, followed by a huge man with remarkably dark skin. The dark man wore eyeglasses with a curiously thick, corklike nosepiece to insulate the necessary metal of the frame from his skin. It would blister if it touched bare flesh.

"This is Dr. Chuka," said Redfeather pleasantly, "Mr. Bordman.

Dr. Chuka's the director of mining and mineralogy here."

Bordman shook hands with the ebony-skinned man. He grinned, showing startlingly white teeth. Then he began to shiver.

"It's like a freeze-box in here," he said in a deep voice. "I'll get a robe and be with you."

He vanished through a doorway, his teeth chattering audibly. Aletha's cousin took half a dozen deliberate deep breaths and grimaced.

"I could shiver myself," he admitted "but Chuka's really acclimated to Xosa. He was raised on Timbuk."

Bordman said curtly:

"I'm sorry I collapsed on landing. It won't happen again. I came here to do a degree-of-completion survey that should open the colony to normal commerce, let the colonists' families move in, tourists, and so on. But I was landed by boat instead of normally, and I am told the colony is doomed. I would like an official statement of the degree of completion of the colony's facilities and an explanation of the unusual points I have just mentioned."

The Indian blinked at him. Then he smiled faintly. The dark man came back, zipping up an indoor warmth-garment. Redfeather dryly brought him up to date by repeating what Bordman had just said. Chuka grinned and sprawled comfortably in a chair.

"I'd say," he remarked humorously, in that astonishingly deep-toned voice of his, "sand got in our hair. And our colony. And the landing grid. There's a lot of sand on Xosa. Wouldn't you say that was the trouble?"

The Indian said with elaborate gravity:

"Of course wind had something to do with it."

Bordman fumed.

"I think you know," he said fretfully, "that as a senior Colonial Survey officer, I have authority to give any orders needed for my work. I give one now. I want to see the landing grid — if it is still standing. I take it that it didn't fall down?"

Redfeather flushed beneath the bronze pigment of his skin. It would be hard to offend a steelman more than to suggest that his work did not stand up.

"I assure you," he said politely, "that it did not fall down."

"Your estimate of its degree of completion?"

"Eighty per cent," said Redfeather formally.

"You've stopped work on it?"

"Work on it has been stopped," agreed the Indian.

"Even though the colony can receive no more supplies until it is completed?"

"Just so," said Redfeather without expression.

"Then I issue a formal order that I be taken to the landing-grid site immediately," said Bordman angrily. "I want to see what sort of incompetence is responsible! Will you arrange it — at once?"

Redfeather said in a completely emotionless voice:

"You want to see the site of the landing grid. Very good. Immediately."

He turned and walked out into the incredible, blinding sunshine. Bordman blinked at the momentary blast of light, and then began to pace up and down the office. He fumed. He was still ashamed of his collapse from the heat during the travel from the landed rocket-boat to the colony. Therefore he was touchy and irritable. But the order he had given was strictly justifiable.

He heard a small noise. He whirled. Dr. Chuka, huge and black and spectacled, rocked back and forth in his seat, suppressing laughter.

"Now, what the devil does that mean?" demanded Bordman suspiciously. "It certainly isn't ridiculous to ask to see the structure on which the life of the colony finally depends!"

"Not ridiculous," said Dr. Chuka. "It's — hilarious!"

He boomed laughter in the office with the rounded ceiling of a remade robot hull. Aletha smiled with him, though her eyes were grave.

"You'd better put on a heat-suit," she said to Bordman.

He fumed again, tempted to defy all common sense because its dictates were not the same for everybody. But he marched away, back to the cubbyhole in which he had awakened. Angrily, he donned the heat-suit that had not protected him adequately before, but had certainly saved his life. He filled the canteens topping full — he suspected he hadn't done so the last time. He went back to the Project Engineer's office with a feeling of being burdened and absurd.

Out a filter-window, he saw that men with skins as dark as Dr. Chuka's were at work on a ground car. They were equipping it with a sun-shade and curious shields like wings. Somebody pushed a sort of caterwheel handtruck toward it. They put big, heavy tanks into its cargo space. Dr. Chuka had disappeared, but Aletha was back at work making notes from the loose-leaf volume on the desk.

"May I ask," asked Bordman with some irony, "what your work happens to be just now?"

She looked up.

"I thought you knew," she said in surprise. "I'm here for the Amerind Historical Society. I can certify coups. I'm taking coup-records for the Society. They'll go in the record-cache Ralph and Dr. Chuka are arranging, so no matter what happens to the colony, the record of the coups won't be lost."

"Coups?" demanded Bordman. He knew that Amerinds painted feathers on the key-posts of steel structures they'd built, and he knew that the posting of such "coup-marks" was a cherished privilege and undoubtedly a survival or revival of some American Indian tradition back on Earth. But he did not know what they meant.

"Coups," repeated Aletha matter-of-factly. "Ralph wears three eagle-feathers. You saw them. He has three coups. Pinions, too! He built the landing grids on Norlath and — Oh, you don't know!"

"I don't," admitted Bordman, his temper not of the best because of what seemed unnecessary condescensions on Xosa II.

Aletha looked surprised.

"In the old days," she explained, "back on Earth, if a man scalped an enemy, he counted coup. The first to strike an enemy in a battle counted coup, too — a lesser one. Nowadays a man counts coups for different things, but Ralph's three eagle-feathers mean he's entitled to as much respect as a warrior in the old days who, three separate times, had killed and scalped an enemy warrior in the middle of his own camp. And he is, too!"

Bordman grunted.

"Barbarous, I'd say!"

"If you like," said Aletha. "But it's something to be proud of — and one doesn't count coup for making a lot of money!" Then she paused and said curtly: "The word 'snobbish' fits it better than 'barbarous.' We are snobs! But when the head of a clan stands up in Council in the Big Tepee on Algonka, representing his clan, and men have to carry the ends of the feather headdress with all the coups the members of his clan have earned — why one is proud to belong to that clan!" She added defiantly, "Even watching it on a vision-screen!"

Dr. Chuka opened the outer door. Blinding light poured in. He did not enter — and his body glistened with sweat.

"Ready for you, Mr. Bordman!"

Bordman adjusted his goggles and turned on the motors of his heat-suit. He went out the door.

The heat and light outside were oppressive. He darkened the goggles again and made his way heavily to the waiting, now-shaded ground car. He noted that there were other changes beside the sunshade. The cover-deck of the cargo space was gone, and there were cylindrical riding seats like saddles in the back. The odd lower shields reached out sidewise from the body, barely above the caterwheels. He could not make out their purpose and irritably failed to ask.

"All ready," said Redfeather coldly. "Dr. Chuka's coming with us. If you'll get in here, please —"

Bordman climbed awkwardly into the boxlike back of the car. He bestrode one of the cylindrical arrangements. With a saddle on it, it would undoubtedly have been a comfortable way to cover impossibly bad terrain in a mechanical carrier. He waited. About him there were the squatty hulls of the space-barges which had been towed here by a colony ship, each one once equipped with rockets for landing. Emptied of their cargoes, they had been huddled together into the three separate, adjoining communities. There were separate living quarters and mess halls and recreation rooms for each, and any colonist lived in the community of his choice and shifted at pleasure, or visited, or remained solitary. For mental health a man has to be assured of his free will, and over-regimentation is deadly in any society. With men psychologically suited to colonize, it is fatal.

Above — but at a distance, now — there was a monstrous scarp of mountains, colored in glaring and unnatural tints. Immediately about there was raw rock. But it was peculiarly smooth, as if sand grains had rubbed over it for uncountable aeons and carefully worn away every trace of unevenness. Half a mile to the left, dunes began and went away to the horizon. The nearer ones were small, but they gained in size with distance from the mountains — which evidently affected the surface-winds hereabouts — and the edge of seeing was visibly not a straight line. The dunes yonder must be gigantic. But of course on a world the size of ancient Earth, and which was waterless save for snow-patches at its poles, the size to which sand dunes could grow had no limit. The surface of Xosa II was a sea of sand, on which islands and small continents of wind-swept rock were merely minor features.

Dr. Chuka adjusted a small metal object in his hand. It had a tube dangling from it. He climbed into the cargo space and fastened it to one of the two tanks previously loaded.

"For you," he told Bordman. "Those tanks are full of compressed air at rather high pressure — a couple of thousand pounds. Here's a reduction-valve with an adiabatic expansion feature, to supply extra air to your heat-suit. It will be pretty cold, expanding from so high a pressure. Bring down the temperature a little more."

Bordman again felt humiliated. Chuka and Redfeather, because of their races, were able to move about nine-tenths naked in the open air on this planet, and they thrived. But he needed a special refrigerated costume to endure the heat. More, they provided him with sunshades and refrigerated air that they did not need for themselves. They were thoughtful of him. He was as much out of his element, where they fitted perfectly, as he would have been making a degree-of-completion survey on an underwater project. He had to wear what was practically a diving suit and use a special air supply to survive!

He choked down the irritation his own inadequacy produced.

"I suppose we can go now," he said as coldly as he could.

Aletha's cousin mounted the control-saddle — though it was no more than a blanket — and Dr. Chuka mounted beside Bordman. The ground car got under way. It headed for the mountains.

The smoothness of the rock was deceptive. The caterwheel car lurched and bumped and swayed and rocked. It rolled and dipped and wallowed. Nobody could have remained in a normal seat on such terrain, but Bordman felt hopelessly undignified riding what amounted to a hobbyhorse. Under the sunshade it was infuriatingly like a horse on a carousel. That there were three of them together made it look even more foolish. He stared about him, trying to take his mind from his own absurdity. His goggles made the light endurable, but he felt ashamed.

"Those side-fins," said Chuka's deep voice pleasantly, "the bottom ones, make things better for you. The shade overhead cuts off direct sunlight, and they cut off the reflected glare. It would blister your skin even if the sun never touched you directly."

Bordman did not answer. The caterwheel car went on. It came to a patch of sand — tawny sand, heavily mineralized. There was a dune here. Not a big one for Xosa II. It was no more than a hundred feet high. But they went up its leeward, steeply slanting side. All the planet seemed to tilt insanely as the caterwheels spun. They reached the dune's crest, where it tended to curl over and break like a water-comber, and here the wheels struggled with sand precariously ready to fall, and Bordman had a sudden perception of the sands of Xosa II as the oceans that they really were. The dunes were waves which moved with infinite slowness, but the irresistible force of storm-seas. Nothing could resist them. Nothing!

They traveled over similar dunes for two miles. Then they began to climb the approaches to the mountains. And Bordman saw for the second time — the first had been through the ports of the landing-boat — where there was a notch in the mountain wall and sand had flowed out of it like a waterfall, making a beautifully symmetrical cone-shaped heap against the lower cliffs. There were many such falls. There was one place where there was a sand-cascade. Sand had poured over a series of rocky steps, piling up on each in turn to its very edge, and then spilling again to the next.

They went up a crazily slanting spur of stone, whose sides were too steep for sand to lodge on, and whose narrow crest had a bare thin coating of powder.

The landscape looked like a nightmare. As the car went on, wabbling and lurching and dipping on its way, the heights on either side made Bordman tend to dizziness. The coloring was impossible. The aridness, the desiccation, the lifelessness of everything about was somehow shocking. Bordman found himself straining his eyes for the merest, scrubbiest of bushes and for however stunted and isolated a wisp of grass.

The journey went on for an hour. Then there came a straining climb up a now-windswept ridge of eroded rock, and the attainment of its highest point. The ground car went onward for a hundred yards and stopped.

They had reached the top of the mountain range, and there was doubtlessly another range beyond. But they could not see it. Here, at the place to which they had climbed so effortfully, there were no more rocks. There was no valley. There was no descending slope. There was sand. This was one of the sand plateaus which were a unique feature of Xosa II. And Bordman knew, now, that the disputed explanation was the true one.

Winds, blowing over the mountains, carried sand as on other worlds they carried moisture and pollen and seeds and rain. Where two mountain ranges ran across the course of long-blowing winds, the winds eddied above the valley between. They dropped sand into it. The equivalent of trade winds, Bordman considered, in time would fill a valley to the mountain tops, just as trade winds provide moisture in equal quantity on other worlds, and civilizations have been built upon it. But —

"Well?" said Bordman challengingly.

"This is the site of the landing grid," said Redfeather.

"Where?"

"Here," said the Indian dryly. "A few months ago there was a valley here. The landing grid had eighteen hundred feet of height built. There was to be four hundred feet more — the lighter top construction justifies my figure of eighty per cent completion. Then there was a storm."

It was hot. Horribly, terribly hot, even here on a plateau at mountaintop height. Dr. Chuka looked at Bordman's face and bent down in the vehicle. He turned a stopcock on one of the air tanks brought for Bordman's necessity. Immediately Bordman felt cooler. His skin was dry, of course. The circulated air dried sweat as fast as it appeared. But he had the dazed, feverish feeling of a man in an artificial-fever box. He'd been fighting it for some time. Now the coolness of the expanded air was almost deliriously refreshing.

Dr. Chuka produced a canteen. Bordman drank thirstily. The water was slightly salted to replace salt lost in sweat.

"A storm, eh?" asked Bordman, after a time of contemplation of his inner sensations as well as the scene of disaster before him. There'd be some hundreds of millions of tons of sand in even a section of this plateau. It was unthinkable that it could be removed except by a long-time sweep of changed trade winds along the length of the valley. "But what has a storm to do —"

"It was a sandstorm," said Redfeather coldly. "Probably there was a sunspot flare-up. We don't know. But the pre-colonization survey spoke of sandstorms. The survey team even made estimates of sandfall in various places as so many inches per year. Here all storms drop sand instead of rain. But there must have been a sunspot flare because this storm blew for" — his voice went flat and deliberate because it was stating the unbelievable — "for two months. We did not see the sun in all that time. And we couldn't work, naturally. The sand would flay a man's skin off his body in minutes. So we waited it out.

"When it ended, there was this sand plateau where the survey had ordered the landing grid to be built. The grid was under it. It is under it. The top of eighteen hundred feet of steel is still buried two hundred feet down in the sand you see. Our unfabricated building-steel is piled ready for erection — under two thousand feet of sand. Without anything but stored power it is hardly practical" — Redfeather's tone was sardonic — "for us to try to dig it out. There are hundreds of millions of tons of stuff to be moved. If we could get the sand away, we could finish the grid. If we could finish the grid, we'd have power enough to get the sand away — in a few years, and if we could replace the machinery that wore out handling it. And if there wasn't another sandstorm."

He paused. Bordman took deep breaths of the cooler air. He could think more clearly.

"If you will accept photographs," said Redfeather politely, "you can check that we actually did the work."

Bordman saw the implications. The colony had been formed of Amerinds for the steel work and Africans for the labor the Amerinds were congenitally averse to — the handling of complex mining-machinery underground and the control of modern high-speed smelting operations. Both races could endure this climate and work in it — provided that they had cooled sleeping quarters. But they had to have power. Power not only to work with, but to live by. The air-cooling machinery that made sleep possible also condensed from the cooled air the minute trace of water vapor it contained and that they needed for drink. But without power they would thirst. Without the landing grid and the power it took from the ionosphere, they could not receive supplies from the rest of the universe. So they would starve.

And the *Warlock*, now in orbit somewhere overhead, was well within the planet's gravitational field and could not use its Lawlor drive to escape with news of their predicament. In the normal course of events it would be years before a colony ship capable of landing or blasting out of a planetary gravitational field by rocket-power was dispatched to find out why there was no news from Xosa II. There was no such thing as interstellar signaling, of course. Ships themselves travel faster than any signal that could be sent, and distances were so great that mere communication took enormous lengths of time. A letter sent to Earth from the Rim even now took ten years to make the journey, and another ten for a reply. Even the much shorter distances involved in Xosa II's predicament still ruled out all hope. The colony was strictly on its own.

Bordman said heavily:

"I'll accept the photographs. I even accept the statement that the colony will die. I will prepare my report for the cache Aletha tells me you're preparing. And I apologize for any affront I may have offered you."

Dr. Chuka nodded approvingly. He regarded Bordman with benign warmth. Ralph Redfeather said cordially enough:

"That's perfectly all right. No harm done."

"And now," said Bordman shortly, "since I have authority to give any orders needed for my work, I want to survey the steps you've taken to carry out those parts of your instructions dealing with emergencies. I want to see right away what you've done to beat this state of things. I know they can't be beaten, but I intend to leave a report on what you've tried!"

The *Warlock* swung in emptiness around the planet Xosa II. It was barely five thousand miles above the surface, so the mottled terrain of the dry world flowed swiftly and perpetually beneath it. It did not seem beneath, of course. It simply seemed out — away — removed from the ship. And in the ship's hull there was artificial gravity, and light, and there were the humming sounds of fans which kept the air in motion and flowing through the air apparatus. Also there was food, and adequate water, and the temperature was admirably controlled. But nothing happened. Moreover, nothing could be expected to happen. There were eight men in the crew, and they were accustomed to space-voyages which lasted from one month to three. But they had traveled a good two months from their last port. They had exhausted the visireels, playing them over and over until they were intolerable. They had read and reread all the bookreels they could bear. On previous voyages they had played chess and similar games until it was completely predictable who would beat whom in every possible contest.

Now they viewed the future with bitterness. The ship could not land, because there was no landing grid in operation on the planet below them. They could not depart, because the Lawlor drive simply does not work within five diameters of an Earth-gravity planet. Space is warped only infinitesimally by so thin a field, but a Lawlor drive needs almost perfectly unstressed emptiness if it is to take hold. They did not have fuel enough to blast out the necessary thirty-odd thousand miles against gravity. The same consideration made their lifeboats useless. They could not escape by rocket-power and their Lawlor drives, also, were ineffective.

The crew of the *Warlock* was bored. The worst of the boredom was that it promised to last without limit. They had food and water and physical comfort, but they were exactly in the situation of men sentenced to prison for an unknown but enormous length of time. There was no escape. There could be no alleviation. The prospect invited frenzy by anticipation.

A fist fight broke out in the crew's quarters within two hours after the *Warlock* had established its orbit — as a first reaction to their catastrophe. The skipper went through the ship and painstakingly confiscated every weapon. He locked them up. He, himself, already felt the nagging effect of jangling nerves. There was nothing to do. He didn't know when there would ever be anything to do. It was a condition to produce hysteria.

There was night. Outside and above the colony there were uncountable myriads of stars. They were not the stars of Earth, of course, but Bordman had never been on Earth. He was used to unfamiliar constellations. He stared out a port at the sky, and noted that there were no moons. He remembered, when he thought, that Xosa II had no moons. There was a rustling of paper behind him. Aletha Redfeather turned a page in a loose-leaf volume and painstakingly made a note. The wall behind her held many more such books. From them could be extracted the detailed history of every bit of work that had been done by the colony-preparation crews. Separate, tersely-phrased items could be assembled to make a record of individual men.

There had been incredible hardships, at first. There were heroic feats. There had been an attempt to ferry water supplies down from the pole by aircraft. It was not practical, even to build up a reserve of fluid. Winds carried sand particles here as on other worlds they carried moisture. Aircraft were abraded as they flew. The last working flier made a forced landing five hundred miles from the colony. A caterwheel expedition went out and brought the crew in. The caterwheel trucks were armored with silicone plastic, resistant to abrasion, but when they got back they had to be scrapped. There had been men lost in sudden sand-squalls, and heroic searches for them, and once or twice rescues. There had been cave-ins in the mines. There had been accidents. There had been magnificent feats of endurance and achievement.

Bordman went to the door of the hull which was Ralph Redfeather's Project Engineer office. He opened it. He stepped outside.

It was like stepping into an oven. The sand was still hot from the sunshine just ended. The air was so utterly dry that Bordman instantly felt it sucking at the moisture of his nasal passages. In ten seconds his feet — clad in indoor footwear — were uncomfortably hot. In twenty the soles of his feet felt as if they were blistering. He would die of the heat at night, here! Perhaps he could endure the outside near dawn, but he raged a little. Here where Amerinds and Africans lived and throve, he could live unprotected for no more than an hour or two — and that at one special time of the planet's rotation!

He went back in, ashamed of the discomfort of his feet and angrily letting them feel scorched rather than admit to it.

Aletha turned another page.

"Look, here!" said Bordman angrily. "No matter what you say, you're going to go back on the *Warlock* before —"

She raised her eyes.

"We'll worry about that when the time comes. But I think not. I'd rather stay here."

"For the present, perhaps," snapped Bordman. "But before things get too bad you go back to the ship! They've rocket fuel enough for half a dozen landings of the landing boat. They can lift you out of here!"

Aletha shrugged.

"Why leave here to board a derelict? The *Warlock*'s practically that. What's your honest estimate of the time before a ship equipped to help us gets here?"

Bordman would not answer. He'd done some figuring. It had been a two-month journey from Trent — the nearest Survey base — to here. The *Warlock* had been expected to remain aground until the smelter it brought could load it with pig metal. Which could be as little as two weeks, but would surprise nobody if it was two months instead. So the ship would not be considered due back on Trent for four months. It would not be considered overdue for at least two more. It would be six months before anybody seriously wondered why it wasn't back with its cargo. There'd be a wait for lifeboats to come in, should there have been a mishap in space. There'd eventually be a report of noncommunication to the Colony Survey headquarters on Canna III. But it would take three months for that report to be received, and six more for a confirmation — even if ships made the voyages exactly at the most favorable intervals — and then there should at least be a complaint from the colony. There were lifeboats aground on Xosa II, for emergency communication, and if a lifeboat didn't bring news of a planetary crisis, no crisis would be considered to exist. Nobody could imagine a landing grid failing!

Maybe in a year somebody would think that maybe somebody ought to ask around about Xosa II. It would be much longer before somebody put a note on somebody else's desk that would suggest that when, or if, a suitable ship passed near Xosa II, or if one should be available for the inquiry, it might be worth while to have the noncommunication from the planet looked into. Actually, to guess at three years before another ship arrived would be the most optimistic of estimates.

"You're a civilian," said Bordman shortly. "When the food and water run low, you go back to the ship. You'll at least be alive when somebody does come to see what's the matter here!"

Aletha said mildly:

"Maybe I'd rather not be alive. Will you go back to the ship?"

Bordman flushed. He wouldn't. But he said doggedly;

"I can order you sent on board, and your cousin will carry out the order!"

"I doubt it very much," said Aletha pleasantly.

She returned to her task.

There were crunching footsteps outside the hulk. Bordman winced a little. With insulated sandals, it was normal for these colonists to move from one part of the colony to another in the open, even by daylight. He, Bordman, couldn't take out-of-doors at night! His lips twisted bitterly.

Men came in. There were dark men with rippling muscles under glistening skin, and bronze Amerinds with coarse straight hair. Ralph Redfeather was with them. Dr. Chuka came in last of all.

"Here we are," said Redfeather. "These are our foremen. Among us, I think we can answer any questions you want to ask."

He made introductions. Bordman didn't try to remember the names. Abeokuta and Northwind and Sutata and Tallgrass and T'ckka and Spottedhorse and Lewanika T — hey were names which in combination would only be found in a very raw, new colony. But the men who crowded into the office were wholly at ease, in their own minds as well as in the presence of a senior Colonial Survey officer. They nodded as they were named, and the nearest shook hands. Bordman knew that he'd have liked their looks under other circumstances. But he was humiliated by the conditions on this planet. They were not. They were apparently only sentenced to death by them.

"I have to leave a report," said Bordman curtly — and he was somehow astonished to know that he did expect to leave a report rather than make one; he accepted the hopelessness of the colony's future — "on the degree-of-completion of the work here. But since there's an emergency, I have also to leave a report on the measures taken to meet it."

The report would be futile, of course. As futile as the coup-records Aletha was compiling, which would be read only after everybody on the planet was dead. But Bordman knew he'd write it. It was unthinkable that he shouldn't.

"Redfeather tells me," he added, again curtly, "that the power in storage can be used to cool the colony buildings — and therefore condense drinking water from the air — for just about six months. There is food for about six months. If one lets the buildings warm up a little, to stretch the fuel, there won't be enough water to drink. Go on half rations to stretch the food, and there won't be enough water to last and the power will give out anyhow. No profit there!"

There were nods. The matter had been thrashed out long before.

"There's food in the *Warlock* overhead," Bordman went on coldly, "but they can't use the landing boat more than a few times. It can't use ship fuel. No refrigeration to hold it stable. They couldn't land more than a ton of supplies all told. There are five hundred of us here. No help there!"

He looked from one to another.

"So we live comfortably," he told them with irony, "until our food and water and minimum night-comfort run out together. Anything we do to try to stretch anything is useless because of what happens to something else. Redfeather tells me you accept the situation. What are you doing — since you accept it?"

Dr. Chuka said amiably:

"We've picked a storage place for our records, and our miners are blasting out space in which to put away the record of our actions to the last possible moment. It will be sandproof. Our mechanics are building a broadcast unit we'll spare a tiny bit of fuel for. It will run twenty-odd years, broadcasting directions so it can be found regardless of how the terrain is changed by drifting sand."

"And," said Bordman, "the fact that nobody will be here to give directions."

Chuka added benignly:

"We're doing a great deal of singing, too. My people are . . . ah . . . religious. When we are . . . ah . . . no longer here . . . there have been boastings that there'll be a well-practiced choir ready to go to work in the next world."

White teeth showed in grins. Bordman was almost envious of men who could grin at such a thought. But he went on grimly:

"And I understand that athletics have also been much practiced."

Redfeather said:

"There's been time for it. Climbing teams have counted coup on all the worst mountains within three hundred miles. There's been a new record set for the javelin, adjusted for gravity constant, and Johnny Cornstalk did a hundred yards in eight point four seconds. Aletha has the records and has certified them."

"Very useful!" said Bordman sardonically. Then he disliked himself for saying it even before the bronze-skinned men's faces grew studiedly impassive.

Chuka waved his hand.

"Wait, Ralph! Lewanika's nephew will beat that within a week!"

Bordman was ashamed again because Chuka had spoken to cover up his own ill-nature.

"I take it back!" he said irritably. "What I said was uncalled for. I shouldn't have said it! But I came here to do a completion survey and what you've been giving me is material for an estimate of morale! It's not my line! I'm a technician, first and foremost! We're faced with a technical problem!"

Aletha spoke suddenly from behind him.

"But these are men, first and foremost, Mr. Bordman. And they're faced with a very human problem — how to die well. They seem to be rather good at it, so far."

Bordman ground his teeth. He was again humiliated. In his own fashion he was attempting the same thing. But just as he was genetically not qualified to endure the climate of this planet, he was not prepared for a fatalistic or pious acceptance of disaster. Amerind and African, alike, these men instinctively held to their own ideas of what the dignity of a man called upon him to do when he could not do anything but die. But Bordman's idea of his human dignity required him to be still fighting: still scratching at the eyes of fate or destiny when he was slain. It was in his blood or genes or the result of training. He simply could not, with self-respect, accept any physical situation as hopeless even when his mind assured him that it was.

"I agree," he said coldly, "but still I have to think in technical terms. You might say that we are going to die because we cannot land the *Warlock* with food and equipment. We cannot land the *Warlock* because we have no landing grid. We have no landing grid because it and all the material to complete it is buried under millions of tons of sand. We cannot make a new light-supply-ship type of landing grid because we have no smelter to make beams, nor power to run it if we had, yet if we had the beams we could get the power to run the smelter we haven't got to make the beams. And we have no smelter, hence no beams, no power, no prospect of food or help because we can't land the *Warlock*. It is strictly a circular problem. Break it at any point and all of it is solved."

One of the dark men muttered something under his breath to those near him. There were chuckles.

"Like Mr. Woodchuck," explained the man, when Bordman's eyes fell on him. "When I was a little boy there was a story like that."

Bordman said icily:

"The problem of coolness and water and food is the same sort of problem. In six months we could raise food — if we had power to condense moisture. We've chemicals for hydroponics — if we could keep the plants from roasting as they grew. Refrigeration and water and food are practically another circular problem."

Aletha said tentatively:

"Mr. Bordman"

He turned, annoyed. Aletha said almost apologetically:

"On Chagan there was a — you might call it a woman's coup given to a woman I know. Her husband raises horses. He's mad about them. And they live in a sort of home on caterwheels out on the plains — the llanos. Sometimes they're months away from a settlement. And she loves ice cream and refrigeration isn't too simple. But she has a Doctorate in Human History. So she had her husband make an insulated tray on the roof of their trailer and she makes her ice cream there."

Men looked at her. Her cousin said amusedly:

"That should rate some sort of technical-coup feather!"

"The Council gave her a brass pot — official," said Aletha. "Domestic science achievement." To Bordman she explained: "Her husband put a tray on the roof of their house, insulated from the heat of the house below. During the day there's an insulated cover on top of it, insulating it from the heat of the sun. At night she takes off the top cover and pours her custard, thin, in the tray. Then she goes to bed. She has to get up before daybreak to scrape it up, but by then the ice cream is frozen. Even on a warm night." She looked from one to another. "I don't know why. She said it was done in a place called Babylonia on Earth, many thousands of years ago."

Bordman blinked. Then he said decisively:

"Damn! Who knows how much the ground-temperature drops here before dawn?"

"I do," said Aletha's cousin, mildly. "The top-sand temperature falls forty-odd degrees. Warmer underneath, of course. But the air here is almost cool when the sun rises. Why?"

"Nights are cooler on all planets," said Bordman, "because every night the dark side radiates heat to empty space. There'd be frost everywhere every morning if the ground didn't store up heat during the day. If we prevent daytime heat-storage — cover a patch of ground before dawn and leave it covered all day — and uncover it all night while shielding it from warm winds — We've got refrigeration! The night sky is empty space itself! Two hundred and eighty below zero!"

There was a murmur. Then argument. The foremen of the Xosa II colony-preparation crew were strictly practical men, but they had the habit of knowing why some things were practical. One does not do modern steel construction in contempt of theory, nor handle modern mining tools without knowing why as well as how they work. This proposal sounded like something that was based on reason — that should work to some degree. But how well? Anybody could guess that it should cool something at least twice as much as the normal night temperature-drop. But somebody produced a slipstick and began to juggle it expertly. He astonishedly announced his results. Others questioned, and then verified it. Nobody paid much attention to Bordman. But there was a hum of absorbed discussion, in which Redfeather and Chuka were immediately included. By calculation, it astoundingly appeared that if the air on Xosa II was really as clear as the bright stars and deep day-sky color indicated, every second night a total drop of one hundred and eighty degrees temperature could be secured by radiation to interstellar space — if there were no convection-currents, and they could be prevented by —

It was the convection-current problem which broke the assembly into groups with different solutions. But it was Dr. Chuka who boomed at all of them to try all three solutions and have them ready before daybreak, so the assembly left the hulk, still disputing enthusiastically. But somebody had recalled that there were dewponds in the one arid area on Timbuk, and somebody else remembered that irrigation on Delmos III was accomplished that same way. And they recalled how it was done —

Voices went away in the ovenlike night outside. Bordman grimaced, and again said:

"Damn! Why didn't I think of that myself?"

"Because," said Aletha, smiling, "you aren't a Doctor of Human History with a horse-raising husband and a fondness for ice cream. Even so, a technician was needed to break down the problem here into really simple terms." Then she said, "I think Bob Running Antelope might approve of you, Mr. Bordman."

Bordman fumed to himself.

"Who's he? Just what does that whole comment mean?"

"I'll tell you," said Aletha, "when you've solved one or two more problems."

Her cousin came back into the room. He said with gratification:

"Chuka can turn out silicone-wool insulation, he says. Plenty of material, and he'll use a solar mirror to get the heat he needs. Plenty of temperature to make silicones! How much area will we need to pull in four thousand gallons of water a night?"

"How do I know?" demanded Bordman. "What's the moisture-content of the air here, anyhow?" Then he said vexedly, "Tell me! Are you using heat-exchangers to help cool the air you pump into the buildings, before you use power to refrigerate it? It would save some power —"

The Indian project engineer said absorbedly:

"Let's get to work on this! I'm a steel man myself, but —"

They settled down. Aletha turned a page.

The *Warlock* spun around the planet. The members of its crew withdrew into themselves. In even two months of routine tedious voyaging to this planet, there had been the beginnings of irritation with the mannerisms of other men. Now there would be years of it. At the beginning, every man tended to become a hermit so that he could postpone as long as possible the time when he would hate his shipmates. Monotony was already so familiar that its continuance was a foreknown evil. The crew of the *Warlock* already knew how intolerable they would presently be to each other, and the foreknowledge tended to make them intolerable now.

Within two days of its establishment in orbit, the *Warlock* was manned by men already morbidly resentful of fate; with the psychology of prisoners doomed to close confinement for an indeterminate but ghastly period. On the third day there was a second fist fight. A bitter one.

Fist fights are not healthy symptoms in a spaceship which cannot hope to make port for a matter of years.

Most human problems are circular and fall apart when a single trivial part of them is solved. There used to be enmity between races because they were different, and they tended to be different because they were enemies, so there was enmity — The big problem of interstellar flight was that nothing could travel faster than light, and nothing could travel faster than light because mass increased with speed, and mass increased with speed — obviously! — because ships remained in the same time-slot, and ships remained in the same time-slot long after a one-second shift was possible because nobody realized that it meant traveling faster than light. And even before there was interstellar travel, there was practically no interplanetary commerce because it took so much fuel to take off and land. And it took more fuel to carry the fuel to take off and land, and more still to carry the fuel for that, until somebody used power on the ground for heave-off instead of take-off, and again on the ground for landing. And then interplanetary ships carried cargoes. And on Xosa II there was an emergency because a sandstorm had buried the almost completed landing grid under some megatons of sand, and it couldn't be completed because there was only storage power because it wasn't completed, because there was only storage power because —

But it took three weeks for the problem to be seen as the ultimately simple thing it really was. Bordman had called it a circular problem, but he hadn't seen its true circularity. It was actually — like all circular problems — inherently an unstable set of conditions. It began to fall apart when he saw that mere refrigeration would break its solidity.

In one week there were ten acres of desert covered with silicone-wool-felt in great strips. By day a reflective surface was uppermost, and at sundown caterwheel trucks hooked on to towlines and neatly pulled it over on its back, to expose gridded black-body surfaces to the starlight. And the gridding was precisely designed so that winds blowing across it did not make eddies in the grid-squares, and the chilled air in those pockets remained undisturbed and there was no conduction of heat downward by eddy currents, while there was admirable radiation of heat out to space. And this was in the manner of the night sides of all planets, only somewhat more efficient.

In two weeks there was a water yield of three thousand gallons per night, and in three weeks more there were similar grids over the colony houses and a vast roofed cooling-shed for pre-chilling of air to be used by the refrigeration systems themselves. The fuel-store — stored power — was thereupon stretched to three times its former calculated usefulness. The situation was no longer a simple and neat equation of despair.

Then something else happened. One of Dr. Chuka's assistants was curious about a certain mineral. He used the solar furnace that had made the silicone wool to smelt it. And Dr. Chuka saw him. And after one blank moment he bellowed laughter and went to see Ralph Redfeather. Whereupon Amerind steel-workers sawed apart a robot hull that was no longer a fuel tank because its fuel was gone, and they built a demountable solar mirror some sixty feet across — which African mechanics deftly powered — and suddenly there was a spot of incandescence even brighter than the sun of Xosa II, down on the planet's surface. It played upon a mineral cliff, and monstrous smells developed and even the African mining-technicians put on goggles because of the brightness, and presently there were threads of molten metal and slag trickling — and separating as they trickled — hesitantly down the cliffside.

And Dr. Chuka beamed and slapped his sweating thighs, and Bordman went out in a caterwheel truck, wearing a heat-suit, to watch it for all of twenty minutes. When he got back to the Project Engineer's office he gulped iced salt water and dug out the books he'd brought down from the ship. There was the specbook for Xosa II, and there were the other volumes of definitions issued by the Colonial Survey. They were definitions of the exact meanings of terms used in briefer specifications, for items of equipment sometimes ordered by the Colony Office.

*****

When Chuka came into the office, presently, he carried the first crude pig of Xosa II iron in his gloved hand. He gloated. Bordman was then absent, and Ralph Redfeather worked feverishly at his desk.

"Where's Bordman?" demanded Chuka in that resonant bass voice of his. "I'm ready to report for degree-of-completion credit that the mining properties on Xosa II are prepared as of today to deliver pig iron, cobalt, zirconium and beryllium in commercial quantities! We require one day's notice to begin delivery of metal other than iron at the moment, because we're short of equipment, but we can furnish chromium and manganese on two days' notice — the deposits are farther away."

He dumped the pig of metal on the second desk, where Aletha sat with her perpetual loose-leafed volumes before her. The metal smoked and began to char the desk-top. He picked it up again and tossed it from one gloved hand to the other.

"There y'are, Ralph!" he boasted. "You Indians go after your coups! Match this coup for me! Without fuel and minus all equipment except of our own making — I credit an assist on the mirror, but that's all — we're set to load the first ship that comes in for cargo! Now what are you going to do for the record? I think we've wiped your eye for you!"

Ralph hardly looked up. His eyes were very bright. Bordman had shown him and he was copying feverishly the figures and formulae from a section of the definition book of the Colonial Survey. The books started with the specifications for antibiotic growth equipment for colonies with problems in local bacteria. It ended with definitions of the required strength-of-material and the designs stipulated for cages in zoos for motile fauna, subdivided into flying, marine, and solid-ground creatures: sub-sub-divided into carnivores, herbivores, and omnivores, with the special specifications for enclosures to contain abyssal creatures requiring extreme pressures, and the equipment for maintaining a healthfully re-poisoned atmosphere for creatures from methane planets.

Redfeather had the third volume open at, "Landing Grids, Lightest Emergency, Commerce Refuges, For Use Of." There were some dozens of non-colonized planets along the most-traveled spaceways on which refuges for shipwrecked spacemen were maintained. Small forces of Patrol personnel manned them. Space lifeboats serviced them. They had the minimum installations which could draw on their planets' ionospheres for power, and they were not expected to handle anything bigger than a twenty-ton lifeboat. But the specifications for the equipment of such refuges were included in the reference volumes for Bordman's use in the making of Colonial surveys. They were compiled for the information of contractors who wanted to bid on Colonial Survey installations, and for the guidance of people like Bordman who checked up on the work. So they contained all the data for the building of a landing grid, lightest emergency, commerce refuge for use of, in case of need. Redfeather copied feverishly.

Chuka ceased his boasting, but still he grinned.

"I know we're stuck, Ralph," he said amiably, "but it's nice stuff to go in the records. Too bad we don't keep coup-records like you Indians!"

Aletha's cousin — Project Engineer — said crisply:

"Go away! Who made your solar mirror? It was more than an assist! You get set to cast beams for us! Girders! I'm going to get a lifeboat aloft and away to Trent! Build a minimum size landing grid! Build a fire under somebody so they'll send us a colony ship with supplies! If there's no new sandstorm to bury the radiation refrigerators Bordman brought to mind, we can keep alive with hydroponics until a ship can arrive with something useful!"

Chuka stared.

"You don't mean we might actually live through this! Really?"

Aletha regarded the two of them with impartial irony.

"Dr. Chuka," she said gently, "you accomplished the impossible. Ralph, here, is planning to attempt the preposterous. Does it occur to you that Mr. Bordman is nagging himself to achieve the inconceivable? It is inconceivable, even to him, but he's trying to do it!"

"What's he trying to do?" demanded Chuka, wary but amused.

"He's trying," said Aletha, "to prove to himself that he's the best man on this planet. Because he's physically least capable of living here! His vanity's hurt. Don't underestimate him!"

"He the best man here?" demanded Chuka blankly. "In his way he's all right. The refrigeration proves that! But he can't walk out-of-doors without a heat-suit!"

Ralph Redfeather said dryly, without ceasing his feverish work:

"Nonsense, Aletha. He has courage. I give him that. But he couldn't walk a beam twelve hundred feet up. In his own way, yes. He's capable. But the best man —"

"I'm sure," agreed Aletha, "that he couldn't sing as well as the worst of your singing crew, Dr. Chuka, and any Amerind could outrun him. Even I could! But he's got something we haven't got, just as we have qualities he hasn't. We're secure in our competences. We know what we can do, and that we can do it better than any —" her eyes twinkled — "paleface. But he doubts himself. All the time and in every way. And that's why he may be the best man on this planet! I'll bet he does prove it!"

Redfeather said scornfully:

"You suggested radiation refrigeration! What does it prove that he applied it?"

"That," said Aletha, "he couldn't face the disaster that was here without trying to do something about it — even when it was impossible. He couldn't face the deadly facts. He had to torment himself by seeing that they wouldn't be deadly if only this one or that or the other were twisted a little. His vanity was hurt because nature had beaten men. His dignity was offended. And a man with easily-hurt dignity won't ever be happy, but he can be pretty good!"

Chuka raised his ebony bulk from the chair in which he still shifted the iron pig from gloved hand to gloved hand.

"You're kind," he said, chuckling. "Too kind! I don't want to hurt his feelings. I wouldn't, for the world! But really . . . I've never heard a man praised for his vanity before, or admired for being touchy about his dignity! If you're right . . . why . . . it's been convenient. It might even mean hope. But . . . hm-m-m — Would you want to marry a man like that?"

"Great Manitou forbid!" said Aletha firmly. She grimaced at the bare idea. "I'm an Amerind. I'll want my husband to be contented. I want to be contented along with him. Mr. Bordman will never be either happy or content. No paleface husband for me! But I don't think he's through here yet. Sending for help won't satisfy him. It's a further hurt to his vanity. He'll be miserable if he doesn't prove himself — to him-self — a better man than that!"

Chuka shrugged his massive shoulders. Redfeather tracked down the last item he needed and fairly bounced to his feet.

"What tonnage of iron can you get out, Chuka?" he demanded. "What can you do in the way of castings? What's the elastic modulus — how much carbon in this iron? And when can you start making cast-ings? Big ones?"

"Let's go talk to my foremen," said Chuka complacently. "We'll see how fast my . . . ah . . . mineral spring is trickling metal down the cliff-face. If you can really launch a lifeboat, we might get some help here in a year and a half instead of five —"

They went out-of-doors together. There was a small sound in the next office. Aletha was suddenly very, very still. She sat motionless for a long half-minute. Then she turned her head.

"I owe you an apology, Mr. Bordman," she said ruefully. "It won't take back the discourtesy, but — I'm very sorry."

Bordman came into the office from the next room. He was rather pale. He said wryly:

"Eavesdroppers never hear good of themselves, eh? Actually I was on the way in here when I heard — references to myself it would embarrass Chuka and your cousin to know I heard. So I stopped. Not to listen, but to keep them from knowing I'd heard their private opin-ions of me. I'll be obliged if you don't tell them. They're entitled to their opinions of me. I've mine of them." He added grimly, "Apparently I think more highly of them than they do of me!"

Aletha said contritely:

"It must have sounded horrible! But they . . . we . . . all of us think better of you than you do of yourself!"

Bordman shrugged.

"You in particular. 'Would you marry someone like me? Great Manitou, no!'"

"For an excellent reason," said Aletha firmly. "When I get back from here — *if* I get back from here — I'm going to marry Bob Running Antelope. He's nice. I like the idea of marrying him. I want to! But I look forward not only to happiness but to contentment. To me that's important. It isn't to you, or to the woman you ought to marry. And I . . . well . . . I simply don't envy either of you a bit!"

"I see," said Bordman with irony. He didn't. "I wish you all the contentment you look for." Then he snapped: "But what's this business about expecting more from me? What spectacular idea do you expect me to pull out of somebody's hat now? Because I'm frantically vain!"

"I haven't the least idea," said Aletha calmly. "But I think you'll come up with something we couldn't possibly imagine. And I didn't say it was because you were vain, but because you are discontented with yourself. It's born in you! And there you are!"

"If you mean neurotic," snapped Bordman, "you're all wrong. I'm not neurotic! I'm not. I'm annoyed. I'll get hopelessly behind schedule because of this mess! But that's all!"

Aletha stood up and shrugged her shoulders ruefully.

"I repeat my apology," she told him, "and leave you the office. But I also repeat that I think you'll turn up something nobody else expects — and I've no idea what it will be. But you'll do it now to prove that I'm wrong about how your mind works."

She went out. Bordman clamped his jaws tightly. He felt that especially haunting discomfort which comes of suspecting that one has been told something about himself which may be true.

"Idiotic!" he fumed, all alone. "Me neurotic? Me wanting to prove I'm the best man here out of vanity?" He made a scornful noise. He sat impatiently at the desk. "Absurd!" he muttered wrathfully. "Why should I need to prove to myself I'm capable? What would I do if I felt such a need, anyhow?"

Scowling, he stared at the wall. It was irritating. It was a nagging sort of question. What would he do if she were right? If he did need constantly to prove to himself —

He stiffened, suddenly. A look of intense surprise came upon his face. He'd thought of what a self-doubtful, discontented man would try to do, here on Xosa II at this juncture.

The surprise was because he had also thought of how it could be done.

The *Warlock* came to life. Her skipper gloomily answered the emergency call from Xosa II. He listened. He clicked off the communicator and hastened to an exterior port, deeply darkened against those times when the blue-white sun of Xosa shone upon this side of the hull. He moved the manual control to make it more transparent. He stared down at the monstrous, tawny, mottled surface of the planet five thousand miles away. He searched for the spot he bitterly knew was the colony's site.

He saw what he'd been told he'd see. It was an infinitely fine, threadlike projection from the surface of the planet. It rose at a slight angle — it leaned toward the planet's west — and it expanded and widened and formed an extraordinary sort of mushroom-shaped object that was completely impossible. It could not be. Humans do not create visible objects twenty miles high, which at their tops expand like toadstools on excessively slender stalks, and which drift westward and fray and grow thin, and are constantly renewed.

But it was true. The skipper of the *Warlock* gazed until he was completely sure. It was no atomic bomb, because it continued to exist. It faded, but was constantly replenished. There was no such thing!

He went through the ship, bellowing, and faced mutinous snarlings. But when the *Warlock* was around on that side of the planet again, the members of the crew saw the strange appearance, too. They examined it with telescopes. They grew hysterically happy. They went frantically to work to clear away the signs of a month and a half of mutiny and despair.

It took them three days to get the ship to tidiness again, and during all that time the peculiar tawny jet remained. On the sixth day the jet was fainter. On the seventh it was larger than before. It continued larger. And telescopes at highest magnification verified what the emergency communication had said.

Then the crew began to experience frantic impatience. It was worse, waiting those last three or four days, than even all the hopeless time before. But there was no reason to hate anybody, now. The skipper was very much relieved.

There was eighteen hundred feet of steel grid overhead. It made a crisscross, ring-shaped wall more than a quarter-mile high and almost to the top of the surrounding mountains. But the valley was not exactly a normal one. It was a crater, now: a steeply sloping, conical pit whose walls descended smoothly to the outer girders of the red-painted, glistening steel structure. More girders for the completion of the grid projected from the sand just outside its half-mile circle. And in the landing grid there was now a smaller, elaborate, truss-braced object. It rested on the rocky ground, and it was not painted, and it was quite small. A hundred feet high, perhaps, and no more than three hundred across. But it was visibly a miniature of the great, now-uncovered, re-painted landing grid which was qualified to handle interstellar cargo ships and all the proper space-traffic of a minerals-colony planet.

A caterwheel truck came lurching and rolling and rumbling down the side of the pit. It had a sunshade and ground-reflector wings, and Bordman rode tiredly on a hobbyhorse saddle in its back cargo section. He wore a heat-suit.

The truck reached the pit's bottom. There was a tool shed there. The caterwheel-truck bumped up to it and stopped. Bordman got out, visibly cramped by the jolting, rocking, exhausting-to-unaccustomed-muscles ride.

"Do you want to go in the shed and cool off?" asked Chuka brightly.

"I'm all right," said Bordman curtly. "I'm quite comfortable, so long as you feed me that expanded air." It was plain that he resented needing even a special air supply. "What's all this about? Bringing the *Warlock* in? Why the insistence on my being here?"

"Ralph has a problem," said Chuka blandly. "He's up there. See? He needs you. There's a hoist. You've got to check degree-of-completion anyhow. You might take a look around while you're up there. But he's anxious for you to see something. There where you see the little knot of people. The platform."

Bordman grimaced. When one was well started on a survey, one got used to heights and depths and all sorts of environments. But he hadn't been up on steel-work in a good many months. Not since a survey on Kalka IV nearly a year ago. He would be dizzy at first.

He accompanied Chuka to the spot where a steel cable dangled from an almost invisibly thin beam high above. There was a strictly improvised cage to ascend in — planks and a handrail forming an insecure platform that might hold four people. He got into it, and Dr. Chuka got in beside him. Chuka waved his hand. The cage started up.

Bordman winced as the ground dropped away below. It was ghastly to be dangling in emptiness like this. He wanted to close his eyes. The cage went up and up and up. It took many long minutes to reach the top.

There was a platform there. Newly-made. The sunlight was blindingly bright. The landscape was an intolerable glare. Bordman adjusted his goggles to maximum darkness and stepped gingerly from the swaying cage to the hardly more solid-seeming area. Here he was in mid-air on a platform barely ten feet square. It was rather more than twice the height of a metropolitan skyscraper from the ground. There were actual mountain-crests only half a mile away and not much higher. Bordman was acutely uncomfortable. He would get used to it, but —

"Well?" he asked fretfully. "Chuka said you needed me here. What's the matter?"

Ralph Redfeather nodded very formally. Aletha was here, too, and two of Chuka's foremen — one did not look happy — and four of the Amerind steel-workers. They grinned at Bordman.

"I wanted you to see," said Aletha's cousin, "before we threw on the current. It doesn't look like that little grid could handle the sand it took care of. But Lewanika wants to report."

A dark man who worked under Chukaan — d looked as if he belonged on solid ground — said carefully:

"We cast the beams for the small landing grid, Mr. Bordman. We melted the metal out of the cliffs and ran it into molds as it flowed down."

He stopped. One of the Indians said:

"We made the girders into the small landing grid. It bothered us because we built it on the sand that had buried the big grid. We didn't understand why you ordered it there. But we built it."

The second dark man said with a trace of swagger:

"We made the coils, Mr. Bordman. We made the small grid so it would work the same as the big one when it was finished. And then we made the big grid work, finished or not!"

Bordman said impatiently:

"All right. Very good. But what is this? A ceremony?"

"Just so," said Aletha, smiling. "Be patient, Mr. Bordman!"

Her cousin said conversationally:

"We built the small grid on the top of the sand. And it tapped the ionosphere for power. No lack of power then! And we'd set it to heave up sand instead of ships. Not to heave it out into space, but to give it up to mile a second vertical velocity. Then we turned it on."

"And we rode it down, that little grid," said one of the remaining Indians, grinning. "What a party! Manitou!"

Redfeather frowned at him and took up the narrative.

"It hurled the sand up from its center. As you said it would, the sand swept air with it. It made a whirlwind, bringing more sand from outside the grid into its field. It was a whirlwind with fifteen mega-kilowatts of power to drive it. Some of the sand went twenty miles high. Then it made a mushroom-head and the winds up yonder blew it to the west. It came down a long way off, Mr. Bordman. We've made a new dune-area ten miles downwind. And the little grid sank as the sand went away from around it. We had to stop it three times, because it leaned. We had to dig under parts of it to get it straight up again. But it went down into the valley."

Bordman turned up the power to his heat-suit motors. He felt uncomfortably warm.

"In six days," said Ralph, almost ceremonially, "it had uncovered half the original grid we'd built. Then we were able to modify that to heave sand and to let it tap the ionosphere. We were able to use a good many times the power the little grid could apply to sand-lifting! In two days more the landing grid was clear. The valley bottom was clean. We shifted some hundreds of millions of tons of sand by landing grid, and now it is possible to land the *Warlock*, and receive her supplies, and the solar-power furnace is already turning out pigs for her loading. We wanted you to see what we have done. The colony is no longer in danger, and we shall have the grid completely finished for your inspection before the ship is ready to return."

Bordman said uncomfortably:

"That's very good. It's excellent. I'll put it in my survey report."

"But," said Ralph, more ceremonially still, "we have the right to count coup for the members of our tribe and clan. Now —"

Then there was confusion. Aletha's cousin was saying syllables that did not mean anything at all. The other Indians joined in at intervals, speaking gibberish. Aletha's eyes were shining and she looked incredibly pleased and satisfied.

"But what . . . what's this?" demanded Bordman when they stopped.

Aletha spoke proudly.

"Ralph just formally adopted you into the tribe, Mr. Bordman — and into his clan and mine! He gave you a name I'll have to write down for you, but it means, 'Man-who-believes-not-his-own-wisdom.' And now —"

Ralph Redfeatherli — censed interstellar engineer, graduate of the stiffest technical university in this quarter of the galaxy, wearer of three eagle-pinion feathers and clad in a pair of insulated sandals and a breechcloth — whipped out a small paint-pot and a brush from somewhere and began carefully to paint on a section of girder ready for the next tier of steel. He painted a feather on the metal.

"It's a coup," he told Bordman over his shoulder. "Your coup. Placed where it was earned — up here. Aletha is authorized to certify it. And the head of the clan will add an eagle-feather to the headdress he wears in council in the Big Tepee on Algonka, and — your clan-brothers will be proud!"

Then he straightened up and held out his hand.

Chuka said benignly:

"Being civilized men, Mr. Bordman, we Africans do not go in for uncivilized feathers. But we . . . ah . . . rather approve of you, too. And we plan a corroboree at the colony after the Warlock is down, when there will be some excellently practiced singing. There is . . . ah . . . a song, a sort of choral calypso, about this . . . ah . . . adventure you have brought to so satisfying a conclusion. It is quite a good calypso. It's likely to be popular on a good many planets."

Bordman swallowed. He was acutely uncomfortable. He felt that he ought to say something, and he did not know what.

But just then there was a deep-toned humming in the air. It was a vibrant tone, instinct with limitless power. It was the eighteen-hundred-foot landing grid, giving off that profoundly bass and vibrant, note it uttered while operating. Bordman looked up.

The *Warlock* was coming down.

ATMOSPHERE

It was all in the atmosphere. People don't take incredible revenges in civilized places. Anywhere else in the world the thing would have been impossible.

The heat and the sun, combined with the neat, well-kept horror across the water, with a background of riotous green, and waves constantly plashing gently against the shore, made an atmosphere in which strange things occurred. If it hadn't been for the horror we saw every time we looked across the water, the whole affair I'm going to tell you about would never have happened.

That thing got on our nerves and rendered us unfit for sober thought or intelligent action. It was the leper village of Molokai. Our little settlement was just back from the beach that faced the small iron wharf of the Molokai village. We could see the road leading down to the wharf, the neat, sanitary, comfortable houses, and if we took glasses to it we could sometimes see figures moving about.

We did not take glasses. Every one of us had at one time or another been to Molokai and see the things that live there. I'll not try to describe them to you. Kipling once said something about men with mildew on their faces. London once wrote a story in which all the people were lepers; a woman, full-breasted, mature, well-formed, with no face; a man who struck out with a hand which had no fingers. Those were appetizing beside some of the things on Molokai.

Mind you, I'm not criticizing the colony. The creatures are probably better looked after there than they would be anywhere else, and they can't pass on their disease to clean people. They have comfortable cottages, their food is supplied them, with little occupations to pass the time, and so on. I even believe they have organized a band.

Molokai hasn't anything really, to do with my story. It was the fact that we could see it by looking across the water, and the effect of having it constantly before our eyes and minds, that makes me tell you about it.

Once a month a boat came to the wharf across the way and dropped foot and supplies — perhaps another patient or two. We would sit on the veranda of Colin Drew's house and watch it. Drew's was a sort of club for us, you understand. We never spoke of Molokai. About six o'clock in the evening we'd begin to gather at Drew's. We'd have drinks, and smoke, and possibly play cards or pool, then scatter for dinner, and come back again afterward unless one or two of us had to stay at home to write up reports, or something of that sort that had to be done.

Our gathering was a regular nightly affair. We chipped in for the drinks, and considered that our company paid Drew fro the use of his house and servants. There is no doubt it did. When there are no other white men but a Spaniard who has "gone native" within thirty miles, four men who will come to one's house night after night are god-sends.

We made a regular society circle. Because the heat and sun rendered us irritable, we were nearly always polite. We knew each other far too well to need to stand on ceremony anywhere else; but with the sun broiling out our brains all day, the hot calm for an hour after sunset until the see breeze came, and Molokai across the way, we had to be careful.

You don't know how irritable a man can be until you've ridden about for hours in a hot sun that threatens to fry your brains inside your skull, then gone to an office and labored over figures and reports, and above all, striven with the stupidity of natives. Mental work in hot climates is damnable.

We were polite until the sea breeze came. When the palms began to sigh — they always got the breeze a little before we did — we would sigh, too, with relief, and relax. The best stories and the keenest talk always came after the sea breeze set in.

We never mentioned the horror across the way. Before sundown we could see it plainly, and after dark we could still see the twinkle of lights, but we never spoke of it. Perhaps that was why it rode our nerves so badly.

Drew was more inclined to overdo the drinking than the rest of us. I think that was because his house was nearest the beach and he had to see more of Molokai than we did.

It did get on his nerves badly. The doctors say leprosy is found among people who eat fish, particularly raw fish. Drew, after he heard that, would no eat fish at all. He had been through the settlement twice and it had gripped his imagination.

I remember one time we were all sitting on his veranda, sipping our drinks and waiting for the breeze. The sun had just set, and dusk was not yet over. The boat had been tied up at the wharf at Molokai all the afternoon, and we saw a white plume of steam shoot up. The whistle was being blown.

The sound did not reach us because of the distance, but we saw the boat swing away from the wharf, begin to forge ahead, and then she steamed off. We did not speak, but presently I heard Drew whisper to himself in an unconsciously horrified fashion:

"There are people being left behind to become things!"

I glanced sharply at him. He was staring across the water with a fascinated gaze. As I looked, he jerked his eyes away. Stealthily, he reached out his fingers and touched the lighted tip of his cigarette lying on the table by his hand.

What for?

It was a sign of blue funk. The first, absolutely the first symptom of leprosy is anesthesia at the tips of the fingers and toes — loss of sensation in the fingertips. Drew, with no cause but panic, was testing his sensation.

After anesthesia comes a tiny whitening or silvering of the skin at the tips of the fingers, and then the darkening of a band of skin across the forehead. That last gives a peculiar expression to the face. It's call the leonine look, I believe.

When I saw Drew deliberately burn his finger with his cigarette to assure himself that he was absolutely safe, I had a moment of fright. I waited until the others had left and hinted that he'd better take a vacation. He said he would. He admitted that he needed it, but he did not. Instead, be began to make love to Maria.

Maria was the daughter of Don José.

It's odd how some forms cling to one. This man had married a native woman, lived in a native hut, though he seemed to have plenty of money, and dressed himself almost like a native, yet he still trimmed his beard in a jaunty imperial and still expected to be given the courtesy of a don.

We gave it to him. He had been a gentleman. Maria showed his blood in her carriage.

She hardly looked like a *hapa-haole* — a half-breed. Her skin was dark, but no darker than many a Spanish señora of the greatest pretensions to blue blood. Her hair was black, but it was a fine, delicately spun hair that hung in soft masses instead of coarse bunches of the wholly native girls.

We white men left her alone. One does not marry a *hapa-haole* girl in Hawaii if one can help it. As they are often startlingly pretty, the best plan is to avoid them, to keep the temptation away, unless they are of the sort that one needn't marry.

Maria was distinctly not of this last class. Her father had been a gentleman, and Maria was a lady. You saw it instantly, the way she walked, the way she moved her hands, in the very inflection of her voice. Drew should have left her alone. As I said, one does not marry a *hapa-haole*, and Maria was too fine to regard as less than a girl to marry.

It may be that I put the objection to marriage with Maria too strongly. White men may marry *hapa-haoles*; they have done so, and they do it even now; but it is horribly uncomfortable for everyone concerned. Of course, if one loves the girl enough it's another matter; but a common-place romance would not last the ostracism of the wholly white people, and a gentleman would hardly care to make the average *hapa-haole* society his own.

I dare say Drew loved Maria in his way. She was the daintiest, dearest little creature you ever saw when she was fifteen. I hadn't seen much of her after she came back from school, however.

Did I mention that her father seemed to have what even we whites would have considered plenty of money? I don't believe I saw Maria on more than half a dozen occasions between the time she was fifteen, when she used to swim with the native children, until the last time anyone saw her, which I'm going to tell you about.

Her love for Drew must have been a quick, hot-blooded passion, sprung up in a moment and complete within the hour. Sometimes we hear about love at first sight. That's absurd, of course. But love may burst through the barrier of ignorance in an instant.

Maria had been seeing Drew at intervals for months. His work brought him into closer contact with her father than that of any of the rest of us. He must have seen Maria and talked idly with her as he did with any number of native girls. She must have been talking with him as she would chat with any of us, quite ignorant of emotion lying in wait. And then, in an instant —

You can't conceive of the full tide of passion until you've seen no woman that you consider as other than natives for month, and then suddenly realize that you love one of them. It's amazing and almost unbelievable, the overpowering longing that comes over one.

It came to me once. Luckily for both the girl and myself, I was transferred from that station almost as soon as I found I loved her. Drew had no such luck.

What I am telling you I learned later. They met under the tall palms by the beach, where it jutted out and formed a small peninsula. They would sit side by side, with the waves breaking before them, the long palm fronds above them moving back and forth in mysterious fashion, stirred by the sea breeze. Behind them all was mystery and shadow. They talked of love.

Of course it was all very improper, but what would you have done? Consider Maria's position, the only girl of her kind. The native young men were far beneath her, the rest of us avoided her for her own good as well as our own, and when one of the only men she could possibly consider as a companion of any sort showed interest in her, what could she do? Have him come to her home?

You do not know what a native hut is like. Maria lived in one. I will not go into details, but I assure you that for the reception of a European making a social call upon a young lady, they leave many things to be desired.

So Maria met Drew out on the peninsula. They talked. They loved. The waves broke at their feet: the palms rustled overhead. There was darkness and mystery behind them — and they were in love.

If Don José had not been a European, the thing might have been arranged. If Maria had not been a lady the thing might still have been arranged. If Drew had been decent, there would never have been any difficulty.

Natives do not gossip — if orders are given with sufficient authority. I repeat that the whole thing could have been settled in some way if any of three things had not been; that Don José was a European, and had been a gentleman; that Maria was a lady, and that Drew was a cad. He proved this last conclusively when Maria made a discovery and told him of it. He broke with her immediately, instead of seeing her through her difficulty.

Drew's absences while his affair with Maria had been goin on had pretty thoroughly disorganized things. We gathered at night as usual, but felt vaguely uncomfortable because one of us was missing. The talk was fragmentary, unsatisfying. Then Drew broke with Maria and came back to us.

The first night he rejoined us after the break was not a propitious one for the complete restoration of the old order of things. A storm was forming somewhere, and the electric tension in the air intensified our normal weariness at the end of the day.

Because of the storm, wherever it was, the sea breeze failed us. We sat on Drew's veranda, sipping our lukewarm drinks, sweating, waiting for the breeze that never came, and listening to the damp flopping of an occasional palm-frond.

We were silent because experience had taught us to keep our mouths shut at times like this. Anything might result in a quarrel. With nothing whatever to annoy us, and simply because of the atmosphere, we felt anger stirring. The stillness, every man holding himself in check, fighting against a peevishness he knew came from sheer nervous strain, was an irritation in itself.

Suddenly Drew slammed his fist down on the table. His quarrel with Maria must have upset him badly, and the hot, still electric air had completed the job.

"Damn it," he cried sharply, his voice a trifle thin, "I can't stand this! It's —"

In an irritated and peevish chorus we spoke to him adjuring him to shut up. We were all on edge. The whining discontent of his voice provoked me. Heat does unholy things to a man's nerves.

A native boy ran up to the steps with a note. Drew took it and crumpled it in his hand while he stared fretfully at us for a moment. The interruption had in a measure relieved the tension, however, and we relapsed into silence.

Drew red the note and his face when white. "Listen," he said.

"Dear Señor Drew:

My daughter Maria is dead. Will you please come to me? I need someone of my own race near. If one or two of the other gentlemen will come, too, please have them do so.

"I dare ask this for the friendship I have received from all of them. I am heartbroken. Please some quickly.

"José Felipe Gomez."

Drew stared at us. Even in the lamplight we could see the ghastly expression on his face. In fretful silence we rose, and all five of us prodded distastefully down the road toward Don José's hut.

He was waiting for us before the door. When we came he shook hands with each of us in turn and led the way inside. He had put candles about a sort of pallet in the center of the room, on which was an object covered with a cloth.

"My daughter," said Don José, with an air of calm grief, indicating the bier.

Drew hesitatingly asked how she had come to die.

"She stabbed herself," said Don José, looking quietly at Drew.

Drew blanched even whiter, and began to pick at his nails furtively. Something is the stealthiness of his movements reminded me of the time I had seen him burn himself with his cigarette.

That had been in a rush of causeless fright about Molokai. He seemed to have forgotten Molokai since then. It weighed on the minds of the rest of us just as before, but still, according to our tacit etiquette, we never spoke of it.

Don José drew out a small piece of paper.

"I wish to read you," he said in a rather hard voice, "her last message to me."

He read. Maria had written in a weary strain that she had loved too well; that disgrace was coming upon her; that she had died rather than cause her father dishonor.

"Dishonor!" said Don José, and smiled very bitterly. For the first time I wondered what his story was.

I could not see, at first, the object in his telling us what Maria had said, of publishing her disgrace; but then I understood. Drew looked utterly crushed and absolutely ghastly.

"I know," said Don José, "that Maria would never have loved one of the Hawaiians. It must have been one of you gentlemen."

He knew, of course, that it was Drew. We waited for him to kill Drew. In our mental state it would have seem the logical thing to do, and none of us would have tried to stop him.

Don José went on:

"For the benefit of that gentleman I have something to say; something that Maria herself did not know. Some time ago I made a discovery which I had not yet broken to her. I considered my duty, however, and communicated with the proper persons."

Don José stood there, quiet and well-mannered, and in eight words he took his revenge for the death of Maria.

"My daughter was to go to Molokai tomorrow."

He lifted the cloth that covered the bier and raised one of the hands underneath. The tips of the fingers were just beginning to show silvery, like the scales of a fish.

Wasn't that a perfect revenge? Don José had put ashes on Maria's fingertips to whiten them. No, of course Maria wasn't a leper. Don José explained the whole thing to me the day after Drew went made from fear.

ATTENTION SAINT PATRICK.

President O'Hanrahan of the planetary government of Eire listened unhappily to his official guest. He had to, because Sean O'Donohue was chairman of the Dail — of Eire on Earth — Committee on the Condition of the Planet Eire. He could cut off all support from the still-struggling colony if he chose. He was short and opinionated, he had sharp, gimlet eyes, he had bristling white hair that once had been red, and he was the grandfather of Moira O'Donohue, who'd traveled to Eire with him on a very uncomfortable spaceship. That last was a mark in his favor, but now he stood four-square upon the sagging porch of the presidential mansion of Eire, and laid down the law.

"I've been here three days." he told the president sternly, while his granddaughter looked sympathetic, "and I'm of the opinion that there's been shenanigans goin' on to keep this fine world from becomin' what it was meant for — a place for the people of Eire on Earth to emigrate to when there was more of them than Erin has room for. Which is now!"

"We've had difficulties —" began the president uneasily.

"This world should be ready!" snapped Sean O'Donohue accusingly. "It should be waitin' for the Caseys and Bradys and Fitzpatricks and other fine Erse people to move to and thrive on while the rest of the galaxy goes to pot with its new-fangled notions. That's the reason for this world's very existence. What set aside Erin on Earth, where our ancestors lived an' where their descendants are breathin' down each other's necks because there's so many of them? There was no snakes there! St. Patrick drove them out. What sets this world apart from all the other livable planets men have put down their smelly spaceships on? There's no snakes here! St. Patrick has great influence up in Heaven. He knew his fine Erse people would presently need more room than there was on Earth for them. So he'd a world set aside, and marked by the sign that no least trace of a serpent could exist on it. No creature like the one that blarneyed Mother Eve could be here! No —"

"Our trouble's been dinies," began the president apologetically.

But he froze. Something dark and sinuous and complacent oozed around the corner of the presidential mansion. The president of Eire sweated. He recognized the dark object. He'd believed it safely put away in pleasant confinement until the Dail Committee went away. But it wasn't. It was Timothy, the amiable six-foot black snake who faithfully and cordially did his best to keep the presidential mansion from falling down. Without him innumerable mouse-sized holes, gnawed by mouse-sized dinies, would assuredly have brought about its collapse. The president was grateful, but he'd meant to keep Timothy out of sight. Timothy must have escaped and as a faithful snake, loyal to his duty, he'd wriggled straight back to the presidential mansion.

Like all Eire, he undoubtedly knew of the pious tradition that St. Patrick had brought the snakes to Eire, and he wasn't one to let St. Patrick down. So he'd returned and doubtless patrolled all the diny tunnels in the sagging structure. He'd cleaned out any miniature, dinosaurlike creatures who might be planning to eat some more nails. He now prepared to nap, with a clear conscience. But if Sean O'Donohue saw him — !

Perspiration stood out on President O'Hanrahan's forehead. The droplets joined and ran down his nose.

"It's evident," said the chairman of the Dail Committee, with truculence, "that we're a pack of worthless, finagling' and maybe even Protestant renegades from the ways an' the traditions of your fathers! There is been shenanigans goin' on! I'll find 'em!"

The president could not speak, with Timothy in full view. But then what was practically a miracle took place. A diny popped out of a hole in the turf. He looked interestedly about. He was all of three inches long, with red eyes and a blue tail, and in every proportion he was a miniature of the extinct dinosaurs of Earth. But he was an improved model. The dinies of Eire were fitted by evolution — or Satan — to plague human settlers. They ate their crops, destroyed their homes, devoured their tools, and when other comestibles turned up they'd take care of them, too.

This diny surveyed its surroundings. The presidential mansion looked promising. The diny moved toward it. But Timothy — nap plans abandoned — flung himself at the diny like the crack of a whip. The diny plunged back into its hole. Timothy hurtled after it in pursuit. He disappeared.

The president of Eire breathed. He'd neglected that matter for some minutes, it seemed. He heard a voice continuing, formidably:

"And I know ye'll try to hide the shenanigans that've destroyed all the sacrifices Earth's made to have Eire a true Erse colony, ready for Erse lads and colleens to move to and have room for their children and their grandchildren too. I know ye'll try! But unless I do find out — not another bit of help will this colony get from Earth! No more tools! No more machinery that ye can't have worn out! No more provisions that ye should be raisin' for yourselves! Your cold-storage plant should be bulgin' with food! It's near empty! It will not be refilled! And even the ship that we pay to have stop here every three months, for mail — no ship!"

"It's the dinies," said the president feebly. "They're a great trouble to us, sir. They're our great handicap."

"Blather and nonsense!" snapped Sean O'Donohue. "They're no bigger than mice! Ye could've trapped 'em! Ye could've raised cats! Don't tell me that fancy-colored little lizards could hinder a world especially set aside by the intercession of St. Patrick for the Erse people to thrive on! The token's plain! There's no snakes! And with such a sign to go by, there must've been shenanigans goin' on to make things go wrong! And till those shenanigans are exposed an' stopped — there'll be no more help from Earth for ye blaggards!"

He stamped his way into the presidential mansion. The door slammed shut. Moira, his granddaughter, regarded the president with sympathy. He looked bedraggled and crushed. He mopped his forehead. He did not raise his eyes to her. It was bad enough to be president of a planetary government that couldn't even pay his salary, so there were patches in his breeches that Moira must have noticed. It was worse that the colony was, as a whole, entirely too much like the remaining shanty areas in Eire back on Earth. But it was tragic that it was ridiculous for any man on Eire to ask a girl from Earth to join him on so unpromising a planet.

He said numbly:

"I'll be wishing you good morning, Moira."

He moved away, his chin sunk on his breast. Moira watched him go. She didn't seem happy. Then, fifty yards from the mansion, a luridly colored something leaped out of a hole. It was a diny some eight inches long, in enough of a hurry to say that something appalling was after it. It landed before the president and took off again for some far horizon. Then something sinuous and black dropped out of a tree upon it and instantly violent action took place in a patch of dust. A small cloud arose. The president watched, with morbid interest, as the sporting event took place.

Moira stared, incredulous. Then, out of the hole from which the diny had leaped, a dark round head appeared. It could have been Timothy. But he saw that this diny was disposed of. That was that. Timothy — if it was Timothy — withdrew to search further among diny tunnels about the presidential mansion.

Half an hour later the president told the solicitor general of Eire about it. He was bitter.

"And when it was over, there was Moira starin' dazed-like from the porch, and the be-damned snake picked up the diny it'd killed and started off to dine on it in private. But I was in the way. So the snake waited, polite, with the diny in its mouth, for me to move on. But it looked exactly like he'd brought over the diny for me to admire, like a cat'll show dead mice to a person she thinks will be interested!"

"Holy St. Patrick!" said the solicitor general, appalled. "What'll happen now?"

"I reason," said the president morbidly, "she'll tell her grandfather, and he'll collar somebody and use those gimlet eyes on him and the poor *omadhoum* will blurt out that on Eire here it's known that St. Patrick brought the snakes and is the more reverenced for it. And that'll mean there'll be no more ships or food or tools from Earth, and it'll be lucky if we're evacuated before the planet's left abandoned."

The solicitor general's expression became one of pure hopelessness.

"Then the jig's up," he said gloomily. "I'm thinkin', Mr. President, we'd better have a cabinet meeting on it."

"What's the use," demanded the president. "I won't leave! I'll stay here, alone though I may be. There's nothing left in life for me anywhere, but at least, as the only human left on Eire I'll be able to spend the rest of my years knockin' dinies on the head for what they've done!" Then, suddenly, he bellowed. "Who let loose the snakes! I'll have his heart's blood —"

The Chancellor of the Exchequer peered around the edge of the door into the cabinet meeting room. He saw the rest of the cabinet of Eire assembled. Relieved, he entered. Something stirred in his pocket and he pulled out a reproachful snake. He said:

"Don't be indignant, now! You were walkin' on the public street. If Sean O'Donohue had seen you —" He added to the other members of the cabinet: "The other two members of the Dail Committee seem to be good, honest, drinkin' men. One of them now — the shipbuilder I think it was — wanted a change of scenery from lookin' at the bottom of a glass. I took him for a walk. I showed him a bunch of dinies playin' leapfrog tryin' to get one of their number up to a rain spout so he could bite off pieces and drop 'em down to the rest. They were all colors and it was quite somethin' to look at. The committeeman — good man that he is! — staggered a bit and looked again and said grave that whatever of evil might be said of Eire, nobody could deny that its whisky had imagination!"

He looked about the cabinet room. There was a hole in the baseboard underneath the sculptured coat of arms of the colony world. He put the snake down on the floor beside the hole. With an air of offended dignity, the snake slithered into the dark opening.

"Now — what's the meeting for?" he demanded. "I'll tell you immediate that if money's required it's impractical."

President O'Hanrahan said morbidly:

"'Twas called, it seems, to put the curse o' Cromwell on whoever let the black snakes loose. But they'd been cooped up, and they knew they were not keepin' the dinies down, and they got worried over the work they were neglectin'. So they took turns diggin', like prisoners in a penitentiary, and presently they broke out and like the faithful creatures they are they set anxious to work on their backlog of diny-catchin'. Which they're doin'. They've ruined us entirely, but they meant well."

The minister of Information asked apprehensively: "What will O'Donohue do when he finds out they're here?"

"He's not found out — yet," said the president without elation. "Moira didn't tell him. She's an angel! But he's bound to learn. And then if he doesn't detonate with the rage in him, he'll see to it that all of us are murdered — slowly, for treason to the Erse and blasphemy directed at St. Patrick." Then the president said with a sort of yearning pride: "D'ye know what Moira offered to do? She said she'd taken biology at college, and she'd try to solve the problem of the dinies. The darlin'!"

"Bein' gathered together," observed the chief justice, "we might as well try again to think of somethin' plausible."

"We need a good shenanigan," agreed the president unhappily. "But what could it be? Has anybody the trace of an idea?"

The cabinet went into session. The trouble was, of course, that the Erse colony on Eire was a bust. The first colonists built houses, broke ground, planted crops — and encountered dinies. Large ones, fifty and sixty feet long, with growing families. They had thick bodies with unlikely bony excrescences, they had long necks which ended in very improbable small heads, and they had long tapering tails which would knock over a man or a fence post or the corner of a house, impartially, if they happened to swing that way. They were not bright.

That they ate the growing crops might be expected, though cursed. But they ate wire fences. The colonists at first waited for them to die of indigestion. But they digested the fences. Then between bales of more normal foodstuffs they browsed on the corrugated-iron roofs of houses. Again the colonists vengefully expected dyspepsia. They digested the roofs, too. Presently the lumbering creatures nibbled at axes — the heads, not the handles. They went on to the plows. When they gathered sluggishly about a ground-car and began to lunch on it, the colonists did not believe. But it was true.

The dinies' teeth weren't mere calcium phosphate, like other beasts. An amateur chemist found out that they were an organically deposited boron carbide, which is harder than any other substance but crystallized carbon — diamond. In fact, diny teeth, being organic, seemed to be an especially hard form of boron carbide. Dinies could chew iron. They could masticate steel. They could grind up and swallow anything but tool-steel reinforced with diamond chips. The same amateur chemist worked it out that the surface soil of the planet Eire was deficient in iron and ferrous compounds. The dinies needed iron. They got it.

The big dinies were routed by burning torches in the hands of angry colonists. When scorched often enough, their feeble brains gathered the idea that they were unwelcome. They went lumbering away.

They were replaced by lesser dinies, approximately the size of kangaroos. They also ate crops. They also hungered for iron. To them steel cables were the equivalent of celery, and they ate iron pipe as if it were spaghetti. The industrial installations of the colony were their special targets. The colonists unlimbered guns. They shot the dinies. Ultimately they seemed to thin out. But once a month was shoot-a-diny day on Eire, and the populace turned out to clear the environs of their city of Tara.

Then came the little dinies. Some were as small as two inches in length. Some were larger. All were cute. Colonists' children wanted to make pets of them until it was discovered that miniature they might be, but harmless they were not. Tiny diny-teeth, smaller than the heads of pins, were still authentic boron carbide. Dinies kept as pets cheerily gnawed away wood and got at the nails of which their boxes were made. They ate the nails.

Then, being free, they extended their activities. They and their friends tunneled busily through the colonists' houses. They ate nails. They ate screws. They ate bolts, nuts, the nails out of shoes, pocket knives and pants buttons, zippers, wire staples and the tacks out of upholstery. Gnawing even threads and filings of metal away, they made visible gaps in the frames and moving parts of farm tractors.

Moreover, it appeared that their numbers previously had been held down by the paucity of ferrous compounds in their regular diet. The lack led to a low birth rate. Now, supplied with great quantities of iron by their unremitting industry, they were moved to prodigies of multiplication.

The chairman of the Dail Committee on the Condition of the Planet Eire had spoken of them scornfully as equal to mice. They were much worse. The planetary government needed at least a pied piper or two, but it tried other measures. It imported cats. Descendants of the felines of Earth still survived, but one had only to look at their frustrated, neurotic expressions to know that they were failures. The government set traps. The dinies ate their springs and metal parts. It offered bounties for dead dinies. But the supply of dinies was inexhaustible, and the supply of money was not. It had to be stopped.

Then upon the spaceport of Eire a certain Captain Patrick Brannicut, of Boston, Earth, descended. It was his second visit to Eire. On the first he'd learned of the trouble. On his second he brought what still seemed the most probable solution. He landed eighteen hundred adult black snakes, two thousand teen-agers of the same species, and two crates of soft-shelled eggs he guaranteed to hatch into fauna of the same kind. He took away all the cash on the planet. The government was desperate.

But the snakes chased dinies with enthusiasm. They pounced upon dinies while the public watched. They lay in wait for dinies, they publicly digested dinies, and they went pouring down into any small hole in the ground from which a diny had appeared or into which one vanished. They were superior to traps. They did not have to be set or emptied. They did not need bait. They were self-maintaining and even self-reproducing — except that snakes when overfed tend to be less romantic than when hungry. In ten years a story began — encouraged by the Ministry of Information — to the effect that St. Patrick had brought the snakes to Eire, and it was certain that if they didn't wipe out the dinies, they assuredly kept the dinies from wiping out the colony. And the one hope of making Eire into a splendid new center of Erse culture and tradition — including a reverence for St. Patrick — lay in the belief that some day the snakes would gain a permanent upper hand.

Out near the spaceport there was an imported monument to St. Patrick. It showed him pointing somewhere with his bishop's staff, while looking down at a group of snakes near his feet. The sculptor intended to portray St. Patrick telling the snakes to get the hell out of Eire. But on Eire it was sentimentally regarded as St. Patrick telling the snakes to go increase and multiply.

But nobody dared tell that to Sean O'Donohue! It was past history, in a way, but also it was present fact. On the day of the emergency cabinet meeting it was appalling fact. Without snakes the planet Eire could not continue to be inhabited, because of the little dinies. But the Republic of Eire on Earth would indignantly disown any colony that had snakes in it. And the colony wasn't ready yet to be self-supporting. The cabinet discussed the matter gloomily. They were too dispirited to do more. But Moira — the darlin' — did research.

It was strictly college-freshman-biology-lab research. It didn't promise much, even to her. But it gave her an excuse to talk anxiously and hopefully to the president when he took the Dail Committee to McGillicuddy Island to look at the big dinies there, while the populace tried to get the snakes out of sight again.

Most of the island lay two miles off the continent named for County Kerry back on Earth. At one point a promontory lessened the distance greatly, and at one time there'd been a causeway there. It had been built with great pains, and with pains destroyed.
The president explained as the boat bearing the committee neared the island.

"The big dinies," he said sadly, "trampled the fences and houses and ate up the roofs and tractors. It could not be borne. They could be driven away with torches, but they came back. They could be killed, but the people could only dispose of so many tons of carcasses. Remember, the big males run sixty feet long, and the most girlish females run forty. You wouldn't believe the new-hatched babies! They were a great trial, in the early days!"

Sean O'Donohue snorted. He bristled. He and the other two of the committee had been dragged away from the city of Tara. He suspected shenanigans going on behind his back. They did. His associates looked bleary-eyed. They'd been treated cordially, and they were not impassioned leaders of the Erse people, like the O'Donohue. One of them was a ship builder and the other a manufacturer of precision machinery, elected to the Dail for no special reason. They'd come on this junket partly to get away from their troubles and their wives. The shortage of high-precision tools was a trouble to both of them, but they were forgetting it fully.

"So the causeway was built," explained President O'Hanrahan. "We drove the big beasts over, and rounded up all we could find —

drivin' them with torches — and then we broke down the causeway. So there they are on McGillicuddy Island. They don't swim."

The boat touched ground — a rocky, uninviting shore. The solicitor general and the Chancellor of the Exchequer hopped ashore. They assisted the committee members to land. They moved on. The president started to follow but Moira said anxiously:

"Wait a bit. I've something to tell you. I . . . said I'd experiment with the dinies. I did. I learned something."

"Did you now?" asked the president. His tone was at once admiration and despair. "It's a darlin' you are, Moira, but —"

"I . . . wondered how they knew where iron was," said Moira hopefully, "and I found out. They smell it."

"Ah, they do, do they!" said the president with tender reverence. "But I have to tell you, Moira, that —"

"And I proved it!" said Moira, searching his face with her eyes. "If you change a stimulus and a specimen reacts, then its reaction is to the change. So I made the metal smell stronger."

President O'Hanrahan blinked at her.

"I . . . heated it," said Moira. "You know how hot metal smells. I heated a steel hairpin and the dinies came out of holes in the wall, right away! The smell drew them. It was astonishing!"

The president looked at her with a strange expression.

"That's . . . that's all I had time to try," said Moira. "It was yesterday afternoon. There was an official dinner. I had to go. You remember! So I locked up the dinies —"

"Moira darlin'," said President O'Hanrahan gently, "you don't lock up dinies. They gnaw through steel safes. They make tunnels and nests in electric dynamos. You don't lock up dinies, darlin'!"

"But I did!" she insisted. "They're still locked up. I looked just before we started for here!"

The president looked at her very unhappily.

"There's no need for shenanigans between us, Moira!" Then he said: "Couldn't ye be mistaken? Keepin' dinies locked up is like bottlin' moonlight or writin' down the color of Moira O'Donohue's eyes or —" He stopped. "How did ye do it?"

"The way you keep specimens," she told him. "When I was in college we did experiments on frogs. They're cold-blooded just like dinies. If you let them stay lively, they'll wear themselves out trying to get away. So you put them in a refrigerator. In the vegetable container. They don't freeze there, but they do . . . get torpid. They just lay still till you let them warm up again. To room temperature."

The president of the planet Eire stared. His mouth dropped open. He blinked and blinked and blinked. Then he whooped. He reached forward and took Moira into his arms. He kissed her thoroughly.

"Darlin'!" he said in a broken voice. "Sit still while I drive this boat back to the mainland! I've to get back to Tara immediate! You've done it, my darlin', you've done it, and it's a great day for the Irish!

It's even a great day for the Erse! It's your birthday will be a planetary holiday long after we're married and our grandchildren think I'm as big a nuisance as your grandfather Sean O'Donohue! It's a fine grand marriage we'll be havin' —"

He kissed her again and whirled the boat about and sent it streaking for the mainland. From time to time he whooped. Rather more frequently, he hugged Moira exuberantly. And she tended to look puzzled, but she definitely looked pleased.

Behind them, of course, the Committee of the Dail on the Condition of the Planet Eire explored McGillicuddy Island. They saw the big dinies — sixty-footers and fifty-footers and lesser ones. The dinies ambled aimlessly about the island. Now and again they reached up on elongated, tapering necks with incongruously small heads on them, to snap off foliage that looked a great deal like palm leaves. Now and again, without enthusiasm, one of them stirred the contents of various green-scummed pools and apparently extracted some sort of nourishment from it. They seemed to have no intellectual diversions. They were not interested in the visitors, but one of the committee members — not Moira's grandfather — shivered a little.

"I've dreamed about them," he said plaintively, "but even when I was dreamin' I didn't believe it!"

Two youthful dinies — they would weigh no more than a couple of tons apiece — engaged in languid conflict. They whacked each other with blows which would have destroyed elephants. But they weren't really interested. One of them sat down and looked bored. The other sat down. Presently, reflectively, he gnawed at a piece of whitish rock. The gnawing made an excruciating sound. It made one's flesh crawl. The diny dozed off. His teeth had cut distinct, curved grooves in the stone. The manufacturer of precision machinery — back on Earth — turned pale.

"L-let's get out of here!"

The committee and the two members of the cabinet returned to the shore. There was no boat. It was far away, headed for the mainland.

"Shenanigans!" said Sean O'Donohue in a voice that would have curdled sulphuric acid. "I warned him no shenanigans! The dirty young bog-trotter's left us here to be eaten up by the beasts!"

The solicitor general said hastily: "Divvil a bit of it, sir. We're his friends and he left us in the same boat — no, he left us out of the same boat. It must've been that something important occurred to him —"

But it was not convincing. It seemed highly unconvincing, later, because some long-delayed perception produced a reaction in the dinies' minuscule brains. They became aware of their visitors. They appeared, in a slow-motion fashion, to become interested in them. Slowly, heavily, numbly, they congregated about them — the equivalent of a herd of several hundred elephants of all the colors of the rainbow, with small heads wearing plaintive but persistent expressions. Long necks reached out hopefully.

"The devil!" said the Chancellor of the Exchequer, fretfully. "I'm just thinkin'. You've iron in your shoes and mainsprings in your watches and maybe pocket knives in your pockets. The dinies have a longin' for iron, and they go after it. They'll eat anything in the world that's got the barest bit of a taste of iron in it! Oh, it's perfectly all right, of course, but ye'll have to throw stones at them till the boat comes back. Better, find a good stout stick to whack them with. Only don't let 'em get behind ye!"

"Ye will?" roared the solicitor general, vengefully. "Take that!" *Whack!* "Tryin' to take somethin' out of the gentleman's hip pocket an' aimin' to grab the rump beyond it just to make sure!"

Whack! A large head moved plaintively away. But another reached hopefully forward, and another. The dinies were not bright. The three committeemen and two members of the cabinet were thigh-deep in water when the boat came back. They still whacked valorously if wearily at intrusive diny heads. They still had made no progress in implanting the idea that the dinies should go away.

The men from the mainland hauled them into the boat. They admitted that the president had returned to Tara. Sean O'Donohue concluded that he had gone back to supervise some shenanigans. He had. On the way to the mainland Sean O'Donohue ground his teeth. On arrival he learned that the president had taken Moira with him. He ground his teeth. "Shenanigans!" he cried hoarsely. "After him!" He stamped his feet. His fury was awe-inspiring. When the ground-car drivers started back to Tara, Sean O'Donohue was a small, rigid embodiment of raging death and destruction held only temporarily in leash.

On the way, even his companions of the committee were uneasy. But one of them, now and again, brought out a small piece of whitish rock and regarded it incredulously. It was not an unusual kind of rock. It was ordinary milky quartz. But it had tooth marks on it. Some diny, at some time, had gnawed casually upon it as if it were soft as cheese.

Faint cheering could be heard in the distance as the ground-cars carrying the committee neared the city of Tara. To those in the vehicles, it seemed incredible that anybody should dare to rejoice within at least two light-years of Sean O'Donohue as he was at this moment. But the cheering continued. It grew louder as the cars entered a street where houses stood side by side. But there came a change in the chairman of the Dail Committee, too.

The cars slowed because the pavement was bad to nonexistent. Trees lined the way. An overhanging branch passed within two yards of Moira's grandfather. Something hung on it in a sort of graceful drapery. It was a black snake. On Eire! Sean O'Donohue saw it. It took no notice of him. It hung comfortably in the tree and looked with great interest toward the sounds of enthusiasm.

The deathly pallor of Sean O'Donohue changed to pale lavender. He saw another black snake. It was climbing down a tree trunk with a purposeful air, as if intending to look into the distant uproar. The ground-cars went on, and the driver of the lead car swerved automatically to avoid two black snakes moving companionably along together toward the cheering. One of them politely gave the ground-car extra room, but paid no other attention to it. Sean O'Donohue turned purple.

Yet another burst of cheering. The chairman of the Dail Committee almost, but not quite, detonated like a fission bomb. The way ahead was blocked by people lining the way on a cross street. The cars beeped, and nobody heard them. With stiff, jerky motions Sean O'Donohue got out of the enforcedly stopped car. It had seemed that he could be no more incensed, but he was. Within ten feet of him a matronly black snake moved along the sidewalk with a manner of such assurance and such impeccable respectability that it would have seemed natural for her to be carrying a purse.

Sean O'Donohue gasped once. His face was then a dark purple. He marched blindly into the mob of people before him. Somehow, the people of Tara gave way. But the sides of this cross street were crowded. Not only was all the population out and waiting to cheer, but the trees were occupied. By black snakes. They hung in tasteful draperies among the branches, sometimes two or three together. They gazed with intense interest at the scene below them. The solicitor general, following Sean O'Donohue, saw a black snake wriggling deftly between the legs of the packed populace — packed as if to observe a parade — to get a view from the very edge of the curb. The Chancellor of the Exchequer came apprehensively behind the solicitor general.

Sean O'Donohue burst through the ranks of onlookers. He stalked out onto the empty center of the street. He looked neither to right nor left. He was headed for the presidential mansion, there to strangle President O'Hanrahan in the most lingering possible manner.

But there came a roar of rejoicing which penetrated even his single-tracked, murder-obsessed brain. He turned, purple-face and explosive, to see what the obscene sound could mean.

He saw. The lean and lanky figure of the chief justice of the supreme court of the Planet Eire came running down the street toward him. He bore a large slab of sheet-iron.

As he ran, he played upon it the blue flame of a welding torch. The smell of hot metal diffused behind him. The chief justice ran like a deer. But he wasn't leaving anything behind but the smell. Everything else was close on his heels.

A multicolored, multitudinous, swarming tide of dinies filled the highway from gutter to gutter. From the two-inch dwarfs to the purple-striped variety which grew to eight inches and sometimes fought cats, the dinies were in motion. They ran in the wake of the chief justice, enthralled and entranced by the smell of hot sheet iron. They were fascinated. They were bemused. They were aware of nothing but that ineffable fragrance. They hopped, ran, leaped, trotted and galloped in full cry after the head of the planet's supreme court.

He almost bumped into the stunned Sean O'Donohue. As he passed, he cried: "Duck, man! The dinies are comin' tra-la, tra-la!"

But Sean O'Donohue did not duck. He was fixed, stuck, paralyzed in his tracks. And the dinies arrived. They ran into him. He was an obstacle. They played leapfrog over each other to surmount him. He went down and was merely a bump in the flowing river of prismatic colorings which swarmed after the racing chief justice.

But there was a limit to things. This was not the first such event in Tara, this day. The dinies, this time, filled no more than a block of the street. They swarmed past him, they raced on into the distance, and Sean O'Donohue struggled to a sitting position.

His shoes were shreds. Dinies had torn them swiftly apart for the nails in them. His garters were gone. Dinies had operated on his pants to get at the metal parts. His pockets were ripped. The bright metal buttons of his coat were gone. His zippers had vanished. His suspenders dangled without any metal parts to hold them together, nor were there any pants buttons for them to hold onto. He opened his mouth, and closed it, and opened it again and closed it. His expression was that of a man in delirium.

And, even before the Chancellor of the Exchequer and the solicitor general could lift him gently and bear him away, there came a final catastrophe, for the O'Donohue. The snakes who had watched events from the curbs, as well as those which had gazed interestedly from aloft, now began to realize that this was an affair which affected them. They came out and began to follow the vanishing procession, very much as small dogs and little boys pursue a circus parade. But they seemed to talk uneasily to each other as they flowed past Sean O'Donohue, sitting in the dust of the street, all his illusions vanished and all his hopes destroyed.

But the people of Tara did not notice. They cheered themselves hoarse.

President O'Hanrahan held himself with some dignity in the tumbledown reception hall of the presidential mansion. Moira gazed proudly at him. The two still-active members of the Dail Committee looked uncomfortably around them. The cabinet of Eire was assembled.

"It's sorry I am," said the President of Eire, "to have to issue a defiance to the Eire on Earth we owe so much to. But it can't be helped. We had to have the black creatures to keep the dinies from eating us out of house and home altogether. We've been fightin' a rear-guard battle, and we needed them. In time we'd have won with their help, but time we did not have. So this mornin' Moira told me what she'd done yesterday. The darlin' had used the brains God gave her, and maybe holy St. Patrick put a flea in her ear. She figured out that dinies must find metal by its smell, and if its smell was made stronger by simple heatin' they'd be unable to resist it. And it was so. Ye saw the chief justice runnin' down the street with all the dinies after him."

The two members of the committee nodded.

"He was headin'," said the president, "for the cold-storage plant that Sean O'Donohue had twitted me was empty of the provisions we'd had to eat up because of the dinies. It's no matter that it's empty now though. We can grow victuals in the fields from now on, because now the cold rooms are packed solid with dinies that ran heedless into a climate they are not used to an' fell — what was the word, Moira darlin'?"

"Torpid," said Moira, gazing at him.

"Torpid," agreed the president. "From now on when there's too many dinies we can send somebody runnin' through the streets with a hot plate to call them into cold storage. We've pied pipers at will, to help out the black creatures that've done so much for us. If we've offended Eire on Earth, by havin' the black creatures to help us, we're sorry. But we had to — till Moira and doubtless St. Patrick gave us the answer ye saw today. If we're disowned, bedamned if we don't hang on! We can feed ourselves now. We can feed some extra mouths. There'll be a ship droppin' by out of curiosity now and then, and we'll trade with 'em. If were disowned — we'll be poor. But when were the Irish ever rich?"

The committeeman who was a manufacturer of precision machinery mopped his forehead.

"We're rich now," he said resignedly. "You'd be bound to learn it. D'you know what the dinies' teeth are made of?"

"It's been said," said President O'Hanrahan, "that it's bor . . . boron carbide in organic form. What that means I wouldn't know, but we've got a fine crop of it!"

"It's the next hardest substance to diamond," said the committeeman dourly. "It's even been guessed that an organic type might be harder. It's used for the tools for lathes and precision machinery, and it sells at close to the price of diamonds of industrial quality — and I'll make a deal to handle all we've got. What Earth don't need, other planets will. You're rich."

The president stared. Then he gazed at Moira.

"It's a pity we're bein' disowned," he said mournfully. "It would be a fine thing to be able to tell the grandfather Eire's rich and can feed more colonists and even maybe pay back what it's cost to keep us here so long. It would be a fine thing to hire colonists to build the houses they'll be given free when they're finished. But since Sean O'Donohue is a stern man —"

The ship owner scratched his head. He'd paused on the way to the presidential mansion. He'd had restoratives for his distress. He'd looked at the bottom of a bottle and seen the facts.

"I'll tell yea," he said warmly. "It's the O'Donohue's been battlin' to keep the colony goin' against the politicians that wanted to econo-mize. He's made a career of believin' in this world. He's ruined if he stops. So it might be that a little bit of blarneyin' — with him desperate to find reason to stay friends, black creature or no black creatures —"

The president took Moira's hand.

"Come, my darlin'," he said sadly. "We'll reason with him."

Long, long minutes later he shook his head as Sean O'Donohue stormed at him.

"The back o' my hand to you!" said Sean O'Donohue in the very quintessence of bitterness. "And to Moira, too, if she has more to do with you! I'll have naught to do with shenanigannin' renegades and blasphemers that actually import snakes into a world St. Patrick had set off for the Erse from ancient days!"

It was dark in the old man's room. He was a small and pathetic figure under the covers. He was utterly defiant. He was irreconcilable, to all seeming.

"Renegades!" he said indignantly. "Snakes, yea say? The devil a snake there is on Eire! I'll admit that we've some good black creatures that in a bad light and with prejudice yea might mistake. But snakes? Ye might as well call the dinies lizards — those same dinies that are native Erin porcupines — bad luck to them!"

There was an astounded silence from the bed.

"It's a matter of terminology," said the president sternly. "And it's not the name that makes a thing, but what it does! *Actio sequitur esse*, as the sayin' goes. You'll not be denyin' that! Now, a diny hangs around a man's house and it eats his food and his tools and it's no sort of good to anybody while it's alive. Is that the action of a lizard? It is not! But it's notorious that porcupines hang around men's houses and eat the han-dles of their tools for the salt in them, ignoring' the poor man whose sweat had the salt in it when he was laborin' to earn a livin' for his family. And when a thing acts like a porcupine, a porcupine it is and nothing else! So a diny is a Eirean porcupine, native to the planet, and no man can deny it!

"And what, then, is a snake?" demanded President O'Hanrahan oratorically. "It's a creature that sneaks about upon the ground and poisons by its bite when it's not blarneyin' unwise females into tasting' apples. Do the black creatures here do anything of that sort? They do not! They go about their business plain and open, givin' a half of the road and a how'd'y-do to those they meet. They're sober and they're industrious. They mind their own business, which is killin' the Eirean porcupines we inaccurate call by the name of dinies. It's their profes-sion! Did yea ever hear of a snake with a profession? I'll not have it said that there's snakes on Eire! And I'll denounce yea as a conscienceless politician if yea dare to put such a name on the honest, friendly, indus-trious Eirean porcupine eaters that up to this moment have been the savin' of the colony! I'll not have it!"

There was a long silence. Then Sean O'Donohue spoke dryly: "Porcupine eaters, you say? Not snakes?"

"Not snakes!" repeated the president defiantly. "Porcupine eaters!"

"Hm-m-m," said Sean O'Donohue. "That's better. The Dail's not immune to blarney when it's needful to accept it — and Eire back on Earth is hard put for breathin' room you say can be had from now on. What would be the reason for Moira standin' so close to you?"

"She's marryin' me," said President O'Hanrahan firmly.

Sean O'Donohue's voice was waspish.

"But I forbid it!" it said sharply. "Until I'm up and about and able to be givin' her in marriage as her grandfather ought to be doin'! Ye'll wait the few days till I'm able! Understand?"

"Yes, sir," said the president. Meekness seemed called for.

"Then begone!" snapped Sean O'Donohue. Then he added sternly: "Remember — no shenanigans!"

The solicitor general watched them depart on a wedding journey to a cottage in Ballyhanninch, which was on Donegal Peninsular, fronting on the Emmett Sea. He waved, like the assembled populace. But when they were out of sight he said darkly to the chief justice and the Chancellor of the Exchequer:

"I didn't have the heart to bring it up before, but there's the devil of a problem buildin' up against the time he comes back."

"Which problem?" asked the Chancellor of the Exchequer, warily.

"It's the sn . . . the porcupine killers," said the solicitor general. "Things look bad for them. They're out of work. Even Timothy. There's no dinies to speak of for them to earn a livin' by killin'. It's technological unemployment. They earned their way faithful, doin' work they knew an' loved. Now they're jobless. There's no work for them. What's to be done? Put 'em on re [remainder of text is missing]

There was a pause. The solicitor general said firmly:

"I mean it! They've a claim on us! A claim of the highest order! They can't starve, it's sure! But would you have them have to hold mass meetin's and set up picket lines and the like, to get justice done them?"

"Ah," said the chief justice. "Some way will turn up to handle the matter. Like Sean O'Donohue was sayin' to me yesterday, at the very bottom of a bottle, we Erse can always depend on St. Patrick to take care of things!"

THE LEADER

   . . . The career of The Leader remains one of the mysteries of history. This man, illegitimate and uneducated, hysterical and superstitious, gathered about him a crowded following of those who had been discontented, but whom he turned into fanatics. Apparently by pure force of personality he seized without resistance the government of one of the world's great nations. So much is unlikely enough. But as the ruler of a civilized country he imposed upon its people the absolute despotism of a primitive sultanate. He honeycombed its society with spies. He imprisoned, tortured, and executed without trial or check. And while all this went on he received the most impassioned loyalty of his subjects! Morality was abandoned at his command with as much alacrity as common sense. He himself was subject to the grossest superstitions. He listened to astrologers and fortunetellers — and executed them when they foretold disaster. But it is not enough to be amazed at the man himself. The great mystery is that people of the Twentieth Century, trained in science and technically advanced, should join in this orgy of what seems mere madness . . .

   — *Concise History of Europe*. Blaisdell.

Letter from Professor Albrecht Aigen, University of Brunn, to the Herr General Johann von Steppberg, retired.

My dear General von Steppberg:

   It is with reluctance that I intrude upon your retirement, but at the request of the Government I have undertaken a scientific examination of the causes which brought about The Leader's rise to power, the extraordinary popularity of his regime, the impassioned loyalty he was able to evoke, and the astounding final developments.

   If you can communicate to me any memories of The Leader which may aid in understanding this most bewildering period of our history, I assure you that it will be appreciated by myself, by the authorities who wish the investigation made, and I dare to hope by posterity.

   I am, my dear general, (Et cetera.)

Letter from General Johann von Steppberg (Retired) to Professor Albrecht Aigen, University of Brunn.

Herr Professor:

   The official yearbooks of the army contain the record of my military career. I have nothing to add to that information. You say the authorities wish more. I refuse it. If they threaten my pension, I will renounce it. If they propose other pressures, I will leave the country. In short, I refuse to discuss in any manner the subject of your recent communication.

I am, Herr Professor, (Et cetera.)

Letter from Professor Albrecht Aigen to Dr. Karl Thurn, Professor of Psychology at University of Laibach.

My dear Karl:

I hope your psionic research goes better than my official project! My business goes nowhere! I have written to generals, ministers, and all kinds of persons who held high office under The Leader. Each and every one refuses to discuss The Leader or his own experiences under him. Why? Surely no one would blame them now! We have had to agree to pretend that no one did anything improper under The Leader, or else that what anyone did was proper at the time. So why should the nabobs of that incredible period refuse to discuss what they should know better than anyone else? I am almost reduced to asking the aid of the astrologers and soothsayers The Leader listened to. Actually, I must make a note to do so in sober earnest. At least they had their own viewpoint of events.

Speaking of viewpoints, I have had some hope of clarifying The Leader's career by comparing it with that of Prime Minister Winston, in power in his country when The Leader ruled ours. His career is splendidly documented. There is astonishingly little documentation about The Leader as a person, however. That is one of the difficulties of my task. Even worse, those who should know him best lock their lips while those —

Here is an unsolicited letter from the janitor of a building in which a former Minister of Education now has his law offices. I have many letters equally preposterous. . . .

Enclosure in letter to Dr. Karl Thurn, University of Laibach.

Herr Professor:

I am the janitor of the building in which Herr Former Minister of Education Werfen has his offices. In cleaning there I saw a letter crumpled into a ball and thrown into a corner. I learned in the time of The Leader that angry actions often mean evil intentions, so I read the letter to see if the police should be notified. It was a letter from you in which you asked Herr Former Minister of Education Werfen for his memories of The Leader.

I remember The Leader, Herr Professor. He was the most holy man who ever lived, if indeed he was only a man. Once I passed the open door of an office in the building I then worked in. I looked in the door — it was the office of the then-struggling Party The Leader had founded — and I saw The Leader sitting in a chair, thinking. There was golden light about his head, Herr Professor. I have told this to other people and they do not believe me. There were shadowy other beings in the room. I saw, very faintly, great white wings. But the other beings were still because The Leader was thinking and did not wish to be disturbed. I assure you that this is true, Herr Professor. The Leader was the holiest of men — if he was only a man.

I am most respectfully, Herr Professor, (Et cetera.)

Letter from Fraulein Lise Grauer, nurse, in the city of Bludenz, to Professor Aigen at Brunn University.

Most respected Herr Professor:

I write this at the request of the Herr Former Police Inspector Grieg, to whom you directed a letter shortly before his death. The Herr Former Police Inspector had been ill for some time. I was his nurse. I had cared for him for months and did many small services for him, such as writing letters at his direction.

When your letter came he read it and went into a black mood of deep and bitter recollection. He would not speak for hours, and I had great difficulty in getting him to take his medicines. Just before his bedtime he called me and said sardonically;

"Lise, write to this Herr Professor for me. Say to him that I was once a decent man. When The Leader took power, I received orders that I would not accept. I submitted my resignation. Then I received orders to come to The Leader. I obeyed these orders because my resignation was not yet accepted. I was received in his office. I entered it with respect and defiance — respect because he was admitted to be the ruler of our nation; defiance because I would not obey such orders as had been sent me in his name.

"The Leader spoke to me, kindly, and as he spoke all my views changed. It suddenly seemed that I had been absurd to refuse the orders sent me. They seemed right and reasonable and even more lenient than would have been justified. . . . I left The Leader in a state in which I could not possibly fail to do anything he wished. From that moment I obeyed his orders. I was promoted. Eventually, as you know, I was in command of the Neusatz prison camp. And you know what orders I carried out there!"

I wept, Herr Professor, because the Herr Grieg's eyes were terrible to look at. He was a gentle and kindly man, Herr Professor! I was his nurse, and he was a good patient and a good man in every way. I had heard of the things that were done at Neusatz, but I could not believe that my patient had commanded them. Now, in his eyes I saw that he remembered them and that the memory was intolerable. He said very bitterly:

"Tell the Herr Professor that I can tell him nothing more. I have no other memories that would be of service to him. I have resolved, anyhow, to get rid even of these. I have kept them too long. Say to him that his letter has decided me."

I did not understand what he meant, Herr Professor. I helped him prepare for the night, and when he seemed to be resting quietly I retired, myself. I was wakened by a very loud noise. I went to see what was the matter. The Herr Former Police Inspector Grieg had managed to get out of his bed and across the room to a bureau. He opened a drawer and took out a revolver. He made his way back to his bed. He blew out his brains.

I called the police, and after investigation they instructed me to carry out his request, which I do.

Herr Professor, I do not myself remember the times of The Leader, but they must have been very terrible. If the Herr Former Police Inspector Grieg was actually in command of the Neusatz prison camp, and did actually order the things done there, — I cannot understand it, Herr Professor! Because he was a good and kindly man! If you write of him, I beg that you will mention that he was a most amiable man. I was only his nurse, but I assure you — (Et cetera.)

Letter from Dr. Karl Thurn, University of Laibach, to Professor Albrecht Aigen, University of Brunn.

My dear friend:

I could have predicted your failure to secure co-operation from eminent figures in The Leader's regime. So long as they keep silent, together, they can pretend to be respectable. And nobody longs so passionately to be respectable as a man who has prospered by being a swine, while he awaits an opportunity to prosper again by more swinishness. I would advise you to expect your best information from little people who suffered most and most helplessly looked on or helped while enormities were committed. Such little people will either yearn over the past like your janitor, or want most passionately to understand so that nothing of the sort can ever happen again.

Winston as a parallel to The Leader? Or as a contrast? Which? I can name one marked contrast. I doubt that anybody really and passionately wishes that Winston had never been born.

You mention my researches. You should see some of our results! I have found a rat with undeniable psychokinetic power. I have seen him move a gram-weight of cheese nearly three centimeters to where he could reach it through the cage bars. I begin to suspect a certain female dog of abilities I would prefer not to name just yet. If you can find any excuse to come to Laibach, I promise you amazing demonstrations of psi phenomena. (Et cetera.)

Quotations from, "Recollections of the Earl of Humber, formerly Prime Minister Winston," *by the Hon. Charles Wilberforce.*

Page 231; ". . . This incredible event took place even while it seemed most impossible. The Prime Minister took it with his usual aplomb. I asked him what he thought of the matter a week later, at a house party in Hertfordshire. He said, 'I consider it most unfortunate. This Leader of theirs is an inherently nasty individual. Therefore he'll make nastiness the avenue to distinction so long as he's in power. The results will be tragic, because when you bottle up decency men seem to go mad. What a pity one can't bottle up nastiness! The world might become a fit place to live in!'"

Page 247; "The Prime Minister disagreed. 'There was Napoleon,' he observed. 'You might despise him, but after he talked to you you served him. He seemed to throw a spell over people. Alexander probably had the same sort of magic personality. When his personality ceased to operate, as a result of too much wine too continuously, his empire fell immediately to pieces. I've known others personally; an Afghan whom I've always thought did us a favor by getting killed by a sniper. He could have caused a great deal of trouble. I'd guess at the Khalifa. Most of the people who have this incredible persuasiveness, however, seem to set up as successful swindlers. What a pity The Leader had no taste for simple crime, and had to go in for crimes of such elaboration!'"

Letter from Professor Albrecht Aigen, University of Brunn, to Dr. Karl Thurn, University of Laibach.

My dear Karl:

You make me curious with your talk of a rat which levitates crumbs of cheese and a she-dog who displays other psi abilities. I assume that you have found the experimental conditions which let psi powers operate without hindrance. I shall hope some day to see and conceivably to understand.

My own affairs are in hopeless confusion. At the moment I am overwhelmed with material about The Leader, the value of which I cannot estimate. Strange! I ask people who should know what I am commissioned to discover, and they refuse to answer. But it becomes known that I ask, and thousands of little people write me to volunteer impassioned details of their experiences while The Leader ruled. Some are bitter because they did what they did and felt as they felt. These seem to believe in magic or demoniac possession as the reason they behaved with such conspicuous insanity. Others gloat over their deeds, which they recount with gusto — and then express pious regret with no great convincingness. Some of these accounts nauseate me. But something utterly abnormal was in operation, somehow, to cause The Leader's ascendancy!

I wish I could select the important data with certainty. Almost anything, followed up, might reveal the key. But I do not know what to follow! I plan to go to Bozen, where the new monstrous computer has been set up, and see if there is any way in which it could categorize my data and detect a pattern of more than bewildered and resentful frenzy.

On the way back to Brunn I shall stop by to talk to you. There is so much to say! I anticipate much of value from your detached and analytic mind. I confess, also, that I am curious about your research. This she-dog with psi powers, of which you give no account . . . I am intrigued.

As always, I am, (Et cetera.)

Letter from Professor Albrecht Aigen, written from The Mathematical Institute at Bozen, to Dr. Karl Thurn, University of Laibach.

My dear Karl:

This is in haste. There is much agitation among the computer staff at the Institute. An assistant technician has been discovered to be able to predict the answer the computer will give to problems set up at random. He is one Hans Schweeringen and it is unbelievable.

Various numerals are impressed on the feed-in tape of the computer. Sections of the tape are chosen at random by someone who is blindfolded. They are fed unread into the computer, together with instructions to multiply, subtract, extract roots, et cetera, which are similarly chosen at random and not known to anyone. Once in twenty times or so, Schweeringen predicts the result of this meaningless computation before the computer has made it. This is incredible! The odds are trillions to one against it! Since nobody knows the sums or instructions given to the computer, it cannot be mind-reading in any form. It must be pure precognition. Do you wish to talk to him?

He is uneasy at the attention he attracts, perhaps because his father was one of The Leader's secretaries and was executed, it is presumed, for knowing too much. Telegraph me if you wish me to try to bring him to you.

Your friend —

Telegram from Dr. Karl Thurn, Professor of Psychology at Laibach University, to Professor Albrecht Aigen, in care of The Mathematical Institute at Bozen:

Take tapes which produced answers Schweeringen predicted. Run them through computer when he knows nothing of it. Wire result.

Thurn.

Telegram. Professor Albrecht Aigen, at The Mathematical Institute in Bozen, to Dr. Karl Thurn, University of Laibach.

How did you know? The tapes do not give the same answers when run through the computer without Schweeringen's knowledge. The only possible answer is that the computer sometimes errs to match his predictions. But this is more impossible than precognition. This is beyond the conceivable. It cannot be! What now?

Aigen.

Telegram from Dr. Karl Thurn, University of Laibach, to Professor Albrecht Aigen, care Mathematical Institute, Bozen.

Naturally I suspect psi. He belongs with my rat and she-dog. Try to

arrange it.
Thurn.

Telegram from Professor Albrecht Aigen, Mathematical Institute, Bozen, to Dr. Karl Thurn, University of Laibach.

Schweeringen refuses further tests. Fears proof he causes malfunctioning of computer will cause unemployment here and may destroy all hope of hoped-for career in mathematics.
Aigen.

Telegram from Professor Albrecht Aigen, at Mathematical Institute, to Dr. Karl Thurn, University of Laibach.

Terrible news. Riding bus to Institute this morning, Schweeringen was killed when bus was involved in accident.
Aigen.

Telegram from Dr. Karl Thurn, University of Laibach, to Professor Albrecht Aigen, care Mathematical Institute, Bozen.

Deeply regret death Schweeringen. When you come here please try to bring all known family history. Psi ability sometimes inherited. Could be tie-in his father's execution and use of psi ability.
Thurn.

Letter from Professor Albrecht Aigen, at Brunn University, to Dr. Karl Thurn, University of Laibach.

My dear Karl:

I have first to thank you for your warm welcome and to express my gratitude for your attention while I was your guest. Since my return I have written many inquiries about Schweeringen's father. There are so far no replies, but I have some hope that people who will not tell of their own experiences may tell about someone else — especially someone now dead. This may be a useful device to get at least some information from people who so far have refused any. Naturally I will pass on to you anything I learn.

I try to work again upon the task assigned me — to investigate the rise and power of The Leader. I find it hard to concentrate. My mind goes back to your laboratory. I am deeply shaken by my experience there. I had thought nothing could be more bewildering than my own work. Consider: Today I received a letter in which a man tells me amazedly of the life he led in a slave-labor camp during the time of The Leader's rule. He describes the attempt of another prisoner to organize a revolt of the prisoners. While he spoke of the brutality of the guards and the intolerably hard labor and the deliberately insufficient food, they cheered him. But when he accused The Leader of having ordered these things — the prisoners fell upon him with cries of fury. They killed him. I had this information verified. It was true.

I cannot hope for a sane explanation of such things. But a sane explanation for my experience seems even less probable. I am impressed by your rat who levitates crumbs of cheese. But I am appalled; I am horrified; I am stupefied by what I did! You asked me to wait for you in a certain laboratory beyond a door. I entered. I saw a small, fat, mangy she-dog in a dog-run. She looked at me and wagged her tail. I thereupon went to the other end of the laboratory, opened a box, and took out a handful of strange objects you later told me are sweetmeats to a dog. I gave them to the animal.

Why did I do it? How was it that I went directly to a box of which I knew nothing, opened it as a matter of course, and took out objects I did not even recognize, to give them to that unpleasant small beast? How did I know where to go? Why did I go? Why should I give those then-meaningless objects to the dog? It is as if I were enchanted!

You say that it is a psi phenomenon. The rat causes small objects to move. The dog, you say, causes persons to give it canine candy. I revolt against the conclusion, which I cannot reason away. If you are right, we are at the mercy of our domestic animals! Dog-lovers are not people who love dogs, but people who are enslaved by dogs. Cat-lovers are merely people who haven't been seized upon by cats to support and pet and cater to them. This is intolerable! I shall fear all pets from now on! I throw myself back into my own work to avoid thinking of it. I —

Later. I did not mail this letter because an appalling idea occurred to me. This could bear upon my investigation! Do you think The Leader — No! It could not be! It would be madness. . . .

Extract from a letter from Dr. Karl Thurn to Professor Albrecht Aigen.

. . . I deplore your reaction. It has the emotional quality of a reaction to witchcraft or magic, but psi is not witchcraft. It is a natural force. No natural force is either nonexistent or irresistible. No natural force is invariably effective. Psi is not irresistible under all circumstances. It is not always effective. My rat cannot levitate cheese-crumbs weighing more than 1.7 grams. My she-dog could not make you give her dog-candy once you were on guard. When you went again into the laboratory she looked at you and wagged her tail as before. You say that you thought of the box and of opening it, but you did not. It was not even an effort of will to refrain.

A lesser will or a lower grade of personality cannot overwhelm a greater one. Not ever! Lesser beings can only urge. The astrologers used to say that the stars incline, but they do not compel. The same can be said of psi — or of magnetism or gravitation or what you will. Schweeringen could not make the computer err when it had to err too egregiously. A greater psi ability was needed than he had. A greater psi power than was available would have been needed to make you give the dog candy, once you were warned.

I do not apply these statements to your so-called appalling idea. I carefully refrain from doing so. It is your research, not mine. . . .

Extract from letter to Professor Albrecht Aigen from the Herr Friedrich Holm, supervisor of electrical maintenance, municipal electrical service, Untersberg.

Herr Professor:

You have written to ask if I knew a certain Herr Schweeringen, attached to The Leader's personal staff during his regime. I did know such a person. I was then in charge of electrical maintenance in The Leader's various residences. Herr Schweeringen was officially one of The Leader's secretaries, but his actual task was to make predictions for The Leader, like a soothsayer or a medium. He had a very remarkable gift. There were times when it was especially needful that there be no electrical failures — when The Leader was to be in residence, for example. On such occasions it was my custom to ask Herr Schweeringen if there was apt to be any failure of apparatus under my care. At least three times he told me yes. In one case it was an elevator, in another refrigeration, in a third a fuse would blow during a State dinner.

I overhauled the elevator, but it failed nevertheless. I replaced the refrigeration motor, and the new motor failed. In the third case I changed the fuse to a new and tested one, and then placed a new, fused line around the fuse Herr Schweeringen had said would blow, and placed a workman beside it. When the fuse did blow as predicted, my workman instantly closed the extra-line switch, so that the lights of the State dinner barely flickered. But I shudder when I think of the result if Herr Schweeringen had not warned me.

He was executed a few days before the period of confusion began, which ended as everyone knows. I do not know the reason for his execution. It was said, however, that The Leader executed him personally. This, Herr Professor, is all that I know of the matter.

Very respectfully, (Et cetera.)

Letter from Herr Theophrastus Paracelsus Bosche, astrologer, to Professor Albrecht Aigen, Brunn University.

Most respected Herr Professor:

I am amused that a so-eminent scientist like yourself should ask information from a so-despised former astrologer to The Leader. It is even more amusing that you ask about a mere soothsayer — a man who displayed an occult gift of prophecy — whom you should consider merely one of the charlatans like myself whom The Leader consulted, and who are unworthy of consideration by a scientific historian. We have no effect upon history, most respected Herr Professor! None at all. Oh, none! I am much diverted.

You ask about the Herr Schweeringen. He was a predictor, using his occult gift of second sight to foreknow events and tell The Leader about them. You will remember that The Leader considered himself to have occult powers of leadership and decision, and that all occult powers should contribute to his greatness. At times of great stress, such as when The Leader demanded ever-increasing concessions from other nations on threat of war, he was especially concerned that occult predictions promise him success.

At a certain time the international tension was greater than ever before. If The Leader could doubt the rightness of any of his actions, he doubted it then. There was great danger of war. Prime Minister Winston had said flatly that The Leader must withdraw his demands or fight. The Leader was greatly agitated. He demanded my prediction. I considered the stars and predicted discreetly that war would be prevented by some magnificent achievement by The Leader. Truly, if he got out of his then situation it would be a magnificent achievement. But astrology, of course, could only indicate it but not describe what it would be.

The Leader was confident that he could achieve anything he could imagine, because he had convinced even himself that only treason or disloyalty could cause him to fail in any matter. He demanded of his generals what achievement would prevent the war. They were not encouraging. He demanded of his civilian political advisers. They dared not advise him to retreat. They offered nothing. He demanded of his occult advisers.

The Herr Schweeringen demanded of me that I tell him my exact prediction. His nerves were bad, then, and he twitched with the strain. Someone had to describe the great achievement The Leader would make. It would be dangerous not to do so. I told him the prediction, I found his predicament diverting. He left me, still twitching and desperately sunk in thought.

I now tell you exact, objective facts, Herr Professor, with no interpretation of my own upon them. The Herr Schweeringen was closeted with The Leader. I am told that his face was shining with confidence when he went to speak to The Leader. It was believed among us charlatans that he considered that he foreknew what The Leader would do to prevent war at this time.

Two hours later there were shots in The Leader's private quarters. The Leader came out, his eyes glaring, and ordered Herr Schweeringen's body removed. He ordered the execution of the four senior generals of the General Staff, of the Minister of Police, and several other persons. He then went into seclusion, from which he emerged only briefly to give orders making the unthinkable retreat that Prime Minister Winston had demanded. No one spoke to him for a week. Confusion began. These are objective facts. I now add one small boast.

My discreet prediction had come true, and it is extremely diverting to think about it. The Leader had achieved magnificently. The war was prevented not only for the moment but for later times, too. The Leader's achievement was the destruction of his regime by destroying the brains that had made it operate!

It is quite possible that you will consider this information a lie. That will be quite droll. However, I am, most respected Herr Professor, (Et cetera.)

Letter from Dr. Karl Thurn, University of Laibach, to Professor Albrecht Aigen, Brunn University.

My dear friend:

Your information about the elder Schweeringen received. The information about his prediction is interesting. I could wish that it were complete, but that would seem to be hopeless. Your question, asked in a manner suggesting great disturbance, is another matter. I will answer it as well as I can, my friend, but please remember that you asked. I volunteer nothing. The question of the rise and power of The Leader is your research, not mine.

Here is my answer. Years back an American researcher named Rhine obtained seemingly conclusive proof that telepathy took place. Tonight he would have a "sender," here, attempt to transmit some item telepathically to a "receiver," there. Tomorrow morning he would compare the record of what the "sender" had attempted to transmit, with the record of what the "receiver" considered he had received. The correspondence was far greater than chance. He considered that telepathy was proven.

But then Rhine made tests for precognition. He secured proof that some persons could predict with greater-than-probability frequency that some particular event, to be determined by chance, would take place tomorrow. He secured excellent evidence for precognition.

Then it was realized that if one could foresee what dice would read tomorrow — dice not yet thrown — one should be able to read what a report would read tomorrow — a report not yet written. In short, if one can foreknow what a comparison will reveal, telepathy before the comparison is unproven. In proving precognition, he had destroyed his evidence for telepathy.

It appears that something similar has happened, which our correspondence has brought out. Young Schweeringen predicted what a computer would report from unknown numerals and instructions. In order for the computer to match his predictions, it had to err. It did. Therefore one reasons that he did not predict what the computer would produce. The computer produced what he predicted. In effect, what appeared to be foreknowledge was psychokinesis — the same phenomenon as the movement of crumbs of cheese by my rat. One may strongly suspect that when young Herr Schweeringen knew in advance what the computer would say, he actually knew in advance what he could make it say. It is possible that one can consciously know in advance only what one can unconsciously bring about. If one can bring about only minor happenings, one can never predict great ones.

This is my answer to your question. I would like very much to know what the elder Schweeringen predicted that The Leader would accomplish!

My she-dog has died. We had a new attendant in the laboratory. He fed her to excess. She died of it. (Et cetera.)

Letter from Professor Albrecht Aigen to Dr. Thurn.

My dear Karl:

I have resolved to dismiss psionic ability from my investigation into The Leader's rise to power. This much I will concede: The Leader could enslave — englamour — enchant anyone who met him personally. He did. To a lesser degree, this irresistible persuasiveness is a characteristic of many successful swindlers. But he could not have englamoured the whole nation. He did not meet enough persons personally to make his regime possible, unless he could cause other persons to apply their own magnetism to further his ambitions, and they others and others and so on — like an endless series of magnets magnetized originally from one. This is not possible. I restrict myself to normal, plausible hypotheses — of which so far I have no faintest trace.

You agree with me, do you not — that it was impossible for The Leader to weave a web of enchantment over the whole nation by his own psi energies controlling the psi energies of others? I would welcome your assurance that it could not be.

Letter from Professor Albrecht Aigen to Dr. Karl Thurn.

My dear Karl:

Did you receive my last letter? I am anxious to have your assurance that it was impossible that The Leader could englamour the whole nation by his psionic gifts.

Telegram, Dr. Albrecht Aigen to Dr. Karl Thurn.

Karl, as you are my friend, answer me!

Letter, Dr. Karl Thurn to Professor Albrecht Aigen.

. . . But what have you discovered, my friend, that you are afraid to face?

Letter. Professor Albrecht Aigen to Dr. Karl Thurn.

My dear Karl:

I appeal to you because I have discovered how nearly our nation and the whole world escaped horrors beside which those of The Leader's actual regime would seem trivial. Give me reasons, arguments, proofs beyond question, which I can put into my report on his career! I must demonstrate beyond question that psi ability did not cause his ascendancy! Help me to contrive a lie which will keep anyone, ever, from dreaming that psi ability can be used to seize a government and a nation. It could seize the world more terribly. . . .

I cannot express the urgency of this need! There are others who possess The Leader's powers in a lesser degree. They must remain only swindlers and such, without ambitions to rule, or they might study The Leader's career as Napoleon studied Alexander's. There must be no hint, anywhere, of the secret I have discovered. There must be nothing to lead to the least thought of it! The Leader could have multiplied his power ten-thousand-fold! Another like him must never learn how it could be done!

I beg your help, Karl! I am shaken. I am terrified. I wish that I had not undertaken this research. I wish it almost as desperately as I wish that The Leader had never been born!

Letter from Colonel Sigmund Knoeller, retired, to Professor Albrecht Aigen, Brunn University.

Herr Professor:

In response to your authorized request for information about certain events; I have the honor to inform you that at the time you mention I was Major in command of the Second Battalion of the 161st Infantry Regiment, assigned to guard duty about the residence of The Leader. Actual guard duty was performed by the secret police. My battalion merely provided sentries around the perimeter of the residence, and at certain places within.

On August 19th I received a command to march three companies of my men into the residence, to receive orders from The Leader in person. This command was issued by the Herr General Breyer, attached to The Leader as a military aide.

I led my men inside according to the orders, guided by the orderly who had brought them. I entered an inner courtyard. There was disturbance. People moved about in a disorderly fashion and chattered agitatedly. This was astonishing in The Leader's residence. I marched up to General Breyer, who stood outside a group biting his nails. I saluted and said: "Major Knoeller reporting for orders, Herr General."

There was then confusion in the nearby squabbling group. A man burst out of it and waved his arms at me. He looked like The Leader. He cried shrilly:

"Arrest these men! All of them! Then shoot them!"

I looked at the Herr General Breyer. He bit his nails. The man who looked so much like The Leader foamed at the mouth. But he was not The Leader. That is, in every respect he resembled The Leader to whom I owed loyalty as did everyone. But no one who was ever in The Leader's presence failed to know it. There was a feeling. One knew to the inmost part of one's soul that he was The Leader who must be reverenced and obeyed. But one did not feel that way about this man, though he resembled The Leader so strongly.

"Arrest them!" shrilled the man ferociously. "I command it! I am The Leader! Shoot them!"

When I still waited for General Breyer to give me orders, the man shrieked at the troopers. He commanded them to kill General Breyer and all the rest, including me. And if he had been The Leader they would have obeyed. But he was not. So my men stood stiffly at attention, waiting for my orders or General Breyer's.

There was now complete silence in the courtyard. The formerly squabbling men watched as if astonished. As if they did not believe their eyes. But I waited for General Breyer to give his commands.

The man screamed in a terrible, frustrated rage. He waved his arms wildly. He foamed at the mouth and shrieked at me. I waited for orders from General Breyer. After a long time he ceased to bite his nails and said in a strange voice:

"You had better have this man placed in confinement, Major Knoeller. See that he is not injured. Double all guards and mount machine guns in case of rioting outside. Dismiss!"

I obeyed my commands. My men took the struggling, still-shrieking man and put him in a cell in the guardhouse. There was a drunken private there, awaiting court-martial. He was roused and annoyed when his new companion shrieked and screamed and shook the bars of the door. He kicked the man who looked so much like The Leader. I then had the civilian placed in a separate cell, but he continued to rave incoherently until I had the regimental surgeon give him an injection to quiet him. He sank into drugged sleep with foam about his lips.

He looked remarkably like The Leader. I have never seen such a resemblance! But he was not The Leader or we would have known him.

There was no disturbance outside the residence. The doubled guards and the mounted machine guns were not needed.

I am, Herr Professor, (Et cetera.)

Letter, with enclosure, from Professor Albrecht Aigen, Brunn University, to Dr. Karl Thurn, University of Laibach.

My dear Karl:

Because of past sharing in my research, you will realize what the enclosed means. It is part of the report of the physicians who examined The Leader three days after his confinement in a military prison. He had recovered much of his self-control. He spoke with precision. He appeared even calm, though he was confused in some matters. The doctors addressed him as "My Leader" because he refused to reply otherwise.

(Enclosure)

Dr. Kundmann: But, My Leader, we do not understand what has happened! You were terribly disturbed. You were even . . . even confused in your behavior! Can you tell us what took place?

The Leader: I suffered a great danger and a temporary damage. That villain Schweeringen — I shot him. It was a mistake. I should have had him worked over — at length!

Dr. Messner: My Leader, will you be so good as to tell us the nature of the danger and the damage?

The Leader: Schweeringen probably told someone what he would propose to me. It was his conviction that because of my special gifts I could cause anyone, not only to obey me, but to pour out to me, directly, his inmost thoughts and memories. Of course this is true. The danger was that of the contact of my mind with an inferior one. But I allowed Schweeringen to persuade me that I should risk even this for the service of my people. Therefore I contacted the mind of Prime Minister Winston, so I could know every scheme and every plan he might have or know to exist to injure my people. I intended, however, to cause him to become loyal to me — though I would later have had him shot. Schweeringen had betrayed me, though. When I made contact with Winston's mind, it was not only inferior, but diseased! There was a contagion which temporarily affected the delicate balance of my intuition. For a short time I could not know, as ordinarily, what was best for my people.

(End of Enclosure)

You will see, my dear Karl, what took place. To you and to me this explains everything. In the background of my research and your information it is clear. Fortunately, The Leader's mind was unstable. The strain and shock of so unparalleled experience as complete knowledge of another brain's contents destroyed his rationality. He became insane. Insane, he no longer had the psi gifts by which he had seized and degraded our nation. He ceased to be The Leader.

But you will see that this must be hidden! Another monster like The Leader, or Napoleon — perhaps even lesser monsters — could attempt the same feat. But they might be less unstable! They might be able to invade the mind of any human being, anywhere, and drain it of any secret or impress upon it any desire or command, however revolting. You see, Karl, why this must never become known! It must be hidden forever.

Letter from Dr. Karl Thurn, University of Laibach, to Professor Albrecht Aigen, Brunn University.

My dear friend:

I am relieved! I feared for your judgment. I thought that perhaps overwork and frustration had set up an anxiety-block to make you cease your work. But you are quite right. Your analysis is brilliant. And now that you have pointed it out, unquestionably a man with The Leader's psi powers could force another man's brain to transmit all its contents to him.

But consider the consequences! Consider the conditions of such an event. One's brain is designed to work within one's own skull, dealing with sensory messages and the like. Very occasionally it acts outside, shifting crumbs of cheese and confusing computers — and securing candy. But even when one's will controls outside actions, it does not fuse with the outside brain or thing. It molds or moves the recipient mind, but there is never a sharing of memory. You have explained why.

Consider what must happen if a brain of limited power and essentially emotional operation is linked to another and more powerful one. Assume for a moment that my she-dog had linked her brain to yours, even momentarily. Do you realize that she would not have gotten your memories, much less your power to reason? She would not even have acquired your knowledge of the meaning of words! When a bright light shines in your eyes, you see nothing else. When thunder rolls in your ears, you do not hear the ticking of a clock. When you suffer pain, you do not notice a feather's tickle. If my she-dog had linked her mind to yours, she would have experienced something which is knowledge more firmly fixed and more continuously known than anything else in your conscious life. This overwhelmingly strong conviction would have been so powerful and so positive that it would be imprinted — branded — burned into every cell of her brain. She could never get it out.

But in receiving this overwhelming experience she would not get your memories or power to reason or even your personality. She would have experienced only your identity. She would have received only the conviction that she was yourself! She would have been like those poor lunatics who believe that they are Napoleon, though they have nothing of Napoleon in them but the conviction of identity. They do not know when he was born or have more than the vaguest notion of what he did, but they try to act as who he was — according to their own ideas of how Napoleon would act in their situation. This is how my she-dog would have behaved.

I am relieved. You have explained everything. Your letter gave me the suspicion. I secured a transcript of the Herr Doctor's report for myself. My suspicion became a certainty. You will find the clue in the report. Consider: The Leader had had the experience I imagined for my she-dog. He had linked his mind with a stronger one and a greater personality — if it must be said, a greater man. For a moment The Leader knew what that man knew most certainly, with most profound conviction, with most positive knowledge. It was burned into his brain. He could never get it out. He did not secure that other man's memories or knowledge or ability. He was blinded, deafened, dazed by the overwhelming conviction that, the other man had of his own identity. It would not be possible for him to get anything else from a stronger mind and a greater person. Nor could anyone else succeed where he failed, my friend! There is no danger of any man seizing the world by seizing the minds of all his fellows! One who tries will meet the fate of The Leader.

You realize what that fate was, of course. He suddenly ceased to be the monster who could cast a spell of blind adoration for himself. He ceased to be The Leader! So the doctors gave him truth-serum so he would not try to conceal anything from them. The result is in the transcript on the third page beyond the place you quoted to me. There the doctors asked The Leader who he was. Read his answer, my friend! It proves everything! He said:

"I am Prime Minister Winston."

THE WAILING ASTEROID

CHAPTER 1

THE SIGNALS from space began a little after midnight, local time, on a Friday. They were first picked up in the South Pacific, just westward of the International Date Line. A satellite-watching station on an island named Kalua was the first to receive them, though nobody heard the first four or five minutes. But it is certain that the very first message was picked up and recorded by the monitor instruments.

The satellite-tracking unit on Kalua was practically a duplicate of all its fellows. There was the station itself with a vertical antenna outside pointing at the stars. There were various lateral antennae held two feet aboveground by concrete posts. In the instrument room in the building a light burned over a desk, three or four monitor lights glowed dimly to indicate that the self-recording instruments were properly operating, and there was a multiple-channel tape recorder built into the wall. Its twin tape reels turned sedately, winding a brown plastic ribbon from one to the other at a moderate pace.

The staff man on duty had gone to the installation's kitchen for a cup of coffee. No sound originated in the room, unless one counted the fluttering of a piece of weighted-down paper on the desk. Outside, palm trees whispered and rustled their long fronds in the southeast trade wind under a sky full of glittering stars. Beyond, there was the dull booming of surf upon the barrier reef of the island. But the instruments made no sound. Only the tape reels moved.

The signals began abruptly. They came out of a speaker and were instantly recorded. They were elfin and brutelike and musical. They were crisp and distinct. They did not form a melody, but nearly all the components of melody were there. Pure musical notes, each with its own pitch, all of different lengths, like quarter-notes and eighth-notes in music. The sounds needed only rhythm and arrangement to form a plaintive tune.

Nothing happened. The sounds continued for something over a minute. They stopped long enough to seem to have ended. Then they began again.

When the staff man came back into the room with a coffee cup in his hand, he heard the flutings instantly. His jaw dropped. He said, "What the hell?" and went to look at the instruments. He spilled some of his coffee when he saw their readings.

The tracking dials said that the signals came from a stationary source almost directly overhead. If they were from a stationary source, no plane was transmitting them. Nor could they be coming from an artificial satellite. A plane would move at a moderate pace across the sky. A satellite would move faster. Much faster. This source, according to the instruments, did not move at all.

The staff man listened with a blank expression on his face. There was but one rational explanation, which he did not credit for an instant. The reasonable answer would have been that somebody, somewhere, had put a satellite out into an orbit requiring twenty-four hours for a circuit of the earth, instead of the ninety to one-hundred-twenty-four-minute orbits of the satellites known to sweep around the world from west to east and pole to pole. But the piping, musical sounds were not the sort of thing that modern physicists would have contrived to carry information about cosmic-particle frequency, space temperature, micrometeorites, and the like.

The signals stopped again, and again resumed. The staff man was galvanized into activity. He rushed to waken other members of the outpost. When he got back, the signals continued for a minute and stopped altogether. But they were recorded on tape, with the instrument readings that had been made during their duration. The staff man played the tape back for his companions.

They felt as he did. These were signals from space where man had never been. They had listened to the first message ever to reach mankind from the illimitable emptiness between the stars and planets. Man was not alone. Man was no longer isolated. Man . . .

The staff of the tracking station was very much upset. Most of the men were white-faced by the time the taped message had been replayed through to its end. They were frightened.

Considering everything, they had every reason to be.

The second pick-up was in Darjeeling, in northern India. The Indian government was then passing through one of its periods of enthusiastic interest in science. It had set up a satellite-observation post in a former British cavalry stable on the outskirts of the town. The acting head of the observing staff happened to hear the second broadcast to reach Earth. It arrived some seventy-nine minutes after the first reception, and it was picked up by two stations, Kalua and Darjeeling.

The Darjeeling observer was incredulous at what he heard — five repetitions of the same sequence of flute-like notes. After each pause — when it seemed that the signals had stopped before they actually did so — the reception was exactly the same as the one before. It was inconceivable that such a succession of sounds, lasting a full minute, could be exactly repeated by any natural chain of events. Five repetitions were out of the question. The notes were signals. They were a communication which was repeated to be sure it was received.

The third broadcast was heard in Lebanon in addition to Kalua and Darjeeling. Reception in all three places was simultaneous. A signal from a nearby satellite could not possibly have been picked up so far around the Earth's curvature. The widening of the area of reception, too, proved that there was no new satellite aloft with an orbit period of exactly twenty-four hours, so that it hung motionless in the sky relative to Earth. Tracking observations, in fact, showed the source of the signals to move westward, as time passed, with the apparent motion of a star. No satellite of Earth could possibly exist with such an orbit unless it was close enough to show a detectable parallax. This did not.

A French station picked up the next batch of plaintive sounds. Kalua, Darjeeling, and Lebanon still received. By the time the next signal was due, Croydon, in England, had its giant radar-telescope trained on the part of the sky from which all the tracking stations agreed the signals came.

Croydon painstakingly made observations during four seventy-nine-minute intervals and four five-minute receptions of the fluting noises. It reported that there was a source of artificial signals at an extremely great distance, position right ascension so-and-so, declination such-and-such. The signals began every seventy-nine minutes. They could be heard by any receiving instrument capable of handling the microwave frequency involved. The broadcast was extremely broadband. It covered more than two octaves and sharp tuning was not necessary. A man-made signal would have been confined to as narrow a wave-band as possible, to save power for one reason, so it could not be imagined that the signal was anything but artificial. Yet no Earth science could have sent a transmitter out so far.

When sunrise arrived at the tracking station on Kalua, it ceased to receive from space. On the other hand, tracking stations in the United States, the Antilles, and South America began to pick up the cryptic sounds.

The first released news of the happening was broadcast in the United States. In the South Pacific and India and the Near East and Europe, the whole matter seemed too improbable for the notification of the public. News pressure in the United States, though, is very great. Here the news rated broadcast, and got it.

That was why Joe Burke did not happen to complete the business for which he'd taken Sandy Lund to a suitable, romantic spot. She was his secretary and the only permanent employee in the highly individual business he'd begun and operated. He'd known her all his life, and it seemed to him that for most of it he'd wanted to marry her. But something had happened to him when he was quite a small boy — and still happened at intervals — which interposed a mental block. He'd always wanted to be romantic with her, but there was a matter of two moons in a strange-starred sky, and trees with foliage like none on Earth, and an overwhelming emotion. There was no rational explanation for it. There could be none. Often he'd told himself that Sandy was real and utterly desirable, and this lunatic repetitive experience was at worst insanity and at the least delusion. But he'd never been able to do more than stammer when talk between them went away from matter-of-fact things.

Tonight, though, he'd parked his car where a river sparkled in the moonlight. There was a scent of pine and arbutus in the air and a faint thread of romantic music came from his car's radio. He'd brought Sandy here to propose to her. He was doggedly resolved to break the chains a psychological oddity had tied him up in.

He cleared his throat. He'd taken Sandy out to dinner, ostensibly to celebrate the completion of a development job for Interiors, Inc. Burke had started Burke Development, Inc., some four years out of college when he found he didn't like working for other people and could work for himself. Its function was to develop designs and processes for companies too small to have research-and-development divisions of their own. The latest, now-finished, job was a wall-garden which those expensive interior decorators, Interiors, Inc., believed might appeal to the very rich. Burke had made it. It was a hydroponic job. A rich man's house could have one or more walls which looked like a grassy sward stood on edge, with occasional small flowers or even fruits growing from its close-clipped surface.

It was done. A production-job room-wall had been shipped and the check for it banked. Burke had toyed with the idea that growing vegetation like that might be useful in a bomb shelter or in an atomic submarine where it would keep the air fresh indefinitely. But such ideas were for the future. They had nothing to do with now. Now Burke was going to triumph over an obsessive dream.

"I've got something to say, Sandy," said Burke painfully.

She did not turn her head. There was moonlight, rippling water, and the tranquil noises of the night in springtime. A perfect setting for what Burke had in mind, and what Sandy knew about in advance. She waited, her eyes turned away from him so he wouldn't see that they were shining a little.

"I'm something of an idiot," said Burke, clumsily. "It's only fair to tell you about it. I'm subject to a psychological gimmick that a girl I — Hm." He coughed. "I think I ought to tell you about it."

"Why?" asked Sandy, still not looking in his direction.

"Because I want to be fair," said Burke. "I'm a sort of crackpot. You've noticed it, of course."

Sandy considered.

"No-o-o-o," she said measuredly, "I think you're pretty normal, except — No. I think you're all right."

"Unfortunately," he told her, "I'm not. Ever since I was a kid I've been bothered by a delusion, if that's what it is. It doesn't make sense. It couldn't. But it made me take up engineering, I think, and . . ."

His voice trailed away.

"And what?"

"Made an idiot out of me," said Burke. "I was always pretty crazy about you, and it seems to me that I took you to a lot of dances and such in high school, but I couldn't act romantic. I wanted to, but I couldn't. There was this crazy delusion . . ."

"I wondered, a little," said Sandy, smiling.

"I wanted to be romantic about you," he told her urgently, "But this damned obsession kept me from it."

"Are you offering to be a brother to me now?" asked Sandy.

"No!" said Burke explosively. "I'm fed up with myself. I want to be different. Very different. With you!"

Sandy smiled again.

"Strangely enough, you interest me," she told him. "Do go on!"

But he was abruptly tongue-tied. He looked at her, struggling to speak. She waited.

"I w-want to ask you to m-m-marry me," said Burke desperately. "But I have to tell you about the other thing first. Maybe you won't want . . ."

Her eyes were definitely shining now. There was soft music and rippling water and soft wind in the trees. It was definitely the time and place for romance.

But the music on the car radio cut off abruptly. A harsh voice interrupted:

"Special Bulletin! Special Bulletin! Messages of unknown origin are reaching Earth from outer space! Special Bulletin! Messages from outer space!"

Burke reached over and turned up the sound. Perhaps he was the only man in the world who would have spoiled such a moment to listen to a news broadcast, and even he wouldn't have done it for a broadcast on any other subject. He turned the sound high.

"This is a special broadcast from the Academy of Sciences in Washington, D. C." boomed the speaker. "Some thirteen hours ago a satellite-tracking station in the South Pacific reported picking up signals of unknown origin and great strength, using the microwave frequencies also used by artificial satellites now in orbit around Earth. The report was verified shortly afterward from India, then Near East tracking stations made the same report. European listening posts and radar telescopes were on the alert when the sky area from which the signals come rose above the horizon. American stations have again verified the report within the last few minutes. Artificial signals, plainly not made by men, are now reaching Earth every seventy-nine minutes from remotest space. There is as yet no hint of what the messages may mean, but that they are an attempt at communication is certain. The signals have been recorded on tape, and the sounds which follow are those which have been sent to Earth by alien, non-human, intelligent beings no one knows how far away."

A pause. Then the car radio, with night sounds and the calls of nightbirds for background, gave out crisp, distinct fluting noises, like someone playing an arbitrary selection of musical notes on a strange wind instrument.

The effect was plaintive, but Burke stiffened in every muscle at the first of them. The fluting noises were higher and lower in turn. At intervals, they paused as if between groups of signals constituting a word. The enigmatic sounds went on for a full minute. Then they stopped. The voice returned:

"These are the signals from space. What you have heard is apparently a complete message. It is repeated five times and then ceases. An hour and nineteen minutes later it is again repeated five times . . ."

The voice continued, while Burke remained frozen and motionless in the parked car. Sandy watched him, at first hopefully, and then bewilderedly. The voice said that the signal strength was very great. But the power for artificial-satellite broadcasts is only a fraction of a watt. These signals, considering the minimum distance from which they could come, had at least thousands of kilowatts behind them.

Somewhere out in space, farther than man's robot rockets had ever gone, huge amounts of electric energy were controlled to send these signals to Earth. Scientists were in disagreement about the possible distance the signals had traveled, whether they were meant solely for Earth or not, and whether they were an attempt to open communication with humanity. But nobody doubted that the signals were artificial. They had been sent by technical means. They could not conceivably be natural phenomena. Directional fixes said absolutely that they did not come from Mars or Jupiter or Saturn. Neptune and Uranus and Pluto were not nearly in the line of the signals' travel. Of course Venus and Mercury were to sunward of Earth, which ruled them out, since the signals arrived only on the night side of mankind's world. Nobody could guess, as yet, where they did originate.

Burke sat utterly still, every muscle tense. He was so pale that even in the moonlight Sandy saw it. She was alarmed.

"Joe! What's the matter?"

"Did you — hear that?" he asked thinly. "The signals?"

"Of course. But what . . ."

"I recognized them," said Burke, in a tone that was somehow despairing. "I've heard signals like that every so often since I was a kid." He swallowed. "It was sounds like that, and what went with them, that has been the — trouble with me. I was going to tell you about it — and ask you if you'd marry me anyway."

He began to tremble a little, which was not at all like the Joe Burke that Sandy knew.

"I don't quite under —"

"I'm afraid I've gone out of my head," he said unsteadily. "Look, Sandy! I was going to propose to you. Instead, I'm going to take you back to the office. I'm going to play you a recording I made a year ago. I think that when you've heard it you'll decide you wouldn't want to marry me anyhow."

Sandy looked at him with astonished eyes.

"You mean those signals from somewhere mean something special to you?"

"Very special," said Burke. "They raise the question of whether I've been crazy, and am suddenly sane, or whether I've been sane up to now, and have suddenly gone crazy."

The radio switched back to dance music. Burke cut it off. He started the car's motor. He backed, swung around, and headed for the office and construction shed of Burke Development, Inc.

Elsewhere, the profoundest minds of the planet gingerly examined the appalling fact that signals came to Earth from a place where men could not be. A message came from something which was not human. It was a suggestion to make cold chills run up and down any educated spine. But Burke drove tensely, and the road's surface sped toward the car's wheels and vanished under them. A warm breeze hummed and thuttered around the windshield. Sandy sat very still.

"The way I'm acting doesn't make sense, does it?" Burke asked. "Do you feel like you're riding with a lunatic?"

"No," she said. "But I never thought that if you ever did get around to asking me to marry you, somebody from outer space would forbid the banns! Can't you tell me what all this is about?"

"I doubt it very much," he told her. "Can you tell me what the signals are about?"

She shook her head. He drove through the night. Presently he said, "Aside from my private angle on the matter, there are some queer things about this business. Why should somebody out in space send us a broadcast? It's not from a planet, they say. If there's a spaceship on the way here, why warn us? If they want to be friends, they can't be sure we'll permit it. If they intend to be enemies, why throw away the advantage of surprise? In either case, it would be foolish to send cryptic messages on ahead. And any message would have to be cryptic."

The car went whirring along the roadway. Soon twinkling lights appeared among the trees. The small and larger buildings of Burke Development, Inc., came gradually into view. They were dark objects in a large empty space on the very edge of Burke's home town.

"And why," he went on, "why send a complex message if they only wanted to say that they were space travelers on the way to Earth?"

The exit from the highway to Burke Development appeared. Burke swung off the surfaced road and into the four-acre space his small and unusual business did not begin to fill up.

"If it were an offer of communication, it should be short and simple. Maybe an arithmetic sequence of dots, to say that they were intelligent beings and would like the sequence carried on if we had brains, too. Then we'd know somebody friendly was coming and wanted to exchange ideas before, if necessary, swapping bombs."

The car's headlights swept over the building in which the experimental work of Burke Development was done and on to the small house in which Sandy kept the books and records of the firm, Burke put on the brakes before the office door.

"Just to see if my head is working right," he said, "I raise a question about those signals. One doesn't send a long message to emptiness, repeated, in the hope that someone may be around to catch it. One calls, and sends a long message only when the call is answered. The call says who's wanted and who's calling, but nothing more. This isn't that sort of thing,"

He got out of the car and opened the door on her side, then unlocked the office door and went in. He switched on the lights inside. For a moment, Sandy did not move. Then she slowly got out of the car and entered the once which was so completely familiar. Burke bent over the office safe, turning the tumbler-wheel to open it. He said over his shoulder, "That special bulletin will be repeated on all the news broadcasts. You've got a little radio here. Turn it on, will you?"

Again slowly, Sandy crossed the office and turned on the miniature radio on her desk. It warmed up and began to make noises. She dimmed it until it was barely audible. Burke stood up with a reel of brown tape. He put it on the office recorder, usually used for the dictation of the day's lab log.

"I have a dream sometimes," said Burke, "A recurrent dream. I've had it every so often since I was eleven. I've tried to believe it was simply a freak, but sometimes I've suspected I was a telepath, getting some garbled message from somewhere unguessable. That has to be wrong. And again I've suspected that — well — that I might not be completely human. That I was planted here on Earth, somehow, not knowing it, to be of use to — something not of Earth. And that's crazy. So I've been pretty leery of being romantic about anybody. Tonight I'd managed to persuade myself all those wild imaginings were absurd. And then the signals came." He paused and said unsteadily, "I made this tape a year ago. I was trying to convince myself that it was nonsense. Listen. Remember, I made this a year ago!"

The reels began to spin on the recorder's face. Burke's voice came out of the speaker, "These are the sounds of the dream," it said, and stopped.

There was a moment of silence, while the twin reels spun silently. Then sounds came from the recorder. They were musical notes, reproduced from the tape. Sandy stared blankly. Disconnected, arbitrary flutelike sounds came out into the office of Burke Development, Inc. It was quite correct to call them elfin. They could be described as plaintive. They were not a melody, but a melody could have been made from them by rearrangement. They were very remarkably like the sounds from space. It was impossible to doubt that they were the same code, the same language, the same vocabulary of tones and durations.

Burke listened with a peculiarly tense expression on his face. When the recording ended, he looked at Sandy.

Sandy was disturbed. "They're alike. But Joe, how did it happen?"

"I'll tell you later," he said grimly. "The important thing is, am I crazy or not?"

The desk radio muttered. It was an hourly news broadcast. Burke turned it up and a voice boomed:

" . . . one o'clock news. Messages have been received from space in the century's most stupendous news event! Full details will follow a word from our sponsor."

There followed an ardent description of the social advantage, personal satisfaction and business advancement that must instantly follow the use of a particular intestinal regulator. The commercial ended.

"From deepest space," boomed the announcer's voice, "comes a mystery! There is intelligent life in the void. It has communicated with us. Today —"

Because of the necessity to give the later details of a cafe-society divorce case, a torch murder and a graft scandal in a large city's municipal budget, the signals from space could not be fully treated in the five-minute hourly news program. But fifteen seconds were spared for a sample of the cryptic sounds from emptiness. Burke listened to them with a grim expression.

"I think," he said measuredly, "that I am sane. I have heard those noises before tonight. I know them — I'll take you home, Sandy."

He ushered her out of the office and into his car.

"It's funny," he said as he drove back toward the highway. "This is probably the beginning of the most important event in human history. We've received a message from an intelligent race that can apparently travel through space. There's no way in the world to guess what it will bring about. It could be that we're going to learn sciences to make old Earth a paradise. Or it could mean that we'll be wiped out and a superior race will take over. Funny, isn't it?"

Sandy said unsteadily, "No. Not funny."

"I mean," said Burke, "when something really significant happens, which probably will determine Earth's whole future, all I worry about is myself — that I'm crazy, or a telepath, or something. But that's convincingly human!"

"What do you think I worry about?" asked Sandy.

"Oh . . ." Burke hesitated, then said uncomfortably, "I was going to propose to you, and I didn't."

"That's right," said Sandy. "You didn't."

Burke drove for long minutes, frowning.

"And I won't," he said flatly, after a time, "until I know it's all right to do so. I've no explanation for what's kept me from proposing to you up to now, but apparently it's not nonsense. I did anticipate the sounds that came in tonight from space and — I've always known those sounds didn't belong on Earth."

Then, driving doggedly through a warm and moonlit night, he told her exactly why the fluting sounds were familiar to him; how they'd affected his life up to now. He'd mentally rehearsed the story, anyhow, and it was reasonably well arranged. But told as fact, it was preposterous.

She listened in complete silence. He finished the tale with his car parked before the boardinghouse in which Sandy lived with her sister

Pam, they being all that was left of a family. If she hadn't known Burke all her life, of course, Sandy would have dismissed him and his story together. But she did know him. It did explain why he felt tongue-tied when he wished to be romantic, and even why he recorded a weird sequence of notes on a tape recorder. His actions were reasonable reactions to an unreasonable, repeated experience. His doubts and hesitations showed a sound mind trying to deal with the inexplicable. And now that the signals from space had come, it was understandable that he should react as if they were a personal matter for his attention.

She had a disheartening mental picture of a place where strange trees waved long and ribbonlike leaves under an improbable sky. Still . . .

"Y-yes," she said slowly when he'd finished his uneasy account. "I don't understand, but I can see how you feel. I — I guess I'd feel the same way if I were a man and what you've experienced happened to me." She hesitated. "Maybe there will be an explanation now, since those signals have come. They do match the ones you recorded from your dream. They're the ones you know about."

"I can't believe it," said Burke miserably, "and I can't dismiss it. I can't do anything until I find out why I know that somewhere there's a place with two moons and queer trees . . ."

He did not mention the part of his experience Sandy was most interested in — the person for whom he felt such anguished fear and such overwhelming joy when she was found. She didn't mention it either.

"You go on home, Joe," she said quietly. "Get a good night's sleep. Tomorrow we'll hear more about it and maybe it will all clear up. Anyhow — whatever turns out, I — I'm glad you did intend to ask me to marry you. I intended to say yes."

CHAPTER 2

BURKE WAS no less disturbed, but his disturbance was of a different kind. After he left Sandy at the house where she and her sister boarded, he headed back to the plant. He wanted to think things out.

The messages from space, of course, must presage events of overwhelming importance. The coming of intelligent aliens to Earth might be comparable to the coming of white men to the American continents. They might bring superior techniques, irresistible weapons, and an assumption of superiority that would bring inevitable conflict with the aborigines of Earth. Judging by the actions of the white race on Earth, if the newcomers were merely explorers it could mean the coming doom of humanity's independence. If they were invaders . . .

Something like this would be pointed out soon after the news itself. Some people would react with total despair, expecting the strangers to act like men. Some might hope that a superior race would have developed a kindliness and altruism that on Earth are rather rare. But there was no one at all who would not be apprehensive. Some would panic.

Burke's reaction was strictly personal. Nobody else in the world would have felt the same appalled, stunned emotion he felt when he heard the sounds from space. Because to him they were familiar sounds.

He paced up and down in the big, partitionless building in which the actual work of Burke Development, Inc., was done. He'd done some reasonably good work in this place. The prototype of the hydroponic wall for Interiors, Inc., still stood against one wall. It was crude, but he'd made it work and then built a production model which had now been shipped off complete. A little to one side was a prototype of a special machine which stamped out small parts for American Tool. That had been a tricky assignment! There were plastic and glass-wool and such oddments with which he'd done a process-design job for Holmes Yachts, and a box of small parts left over from the designing job that gave one aviation company the only practical small-plane retractable landing-gear.

These things had a queer meaning for him now. He'd devised the wanted products. He'd developed certain needed processes. But now he began to be deeply suspicious of his own successes. Each was a new reason for uneasiness.

He grimly questioned whether his highly peculiar obsession had not been planted in him against the time when fluting noises would come from that illimitable void beyond Earth's atmosphere.

He examined, for the thousandth time, his special linkage with the space noises. In previous soul-searchings he'd pin-pointed the time when the whole business began. He'd been eleven years old. He could even work out something close to an exact date. He was living with his aunt and uncle, his own parents being dead. His uncle had made a business trip to Europe, alone, and had brought back souvenirs which were fascinating to eleven-year-old Joe Burke. There was a flint knife, and a carved ivory object which his uncle assured him was mammoth ivory. It had a deer's head incised into it. There were some fragments of pottery and a dull-surfaced black cube. They appealed to the small boy because his uncle said they'd belonged to men who lived when mammoths roamed the Earth and cave men hunted the now-extinct huge beasts. Cro-Magnons, his uncle said, had owned the objects. He'd bought them from a French peasant who'd found a cave with pictures on its walls that dated back twenty thousand years. The French government had taken over the cave, but before reporting it the peasant had thriftily hidden away some small treasures to sell for himself. Burke's uncle bought them and, in time, presented them to the local museum. All but the black cube, which Burke had dropped. It had shattered into a million tissue-thin, shiny plates, which his aunt insisted on sweeping out. He'd tried to keep one of the plates, but his aunt had found it under his pillow and disposed of it.

He remembered the matter solely because he'd examined his memories so often, trying to find something relevant to account for the beginning of his recurrent dream. Somewhere shortly after his uncle's visit he had had a dream. Like all dreams, it was not complete. It made no sense. But it wasn't a normal dream for an eleven-year-old boy.

He was in a place where the sun had just set, but there were two moons in the sky. One was large and motionless. The other was small and moved swiftly across the heavens. From behind him came fluting signals like the messages that would later come from space. In the dream he was full-grown and he saw trees with extraordinary, ribbony leaves like no trees on Earth. They wavered and shivered in a gentle breeze, but he ignored them as he did the fluting sounds behind him.

He was searching desperately for someone. A child knows terror for himself, but not for anybody else. But Burke, then aged eleven, dreamed that he was in an agony of fear for someone else. To breathe was torment. He held a weapon ready in his hand. He was prepared to do battle with any imaginable creature for the person he needed to find. And suddenly he saw a figure running behind the waving foliage. The relief was almost greater pain than the terror had been. It was a kind and amount of emotion that an eleven-year-old boy simply could not know, but Burke experienced it. He gave a great shout, and bounded forward toward her — and the dream ended.

He dreamed it three nights running, then it stopped, for a while.

Then, a week later, he had the dream again, repeated in every detail. He had it a dozen times before he was twelve, and as many more before he was thirteen. It recurred at random intervals all through his teens, while he was in college, and after. When he grew up he found out that recurrent dreams are by no means unusual. But this was very far from a usual dream.

From time to time, he observed new details in the dream. He knew that he was dreaming. His actions and his emotions did not vary, but he was able to survey them — like the way one can take note of items in a book one reads while quite absorbed in it. He came to notice the way the trees sent their roots out over the surface of the ground before dropping suckers down into it. He noticed a mass of masonry off to the left. He discovered that a hill in the distance was not a natural hill. He was able to remember markings on the large, stationary moon in the sky, and to realize that the smaller one was jagged and irregular in shape. The dream did not change, but his knowledge of the place of the dream increased.

As he grew older, he was startled to realize that though the trees, for example, were not real, they were consistent with reality. The weapon he held in his hand was especially disturbing. Its grip and barrel were transparent plastic, and in the barrel there was a sequence of peculiarly-shaped forms, in and about which wire had been wound. As a grown man he'd made such shapes in metal, once. He'd tried them out as magnets in a job for American Tool. But they weren't magnets. They were something specific and alarming instead. He also came to know exactly what the mass of masonry was, and it was a sober engineering feat. No boy of eleven could have imagined it.

And always there were the flutelike musical sounds coming from behind him, When he was twenty-five he'd memorized them. He'd heard them — dreamed them — hundreds of times. He tried to duplicate them on a flute and devised a special mute to get exactly the tone quality he remembered so well. He made a recording to study, but the study was futile.

In a way, it was unwholesome to be so much obsessed by a dream. In a way, the dream was magnificently irrelevant to messages transmitted through millions of miles of emptiness. But the flutelike sounds linked it — now — to reality! He paced up and down in the empty, resonant building and muttered, "I ought to talk to the space-exploration people."

Then he laughed. That was ironical. All the crackpots in the world would be besieging all the authorities who might be concerned with the sounds from space, impassionedly informing them what Julius Caesar, or Chief Sitting Bull, or some other departed shade, had told them about the matter via automatic writing or Ouija boards. Those who did not claim ghostly authority would explain that they had special talents, or a marvelous invention, or that they were members of the race which had sent the messages the satellite-tracking stations received.

No. It would serve no purpose to inform the Academy of Sciences that he'd been dreaming signals like the ones that now agitated humanity. It was too absurd. But it was unthinkable for a person of Burke's temperament to do nothing. So he set to work in exactly the fashion of one of the crackpots he disliked.

Actually, the job should have been undertaken in ponderous secrecy by committees from various learned societies, official bureaus, and all the armed forces. There should have been squabbles about how the task was to be divided up, bitter arguments about how much money was to be spent by whom, violent disagreements about research-and-development contracts. It should have been treated as a program of research, in which everybody could claim credit for all achievements and nobody was to blame for blunders.

Burke could not command resources for so ambitious an undertaking. And he knew that as a private project it was preposterous. But he began the sort of preliminary labor that an engineer does before he really sets to work.

He jotted down some items that he didn't have to worry about. The wall-garden he'd made for Interiors, Inc., would fit neatly into whatever final result he got — if he got a final result. He had a manufacturing process available for glass-wool and plastics. If he could get hold of an inertia-controlled computer he'd be all set, but he doubted that he could. The crucial item was a memo he'd made from a memory of the dream weapon. It concerned certain oddly-shaped bits of metal, with fine wires wound eccentrically about them, which flew explosively to pieces when a current went through them. That was something to worry about right away.

At three o'clock in the morning, then, Burke routed out the laboratory notes on the small-sized metal-stamping machine he had designed for American Tool. He'd tried to do the job with magnets, but they flew apart. He'd wound up with blank cartridges to provide the sudden, explosive stamping action required, but the notes on the quasi-magnets were complete.

He went through them carefully. An electromagnet does not really attain its full power immediately after the current is turned on. There is an inductive resistance, inherent in a wound magnet, which means that the magnetism builds up gradually. From his memory of the elements in a transparent-plastic hand-weapon barrel, Burke had concluded that it was possible to make a magnet without inductive resistance. He tried it. When the current went on it went to full strength immediately. In fact, it seemed to have a negative-induction effect. But the trouble was that it wasn't a magnet. It was something else. It wound up as scrap.

Now, very reflectively, he plugged in a metal lathe and carefully turned out a very tiny specimen of the peculiarly-shaped magnetic core. He wound it by hand, very painstakingly. It was a tricky job. It was six o'clock Saturday morning when the specimen was finished. He connected the leads to a storage battery and threw the switch. The small object tore itself to bits, and the core landed fifteen feet from where it had been. Burke beamed.

He wasn't tired, but he wanted to think things over so he drove to a nearby diner and got coffee and a roll and reflected with satisfaction upon his accomplishment. At the cost of several hours' work he'd made a thing like a magnet, which wasn't a magnet, and which destroyed itself when turned on. As he drank his coffee, a radio news period came on. He listened.

The signals still arrived from space, punctually, seventy-nine minutes apart. At this moment, 6:30 A.M., they were not heard an the Atlantic coast, but the Pacific coast still picked them up and they were heard in Hawaii and again on the South Pacific island of Kalua.

Burke drove back to the plant. He was methodical, now. He reactivated the prototype wall-garden which he'd neglected while building the larger one for Interiors, Inc. The experimental one had been made in four sections so he could try different pumping systems and nutrient solutions. Now he set the pumps to work. The plants looked ragged, but they'd perk up with proper lighting and circulation of the hydroponic liquid.

Then he went into the plant's small office building and sat down with drawing instruments to modify the design of the magnetic core. At eleven he'd worked out a rough theory and refined the design, with curves and angles all complete. At four the next morning a second, modified magnet-core was formed and polished.

He'd heard the first newscast on Friday night. It was now early Sunday morning, and although he was tired, he was still not sleepy. He worked on doggedly, winding fine magnet wire on a noticeably complicated metal form. Just before sunrise he tested it.

When the current went on the wire windings seemed to swell. He'd held it in a small clamp while he tested it. The clamp overturned and broke the contact with the battery before the winding wire stretched to breaking-point. But it had not torn itself or anything else to bits.

He was suddenly enormously weary and bleary-eyed. To anyone else in the world, the consequence of this second attempt to make what he thought of as a negative-induction magnet would seem an absolute failure. But Burke now knew why the first had failed and what was wrong with the second. The third would work, just as the unfired hand-weapon of his dream would have worked. Now he could justify to himself the association of a recurrent dream with a message from outer space. The dream now had two points of contact with reality. One was the sounds from emptiness, which matched those in the dream. The other was the hand-weapon of the dream, whose essential working part now plainly did something unknown in a normal world.

But it would be impossible to pass on his information to anybody else. Too many crackpots have claimed too many triumphs. His actual, unpredictable technical achievement would have little chance of winning official acceptance. Especially since he would be considered a non-accredited source. Burke had a small business of his own. He had an engineering degree. But he had no background of learned futility to gain a hearing for what he now knew.

"Crackpots of the world, unite!" he muttered to himself.

He dragged himself out-of-doors to a cool, invigorating morning and drove somnolently to the diner he'd patronized before. The coffee he ordered was atrocious, but it waked him. He heard two truck drivers at the counter.

"It's baloney!" said one of them scornfully. "There ain't no people out there! We'd'a heard from them before if there was. Them scientists are crazy!"

"Nuts!" said the other earnestly. "One of their idle thoughts would crack your brain wide open, mac! They know what's up, and they're scared! If you wanna know, I'm scared too!"

"Of what?"

"Hell! Did you ever drive at night, and have all the stars come in pairs like snake-eyes — like little mean eyes, lookin' down at you an' despisin' you? You've seen that, ain't you? Whoever's signalin' could be lookin' down at us just like the stars do."

The first man grunted.

"I don't like it!" said the second man, fretfully. "If it was a man headin' out to go huntin' among the stars for somethin' he wanted, that's all right. That's like a man goin' huntin' in the woods with a gun.

But I don't like somebody comin' our way from somewhere else. Maybe he's huntin' us!"

The two drivers paid for their coffee and went out. And Burke reflected wryly that the second man had, after all, expressed a universal truth. We humans do not like to be hunted. The passion with which a man-killing wild beast is pursued comes from human vanity. We do not like the idea that any other creature can be better than we are. It is highly probable that if we ever have to face a superior race, we will die of it.

So Burke went back to the plant and began to make yet another of the peculiarly wound magnets-which-were-not-magnets. This was to have three of the odd-shaped cores, formed in line, of a single piece of Swedish iron. As the windings were put on they'd be imbedded in plastic. Over that would go a casing to keep them from expanding or stretching. It ought to be distinctively different from a magnet.

It was an extremely long and utterly tedious job. He knew what he was doing, but he had doubts about the why. As he worked, though, he wrestled out a detailed theory. Discoverers often work like that. It was said that Columbus didn't know where he was going when he started out, didn't know where he was when he got there, and didn't know where he'd been when he got back. The history of the discovery of the triode tube has points of similarity. Burke had begun with a device which destroyed itself when turned on, developed the idea into a device which swelled to uselessness when energized, and now hoped that it would turn out at the third try to be something the textbooks said was impossible.

Outside the construction shed, the world went about its business. While Burke worked on through the Sunday noon hour, a Japanese radar telescope aimed at the night sky and made six successive position-findings on the source of the space signals. When sunset found him laboring doggedly at a metal lathe, Croydon made eight. American radar telescopes had made others. Carefully computed, the observations added up to the discovery of an independent motion of the signal source. It moved against the stars as if it were a solar-system body with an orbit in the asteroid belt some three hundred sixty million miles from the sun — as compared to Earth's ninety-two million,

At midnight on Sunday, while Burke painstakingly made micro-metric examination of the triple magnet-core, Harvard Observatory reported that there should be a very minor asteroid at the spot in space from which the signals came.

The coincidental asteroid was known as Schull's object. It was listed as M-387 in the catalogs. It had been discovered in 1913, was a very minor celestial body, had an estimated greatest diameter of less than two miles, and its brightness had been noticed to vary, suggesting that it was of irregular shape. It was too insignificant to have been kept under constant observation, but the signals from space appeared definitely to originate from its position.

An hour after midnight, Eastern Standard time, Palomar detected the infinitesimal speck of light which was Schull's object at exactly the place the radar telescopes insisted was the signal source. Satellite-watching stations now monitored the cryptic signals around the clock, and radar telescopes began to sweep space for possible answers to the space broadcast. There was an uncomfortable possibility that the transmitter might not be signaling Earth, after all, but a fellow mystery of space — an associate or a sister-ship.

More data turned up. M.I.T. made examination of the signals themselves. Timed, the intervals between notes varied as if keyed by something alive. But successive broadcasts were identical to microseconds. The conclusion was that the original broadcast had been set up by hand, as it were, but that all were now transmitted mechanically — automatically — by a robot transmitter.

It was Monday morning when Burke completed the last turn of the last winding of his three-element pseudo-magnet. There are many things which become something else when they change in degree. Electromagnetic radiation may be long radio waves or radiant heat or yellow light or ultraviolet or X-rays, or who knows what, according to its frequency. It is different things with different properties at different wavelengths. Burke believed that his cores and windings were something other than magnets because the "flux" they produced was of a different intensity. He did not believe it to be magnetism.

At nine o'clock Monday morning, he was clumsy from pure weariness when he began to fit the outer case on the thing he'd worked so long to complete. The hand-weapon in his dream undoubtedly flung bullets through a rifled bore penetrating the very center of the multiple core. The design of the hand-weapon ruled out any possibility of a considerable recoil. It wasn't built to allow the hand to take a recoil. So there must be no recoil. On that basis, Burke had made what finally amounted to a thick rod some six inches long and two in diameter. With the casing in place, it was absolutely solid. There was no play for the windings to expand into. He blinked at it. Common sense said he ought to put it aside and test it when his mind was not nearly numb from fatigue.

Then Sandy came into the constructions shed, looking for him. She'd arrived for work and seen his car outside the shed. Her expression indicated several things: a certain uneasiness, and some embarrassment, and more than a little indignation. When she saw him unshaven and wobbly with weariness, she protested.

"Joe! You've been working since Heaven knows when!"

"Since I left you," he admitted. "I got interested."

"You look dreadful!"

"Maybe I'll look worse after I try out this thing I've made, I'm not sure."

"When did you eat last?" she demanded. "And when did you sleep?"

He shrugged tiredly, regarding the thing in his hands. He'd had enough experience contriving new things to know that no theory is right until something that depends on it has been made and works. He tended to be pessimistic. But this time he thought he had it.

"Is this working night and day a part of your reaction to those signals?" asked Sandy unhappily. "If it is —"

"Let's try it," Burke interrupted. "It's something I worked out from the dream. Now I'll find out whether I'm crazy or not — maybe." He drew a deep breath. He had a sodden, deep and corrosive doubt of things which didn't make sense, like space signals and magnets which weren't magnets because they were capable of negative self-induction. "If this shows no sign of working, Sandy . . ."

"What?"

He didn't answer. He went heavily over to the table where he had storage-battery current available. He plucked a momentary-contact switch out of a drawer and connected it to the wires from the small thing he'd made. Then he hooked on the storage battery.

"Stand back, Sandy," he said tiredly. "We'll see what happens."

He flipped the momentary-contact switch. There was a crash and a roar. The six-inch thing leaped. It grazed Burke's head and drew blood. It flashed across the room, a full thirty feet, and then smashed a water-cooler and imbedded itself in the brick wall beyond. A tool cabinet tottered and crashed to the floor. The storage battery spouted steam, swelled. Burke grabbed Sandy and plunged outside with her as the building filled with vaporized battery acid.

Outside, he put her down and rubbed his nose with his finger.

"That was a surprise," he said with some animation. "Are you all right?"

"You — could have been killed!" she said in a whisper.

"I wasn't," said Burke. "If you're not hurt there's no harm done. It looks like the thing worked! Lucky that was only a millisecond contact! Negative self-induction . . . I'll break some windows and come to the office."

He did break windows, from the outside, so air could flow through the building and clear away the battery-acid steam. Sandy watched him anxiously.

"Okay," he said. "I'll come quietly."

He followed her to the office. He was so physically worn out, he tripped on the office step as he went in.

"Tell me the news on the signals," he said. "Still coming in?"

"Yes." She looked at him again, worried. "Joe . . . Sit down. Here. What's happened?"

"Nothing except that I'm a genius at second hand. I didn't intend it that way, and maybe it can be covered up, but I've turned out to be sane. So I think, maybe you'd better get another job. Since I'm sane I'll surely go bankrupt and maybe I'll end up in jail. But it's going to be interesting." His head drooped and he jerked it upright. "This is reaction," he said distinctly. "I'm tired, I wanted badly to find out whether I was crazy or not. I found out I haven't been. I'm not so sure I won't be presently." He made a stiff gesture and said, "Take the day off, Sandy. I'm going to rest awhile."

Then his head fell forward and he was asleep.

Burke slept for a long time. And this time dreamlessly.

The thing he made had worked for much less than the tenth of a second, but it came out of his dream, ultimately, and it was linked with whatever sent messages from Asteroid M-387. There was still nothing intelligible about the whole affair. It contained no single rational element. But if there was no rational explanation, there was what now seemed reasonable action that could be taken.

So he slept, and as usual the world went on its way unheeding. The fluting sounds from the sky remained the top news story of the day. There was no doubt of their artificiality, nor that they came from a small, tumbling, jagged rock which was one of the least of the more than fifteen hundred asteroids of the solar system. It was two hundred and seventy million miles from Earth. The latest computations said that not less than twenty thousand kilowatts of power had been put into the transmitter to produce so strong and loud a signal on Earth. No power-source of that order had been carried out to make the signals. But they were there.

Astronomers became suddenly important sources of news. They contradicted each other violently. Eminent scientists observed truthfully that Schull's object, as such, could not sustain life. It could not have an atmosphere, and its gravitational field would not hold even a moderately active microbe on its surface. Therefore any life and any technology now on it must have come from somewhere else. The most eminent scientists said reluctantly that they could not deny the possibility that a spaceship from some other solar system had been wrecked on M-387, and was now sending hopeless pleas for help to the local planetary bodies.

Others observed briskly that anything which smashed into an asteroid would vaporize, if it hit hard enough, or bounce away if it did not. So there was no evidence for a spaceship. There was only evidence for a transmitter. There was no explanation for that. It could be mentioned, said these skeptics, that there were other sources of radiation in space. There was the Jansky radiation from the Milky Way, and radiations from clouds of ionized material in emptiness, and radio stars were well known. A radio asteroid was something new, but —

It was working astronomers, so to speak, who took action. They had been bouncing signals off of Earth's moon, and various artificial satellites, and they'd flicked signals in the direction of Mars and Venus and believed that they got them back. The most probable returned radar signal from Mars had been received by a radar telescope in West Virginia. It had been turned temporarily into a transmitter and some four hundred kilowatts were poured into it to go out in a tight beam.

The working astronomers took over that parabolic bowl again. They borrowed, begged, wheedled, and were suspected of stealing necessary equipment to put nearly eight hundred kilowatts into a microwave signal, this time beamed at Asteroid M-387. If intelligent beings received the signal, they might reply. If they did, the working astronomers would figure out what to do next.

Burke slept in the office of Burke Development, Inc. His features were relaxed and peaceful. Sandy was completely helpless before his tranquil exhaustion. But presently she used the telephone and spoke in a whisper to her younger sister, Pam. In time, Pam came in a cab bringing blankets and a pillow. She and Sandy got Burke to a pallet on the floor with a pillow under his head and a thickness of blanket over him. He slept on, unshaven and oblivious.

Pam said candidly, "If you can feel romantic about anything like that, Sandy, I'll still love you, but I'll join the men in thinking that women are mysterious!"

She departed in the cab and Sandy took up a vigil over Burke's slumbering form.

Pravda announced in its evening edition of Monday that Soviet scientists would send out a giant space-probe, intended to orbit around Venus, to investigate the space-signal source. The probe would carry a man. It would blast off within six weeks, preceded by drone fuel-carriers which would be overtaken by the probe and furnish fuel to it. Pravda threw in a claim that Russians had been first to refuel an aeroplane in flight, and asserted that Soviet physical science would make a space-voyage of two hundred seventy million miles mere ducksoup for their astronaut.

Editorially, American newspapers mentioned that the Russians had tried similar things before, and that at least three coffins now floated in orbit around Earth, not to mention the one on the moon. But if they tried it . . . The American newspapers waited for a reaction from Washington.

It came. The most eminent of civilian scientists announced proudly that the United States would proceed to the design and testing of multi-stage rockets capable of landing a party on Mars when Earth and Mars were in proper relative position. This having been accomplished, a rocket would then take off from Mars for Asteroid M-387 to investigate the radio transmissions from that peculiar mass of tumbling rock. It was blandly estimated that the Americans might take off for Mars in eighteen months.

Sandy watched over Burke. There was nothing to do in the office. She did not read. Near seven the telephone rang, and she frantically muffled its sound. It was Pam, asking what Sandy meant to do about dinner. Sandy explained in an almost inaudible voice. Pam said resignedly, "All right. I'll come out and bring something. Lucky it's a warm day. We can sit in your car and eat. If I had to watch Joe sleeping like that and needing a shave as he does, I'd lose my appetite."

She hung up. When she arrived, Burke was still asleep. Sandy went outside. Pam had brought hero sandwiches and coffee. They sat on the steps of the office and ate.

"I know," said Pam between sympathy and scorn, "I know you like the poor goof, Sandy, but there ought to be some limit to your amorous servitude! There are office hours! You're supposed to knock off at five. It's seven-thirty now. And what will being decent to that unshaven Adonis get you? He'll take you for granted, and go off and marry a nitwit of a blonde who'll hate you because you'd have been so much better for him. And she'll get you fired and what then?"

"Joe won't marry anybody else," said Sandy forlornly. "If he could fall for anybody, it'd be me. He told me so. He started to propose to me Friday night."

"So?" said Pam, with the superior air of a younger sister. "Did he say enough for you to sue him?"

"He can't fall in love with anybody," said Sandy. "He wants to marry me, but he's emotionally tangled up with a female he's had dreams about since he was eleven."

"I thought I'd heard everything," said Pam. "But that —"

Sandy explained morosely. As she told it, it was not quite the same picture Burke had given her. Her account of the trees in Burke's recurrent dream was accurate enough, and the two moons in the sky, and the fluting, arbitrary tones from behind him. Pam had heard their duplicates, along with all the broadcast listeners in the United States. But as Sandy told it, the running figure beyond the screen of foliage was not at all the shadowy movement Burke described. Sandy had her own ideas, and they colored her account.

There was a stirring inside the small office building. Burke had waked. He turned over and blinked, astonished to find himself with blankets over him and a pillow under his head. It was dark inside the office, too.

"Joe," called Pam in the darkness, "Sandy and I have been waiting for you to wake up. You took your time about it! We've got some coffee for you."

Burke got to his feet and stumbled to the light switch. "Fine!" he said ruefully. "Somebody got blankets for me, too! Nice business, this!"

They heard him moving about. He folded the blankets that had been laid on the floor for him. He moved across the room and turned on Sandy's desk radio. It hummed, preliminary to playing. He came to the door.

"I'm sorry," he apologized. "I worked pretty hard pretty long, and when the thing was finished I passed out. I feel better now. Did you actually say you had some coffee?"

Sandy passed up a cardboard container.

"Pam's compliments," she said. "We've been waiting until you slept off your working binge. We didn't want to leave you. Booger-men sound likelier than they used to."

A voice from the radio broke in.

" . . . o'clock news. A signal has been beamed toward the space-broadcast transmitter by the parabolic reflector of the Bradenville radar telescope, acting as a mirror to concentrate the message toward Asteroid M-387. So far there has been no reply. We are keeping a circuit open, and if or when an answer is received we will issue a special bulletin. . . . The San Francisco Giants announced today that in a three-way trade —"

Burke had listened to nothing else while the news broadcast dealt with space signals, but other news did not mean very much to him just now. He sipped at the cardboard cup of coffee.

"I think," said Pam, "that since you've waked up I'll take my big sister home. You'll be all right now."

"Yes," said Burke abstractedly. "I'll be all right now."

"Really, Joe, you shouldn't work day and night without a break!" Sandy said.

"And you shouldn't have bothered to stand watch over me," he answered. "Well, I guess the shed should be clear of battery fumes by now. I'll go over and see."

Burke came back in a few minutes.

"This thing I made is pretty tough," he observed. "It smashed into a brick wall, but it was the wall that suffered." He fingered it thoughtfully. "I had that dream again just now," he volunteered. "While I was asleep on the floor. Sandy, you know about such things better than I do. How much money have I in the bank? I'm going to build something and it'll probably cost a lot."

Sandy's hands had clenched when he mentioned the dream. So far, it had done more damage than any dream had a right to do. But it looked as if it were about to do more. She told him his balance in the bank. He nodded.

"Maybe I can stretch it," he observed. "I'm going to —"

The music had stopped inside the office. The voice of an announcer interrupted.

"Special Bulletin! Special Bulletin! Our signal to space have been answered! Special Bulletin! Here is a direct report from the Bradenton radar telescope which, within the hour, broadcast a message to space!"

A tinny, agitated voice came from the radio, punctuated by those tiny beeping sounds that say that a telephone talk is being recorded.

"A definite reply to the human signal to Asteroid M-387 has been received. It is cryptic, like the first message from space, but is unmistakably a response to the eight-hundred-kilowatt message beamed toward the source of those world-wide-received strange sounds. . . ."

The tinny voice went on.

CHAPTER 3

IN RETROSPECT, events moved much faster than reason would suggest. The first signal from space had been received on a Friday. At that time — when the first flutings were picked up by a tape recorder on Kalua — the world had settled down to await the logical consequences of its history. It was not a comfortable settling-down, because the consequences were not likely to be pleasant. Earth was beginning to be crowded, and there were whole nations whose populations labored bitterly with no hope of more than subsistence during their lifetime, and left a legacy of equal labor and scarcer food for their descendants. There were hydrogen bombs and good intentions, and politics and a yearning for peace, and practically all individual men felt helpless before a seemingly merciless march of ominous events. At that time, too, nearly everybody worked for somebody else, and a large part of the employed population justified its existence by the length of time spent at its place of employment. Nobody worried about what he did there.

In the richer nations, everybody wanted all the rewards earned for them by generations gone by, but nobody was concerned about leaving his children better off. An increasingly smaller number of people were willing to take responsibility for keeping things going. There'd been a time when half of Earth fought valiantly to make the world safe for democracy. Now, in the richer nations, most men seemed to believe that the world had been made safe for a four-card flush, which was the hand they'd been dealt and which nobody tried to better.

Then the signals came from space. They called for a showdown, and very few people were prepared for it. Eminent men were called on to take command and arrange suitable measures. They immediately acted as eminent men so often do; they took action to retain their eminence. Their first instinct was caution. When a man is important enough, it does not matter if he never does anything. It is only required of him that he do nothing wrong. Eminent figures all over the world prepared to do nothing wrong. They were not so concerned to do anything right.

Burke, however, was not important enough to mind making a mistake or two. And there were other non-famous people to whom the extra-terrestrial sounds suggested action instead of precautions. Mostly they were engineers with no reputations to lose. They'd scrabbled together makeshift equipment, ignored official channels, and in four days — Friday to Monday — they had eight hundred kilowatts ready to fling out toward emptiness, in response to the signal from M-387.

The transmission they'd sent out was five minutes long. It began with a re-transmission of part of the message Earth had received. This plainly identified the signal from Earth as a response to the cryptic flutings. Then there were hummings. One dot, two dots, three, and so on. These hummings assured whoever or whatever was out yonder that the inhabitants of Earth could count. Then it was demonstrated that two dots plus two dots were known to equal four dots, and that four and four added up to eight. The inhabitants of Earth could add. There followed the doubtless interesting news that two and two and two and two was eight. Humanity could multiply.

Arithmetic, in fact, filled up three minutes of the eight-hundred-kilowatt beam-signal. Then a hearty human voice — the president of a great university — said warmly:

"Greetings from Earth! We hope for splendid things from this opening of communication with another race whose technical achievements fill us with admiration."

More flutings repeated that the Earth signal was intended for whoever or whatever used flutelike sounds for signaling purposes, and the message came to an end with an arch comment from the university president: "We hope you'll answer!"

When this elaborate hodge-podge had been flung out to immensity, the prominent persons who'd devised it shook hands with each other. They were confident that if intelligent beings did exist where the mournful musical notes came from, interplanetary or interstellar communication could be said to have begun. The engineers who'd sweated together the equipment simply hoped their signal would reach its target.

It did. It went out just after the end of a reception of a five-minute broadcast from M-387. Seventy-nine minutes should have passed before any other sound from M-387. But an answer came much more quickly than that. In thirty-four minutes, five and three-tenth seconds, a new signal came from beyond the sky. It came in a rush. It came from the transmitter out in orbit far beyond Mars. It came with the same volume.

It started with an entirely new grouping of the piping tones. There was a specific crispness in their transmission, as if a different individual handled the transmitter-keys. The flutings went on for three minutes, then were replaced by entirely new sounds. These were sharp, distinct, crackling noises. A last sequence of the opening flutings, and the message ended abruptly. But silence did not follow. Instead, a steady, sonorous, rhythmic series of beeping noises began and kept on interminably. They were remarkably like the directional signals of an airway beacon. When the news broadcasts of the United States reported the matter, the beeping sounds were still coming in.

And they continued to come in for seventy-nine minutes. Then they broke off and the new transmission was repeated. The original message was no longer sent. Robot transmitter or no robot transmitter, the first message had been transmitted at regular intervals for something like seventy-six hours and then, instantly on receipt of the beginning of an answer, a new broadcast took its place.

The reaction had been immediate. The distance between M-387 and Earth could be computed exactly. The time needed for the Earth signal to arrive was known exactly. And the instant — the very instant — the first sound from Earth reached M-387, the second message had begun. There was no pause to receive all the Earth greeting, or even part of it. The reaction was immediate and automatic.

Automatic. That was the significant thing. The new message was already prepared when the Earth signal arrived. It was set up to be transmitted on receipt of the earliest possible proof that it would be received. The effect of this rapid response was one of tremendous urgency — or absolute arrogance. The implication was that what Earth had to say was unimportant. The Earth signal had not been listened to. Instead, Earth was told something. Something crisp and arbitrary. Maybe there could be amiable chit-chat later on, but Earth must listen first! The beepings could not be anything but a guide, a directional indicator, to be followed to M-387. The message, now changed, might amount to an offer of friendship, but it also could be a command. If it were a command, the implications were horrifying.

At the moment of first release, the news had only a limited effect. Most of Europe was asleep and much of Asia had not waked up yet. But the United States was up and stirring. The news went to every corner of the nation with the speed of light. Radio stations stopped all other transmissions to announce the frightening event. It is of record that four television stations on the North American continent actually broke into filmed commercials to announce that M-387 had made a response to the signal from Earth. Never before in history had a paid advertisement been thrust aside for news.

In the United States, then, there was agitation, apprehension, indignation, and panic. Perhaps the only place where anything like calmness remained was inside and outside the office of Burke Development, Inc., where Burke felt a singular relief at this evidence that he wasn't as much of a fool as he feared.

"Well," he thought. "It looks like there is something or somebody out there. If I'd been sure about it earlier — but it probably wasn't time."

"What does this mean?" asked Sandy. "This horrible spell of around-the-clock working! Are you still trying to do something about the space signals?"

"Listen, Sandy," said Burke. "I've been ashamed of that crazy dream of mine all my life. I've thought it was proof there was something wrong with me. I'll still have to keep it secret, or nice men in white coats will come and get me. But I'm going to do what all enterprising young men are advised to do — dream greatly and then try to realize my dream. It's quite impossible and it'll bankrupt me, but I think I'm going to have fun."

He grinned at the two sisters as he led them firmly to Sandy's car.

"Shoot" he said pleasantly. "You'd better go home now. I'll be leaving in minutes, heading for Schenectady first. I need some electric stuff. Then I'll go elsewhere. There'll be some shipments arriving,

Sandy. Take care of them for me, will you?"

He closed the car door and waved, still grinning. Pam fumed and started the motor. Moments later their car trundled down the highway toward town. Sandy clenched her fists.

"What can you do with a man like that?" she demanded. "Why do I bother with him?"

"Shall I answer," asked Pam, "or shall I be discreetly sympathetic? I wouldn't want him! But unfortunately, if you do —"

"I know," said Sandy forlornly. "I know, dammit!"

Burke was not thinking of either of them then. He opened the office safe, put the six-inch object inside, and took out his checkbook. Then he locked up, got into his car, and headed away from the plant and the town he'd been brought up in. He was unshaven and uncombed and this was an inappropriate time to start out on a drive of some hundreds of miles, but it was a pleasing sensation to know that a job had turned up that nobody else would even know how to start to work on. He drove very cheerfully to a cross-country expressway and turned onto it. He settled down at once to drive and to think.

He drove practically all night. Shortly after sunrise he stopped to buy a razor and brush and comb and to make himself presentable. He was the first customer on hand when a Schenectady firm specializing in electronic apparatus for seagoing ships opened up for business. He ordered certain equipment from a list he'd written on an envelope while eating breakfast.

The morning papers, naturally, were full of the story of the answer to the Earth signal sent out to M-387. The morning comedians made jokes about it, and in every one of the business offices Burke visited there was some mention of it. He listened, but had nothing to say. The oddity of his purchases caused no remark. His was a small firm, but a man working in research and development needs strange stuff sometimes. He ordered two radar units to be modified in a particular fashion, air-circulation pumps of highly specialized design to be changed in this respect and that. He had trouble finding the electric generators he wanted and had to pay heavily for alterations in them, and even more heavily for a promise of delivery in days instead of weeks. He bought a self-contained diving suit.

He was busy for three days, buying things by day, designing by night and finding out new things to order. On the second day, United States counter-intelligence reported that the Russians were trying to signal M-387 on their own. An American satellite picked up the broadcast. The Russians denied it, and continued to try. Burke made arrangements for the delivery of aluminum-alloy bars, rods, girders, and plates; for plaster of Paris in ton lots; for closed-circuit television equipment. Once he called Sandy to give her an order to be filled locally. It was lumber, mostly slender strips of lathing, to be on hand when he returned.

"All kinds of material is turning up," said Sandy. "There've been six deliveries this morning. I'm signing receipts for it because I don't know what else to do. But won't you please give me copies of the orders you've placed so I can check what arrives?"

"I'll put 'em in the mail — airmail," promised Burke. "But only six deliveries? There ought to be dozens! Get after these people on long distance, will you?" And he gave her a list of names.

Burke said suddenly, "I had that dream again last night. Twice in a week. That's unusual."

"No comment," Sandy said.

She hung up, and Burke was taken aback. But there was hardly any comment she could make. Burke himself had no illusion that he would ever come to a place where there were two moons in the sky and trees with ribbon-like leaves. And if he did — unthinkable as that might be — he could not imagine finding the person for whom he felt such agonized anxiety. The dream, recurrent, fantastic, or whatnot, simply could not represent a reality of the past, present, or future. Such things don't happen. But Burke continued to be moved much more by the emotional urge of the repeated experience than by intellectual curiosity about his having dreamed repeatedly of signals exactly like those from space, long before such signals ever were.

He made ready to try to do something about those signals. And, all reason to the contrary notwithstanding, to him they meant a world with two moons and strange vegetation and such emotion as nothing on Earth had ever quite stirred up — though he felt pretty deeply about Sandy, at that. So he went intently from one supplier of exotic equipment to another, spending what money he had for an impossibility. Impossible because Asteroid M-387 was not over two miles through at its largest dimension, and therefore could not possibly have an atmosphere and certainly not trees, and it could not own even a single moon!

He spent one day at a small yachting port with a man for whom he'd worked out a special process of Fiberglas yacht construction, Through that process, Holmes yachts could be owned by people who weren't millionaires, Holmes was a large, languid, sunburned individual who built yachts because he liked them. He had much respect for Burke, even after Burke asked his help and explained what for.

But that was the day the Russians launched an unmanned space-probe headed toward M-387. That development may have influenced Holmes to do as Burke asked.

Later on, it transpired that the probe originally had been designed and built as a cargo-carrier to take heavy loads to Earth's moon. The Russian space service had planned to present the rest of Earth with a fait accompli even more startling than the first Sputnik. They had intended to send a fleet of drone cargo-rockets to the moon and then assemble them into a colony. Broadcasts would triumphantly explain that the Soviet social system was responsible for another technical achievement. But to get a man out to M-387 was now so much mare important a propaganda device that the cargo-carriers were converted into fuel-tankers and the first sent aloft.

At ten thousand miles up, when the third booster-stage should have given it a decisive thrust, one of the probe's rocket engines misfired. The space-probe tilted, veered wildly from its course, and went on accelerating splendidly toward nowhere. And still the steady, urgent beeping sounds continued to come to Earth, with every seventy-nine minutes a broadcast containing one section of crackling sounds and a tone of extremest urgency.

The day after the probe's ineffectual departure, Burke got back to his plant. He brought Holmes with him. Together, they looked over the accumulated material for Burke's enterprise and began to sort out the truckloads of plaster of Paris, masses of punched-sheet aluminum, girders, rods, beams of shining metal, cased dynamos, crated pumps, tanks, and elaborately padded objects whose purpose was not immediately clear. Sandy was overwhelmed by the job of inventorying, indexing, and otherwise making the material available for use as desired. There were bales of fluffy white cloth and drums and drums of liquids which insisted on leaking, and smelled very badly when they did. But Burke found some items not yet on hand, and fretted, so Sandy brought her sister Pam into the office to add to the office force.

Sandy and Pam worked quite as hard in the office as Burke and Holmes in the construction shed. They telephoned protests at delays, verified shipments, scolded shipping-clerks, argued with transportation-system expediters, wrote letters, answered letters, compared invoices with orders, sternly battled with negligence and delays of all kinds, and in between kept the books of Burke Development, Inc., up to date so that at any instant Burke could find out how much money he'd spent and how little remained. The two girls in the office were necessary to the operations which at first centered in the construction shed, but shortly began to show up outside.

Four workmen arrived from the Holmes' Yacht shipyard. They looked at blueprints and drawings made by Holmes and Burke together, regarded with pained expressions the material they were to use, and set to work. This was on the day the second Russian space-probe lifted from somewhere in the Caucasus Mountains at 1:10 A.M., local time.

The second probe did not veer off its proper line. Its four boosters fired at appropriate intervals and it went streaking off toward emptiness almost straight away from the sun. It left behind it a thin whining transmission which was not at all like the beepings of the asteroid transmitter.

In two days a framework of struts and laths took form outside the construction shed. It looked more like a mock-up of a radio telescope than anything else, but it was smaller and had a different shape. It was an improbable-looking bowl. Under Holmes' supervision, dozens of sacks of plaster of Paris found their way into it, coating it roughly on the outside and very smoothly within. It was then lined tenderly with carefully cut sections of fluffy cloth, with bars and beams and girders placed between the layers. Then reeking drums of liquid were moved to the working-site and their contents saturated the glass-wool.

The smell was awful, so the workmen knocked off for a day until it diminished. But Sandy and Pam continued to expostulate with shippers by long-distance, type letters threatening lawsuits if orders were not filled immediately, and once found that items Burke indignantly demanded had come in and Holmes had carted them off and used them without notifying anybody. That was the day Pam threatened to resign.

"It looks like a pudding," grumbled Pam, after Sandy had mollified her and Burke had apologized for having made her fight needlessly with two transport-lines, a shipping department, and a vice-president in charge of sales. "And they act like it was a baby!"

"It'll be a ship," said Sandy. "You know what kind."

"I'll believe it when I see it," said Pam. Then she demanded indignantly, "Has Joe looked at you twice since this nonsense started?"

"No," admitted Sandy. "He works all the time. At night he has a receiver tuned to the beepings to make sure he knows if the broadcast changes again. The Russians are still trying to make a two-way contact. But the broadcast just keeps on, ignoring everybody." Then she said, "Anyhow, Joe's going to feel awful if it doesn't work. I've got to be around to pick up the pieces of his vanity and put them together again."

"Huh!" said Pam. "Catch me doing that!"

At just that moment Holmes came into the office with a finger dripping blood. He had been supervising and, at the same time, assisting in the building of an additional section of laths and struts and he was annoyed with himself for the small injury which interfered with his work.

Pam did the bandaging. She cooed over him distressedly, and had him grinning before the dressing was finished. He went back to work very much pleased with himself.

"I," said Sandy, "wouldn't act like you just did!"

"Sister, darling," said Pam, "I won't cramp your act. Don't you criticize mine! That large wounded character is as attractive as anything I've seen in months."

"But I feel," said Sandy, "as if I hadn't seen Joe in years!"

Their viewpoint was strictly feminine and geared to female ideas and aspirations. But, in fact, they were probably as satisfied as two girls could be. They were on the side lines of interesting happenings which were being prepared by interesting men. They were useful enough to the enterprise to belong to it without doing anything outstanding enough to amount to rivalry with the men. From a girl's standpoint, it wasn't at all bad.

But neither Burke nor Holmes even faintly guessed at the appraisal of their work by Sandy and Pam. To Holmes, the task was fascinating because it was a ship he was building. It was not a beautiful object, to be sure. If the lath-and-plaster mould were removed, the thing inside it would look rather like an obese small whale. There were recesses in its rotund sides in which distinctly eccentric apparatus appeared. Its interior was even more curious. And still it was a ship. Holmes found deep satisfaction in fitting its interior parts into place. It was like, but not the same as, equipping a small vessel with fathometers, radars, direction-finders, air-conditioners, stoves, galleys, heads and refrigerators without getting it crowded.

To be sure, no seagoing ship would have sections of hydroponic wall-garden installed, nor would an auxiliary schooner normally have six pairs of closed-circuit television cameras placed outside for a view in each and every direction. This ship had such apparatus. But to Holmes the building of what Burke had designed was an extremely attractive task.

Burke had less fun. He'd set up a huge metal lathe in the construction shed, and he labored at carving out of a specially built-up Swedish-iron shaft a series of twenty-odd magnet-cores like the triple unit he considered successful. Each of the peculiar shapes had to be carved out of the shaft, and all had to remain part of the shaft when completed. Then each had to be wound with magnet-wire, coated with plastic as it was wound. Then a bronze tube had to be formed over all, with no play of any sort anywhere. The task required the workmanship of a jeweller and the patience of Job. And Burke had had enough experience with new constructions to be acutely doubtful that this would be right when it was done.

The Russians sent up a third space-probe, aimed at Asteroid M-387. It functioned perfectly. Three days later, a fourth. Three days later still, a fifth. Their aim with the fifth was not too good.

The beeping sounds continued to come in from space. The second message remained the same but the crackling sounds changed. There was a systematic and consistent variation in what they apparently had to say. M.I.T. discovered the modification. When its report reached the newspapers, Sandy invaded the construction shed to show Burke the news account. Oil-smeared and harassed, he stopped work to read it.

"Hell!" he said querulously. "I should've had somebody watching for this! I figured the second broadcast was telling us something that would change as time went on. They're telemetering something to us. I'd guess there's an emergency or an ultimatum in the works, and this is telling how fast it's coming to a crisis. But I'm already working as fast as I can!"

"Some cases marked 'Instruments' came this morning," Sandy told him. "They're the solidest shipping cases I ever saw. And the bills for them!"

"Wire Keller," said Burke. "Tell him they're here and to come along."

"Who's Keller?" asked Sandy. "And what's his address?"

Burke blew up unreasonably, and Sandy said "I quit!" In seconds, he had apologized and assured Sandy that she was quite right and that he was an idiot. Of course she couldn't know who Keller was. Keller was the man who would install the instruments in the ship outside. Burke gave her his address. Sandy was not appeased.

Burke ran a grimy hand despairingly through his hair.

"Sandy," he protested, "bear with me just a little while! In just a few more days this thing will be finished, and I'll know whether I'm the prize imbecile of history or whether I've actually managed to do something worth while! Bear with me like you would with a half-wit or a delinquent child or something. Please, Sandy —"

She turned her back on him and walked out of the shed. But she didn't quit. Burke turned back to his work.

The Russians sent up another probe. It went off course. There were now six unmanned Russian probes in emptiness, of which four were lined up reasonably well along the route which a manned probe, if one were sent up, should ultimately travel. The advance probes formed an ingenious approach to the problem of getting a man farther out in space than any man had been before, but it was horribly risky. But apparently the Russians could afford to take such risks. The Americans couldn't. They had a settled policy of spending a dollar instead of a man. It was humanitarian, but it had one drawback. There was a tendency to keep on spending dollars and not ever let a man take a chance.

The Russians had four fuel-carrying drones in line out in space. If a ship could grapple them in turn and refuel, it might make the journey to M-387 in eight or ten weeks instead of as many months. But it was not easy to imagine such a success. And as for getting back . . .

The beeping sounds continued to be received by Earth.

A short man with thin hair arrived at Burke Development, Inc. His name was Keller, and his expression was pleasant enough, but he was so sparing of words as to seem almost speechless. Sandy watched as he unpacked the instruments in the massive shipping cases. The instruments themselves were meaningless to her. They had dials, and some had gongs, and one or two had unintelligible things printed on paper strips. At least one in the last category was a computer. Keller unpacked them reverently and made sure that not a speck of dust contaminated any one. When he carried them out to the hull, still concealed by the lath-and-plaster exterior mould, he walked with the solemn care of a man bearing treasure.

That day Sandy saw him talking to Burke. Burke spoke, and Keller smiled and nodded. Only once did he open his mouth to say something. Then he could not have said more than four words, He went happily back to his instruments.

The next day, Burke made what was intended to be a low-power test of the long iron bar he'd machined so painstakingly and wound so carefully before enclosing it in the bronze outer case. He'd worked on it for more than two weeks.

He prepared the test very carefully. The six-inch test model had lain on a workbench and had been energized through a momentary-contact switch. The full-scale specimen was clamped in a great metal lathe, which in turn was shackled with half-inch steel cable to the foundations of the construction shed. If the pseudo-magnet flew anywhere this time it would have to break through a tremendous restraining force. The switch was discarded. A condenser would discharge through the windings via a rectifier. There would be a single damped surge of current of infinitesimal duration.

Holmes passed on the news. He got along very well with Pam these days. At first he'd been completely careless of his appearance. Then Pam took measures to distract him from total absorption in the construction job, and he responded. Nowadays, he tended to work in coveralls and change into more formal attire before approaching the office. Sandy came upon him polishing his shoes, once, and she told Pam. Pam beamed.

Now he came lounging into the office and said amiably, "The moment of truth has arrived, or will in minutes."

Sandy looked anxious. Pam said, "Is that an invitation to look on at the kill?"

"Burke's going to turn juice into the thing he's been winding by hand and jittering over. He's worried. He can think of seven thousand reasons why it shouldn't work. But if it doesn't, he'll be a pretty sick man." He glanced at Sandy. "I think he could do with somebody to hold his hand at the critical moment."

"We'll go," said Sandy.

Pam got up from her desk.

"She won't hold his hand," she explained to Holmes, "but she'll be there in case there are some pieces to be picked up. Of him."

They went across the open space to the construction shed. It was a perfectly commonplace morning. The very temporary mass of lumber and laths and plaster, forming a mould for something unseen inside, was the only unusual thing in sight. There were deep truck tracks by the shed. One of the workmen came out of the airlock door on the bottom of the mould and lighted a cigarette.

"No smoking inside," said Holmes. "We're cementing things in place with plastic."

Sandy did not hear. She was first to enter the shed. Burke was moving around the object he'd worked so long to make. It now appeared to be simply a piece of bronze pipe some fifteen feet long and eight inches in diameter, with closed ends. It lay in the bed of an oversized metal lathe, which was anchored in place by cables. Burke took a painstaking reading of the resistance of a pair of red wires, then of white ones, and then of black rubber ones, which stuck out of one end of the pipe.

"The audience is here," said Holmes.

Burke nodded. He said almost apologetically, "I'm putting in a minimum of power. Maybe nothing will happen, It's pretty silly."

Sandy's hands twisted one within the other when he turned his back to her. He made connections, took a deep breath, and said in a strained voice, "Here goes."

He flipped a switch.

There was a cracking sound. It was horribly loud. There was a crash. Bricks began to fall. The end of the metal-lathe bounced out of a corner. Steel cables gave off high-pitched musical notes which went down in tone as the stress on them slackened. One end of the lathe was gone — snapped off, broken, flung away into a corner. There was a hole in the brick wall, over a foot in diameter.

The fifteen-foot object was gone. But they heard a high-pitched shrilling noise, which faded away into the distance.

That afternoon the Russians announced that their manned space-probe had taken off for Asteroid M-387. Naturally, they delayed the announcement until they were satisfied that the launching had gone well. When they made their announcement, the probe was fifty thousand miles out, they had received a message from its pilot, and they predicted that the probe would land on M-387 in a matter of seven weeks.

In a remote small corner of the afternoon newspapers there was an item saying that a meteorite had fallen in a ploughed field some thirty miles from where Burke's contrivance broke loose. It made a crater twenty feet across. It could not be examined because it was covered with frost.

Burke had the devil of a time recovering it. But he needed it badly. Especially since the Russian probe had gone out from Earth. He explained that it was a shipment to his plant, which had fallen out of an aeroplane, but the owner of the ploughed field was dubious. Burke had to pay him a thousand dollars to get him to believe.

That night he had his recurrent dream again. The fluting signals were very clear.

CHAPTER 4

THE PUBLIC ABRUPTLY ceased to be interested in news of the signals. Rather, it suddenly wanted to stop thinking about them. The public was scared. Throughout all human history, the most horrifying of all ideas has been the idea of something which was as intelligent as a man, but wasn't human. Evil spirits, ghosts, devils, werewolves, ghouls — all have roused maddened terror wherever they were believed in. Because they were intelligent but not men.

Now, suddenly, the world seemed to realize that there was a Something out on a tiny frozen rock in space. It signaled plaintively to Earth. It had to be intelligent to be able to send a signal for two hundred seventy million miles. But it was not a man. Therefore it was a monster. Therefore it was horrible. Therefore it was deadly and intolerable and scarey, and humans abruptly demanded not to hear any more about it.

Perhaps they thought that if they didn't think about it, it would go away.

Newspaper circulations dropped. News-magazine sales practically vanished. A flood of hysterical letters demanded that the broadcasting networks leave such revolting things off the air. And this reaction was not only in America. Violent anti-American feeling arose in Europe, which psychologists analyzed as resentment caused by the fact that the Americans had answered the first broadcast. If they hadn't answered the first, there wouldn't have been a second. But also, even more violent anti-Russian feeling rose up, because the Russians had started a man off to meddle with the monster who piped so pleadingly. This antipathy to space caused a minor political upset in the Kremlin itself, where a man with a name ending in ov was degraded to much lower official rank and somebody with a name ending in sky took his place. This partly calmed the Russian public but had little effect anywhere else. The world was frightened. It looked for a victim, or victims for its fear. Once upon a time, witches were burned to ease the terrors of ignorance, and plague-spreaders were executed in times of pestilence to assure everybody that now the plague would cease since somebody had been killed for spreading it.

Organizations came into being with the official and impassioned purpose of seeing that space research ceased immediately. Even more violent organizations demanded the punishment of everybody who had ever considered space travel a desirable thing. Congress cut some hundreds of millions from a guided-missile-space-exploration appropriation as a starter. A poor devil of a crackpot in Santa Monica, California, revealed what he said was a spaceship he'd built in his back yard to answer the signals from M-387. He intended to charge a quarter admission to inspect it, using the money to complete the drive apparatus. The thing was built of plywood and could not conceivably lift off the ground, but a mob wrecked his house, burned the puerile "spaceship" and would have lynched its builder if they'd thought to look in a cellar vegetable closet. Other crackpots who were more sensitive to public feelings announced the picking up of messages addressed to the distant Something. The messages, said this second class of crackpot, were reports from spies who had been landed on Earth from flying saucers during the past few decades. They did not explain how they were able to translate them. A rush of flying-saucer sightings followed inevitably — alleged to be landing-parties from M-387 — and in Peoria, Illinois, a picnicking party sighted an unidentified flying object shaped like a soup spoon, the handle obviously being its tail. Experienced newspapermen anticipated reports of the sighting of unidentified flying objects shaped like knives and forks as soon as somebody happened to think of it.

Sandy called a conference on the subject of security. She did not look well, nowadays. She worried. Other people thought about the messages from space, but Sandy had to think of something more concrete. Six months earlier, the construction going on within a plaster of

Paris mould would have been laughed at, tolerantly, and some hopeful people might have been respectful about it, But now it was something utterly intolerable to public opinion. Newspapers who'd lost circulation by talking sanely about space travel now got it back by denouncing the people who'd answered the first broadcast. And naturally, with the whole idea of outer space agitatedly disapproved, everybody connected with it was suspected of subversion.

"A reporter called up today," said Sandy. "He said he'd like to do a feature story on Burke Development's new research triumph — the new guided missile that flew thirty miles and froze everything around where it landed. I said it fell out of an aeroplane and the last completed project was for Interiors, inc. Then he said that he'd been talking to one of Mr. Holmes' men and the man said something terrific was under way."

Burke looked uneasy. Holmes said uncomfortably, "There's no law against what we're building, but somebody may introduce a bill in Congress any day."

"That would be reasonable under other circumstances. There's a time for things to be discovered. They shouldn't be accomplished too soon. But the time for the ship out there is right now!" Burke said.

Pam raised her eyebrows. "Yes?"

"Those signals have to be checked up on," explained Burke. "It's necessary now. But it could have been bad if our particular enterprise had started, say, two years ago. Just think what would have happened if atomic fission had been worked out in peacetime ten years before World War Two! Scientific discoveries were published then as a matter of course. Everybody'd have known how to make atom bombs. Hitler would have had them, and so would Mussolini. How many of us would be alive?"

Sandy interrupted, "The reporter wants to do a feature story on what Burke Development is making. I said you were working on a bomb shelter for quantity production. He asked if the rocket you shot off through the construction-shed wall was part of it. I said there'd been no rocket fired. He didn't believe me."

"Who would?" asked Holmes.

"Hmmmmm," said Burke. "Tell him to come look at what we're doing. The ship can pass for a bomb shelter. The wall-garden units make sense. I'm going to dig a big hole in the morning to test the drive-shaft in. It'll look like I intend to bury everything. A bomb shelter should be buried."

"You mean you'll let him inside?" demanded Sandy.

"Sure!" said Burke. "All inventors are expected to be idiots. A lot of them are. He'll think I'm making an impossibly expensive bomb shelter, much too costly for a private family to buy. It will be typical of the inventive mind as reporters think of it. Anyhow, everybody's always willing to believe other people fools. That'll do the trick!"

Pam said blandly, "Sandy and I live in a boardinghouse, Joe. You don't ask about such things, but an awfully nice man moved in a couple of days ago — right after that shaft got away and went flying thirty miles all by itself. The nice man has been trying to get acquainted."

Holmes growled, and looked both startled and angry when he realized it.

Pam added cheerfully, "Most evenings I've been busy, but I think I'll let him take me to the movies. Just so I can make us all out to be idiots," she added.

"I'll make the hole big enough to be convincing," said Burke. "Sandy, you make inquiries for a rigger to lift and move the bomb shelter into its hole when it's ready. If we seem about to bury it, nobody should suspect us of ambitions they won't like."

"Why the hole, really?" asked Sandy.

"To put the shaft in," said Burke. "I've got to get it under control or it won't be anything more than a bomb shelter."

Keller, the instrument man, had listened with cheerful interest and without speaking a word. Now he made an indefinite noise and looked inquiringly at Burke. Burke said, explanatorily, "The shaft seems to be either on or off — either a magnet that doesn't quite magnetize, or something that's hell on wheels. It flew thirty miles without enough power supplied to it to make it quiver. That power came from somewhere. I think there's a clue in the fact that it froze everything around where it landed, in spite of traveling fast enough to heat up from air-friction alone. I've got some ideas about it."

Keller nodded. Then he said urgently, "Broadcast?"

Burke frowned, and turned to Sandy. "That part of the broadcast from space that changes — is it still changing?"

"Still changing," said Sandy.

"I didn't think to ask you to keep a check on that. Thanks for thinking of it, Sandy. Maybe someday I can make up to you for what you've been going through."

"I doubt it very much," said Sandy grimly. "I'll call the reporter back."

She waited for them to leave. When they'd gone, she moved purposefully toward the telephone.

Pam said, "Did you hear that growl when I said I'd go to the movies with somebody else? I'm having fun, Sandy!"

"I'm not," said Sandy.

"You're too efficient," the younger sister said candidly. "You're indispensable. Burke couldn't begin to be able to put this thing through without you. And that's the trouble. You should be irresistible instead of essential."

"Not with Joe," said Sandy bitterly.

She picked up the telephone to call the newspaper. Pam looked very, very reflective.

There was a large deep pit close by the plaster mould when the reporter came next afternoon. A local rigger had come a little earlier and was still there, estimating the cost for lifting up the contents of the mould and lowering it precisely in place to be buried as a bomb shelter under test should be. It was a fortunate coincidence, because the reporter brought two other men who he said were civilian defense officials. They had come to comment on the quality of the bomb shelter under development. It was not too convincing a statement.

When they left, Burke was not happy. They knew too much about the materials and equipment he'd ordered. One man had let slip the fact that he knew about the very expensive computer Burke had bought. It could have no conceivable use in a bomb shelter. Both men painstakingly left it to Burke to mention the thirty-mile flight of a bronze object which arrived coated with frost of such utter frigidity that it appeared to be liquid-air snow instead of water-ice. Burke did not mention it. He was excessively uneasy when the reporter's car took them away.

He went into the office. Pam was in the midst of a fit of the giggles.

"One of them," she explained, "is the nice man who moved into the boardinghouse. He wants to take me to the movies. Did you notice that they came when it ought to be my lunchtime? He asked when I went to lunch . . ."

Holmes came in. He scowled.

"One of my men says that one of those characters has been buying him drinks and asking questions about what we're doing."

Burke scowled too.

"We can let your men go home in three days more."

"I'm going to start loading up," Holmes announced abruptly. "You don't know how to stow stuff. You're not a yachtsman."

"I haven't got the shaft under control yet," said Burke.

"You'll get it," grunted Holmes.

He went out. Pam giggled again.

"He doesn't want me to go to the movies with the nice man from Security," she told Burke. "But I think I'd better. I'll let him ply me with popcorn and innocently let slip that Sandy and I know you've been warned that bomb shelters won't find a mass market unless they sell for less than the price of an extra bathroom. But if you want to go broke we don't care."

"Give me three days more," said Burke harassedly.

"Well try," said Sandy suddenly. "Pam can fix up a double date with one of her friend's friends and well both work on them."

Burke frowned absorbedly and went out. Sandy looked indignant. He hadn't protested.

Burke got Holmes' four workmen out of the ship and had them help him roll the bronze shaft to the pit and let it down onto a cradle of timbers. Now if it moved it would have to penetrate solid earth.

The most trivial of computations showed that when the bronze shaft had flown thirty miles, it hadn't done it on the energy of a condenser shorted through its coils. The energy had come from somewhere else. Burke had an idea where it was.

Presently he verified it. The cores and windings he'd adapted from a transparent hand-weapon seen in an often-repeated dream — those cores and windings did not make electromagnets. They made something for which there was not yet a name. When current flows through a standard electromagnet, the poles of its atoms are more or less aligned. They tend to point in a single direction. But in this arrangement of wires and iron no magnetism resulted, yet, the random motion of the atoms in their framework of crystal structure was coordinated. In any object above absolute zero all the atoms and their constituent electrons and nuclei move constantly in all directions. In such a core as Burke had formed and repeated along the shaft's length, they all tried to move in one direction at the same time. Simultaneously, a terrific surge of current appeared in the coils. A high-speed poleward velocity developed in all the substance of the shaft. It was the heat-energy contained in the metal, all turned instantly into kinetic energy. And when its heat-energy was transformed to something else, the shaft got cold.

Once this fact was understood, control was easy. A single variable inductance in series with the windings handled everything. In a certain sense, the gadget was a magnet with negative — minus — self-inductance. When a plus inductance in series made the self-inductance zero, neither plus nor minus, the immensely powerful device became docile. A small current produced a mild thrust, affecting only part of the random heat-motion of atoms and molecules. A stronger current produced a greater one. The resemblance to an electromagnet remained. But the total inductance must stay close to zero or utterly violent and explosive forward thrust would develop, and it was calculable only in thousands of gravities.

Burke had worked for three weeks to make the thing, but he developed a control system for it in something under four hours.

That same night they got the bronze shaft into the ship. It fitted perfectly into the place left for it. Burke knew now exactly what he was doing. He set up his controls. He was able to produce so minute swayed. But he knew that he could make the whole mass surge unstoppably from its place.

Holmes sent his workmen home. Sandy and Pam went to the movies with two very nice men who pumped them deftly of all sorts of erroneous information about Burke and Holmes and Keller and what they were about. The nice men did not believe that information, but they did believe that Sandy and Pam believed it. For themselves, the combination of an object made by Burke which flew thirty miles plus the presence of Holmes, who built plastic yachts, and the arrival of Keller to adjust instruments of which they had a complete list — these things could not be overlooked. But they did feel sorry for two nice and not over-bright girls who might be involved in very serious trouble.

Holmes and Burke installed directional controls, wiring, recording instruments, etc. Stores and water and oxygen, for emergency use only, went into the lath-and-plaster construction. Holmes took a hammer and chisel and painstakingly cracked the mould so that the top half could be lifted off, leaving the bottom half exposed to the open air and sky.

Then the broadcast from space cut off. It had been coming continuously for something like five weeks; one sharp, monotonous note every two seconds, with a longer, fluting broadcast every seventy-nine minutes. Now a third, new message began. It was yet another grouping of the musical tones, with a much longer interval of specific crackling sounds.

Keller had adjusted every instrument and zestfully re-tested them over and over. Burke asked him to see if the third space message compared in any way with the second. Keller put them through a hook-up of instruments, beaming to himself, and the answer began to appear.

Newspapers burst into new headlines. "Ultimatum from Space" they thundered. "Threats from Alien Space Travelers." And as they presented the situation it seemed believable that the third message from the void was a threat.

The first had been a call, requiring an answer. When the answer went out from Earth, a second message replaced the call. It contained not only flute tones which might be considered to represent words, but cracklings which might be the equivalent of numbers. The continuous beepings between repetitions of the second message were plainly a directional signal to be followed to the message source.

In this context, the newspapers furiously asserted that the third message was a threat. The first had been merely a summons, the second had been a command to repair to the signaling entities, and the third was a stern reiteration of the command, reinforced by threats.

The human race does not take kindly to threats, especially when it feels helpless. In the United States, there was such explosive resentment as to require spread-eagle oratory by all public figures. The President declared that every space missile in store had been fitted with atomic-fusion warheads and that any alien spacecraft which appeared in American skies would be shot down immediately. Congress reported out of committee a bill for rocket weapons which was stalled for six days because every senator and representative wanted to make a speech in its favor. It was the largest appropriation bill ever passed by Congress, which less than five weeks before had cut two hundred millions out of a guided-missile-space-exploration budget.

And in Europe there was frenzy.

For Burke and Holmes and Sandy and Pam and the smiling, inarticulate Keller, the matter was deadly serious. Fury such as the public felt constituted a witch-hunt in itself. Suspicious private persons overwhelmed the FBI and the Space Agency with information about characters they were sure were giving military secrets to the space travelers on M-387. There were reports of aliens skulking about American cities wearing luxuriant whiskers and dark glasses to conceal their non-human features. Artists, hermits, and mere amateur beard-growers found it wise to shave, and spirit mediums, fortunetellers and, in the South, herb doctors reaped harvests by the sale of ominous predictions and infallible advice on how to escape annihilation from space.

And Burke Development, Inc., was building something that neither Civilian Defense nor the FBI believed was a bomb shelter.

The three days Burke had needed passed. A fourth. He and Holmes practically abandoned sleep to get everything finished inside the plaster mould. Keller happily completed his graphs and took them to Burke. They showed that the cracklings, which presumably meant numbers, had been expanded. What they said was now told on a new scale. If the numbers had meant months or years, they now meant days and hours. If they had meant millions of miles, they now meant thousands or hundreds.

Burke was struggling with these implications when there was a tapping at the air-lock, through which all entry and egress from the ship took place. Holmes opened the inner door. Sandy and Pam crawled through the lock which lay on its side instead of upright. Sandy looked at Burke.

Pam said amiably, "We figured the job was about finished and we wanted to see it. How do you fasten this door?"

Holmes showed her. The vessel that had been built inside the mould did not seem as large as the outside structure promised. It looked queer, too, because everything lay on its side. There were two compartments with a ladder between, but the ladder lay on the floor. The wall-gardens looked healthy under the fluorescent lamps which kept the grass and vegetation flourishing. There were instrument dials everywhere.

Sandy went to Burke's side.

"We're all but done," said Burke tiredly, "and Keller's just about proved what the signals are."

"Can we go with you?" asked Sandy.

"Of course not," said Burke. "The first message was a distress call. It had to be. Only in a distress call would somebody go into details so any listener would know it was important. It called for help and said who needed it, and why, and where."

Pam turned to Holmes. "Can that airlock be opened from outside?"

It couldn't. Not when it was fastened, as now.

"Somebody answered that call from Earth," said Burke heavily, "and the second message told more about what was wrong. The clickings, we think, are numbers that told how long help could be waited for, or something on that order. And then there was a beacon signal meant to lead whoever was coming to help to that place."

Keller smiled pleasantly at Pam. He made an electrical connection and zestfully checked the result.

"Now there's a third message," said Burke. "Time's running out for whoever needs whatever help is called for. The clickings that seem to be numbers have changed. The — what you might call the scale of reportage — is new. They're telling us just how long they can wait or just how bad their situation is. They're saying that time is running out and they're saying, 'Hurry!'"

There was a thumping sound. Only Sandy and Pam looked unsurprised. Burke stared.

Sandy said firmly, "That's the police, Joe. We've been going to the movies with people who want to talk about you. Yesterday one of them confided to us that you were dangerous, and since he told us to get away from the office, we did. There might be shooting. He tipped us a little while ago."

Burke swore. There were other thumpings. Louder ones. They were on the airlock door.

"If you try to put us out," said Sandy calmly, "you'll have to open that door and they'll try to fight their way in — and then where'll you be?"

Keller turned from the checking of the last instrument. He looked at the others with excited eyes. He waited.

"I don't know what they can arrest you for," said Sandy, "and maybe they don't either, unless it's unauthorized artillery practice. But you can't put us out! And you know darn well that unless you do something they'll chop their way in!"

Burke said, "Dammit, they're not going to stop me from finding out if this thing works!"

He squirmed in a chair which had its base firmly fastened to a wall and began to punch buttons.

"Hold fast!" he said angrily. "At least well see . . ."

There were loud snapping sounds. There were creakings. The room stirred. It turned in a completely unbelievable fashion. Violent crashings sounded outside. Abruptly, a small television screen before Burke acquired an image. It was of the outside world reeling wildly. Holmes seized a handhold and grabbed Pam. He kept her from falling as a side wall became the floor, and what had been the floor became a side wall, with the ceiling another. It seemed that all the cosmos changed, though only walls and floors changed places.

Suddenly everything seemed normal but new. The surface underfoot was covered with a rubber mat. The hydroponic wall-garden sections were now vertical. Burke sat upright, and something over his head rotated a half-turn and was still. But it became coated with frost.

More crashes. More small television screens acquired images. They showed the office of Burke Development, Inc., against a tilted landscape. The landscape leveled. Another showed the construction shed. One showed cloud formations, very bright and distinct. And two others showed a small, armed, formidable body of men instinctively backing away from the outside television lens.

"So far," said Burke, "it works. Now —"

There was a sensation as of a rapidly rising elevator. Such a sensation usually lasts for part of a second. This kept on. One of the six television screens suddenly showed a view of Burke Development from straight overhead. The buildings and men and the four-acre enclosure dwindled rapidly. They were very tiny indeed and nearly all of the town was in the camera's field of vision when a vague whiteness, a cloud, moved in between.

"The devil!" said Burke. "Now they'll alert fighter planes and rocket installations and decide that we're either traitors or aliens in disguise and better be shot down. I think we simply have to go on!"

Keller made gestures, his eyes bright. Burke looked worried.

"It shouldn't take more than ten minutes to get a Nike aloft and after us. We must have been picked up by radar already. . . . We'll head north. We have to, anyhow."

But he was wrong about the ten minutes. It was fifteen before a rocket came into view, pouring out enormous masses of drive-fumes. It flung itself toward the ship.

CHAPTER 5

FROM A SUFFICIENT height and a sufficient distance, the rocket's repeated attacks must have appeared like the strikings and twistings of a gigantic snake. It left behind it a writhing trail of fumes which was convincingly serpentine. It climbed and struck, and climbed and struck, like a monstrous python flinging itself furiously at some invisible prey. Six, seven, eight times it plunged frenziedly at the minute egg-shaped ship which scuttled for the heavens. Each time it missed and writhed about to dart again.

Then its fuel gave out and for all intents and purposes it ceased to exist. The thick, opaque trail it left behind began to dissipate. The path of vapor scattered. It spread to rags and tatters of unsubstantiality through which the rocket plummeted downward in the long fall which is a spent rocket's ending.

Burke cautiously cut down the drive and awkwardly turned the ship on its side, heading it toward the north. The state of things inside the ship was one of intolerable tenseness.

"I'm a new driver," said Burke, "and that was a tough bit of driving to do." He glanced at the exterior-pressure meter. "There's no air outside to register. We must be fifty or sixty miles high and maybe still rising. But we're not leaking air."

Actually the plastic ship was eighty miles up. The sunlit world beneath it showed white patches of cloud in patterns a meteorologist would have found interesting. Burke could see the valley of the St. Lawrence River between the white areas. But the Earth's surface was curiously foreshortened. What was beneath seemed utterly flat, and at the edge of the world all appeared distorted and unreal.

Holmes, still pale, asked, "How'd we get away from that rocket?"

"We accelerated," said Burke. "It was a defensive rocket. It was designed to knock down jet bomb carriers or ballistic missiles which travel at a constant speed. Target-seeking missiles can lock onto the radar echo from a coasting ship, or one going at its highest speed because their computers predict where their target, traveling at constant speed, can be intercepted. We were never there. We were accelerating. Missile-guidance systems can't measure acceleration and allow for it. They shouldn't have to."

Four of the six television screens showed dark sky with twinkling lights in it. On one there was the dim outline of the sun, reversed to blackness because its light was too great to be registered in a normal fashion. The other screen showed Earth.

There was a buzzing, and Keller looked at Burke.

"Rocket?" asked Burke. Keller shook his head. "Radar?" Keller nodded.

"The DEW line, most likely," said Burke in a worried tone. "I don't know whether they've got rockets that can reach us. But I know fighter planes can't get this high. Maybe they can throw a spread of air-to-air rockets, though . . . I don't know their range."

Sandy said unsteadily, "They shouldn't do this to us! We're not criminals! At least they should ask us who we are and what we're doing!"

"They probably did," said Burke, "and we didn't answer. See if you can pick up some voices, Keller."

Keller twirled dials and set indicators. Voices burst into speech. "Reporting UFO sighted extreme altitude cošrdinates — First rocket exhausted fuel in multiple attacks and fell, sir." Another voice, very brisk, "Thirty-second squadron, scramble! Keep top altitude and get under it. If it descends within range, blast it!" Another voice said crisply, "Cošrdinates three-seven Jacob, one-nine Alfred . . ."

Keller turned the voices down to mutters because they were useless.

Burke said, "Hell! We ought to land somewhere and check over the ship. Keller, can you give me a microphone and a wave-length somebody will be likely to pick up?"

Keller shrugged and picked up masses of wire. He began to work on an as yet unfinished wiring job. Evidently, the ship was not near enough to completion to be capable of a call to ground. It had taken off with many things not finished. Burke, at the controls, found it possible to think of a number of items that should have been examined exhaustively before the ship left the mould in which it had been made. He worried.

Pam said in a strange voice, "I thought I might rate as a heroine for stowing away on this voyage, but I didn't think we'd have to dodge rockets and fighter planes to get away!"

There was no comment.

"I'm a beginner at navigation," said Burke a little later, more worried than before. "I know we have to go out over the north magnetic pole, but how the hell do I find that?"

Keller beamed. He dropped his wiring job and went to the imposing bank of electronic instruments. He set one, and then another, and then a third. The action, of course, was similar to that of an airline pilot when he tunes in broadcasting stations in different cities. From each, a directional reading can be taken. Where the lines of direction cross, there the transport plane must be. But Keller turned to shortwave transmitters whose transmissions could be picked up in space. Presently, eighty miles high, he wrote a latitude and longitude neatly on a slip of paper, wrote "North magnetic pole 93¡W, 71¡N, nearly," and after that a course.

"Hm," said Burke. "Thanks."

Then there was a relative silence inside the ship. Only a faint mutter of voices came from assorted speakers that Keller had first turned on and then turned down, and a small humming sound from a gyro. When they listened, they could also hear a high sweet musical tone. Burke shifted this control here, and that control there, and lifted his hands. The ship moved on steadily. He checked this and that and the other thing. He was pleased. But there were innumerable things to be checked. Holmes went down the ladder to the other compartment below. There were details to be looked into there, too.

One of the screens portrayed Earth from a height of seventy miles instead of eighty, now. Others pictured the heavens, with very many stars shining unwinkingly out of blackness. Keller got at his wires again and resumed the work of installing a ship-to-ground transmitter and its connection to an exterior-reflecting antenna.

Sandy watched Burke as he moved about, testing one thing after another. From time to time he glanced at the screens which had to serve in the place of windows. Once he went back to the control-board and changed an adjustment.

"We dropped down ten miles," he explained to Sandy. "And I suspect we're being trailed by jets down below."

Holmes meticulously inspected all storage places. He'd packed them when the ship lay on her side.

Burke read an instrument and said with satisfaction, "We're running on sunshine!"

He meant that in empty space certain aluminum plates on the outside of the hull were picking up heat from the naked sun. The use of the drive-shaft lowered its temperature. Metallic connection with the outside plates conducted heat inward from those plates. The drive-shaft was cold to the touch, but it could drop four hundred degrees Fahrenheit before it ceased to operate as a drive. It was gratifying that it had cooled so little up to this moment.

Later Keller tapped Burke on the shoulder and jerked his thumb upward.

"We go up now?" asked Burke.

Keller nodded. Burke carefully swung the ship to aim vertically. The views of solid Earth slid from previous screens to new ones. The stars and the dark object which was the sun also moved across their screens to vanish and reappear on others. Then Burke touched the drive-control. Once more they had the sensation of being in a rising elevator. And at just that moment spots appeared on the barren, icy, totally flattened terrain below.

They were rocket-trails from target-seeking missiles which had reached the area of the north magnetic pole by herculean effort and were aimed at the radar-detected little ship by the heavy planes that carried them.

From the surface of the Earth, it would have seemed that monstrous columns of foaming white appeared and rose with incredible swiftness toward the heavens. They reached on, up and up and up, seeming to draw closer together as they became smaller in the distance, until all eight of them seemed to merge into a single point of infinite whiteness in the sunshine above the world's blanket of air.

But nothing happened. Nothing. The ship did not accelerate as fast as the rockets, but it had started first and it kept up longer. It went scuttling away to emptiness and the bottoms of the towers of rocket-smoke drifted away and away over the barren landscape all covered with ice and snow.

When Earth looked like a huge round ball that did not even seem very near, with a night side that was like a curious black chasm among the stars, the atmosphere of tension inside the ship diminished. Keller completed his wiring of a ship-to-ground transmitter. He stood up, brushed off his hands and beamed.

The little ship continued on. Its temperature remained constant. The air in it smelled of growing green stuff. It was moist. It was warm. Keller turned a knob and a tiny, beeping noise could be heard. Dials pointed, precisely.

"We couldn't go on our true course earlier," Burke told Sandy, "because we had to get out beyond the Van Allen bands of cosmic particles in orbit around the world. Pretty deadly stuff, that radiation! In theory, though, all we have to do now is swing onto our proper course and follow those beepings home. We ought to be in harmless emptiness here. Do you want to call Washington?"

She stared.

"We need help to navigate — or astrogate," said Burke. "Call them, Sandy. I'll get on the wire when a general answers."

Sandy went jerkily to the transmitter just connected. She began to speak steadily, "Calling Earth! Calling Earth! The spaceship you just shot all those rockets at is calling! Calling Earth!"

It grew monotonous, but eventually a suspicious voice demanded further identification.

It was a peculiar conversation. The five in the small spaceship were considered traitors on Earth because they had exercised the traditional right of American citizens to go about their own business unhindered. It happened that their private purposes ran counter to the emotional state of the public. Hence voices berated Sandy and furiously demanded that the ship return immediately. Sandy insisted on higher authority and presently an official voice identified itself as general so-and-so and sternly commanded that the ship acknowledge and obey orders to return to Earth. Burke took the transmitter.

"My name's Burke," he said mildly. "If you can arrange some sort of code, I'll tell you how to find the plans, and I'll give you the instructions you'll need to build more ships like this. They can follow us out. I think they should. I believe that this is more important than anything else you can think of at the moment."

Silence. Then more sternness. But ultimately the official voice said, "I'll get a code expert on this."

Burke handed the microphone to Sandy.

"Take over. We've got to arrange a cipher so nobody who listens in can learn about official business. We may use a social security number for a key, or the name of your maiden aunt's first sweetheart, or something we know and Washington can find out but that nobody else can. Hm. Your last year's car-license number might be a starter. They can seal up the records on that!"

Sandy took over the job. What was transmitted to Earth, of course, could be picked up anywhere over an entire hemisphere. Somebody would assuredly pass on what they overheard to, say, nations the United States would rather have behind it than ahead of it in space-travel equipment. Burke's suggestion of a cipher and instructions changed his entire status with authority. They'd rather have had him come back, but this was second best, and they took it.

From Burke's standpoint it was the only thing to do. He had no official standing to lend weight to his claim that lunatic magnet-cores with insanely complicated windings would amount to space-drive units. If he returned, in the nature of things there would be a long delay before mere facts could overcome theoreticians' convictions. But now he was forty-five thousand miles out from Earth.

He had changed course to home on the beeping signals from M-387, was accelerating at one full gravity and had been doing so for forty-five minutes. And the small ship already had a velocity of twenty miles per second and was still going up. All the rockets that men had made, plus the Russian manned-probe drifting outward now, had become as much outdated for space travel as flint arrowheads are for war.

Burke returned to the microphone when Sandy left it to get a pencil and paper.

"By the way," he said briskly. "We can keep on accelerating indefinitely at one gravity. We've got radars. We got them from —" He named the supplier. "Now we want advice on how fast we can risk traveling before we'll be going too fast to dodge meteors or whatnot that the radar may detect. Get that figured out for us, will you?"

He gave back the instrument to Sandy and returned to his inspection of every item of functioning equipment in the ship. He found one or two trivial things to be bettered. The small craft went on in a singularly matter-of-fact fashion. If it had been a bomb shelter buried in the pit beside the mould in which it was built, there would have been very little difference in the feel of things. The constant acceleration substituted perfectly for gravity. The six television screens, to be sure, pictured incredible things outside, but television screens often picture incredible things. The wall-gardens looked green and flourishing. The pumps were noiseless. There were no moving parts in the drive. The gyro held everything steady. There was no vibration.

Nobody could remain upset in such an unexciting environment. Presently Pam explored the living quarters below. Holmes took his place in the control-chair, but found no need to touch anything.

Some time later Sandy reported, "Joe, they say we must be lying, but if we can keep on accelerating, we'd better not hit over four hundred miles a second. They say we can then swing end for end and decelerate down to two hundred, and then swing once more and build up to four again. But they insist that we ought to return to Earth."

"They don't mention shooting rockets at us, do they?" asked Burke. "I thought they wouldn't. Just say thanks and go on working out a code."

Sandy set to work with pencil and paper. Federal agents would be moving, now, to impound all official records that were in any way connected with any of the five on the ship. The key to the code would be contained in such records. It would be an agglomeration of such items as Burke's grandmother's maiden name, Holmes' social-security number, the name of a street Burke had lived on some years before, the exact amount of his federal income taxes the previous year, the title of a book third from the end on the second shelf of a bookcase in Keller's apartment, and such unconsidered items as most people can remember with a little effort, but which can only be found out by people who know where to look. These people would keep anybody else from looking in the same places. Such a code would be clumsy to work with, but it would be unbreakable.

It took hours to establish it without the mention of a single word included in the lengthy key. The ship reached four hundred miles a second, turned about, and began to cut down its speed again.

Pam spoke from beside an electric stove, "Dinner's ready! Come and get it!"

They dined; Sandy weary, Burke absorbed and inevitably worried, Holmes placid and amiable, and Keller beaming and interested in all that went on, which was practically nothing.

They did not see the stars direct, because television cameras were preferable to portholes. Earth had become very small, and as it swung ever more nearly into a direct line between the ship and the sun, night filled more of its disk until only a hairline of sunshine showed at one edge. The microwave receivers ceased to mutter. The working astronomers on Earth who'd sent a message to M-387 were suddenly relieved of their disgrace and set to work again to equip the West Virginia radar telescope for continuous communication with Burke's ship. Other technicians began to prepare multiple receptors to pick up the ship's signals from hitherto unprecedented distances for human two-way communication.

And on Earth an official statement went out from high authority. It announced that a hurriedly completed American ship was on the way to M-387 to investigate the signals from space. It announced that measures long in preparation were now in use, and that an invincible fleet of spacecraft would be completed in months, whereas they had not been hoped for for another generation. An unexpected breakthrough had made it possible to advance the science of space travel by many decades, and a fleet to explore all the planets as well as M-387 was already under construction. It was almost true that they were. The blueprints of Burke's ship had been flown to Washington from the plant, and an enormous number of replicas of the egg-shaped vessel were ordered to be begun immediately, even before the theory of the drive was understood.

There was one minor hitch. A legal-minded official protested that Congressional appropriations had been for rocket-driven spaceships only, and the money appropriated could not be used for other than rockets. An executive order settled the matter. Then theorists began to object to the principle of the drive. It contradicted well-established scientific beliefs. It could not work.

It did, but there was violent opposition to the fact.

Publicly, of course, the shock of such an about-face by the national government was extreme. But newspapers flashed new headlines. "U.S. SHIP SPEEDING TO QUERY ALIENS!" Lesser heads announced, "Critical Velocity Exceeded! Russian Probe Already Passed!" The last was not quite true. The Russian manned probe had started out ten days before. Burke hadn't overtaken it yet.

Broadcasters issued special bulletins, and two networks canceled top evening programs to schedule interviews with prominent scientists who'd had nothing whatever to do with what Burke had managed to achieve.

In Europe, obviously, the political effect was stupendous. Russia was reduced to impassioned claims that the ship had been built from Russian plans, using Russian discoveries, which had been stolen by imperialistic secret agents. And the heads of the Russian spy system were disgraced for not having, in fact, stolen the plans and discoveries from the Americans. All other operatives received threats of what would happen to them if they didn't repair that omission. These threats so scared half a dozen operatives that they defected and told all they knew, thereby wrecking the Russian spy system for the time being.

Essentially, however, the recovery of confidence in America was as extravagant as the previous unhappy desire to hear no more about space. Burke, Holmes, Keller, Sandy and Pam became national heroes and heroines within eighteen hours after guided missiles had failed to shoot them down. The only criticism came from a highly conservative clergyman who hoped that other young girls would not imitate Sandy's and Pam's disregard of convention and maintained that a married woman should have gone along to chaperon them.

The atmosphere in the ship, however, was that of respectability carried to the point where things were dull. The lower compartment of the ship, being smaller, was inevitably appropriated by Sandy and Pam. They retired when the ship was twenty hours out from Earth. Each of them had prepared for stowing away by wearing extra garments in layers.

"Funny," said Pam, yawning as they made ready to turn in, "I thought it was going to be exciting. But it's just like a rather full day at the office."

"Which," said Sandy, "I'm quite used to."

"I do think you ought to have barged in when they designed the ship, Sandy. There's not one mirror in it!"

In the upper compartment Keller took his place in the control-chair and took a trick of duty. It consisted solely of looking at the instruments and listening to the beeping noises which came from remoteness every two seconds, and the still completely cryptic broad-casts which came every seventy-nine minutes. It wasn't exciting. There was nothing to be excited about. But somebody had to be on watch.

On the second day out, Washington was ready to use the new code. The West Virginia radar bowl was powered to handle communications again. Sandy painstakingly took down the gibberish that came in and decoded it. From then on she worked at the coding and transmission of messages and the reception and decoding of others. Presently Pam relieved her at the job. Pam tended to be bored because Holmes was as much absorbed in the business of keeping anything from happening as was Burke.

The messages were almost entirely requests far, and answers to requests for, details about the ship plans. The United States had not yet completed a duplicate drive-shaft. Machinists labored to reproduce the cores, which would then have to be wound in the complicated fashion the plans described. But it was an unhappy experience for the scientific minds assigned to duplicate Burke's ship. No woman ever followed a recipe without making some change. Very few physicists can dupli-cate another's apparatus without itching to change it. There were six copies of the drive under construction at the same time, at the begin-ning. Four were made by skeptics, who adhered to the original plans with strict accuracy. They were sure they'd prove Burke wrong. Two were "improved" in the making. The four, when finished, worked beautifully. The two doctored versions did not. But still there was fretful discussion of the theory of the drive. It seemed flatly to contradict Newton's law that every action has a reaction of equal moment and opposite sign — a law at least as firmly founded as the law of the conservation of energy. But that had lately been revised into the law of the conservation of energy and matter, which now was gospel. Burke's theory required the Newtonian law to be restated to read "every action of a given force has a reaction of the same force, of the same moment," and so on. When the reaction of one force is converted into another force, the results can be interesting. In fact, one can have a space-drive. But there was bitter resistance to the idea. It was demanded that Burke justify his views in a more reasonable way than by mere demonstration that they worked.

After a time, Burke gave up trying to explain things. And when one and then another duplicate drive worked, the argument ceased. But eminent physicists still had a resentful feeling that Burke was cheating on them somehow.

Then for days nothing happened. One of the three men in the ship always stayed in the control-chair where he could check the ship's course against the homing signals from the asteroid. He might have to correct it by the fraction of a hair, or swing ship and put on more drive if the radar should show celestial debris in the spaceship's path. Every so many hours the ship had to be swung about so that instead of accelerating she decelerated, or instead of decelerating gained fresh speed. But that was all.

On the fifth day there was the flash of a meteor on the radar. On the seventh day an object which could have been the second or third unmanned Russian probe showed briefly at the very edge of the radar screens. In essence, however, the journey was pure tedium. Burke wearied of making sure that his work was good, though he congratulated himself that nothing did happen to break the monotony. Holmes admitted that he was disappointed. He'd wanted to make the journey because he'd sailed in everything but a spaceship. But there was no fun in it. Keller alone seemed comfortably absorbed. He prepared daily lists of instrument-readings to be sent back to Earth. They would be of enormous importance to science-minded people. They were not of interest to Sandy.

Even when she talked to Burke, it was necessarily impersonal. There could be no privacy which was not ostentatious. The two girls used the lower compartment, the three men the upper and larger one. For Sandy to talk privately with Burke, she'd have had to go to the small bottom section of the ship. Holmes and Pam faced the same situation. It was uncomfortable. So they developed a perfectly pleasant habit of talking exclusively of things everybody could talk about. It did not bother Keller, who would hardly average a dozen words in twenty-four hours, but Sandy muttered to herself when she and Pam retired for what was a ship-night's rest.

When they went past the orbit of Mars, agitated instructions came out from Earth. The asteroid belts began beyond Mars. Elaborate directions came. The ship was tracked by radar telescopes all around the world, direction-finding on its transmission. Croydon kept track. American radar bowls picked up the ship's voice. South American and Hawaiian and Japanese and Siberian radar telescopes determined the ship's position every time a set of code symbols reached Earth from the ship. Of course, there were also the beepings and the seventy-nine-minute-spaced identical broadcasts from farther out from the sun.

Somebody got a brilliant idea and authority to try it. An interview for broadcast on Earth was sought with somebody on the ship. It was then a hundred thirty million miles from Earth, and ninety-two million more from the sun. Largely out of boredom Sandy agreed to answer questions. But at the speed of light it required eleven minutes to reach her from Earth, and as long for her reply to be received. It did not make for liveliness, so she spoke curtly for five minutes and stopped. She talked at random about housekeeping in space. Without knowing it, she was praised for her domestics in many pulpits the following Sunday, and eight hundred ninety-two proposals of marriage piled up in mail addressed to her in care of the United States government. Twelve were in Russian.

But nothing really exciting happened aboard the spaceship. It was Burke's guess that they could go directly through the asteroid belt along the plane of the ecliptic, and not get nearer than ten thousand miles to any bit of shattered stone or metal in orbit out there. He was almost right. There was only one occasion when his optimism came into doubt.

It was on the ninth day out from Earth. Experimentally, the ship coasted on attained momentum, using no drive. There was, then, no substitute for gravity and everyone and everything in the ship was weightless. The power obtainable from the sun as heat had dwindled to one-ninth of that at the Earth's distance. But what was received could be stored, and was. Meanwhile the ship plunged onward at very nearly four hundred miles per second, Burke, Keller, and Holmes together labored over a self-contained diving suit which they hoped could be used as a space suit in dire emergency and for brief periods. They wanted to get the feel of using it with internal pressure and weightlessness as conditions. Sandy sat at the transmitter, working at code which by now she heartily loathed. Pam sat in the control-chair, watching the instruments.

There was a buzz. Burke snapped his head around to see the radar screen. A line of light appeared on it. It aimed directly at the center of the screen, which meant that whatever had been picked up was on a collision course with the ship. Burke plunged toward the control-chair to take over. But he'd forgotten the condition of no-gravity. He went floating off in mid-air, far wide of the chair.

He barked orders to Pam, who was least qualified of anybody

aboard to meet an emergency of this sort. She panicked. She did nothing. Holmes took precious seconds to drag himself to the controls by what hand-holds could be had. The glowing white line on the radar screen lengthened swiftly. It neared the center. It reached the center. Burke and Holmes froze.

There was a curious flashing change in a vision-screen. An image flashed into view. It was a jagged, tortured, irregularly-shaped mass of stone or metal, distorted in its representation by the speed at which it passed the television lens. It was perhaps a hundred yards in diameter. It could never have been seen from Earth. It might circle the sun in its lonely orbit for a hundred million years and never be seen again.

It went away to nothing. It had missed by yards or fathoms, and Burke found himself sweating profusely. Holmes was deathly white. Keller very carefully took a deep breath, swallowed, and went back to his work on the diving-suit-qua-space-suit. Sandy hadn't noticed anything at all. But Pam burst into abrupt, belated tears, and Holmes comforted her clumsily. She was bitterly ashamed that she'd done nothing to meet the emergency which came while she was at the control-board, and which was the only emergency they'd encountered since the ship's departure from Earth.

After that, they put on the drive and used reserve fuel. It was necessary to check their speed, anyhow. They were very near the source of the beeping signal they'd steered by for so long. The directional receiver pointed to it had long since been turned dawn to its lowest possible volume, and still the beepings were loud.

On the eleventh day after their take-off, they sighted Asteroid M-387. They had traveled two hundred seventy million miles at an averaged-out speed of very close to three hundred miles per second. Despite muting, the beepings from the loud-speakers were monstrous noises.

"Try a call, Holmes," said Burke. "But they ought to know we're here."

He felt strange. He'd brought the ship to a stop about four or five miles from M-387. The asteroid was a mass of dark stuff with white outcroppings at one place and another. The ship seemed to edge itself toward it. The floating mass of stone and metal had no particular shape. It was longer than it was wide, but its form fitted no description. A mountain which had been torn from solidity with its roots of stone attached might look like Scull's Object as it turned slowly against a background of myriads of unblinking stars.

There was no change in the beeping that came from the singular thing. It did rotate, but so slowly that one had to watch for long minutes to be sure of it. There was no outward sign of any reaction to the ship's presence. Holmes took the microphone.

"Hello! Hello!" he said absurdly. "We have come from Earth to find out what you want."

No answer. No change in the beeping calls. The asteroid turned with enormous deliberation.

Sandy said suddenly, "Look there! A stick! No, it's a mast! See, where the patch of white is?"

Burke very, very gingerly drew closer to the monstrous thing which hung in space. It was true. There was a mast of some sort sticking up out of white stone. The direction-indicators pointed to it. The beeping stopped and a broadcast began. It was the standard broadcast Earth heard every seventy-nine minutes.

There was no reply to Holmes' call. There was no indication that the ship's arrival had been noted. On Earth the ignoring of human broadcasts to M-387 had seemed arrogance, indifference, a superior and menacing contempt for man and all his works; somehow, here the effect was different. This irregular mass was a fragment of something that once had been much greater. It suddenly ceased to seem menacing because it seemed oblivious. It acted blindly, by rote, like some mechanism set to operate in a certain way and unable to act in any other.

It did not seem alive. It had signaled like a robot beacon. Now it felt like one. It was one.

"Look, coming around toward us," said Holmes very quietly. "There's something that looks like a tunnel. It's not a crevasse. It was cut."

Burke nodded.

"Yes," he said thoughtfully. "I think we'll explore it. But I don't really expect we'll find any life here. There's nothing outside to see but a single metal mast. We've got some signal lights on our hull. If we're careful —"

No one objected. The appearance of the asteroid was utterly disappointing. Its lifelessness and its obliviousness to their coming and their calls were worse than disappointing. There was nothing to be seen but a metal stick from which signals went out to nowhere.

Burke jockeyed the little ship to the tunnel-mouth. It was fully a hundred feet in diameter. He turned on the ship's signal lights. Gently, cautiously, he worked down the very center of the very large bore.

It was perfectly straight. They went in for what seemed an indefinite distance. Presently the signal lights showed that the wall was smoothed. The bore grew smaller still. They went on and on.

Suddenly Keller grunted. He pointed to one of the six television screens which aimed out the length of the tunnel and showed the stars beyond.

Those stars were being blotted out. Something vast moved slowly and deliberately across the shaft they navigated. It closed the opening. Their retreat was blocked. The ship was shut in, in the center of a mountain of stone which floated perpetually in emptiness. Burke checked the ship's forward motion, judging their speed by the side walls shown by the ship's outside lights.

Very, very slowly, faint illumination appeared outside. In seconds they could see that the light came from long tubes of faint bluish light. The light changed. It grew stronger. It turned green and then yellowish and then became very bright, indeed.

Then nothing more took place. Nothing whatever. The five inside the ship waited more than an hour for some other development, but absolutely nothing happened.

CHAPTER 6

THERE WAS A TINY SHOCK; in a minute, trivial contact of the ship with something outside it. Drifting within the now brightly lighted bore, it had touched the wall. There was no force to the impact.

Keller made an interested noise. When eyes turned to him, he pointed to a dial. A needle on that dial pointed just past the figure "30." Burke grunted.

"The devil! We've been waiting for things to happen, and they already have! It's our move."

"According to that needle," agreed Holmes, "somebody has kindly put thirty point seven mercury inches of air-pressure around the ship outside. We can walk out and breathe, now."

"If," said Burke, "it's air. It could be something else. I'll have to check it."

He got out the self-contained diving apparatus that had been brought along to serve as a strictly temporary space suit.

"I'll try a cigarette-lighter. Maybe it will burn naturally. Maybe it will go out. It could make an explosion. But I doubt that very much."

"We'll hope," said Holmes, "that the lighter burns."

Burke climbed into the diving suit, which had been designed for amateurs of undersea fishing to use in chilly waters. On Earth it would have been intolerably heavy, for a man moving about out of the ocean. But there was no weight here. If M-387 had a gravitational field at all, which in theory it had to have, it would be on the order of millionths of the pull of Earth.

Keller sat in the control-chair, watching the instruments and the outside television screens which showed the bore now reduced to fifty feet. Somehow the more distant parts of the tunnel looked hazy, as if there were a slight mist in whatever gas had been released in it. Sandy watched Burke pull on the helmet and close the face-plate. She grasped a hand-hold, her knuckles turning white. Pam nestled comfortably in a corner of the ceiling of the control-room. Holmes frowned as Burke went into the air-lock and closed the inner door.

His voice came immediately out of a speaker at the control-desk.

"I'm breathing canned air from the suit," he said curtly.

There were scrapings. The outer lock-door made noises. There was what seemed to be a horribly long wait. Then they heard Burke's voice again.

"I've tried it," he reported. "The lighter burns when it's next to the slightly opened door. I'm opening wide now."

More noises from the air-lock.

"It still burns. Repeat. The lighter burns all right. The tunnel is filled with air. I'm going to crack my face-plate and see how it smells."

Silence, while Sandy went white. But a moment later Burke said crisply, "It smells all right. It's lifeless and stuffy, but there's nothing in it with an odor. Hold on — I hear something!"

A long minute, while the little ship floated eerily almost in contact with the walls about it. It turned slowly. Then there came brisk, brief fluting noises. They were familiar in kind. But this was a short message, of some fifteen or twenty seconds length, no more. It ended, was repeated, ended, was repeated, and went on with an effect of mechanical and parrot-like repetition.

"It's good air," reported Burke. "I'm breathing normally. But it might have been stored for ages. It's stale. Do you hear what I do?"

"Yes," said Sandy in a whisper to the control-room. "It's a call. It's telling us to do something. Come back inside, Joe!"

They heard the outer air-lock door closing and its locking-dogs engaging. The fluting noises ceased to be audible. The inner door swung wide. Burke came into the control-room, his helmet face-plate open. He wriggled out of the diving suit.

"Something picked up the fact that we'd entered. It closed a door behind us. Then it turned on lights for us. Then it let air into the entrance lock. Now it's telling us to do something."

The ship surged, ever so gently. Keller had turned on an infinitesimal trace of drive. The walls of the bore floated past on the television screens. There was mist in the air outside. It seemed to clear as the ship moved.

Keller made a gratified small sound. They could see the end of the tunnel. There was a platform there. Stairs went to it from the side of the bore. There was a door with rounded corners in the end wall. That wall was metal.

Keller carefully turned the ship until the stairway was in proper position for a landing, if there had been gravitation to make the stairs usable. Very, very gently, he lowered the ship upon the platform.

There was a singular tugging sensation which ceased, came again, ceased, and gradually built up to a perfectly normal feeling of weight. They stood upon the floor of the control-room with every physical sensation they'd felt during one-gravity acceleration on the way out here, and which they'd have felt if the ship were aground on Earth.

"Artificial gravity! Whoever made this knew something!" Burke said.

Pam swallowed and spoke with an apparent attempt at nonchalance.

"Now what do we do?"

"We — look for the people," said Sandy in a queer tone.

"There's nobody here, Sandy!" Burke said irritably. "Can't you see? There can't be anybody here! They'd have signaled us what to do if there had been! This is machinery working. We do something and it operates. But then it waits for us to do something else. It's like — like a self-service elevator!"

"We didn't come here for an elevator ride," said Sandy.

"I came to find out what's here," said Burke, "and why it's signaling to Earth. Holmes, you stay here with the girls and I'll take a look outside."

"I'd like to mention," said Holmes drily, "that we haven't a weapon on this ship. When they shot rockets at us back on Earth, we didn't have even a pea-shooter to shoot back with. We haven't now. I think the girls are as safe exploring as they are here. And besides, we'll all feel better if we're together."

"I'm going!" said Sandy defiantly.

Burke hesitated, then shrugged. He unlatched the devices which kept both doors to the air-lock from being open at the same time. It was not a completely cautious thing to do, but caution was impractical. The ship was imprisoned. It was incapable of defense. There was simply nothing sensible about precautions that couldn't prevent anything.

Burke threw open the outer lock door. One by one, the five of them climbed down to the platform so plainly designed for a ship of space — a small one — to land upon. Nothing happened. Their surroundings were completely uninformative. This landing-platform might have been built by any race on Earth or anywhere else, provided only that it used stairs.

"Here goes," said Burke.

He went to the door with rounded corners. There was something like a handle at one side, about waist-high. He put his hand to it, tugged and twisted, and the door gave. It was not rusty, but it badly needed lubrication. Burke pulled it wide and stared unbelievingly beyond.

Before him there stretched a corridor which was not less than twenty feet high and just as wide. The long, glowing tubes of light that illuminated the ship-tunnel were here, too, fixed in the ceiling. The corridor reached away, straight and unbroken, until its end seemed a mere point in the distance. It looked about a full mile long. There were doorways in both its side walls, and they dwindled in the distance with a monotonous regularity until they, too, were mere vertical specks. One could not speak of the length of this corridor in feet or yards. It was a mile.

It was incredible. It was overwhelming. And it was empty. It shone in the glare of the light tubes which made a river of brilliance overhead. It seemed preposterous that so vast a construction should have no living thing in it. But it was absolutely vacant.

They stared down its length for long seconds. Then Burke seemed to shake himself.

"Here's the parlor. Let's walk in, even if there's no welcoming committee;"

His voice echoed. It rolled and reverberated and then diminished very slowly to nothing.

Burke strode forward with Sandy close to him. Pam stared blankly, and instinctively moved up to Holmes. Once they were through the door, the sensation was not that of adventure in a remote part of space, but of being in some strange and impossible monument on Earth. The feeling of weight, if not completely normal, was so near it as not to be noticed. They could have been in some previously unknown structure made by men, at home.

This corridor, though, was not built. It was excavated. Some process had been used which did not fracture the stone to be removed. The surface of the rock about them was smooth. In places it glittered. The doorways had been cut out, not constructed. They were of a size which made them seem designed for the use of men. The compartments to which they gave admission were similarly matter-of-fact. They were windowless, of course, but their strangeness lay in the fact that they were empty, as if to insist that all this ingenuity and labor had been abandoned thousands of years before. Yet from somewhere in the asteroid a call still went out urgently, filling the solar system with plaintive fluting sounds, begging whoever heard to come and do something which was direly necessary.

A long, long way down the gallery there were two specks. A quarter-mile from the entrance, they saw that one of the rooms contained a pile of metal ingots, neatly stacked and bound in place by still-glistening wire. At half a mile they came upon the things in the gallery itself. One was plainly a table with a single leg, made of metal. It was unrusted, but showed signs of use. The other was an object with a hollow top. In the hollow there were twisted, shriveled shreds of something unguessable.

"If men had built this," said Burke, and again his voice echoed and rolled, "that hollow thing would be a stool with a vanished cushion, and the table would be a desk."

Sandy said thoughtfully, "If men had built this, there'd be signs somewhere marking things. At least there'd be some sort of numbers on these doorways!"

Burke said nothing. They went on.

The gallery branched. A metal door closed off the divergent branch. Burke tugged at an apparent handle. It did not yield. They continued along the straight, open way.

They came to a larger-than-usual opening in the side wall. Inside it there were rows and rows and rows of metal spheres some ten feet in diameter. There must have been hundreds of them. Beside the door there was a tiny shelf, with a tinier box fastened to it. A long way farther, they came to what had appeared to be the end of this corridor. But it did not end. It slanted upward and turned and they found themselves in the same corridor on a different level, headed back in the direction from which they had come. Their footsteps echoed hollowly in the still-enormous emptiness. There were other closed doors. Burke tried some. Holmes tried others. They did not open. Keller moved raptly, gazing at this and that.

Everything was strange, but not strange enough to be frightening. One could have believed this place the work of men, except that this was beyond the ability of men to make. There must be miles of vacant rooms carved out of solid rock. They came upon some hundreds of yards of doorways, and in every room on which they opened, there were metal frames about the walls. Holmes said suddenly, "If men had built this place, those could be bunks."

They came to another place where there was dust, and a group of six huge rooms communicating not only with the corridor but with each other. They found hollow metal things like cook pans. They found a hollow small object which could have been a drinking vessel. It was broken. It was of a size suitable for men.

"If men built this," said Holmes again, "these could be mess-halls. But I agree with Sandy that there should be signs."

Yet another closed door. It resisted their efforts to open it, just like the others. Keller put out his hand and thoughtfully touched the stone beside it. He looked astonished.

"What?" asked Burke. He touched the stone as Keller had. It was bitterly, bitterly cold. "The air's warm and the stone's cold! What's this?"

Keller wetted the tip of his finger and rubbed it on the rocky side wall. Instantly, frost appeared. But the air remained warm.

The gallery turned again, and again rose. The third-level passageway was shorter; barely half a mile in length. Here they passed door after door, all open, with each compartment containing a huge and somehow malevolent shape of metal. And beside each doorway there was a little shelf with a small box fastened to it.

"These," said Holmes, "could be guns, if there were any way for them to shoot anything. Just by the look of them I'd say they were weapons."

Burke said abruptly, "Keller, the stone being freezing cold while the air's warm means that this place has been heated up lately. Heat's been poured into it. Within hours!"

Keller considered. Then he shook his head.

"Not heat. Warmed air."

Burke went scowling onward. He followed, actually, the only route that was open. Other ways were cut off by doors which refused to open. Sandy, beside him, noted the floor. It was stone like the walls and ceiling. But it was worn. There were slight inequalities in it, beginning a foot or so from the walls. Sandy envisioned thousands of feet moving about these resonant corridors for hundreds or thousands of years in order to wear away the solid stone in this fashion. She felt age about her — incredible age reaching back to time past imagining, while the occupants of this hollow world swarmed about its interior. Doing what?

Burke considered other things. There were the ten-foot metal spheres, ranged by hundreds in what might be a magazine below. There were the squat and ugly metal monsters which seemed definitely menacing to somebody or something. There were the metal frameworks like bunks. There was no rust, here, which could be accounted for if Keller happened to be right and warmed air had been released lately in corridors which before — for ten thousand years or more — had contained only the vacuum of space. And there were those rooms which could be mess-halls.

These items were subject matter for thought. But if what they hinted at was true, there must be other specialized compartments elsewhere. There must be storerooms for food for those who managed the guns — if they were guns — and the spheres, and lived in the bunk-rooms and ate in the mess-halls. There'd be storerooms for equipment and supplies of all sorts. And again, if Keller were right about the air, there must be enormous pressure-tanks which had held the asteroid's atmosphere under high pressure for millennia, only to warm it and release it within the hour so that those who came by ship could use it.

An old phrase occurred to Burke. "A mystery wrapped in an enigma." It applied to these discoveries. Plainly the release of air had been done without the command of any living creature. There could be none here! As plainly, the signals from space had been begun without the interposition of life. The transmitter which still senselessly flung its message to Earth was a robot. The operation of the ship-lock, the warming of air, the lighting of the ship-lock and the corridors — all had been accomplished by machinery, obeying orders given to the transmitter first by some unguessable stimulus.

But why? Other mysteries aside, there had plainly been meticulous preparation for the welcoming of a ship from space. No, not welcoming. Acceptance of a ship from space. Somebody had been expected to respond to those plaintive fluting noises which went wailing through the solar system. Who were those waited-for visitors expected to be? What were they expected to do? For that matter, what was the purpose of the asteroid itself? What had it been built for? At some time or another it must have contained thousands of inhabitants. What were they here for? What became of them? And when the asteroid was left — abandoned — what conceivable situation was to trigger the transmitter to send out urgent calls, and then a directional guiding-signal the instant the call was answered? When Burke's ship came, the asteroid accepted it without question and carried out mechanical operations to make it possible for that ship's crew to roam at will through it. What activated this mechanism of so many eons ago?

The five newly-arrived humans, three men and two girls, trudged along the echoing gallery cut out of the asteroid's heart. Murmurous sounds accompanied them. Once they came to a place where a whispering-gallery effect existed. They heard their footsteps repeated loudly as if the asteroid inhabitants were approaching invisibly, but no one came.

"I don't like this!" Pam said uneasily.

Then her own voice mocked her, and she realized what it was, and giggled nervously. That also was repeated, and sounded like something which seemed to sneer at them. It was unpleasant.

They came to the end of the gallery. There was a stair leading upward. There was nowhere else to go, so Burke started up, Sandy close behind him, and Holmes and Pam behind them. Keller brought up the rear. They climbed, and small noises began to be audible.

They were fluting sounds. They grew louder as the party from Earth went up and up. They reached a landing, and here also there was a metal door with rounded corners. Through it and from beyond it came the piping notes that Burke had heard in his dream some hundreds of times and that lately had come to Earth from emptiness. The sounds seemed to pause and to begin again, and once more to pause. It was not possible to tell whether they came from one source, speaking pathetically, or from two sources in conversation.

Sandy went utterly white and her eyes fixed upon Burke. He was nearly as pale, himself. He stopped. Here and now there was no trace of ribbony-leaved trees or the smell of green things, but only air which was stuffy and lifeless as if it had been confined for centuries. And there was no sunset sky with two moons in it, but only carved and seamless stone Yet there were the familiar fluting sounds. . . .

Burke put his hand to the curiously-shaped handle of the door. It yielded. The door opened inward. Burke went in, his throat absurdly dry. Sandy followed him.

And again there was disappointment. Because there was no living creature here. The room was perhaps thirty feet long and as wide. There were many vision-screens in it, and some of them showed the stars outside with a precision of detail no earthly television could provide. The sun glowed as a small disk a third of its proper diameter. It was dimmer, too. The Milky Way showed clearly. And there were very many screens which showed utterly clear views of the surface of the asteroid, all broken, chaotic, riven rock and massy, un-oxydized metal.

But there was no life. There were not even symbols of life. There were only machines. They noticed a large transparent disk some ten feet across. Specks of light glowed within its substance. Off at one side an angular metal arm held a small object very close to the disk's surface, a third of the way from its edge. It did not touch the disk, but under it and in the disk there was a little group of bright-red specks which quivered and wavered. They were placed in a strict mathematical arrangement which very, very slowly changed so that it would be hours before it had completed a rotation and had exactly the same appearance again.

The flutings came from a tall metal cone on the floor. Another machine nearby held a round plate out toward the cone. "There's nobody here," said Sandy in a strange voice. "What'll we do now, Joe?"

"This must be the transmitter," he murmured. "The sound-record for the broadcasts must be in here, somehow. It's possible that this plate is a sort of microphone —"

Keller, beaming, pointed to a round spot which quivered with an eerie luminescence. It glowed more brightly and dimmed according to the flutings. Burke said "The devil!" and the round spot flickered up very brightly for an instant.

"Yes," said Burke. "It's a mike. It's quite likely —" the round spot flared up and dimmed with the modulations of his voice — "it's quite likely that what I say goes into the broadcast to Earth."

The cone ceased to emit fluting noises. Burke said very steadily — and the spot flickered violently with the sounds — "I think I am transmitting to Earth. If so, this is Joe Burke. I announce the arrival of my ship at Asteroid M-387. The asteroid has been hollowed out and fitted with an air-lock which admitted our ship. It is a — a —"

He hesitated, and Holmes said curtly, "It's a fortress."

"Yes," said Burke heavily. "It's a fortress. There are weapons we haven't had time to examine. There are barracks for a garrison of thousands. But there is no one here. It has been deserted, but not abandoned, because the transmitter was set up to send out a call when some occasion arose. It seems to have arisen. There is a big plate here which may be a star map, with a scale on which light-years may be represented by inches. I don't know. There are certain bright-red specks on it. They are moving. There is a machine to watch those specks. Apparently it actuated the transmitter to make it call to all the solar system."

Keller suddenly put his finger to his lips. Burke nodded and said curtly, "I'll report further."

Keller flipped aver an odd switch with something of a flourish — after which he looked embarrassed. The transmitter went dead.

"He's right," said Holmes. "Back home they knave we're here, I suspect, and you've told enough to give them fits. I think we'd better be careful what we say in the clear."

Burke nodded again. "There'll be calls from Earth shortly and we can decide whether or not to use code then. Keller, can you trace the leads to this transmitter and find the receiver that picked up that West Virginia beam-signal and changed the first broadcast to the second? It should be as sensitive as this transmitter is powerful."

Keller nodded confidently.

"It'll take thirty-some minutes for that report of mine to reach Earth and an answer to get back," observed Burke, "if everything works perfectly and the proper side of Earth is turned this way. I think we can be sure there's nobody but us in the fortress."

His sensations were peculiar. It was exciting to have found a fortress in space, of course. It was the sort of thing that might have satisfied a really dedicated scientist completely. Burke realized the importance of the discovery, but it was an impersonal accomplishment. It did not mean, to Burke, that he'd carried out the purpose behind his coming here. This fortress was linked to a dream about a world with two moons in its sky and someone or something running breathlessly behind unearthly swaying foliage. But this place was not the place of that dream, nor did it fulfill it. Mystery remained, and frustration, and Burke was left in the state of mind of a savage who has found a treasure which means much to civilized men, but doesn't make him any happier because he doesn't want what civilized men can give him.

He grimaced and spoke without elation.

"Let's go back to the ship and get a code message ready for Earth."

He led the way out of this room of many motionless but operating machines. The incredibly perfect vision-screen images still portrayed the cosmos outside with all the stars and the sun itself moving slowly across their plates. They saw sunshine and starlight shining on the broken, chaotic outer surface of the asteroid. Wavering, curiously writhing red specks on the ten-foot disk continued their crawling motion. Keller fairly glowed with enthusiasm as he began to investigate this apparatus.

They all went back to the ship, except for Keller. They retraced their way along the long and brilliantly lighted galleries. They descended ramps and went along more brilliantly lighted corridors. Then they came to the branch which had been blocked off by a door that would not open. It was open now. They could see along the new section for a long, long way. They passed places where other doors had been closed, but now were open. What they could see inside them was almost exclusively a repetition of what they saw outside of them. They passed the place where hundreds of ten-foot metal spheres waited for an unknown use. They passed the table with a single leg, and the compartment with many metal ingots stored in it.

Finally, they came to the door with rounded corners, went through it, and there was their ship with its air-lock doors open, waiting in the brightly lighted tunnel.

They went in, and the feeling was of complete anticlimax. They knew, of course, that they had made a discovery beside which all archaeological discoveries on Earth were trivial. They had come upon operating machines which must be old beyond imagining, unrusted because preserved in emptiness, and infinitely superior to anything that men had ever made. They had come upon a mystery to tantalize every brain on Earth. The consequences of their coming to this place would remake all of Earth's future. But they were singularly un-elated.

"I'll make up a sort of report," said Burke heavily, "of what we saw as we arrived, and our landing, and that sort of thing. We'll get it in code and ready for transmission. We can use the asteroid's transmitter."

Holmes scowled at the floor of the little ship.

"You'll make a report, too," said Burke. "You realized that this is a fortress. There can't be any doubt. It was built and put here to fight something. It wasn't built for fun. But I wonder who it was meant to do battle with, and why it was left by its garrison, and why they set up a transmitter to broadcast when something happened! Maybe it was to call the garrison back if they were ever needed, But thousands of years — You make a report on that!"

Holmes nodded.

"You might add," said Pam, shivering a little, "that it's a terribly creepy place."

"What I don't understand," said Sandy, "is why nothing's labelled. Nothing's marked. Whoever built it must have known how to write, in some fashion. A civilized race has to have written records to stay civilized! But I haven't seen a symbol or a pointer or even a color used to give information."

She got out the papers on which she would code the reports as Burke and Holmes turned them over for transmission. She began to write out, carefully, the elaborate key to the coding. Almost reluctantly, Pam prepared to do the same with Holmes' narrative of what he'd seen.

But if enthusiasm was tempered in the ship, there was no such reserve in the United States. Burke's voice had cut into one of the space broadcasts which arrived every seventy-nine minutes. There had been the usual cryptic, plaintive piping noises, repeating for the thousandth time their meaningless message. Then a human voice said almost inaudibly,

". . . 'll we do now, Joe?" It was heard over an entire hemisphere, where satellite-tracking stations and radar telescopes listened to and recorded every broadcast from space.

It was a stupendous happening. Then Burke's voice came through the flutings. "This must be the transmitter. The sound-record for the broadcasts must be in here, somehow. It's quite possible that this plate is a sort of microphone . . ." A few seconds later he was heard to say, "The devil!" And later still he addressed himself directly to his listeners on Earth.

He'd spoken the words eighteen and a fraction minutes before they arrived, though they traveled at the speed of light. Broadcast and ecstatically reported in the United States, they touched off a popular reaction as widespread as that triggered by the beginning of the signals themselves. Broadcasters abandoned all other subject matter. Announcers with lovely diction stated the facts and then expanded them into gibbering nonsense. Man had reached M-387. Man had spoken to Earth across two hundred seventy million miles of emptiness. Man had taken possession of a fortress in space. Man now had an outpost, a steppingstone toward the stars. Man had achieved. . . . Man had risen. . . . Man now took the first step toward his manifest destiny, which was to occupy and possess all the thousands of thousands of planets all the way to the galaxy's rim.

But this was in the United States. Elsewhere, rejoicing was much less, especially after a prominent American politician was reported to have said that America's leadership of Earth was not likely ever to be challenged again. A number of the smaller nations immediately protested in the United Nations. That august body was forced to put upon its agenda a full-scale discussion of U.S. space developments. Middle European nations charged that the purpose of America was to monopolize not only the practical means of traveling to other members of the solar system, but all natural and technical resources obtained by such journeyings. With a singular unanimity, the nations at the edge of the Russian bloc demanded that there should be equality of information on Earth. No nation should hold back scientific information. In fact, there was bitter denunciation of the use of code by the humans now on M-387. It was demanded that they answer in the clear all scientific inquiries made by any government — in the clear so everybody could eavesdrop.

In effect, the United States rejoiced in and boasted of the achievements of some of its citizens who, after escaping attack by American guided missiles, had found a steppingstone toward the stars. But the rest of the world jealously demanded that the United States reap no benefit from the fact. International tension, in fact, rose to a new high.

And Burke and the others laboriously gathered this bit of information and discovered the lack of that. They found incredible devices whose purpose or workings they could not understand. They found every possible evidence of a civilization beside which that of Earth was intolerably backward. But the civilization had abandoned the asteroid.

By the second day the mass of indigestible information had become alarming. They could marvel, but they could not understand. And not to understand was intolerable. They could comprehend that there was a device with red sparks in it which had made another device send a fluting, plaintive call to all the solar system. Nothing else was understandable. The purpose of the call remained a mystery.

But the communicators hummed with messages from Earth. It seemed that every radar telescope upon the planet had been furnished with a transmitter and that every one bombarded the asteroid with a tight beam carrying arguments, offers, expostulations and threats.

"This ought to be funny," said Burke dourly. "But it isn't. All we know is that we've found a fortress which was built to defend a civilization about which we know nothing except that it isn't in the solar system. We know an alarm went off, to call the fortress' garrison back to duty, but the garrison didn't come. We did. We've some evidence that a fighting fleet or something similar is headed this way and that it intends to smash this fortress and may include Earth. You'd think that that sort of news would calm them down, on Earth!"

The microwave receiver was so jammed with messages that there was no communication at all. None could be understood when all arrived at once. Burke had to send a message to Earth in code, specifying a new and secret wavelength, before it became possible to have a two-way contact with Earth. But the messages continued to came out, every one clamoring for something else of benefit to itself alone.

CHAPTER 7

IN THE BEGINNING there was nothing at all, and then things were created, and the wonder of created things was very great. When men became, they marveled at the richness and the beauty about them, and their lives were filled with astonishment at the myriads of things in the air and on the earth and in the sea. For many centuries they were busy taking note of all the created things that were. They forgot that there was such a condition as emptiness.

But there were six people in a certain solar system who really knew what emptiness amounted to. Five of them were in a fortress which was an asteroid and a mystery. One was in a small, crude object which floated steadily out from Earth. This one's name was Nikolai. The rest of it does not matter. He had been born in a small village in the Urals, and as a little boy he played games with mud and reeds and sticks and dogs and other little boys. As a growing youth he dutifully stuffed his head with things out of books, and some seemed to him rational and marvelous, and some did not make much sense but were believed by everybody. And who was he to go against the wise comrades who ran the government and protected the people from wars and famines and the schemes of villainous capitalists?

As a young man he was considered promising. If he had been interested in such matters, he might have had a moderately successful career in politics, as politics was practised in his nation. But he liked things. Real things.

When he was a student in the university he kept a canary in his lodgings. He loved it very much. There was a girl, too, about whom he dreamed splendidly. But there was a need for school teachers in Bessarabia, and she went there to teach. She wept when she left him. After that Nikolai studied with something of desperation, trying to forget her because he could not have her.

He thought of such past events as he drifted outward from Earth. He was the passenger, he was the crew of the manned space-probe his government had prepared to go out and investigate strange signals coming from emptiness. He was a volunteer, of course. It was a great honor to be accepted, and for a while he'd almost forgotten the girl who was teaching school in Bessarabia. But that was a long time ago, now. At first he'd liked to remember the take-off, when brisk, matter-of-fact men tucked him in his acceleration-chair and left him, and he lay staring upward in dead silence — save far the ticking of an insanely emotionless clock — until there was a roar to end all roars and a shock to crush anything made of flesh and bones, and then a terrible, horrible feeling of weight that kept on and on until he lost consciousness.

He could remember all this, if he chose. He had a distinct recollection of coming back to life, and of struggling to send off the signal which would say that he had survived the take-off. There were telemetering devices which reported what information was desired about the bands and belts of deadly radiation which surrounded the planet Earth. But Nikolai reported by voice, because that was evidence that he had passed through those murderous places unharmed. And his probe went on and on outward, away from the Earth and the sun.

He received messages from Earth. Tinny voices assured him that his launching had gone well. His nation was proud of him. Enormous rewards awaited him on his return. Meanwhile — The tinny voices instructed him in what he was to say for them to record and broadcast to all the world in his honor.

He said it, with the Earth a small crescent-shaped bit of brightness behind him. He drifted on. The crescent which was Earth grew smaller and smaller as days went by. He took due care of the instruments of his space-vehicle. He made sure that the air apparatus behaved properly. He disposed of wastes. From time to time he reported, by voice, information which automatic devices had long since given in greater detail and with superior accuracy.

And he thought more and more about the girl — teaching school in Bessarabia — and his canary, which had died. Days went by. He was informed that it was time for him to make contact with a drone fuel-rocket sent on before him. He watched the instruments which would point out where it was.

He found it, and with small auxiliary rockets he made careful tiny blastings which guided his vehicle to contact with it. The complex machinery for refueling took effect. Presently he cast off the emptied drone, aimed very, very carefully and blasted outward once more. The shock was worse than that on Earth, and he knew nothing for a long, long time. He was horribly weak when he regained consciousness. He mentioned it in his reports. There was no comment on the fact in the replies he received from Earth.

He continued to float away from the sun. It became impossible to pick out Earth among the stars. The sun was smaller than he remembered. There was nothing to be seen anywhere but stars and more stars and the dwindling disk of the sun that used to rise and set but now remained stationary, shrinking.

So Nikolai came to know emptiness. There were points of light which were stars. They were illimitable distances away. In between was emptiness. He had no sensation of movement. Save that as days went by the sun grew smaller, there was no change in anything. All was emptiness. If his vehicle floated like this for ten thousand times ten thousand years, the stars would appear no nearer. If he got out and ran upon nothingness to get back to where he could see Earth again, he would have to run for centuries, and generations would die and nations fall before he caught the least glimmer of that thin crescent which was his home.

If he shouted, no man would ever hear, because emptiness does not carry sound. If he died, there was no earth into which his body could be lowered. If he lived, there was nowhere he could stand upright and breathe clean air and feel solidity beneath his feet. He had a destination, to be sure, but he did not really believe that he would ever reach it, nor did he imagine he would ever return. Now he dismissed it from his thoughts.

He found that he was feverish, and he mentioned it when the tinny voices talked urgently to him. He guessed, without emotion, that he had not passed through the deadly radiation-belts around Earth unburned. He had been assured that he would pass through them so swiftly that they would be quite harmless. Now he knew that this was a mistake. His body obeyed him only sluggishly. He was dying of deep-seated radiation burns. But he felt nothing.

Voices waked him to insist that he make contact with another fuel-drone. He exhausted himself as he dutifully obeyed commands. He was clumsy. He was feeble. But he managed a second refueling. And even as he performed the highly technical operation with seemingly detached and reluctant hands, he thought of a schoolteacher in Bessarabia.

Before he fired the new fuel which would send him onward at what would be more than escape velocity, he almost humorously — yet quite humorlessly — reviewed his life. He considered that he might have no later opportunity to do so. There were three things he had done which no man had done before him. He had loved a certain small canary, and he remembered it distinctly. He had loved a certain girl, and in his weakened and dying state he could see her much more clearly than the grubby interior of the space-probe. And the third thing —

He had to cast about in his mind to remember what it was. His hand poised upon the rocket-firing key, he debated. Ah, yes! The third thing was that he had learned what emptiness was.

He pressed the firing-key. And the space-probe spouted flames and went on. Before the fuel was exhausted it had reached a velocity so great that it would go on forever through interstellar space. It would never fall back toward the sun, not even after thousands of years.

The knowledge of emptiness possessed by the five in the asteroid was different. A totally empty room is intimidating. A vacant house is depressing. The two-mile-long asteroid, honeycombed with tunnels and corridors and galleries and rooms, was like a deserted city. Those who had left it had carefully stripped it of personal possessions, but they'd left weapons behind, ready to be manned and used. They'd left a warning device to call them. The recall device was proof that the danger had not been destroyed and might return. And the plaintive call through all the solar system proved that it was returning.

There was irony in the fact that Earth had panicked when it seemed that intelligent non-human beings signaled from space, and that shrill disputes for advantage began instantly Burke reported no living monsters at the signals' source. The fortress and its call meant more than the mere existence of aliens. It was proof that there were entities of space who needed to be fought. It proved the existence of fighting ships of space; of deadly war in emptiness; of creatures who crossed the void between star systems to conquer and to murder and destroy.

And such creatures were coming.

Burke ground his teeth. Earth had fusion bombs and rockets which could carry them for pitifully short distances on the cosmic scale. This fortress was incomparably more powerful than all of Earth's armament put together. A fleet which dared to attack it must feel itself stronger still. What could Earth do against a fleet which dared attack this asteroid?

And what could he and Holmes and Keller do against such a fleet, even with the fortress, when they did not yet understand a single one of its weapons?

Burke worked himself to exhaustion, trying to unravel even the simplest principles of the fortress' armament. There were globes which were, obviously, the long-range weapons of the garrison. They were stored in a launching-tube at the far back of the compartment. But Keller could not unravel the method of their control. There was no written matter in the fortress. None. A totally unknown language and an unfamiliar alphabet would prevent written matter from being useful, ordinarily, but in technical descriptions there are bound to be diagrams. Burke felt desperately that in even the most meaningless of scripts there would be diagrams which could be puzzled out. But there was nothing. The builders of the fortress could have been illiterate, for all the signs of writing that they'd left.

Keller continued to labor valiantly. But there was no clue to the operation of anything but the transmitter. That was understandable because one knew where the message went in, and where it came out for broadcast. With the apparatus before one, one could deduce how it operated. But no one could guess how weapons were controlled when he hadn't the least idea of what they did.

On the third night in the asteroid — the third night by ship-time, since there was neither day nor night in the great empty corridors of the fortress — Burke dreamed his dream again. It was perfectly familiar, from the trees with their trailing leaves, to the markings on the larger moon. He felt the anguished anxiety he'd so often known before. He grasped the hand-weapon and knew that he was ready to fight anything imaginable for the person he feared for. He heard small fluting sounds behind him, and then he knew that someone ran breathlessly behind the swaying foliage just ahead. He felt such relief and exultation that his heart seemed about to burst. He gave a great shout and bounded to meet her —

He waked in the small ship in the entrance tunnel. All was silent. All was still. The lights in the control-compartment of the ship were turned to dim. There was no sound anywhere. The opened air-lock doors, both inner and outer, let in a fan-shaped streak of brightness which lay on the floor.

Burke lay quiet, still wrought up by the vivid emotions of the dream.

He heard a stirring in the compartment below, occupied by Sandy and Pam. Someone came very quietly up the ladder-like stairway. Burke blinked in the semi-darkness. He saw that it was Sandy. She crossed the compartment to the air-lock. Very quietly, she closed the outer door and then the inner. She fastened them.

Burke said, sitting up, "Why'd you do that, Sandy?"

She started violently, and turned.

"Pam can't sleep," she said in a low tone. "She says the fortress is creepy. She feels that there's something hiding in it, something deadly and frightening. When you leave the air-lock open, she's afraid. So I closed it."

"Holmes and Keller are out," said Burke. "Keller's trying to trace down power-leads from the instrument-room to whatever power-source warms and lights everything. We can't lock him out."

Sandy obediently opened the air-lock doors again. She turned toward the ladder leading downward.

"Sandy," said Burke unhappily, "I know I'm acting like a fool."

"You're doing all right," said Sandy. She paused at the top of the ladder. "Finding this —" she waved her hand about her — "ought to put your name in the history books. Of course you'll be much disliked by people who intended to invent space travel themselves. But you're doing all right."

"I'm not thinking of that," said Burke. "I'm thinking of you. I was going to ask you to marry me. I didn't. If we live through this, will you?"

Sandy regarded him carefully in the dim light of the ship's interior, most of which came through the air-lock doors.

"There are some conditions," she said evenly. "I won't play second fiddle to an imaginary somebody behind a veil of dreamed-of leaves. I don't want to make conditions, Joe. But I couldn't stand your feeling that maybe in marrying me you'd give up your chance of finding her — whatever or whoever she is."

"But I wouldn't feel that way!" protested Burke.

"I'd believe you did," said Sandy. "And it would amount to the same thing. I think I made a mistake in coming along in the ship, Joe. If I weren't along you might have missed me. You might even —" she grimaced — "you might even have dreamed about me. But here I am. And I can't compete with somebody in a dream. I won't even try. I — I can't imagine marrying anybody else, but if I do get married I want to be the only girl my guy dreams about!"

She turned again to the ladder. Then said abruptly, "You didn't ask why Pam feels creepy, or where. There's a place up on the second gallery where there's a door that's still locked. Pam gets the shivers when she goes by it. I don't. The whole place is creepy, to me."

She went down the ladder. Minutes later Holmes and Keller arrived.

Holmes said curtly, "The machinery in the transmitter-room reached a change-point just now. Those red dots in that plastic plate apparently started the transmitter in the first place. When its calls were answered it changed the broadcast, adding a directional signal. Just before we started out from Earth the red sparks passed another place and changed the broadcast again. Now they've passed a third place. We were there when the machinery shifted all around on a signal from that thing which hovers close to the red sparks and watches them. The transmitter probably blasted out at four or five times its original volume. There must have been a hundred thousand kilowatts in it, at least. It looks serious Whatever those red sparks represent must be close."

Keller nodded in agreement, frowning, then he and Holmes wearily prepared to turn in. But Burke was upset. He knew he wouldn't be able to sleep.

"Pam gets the creeps when she passes a certain locked door up on the second gallery. I never noticed it, but I'm going to get that door open. We got to look into every compartment of this thing! There's bound to be something informative somewhere! Close the air-lock behind me so Pam can sleep."

He went out. Behind him, Holmes looked at Keller.

"Funny!" he said drily. "We're all scared. I feel uneasy all the time, without knowing why. But if he's as scared as I am, why doesn't he worry about going places alone?"

The same question occurred to Burke. The atmosphere of the brightly lighted halls was ominous and secretive. A man alone in a vast empty building would feel queer even in broad daylight with sunshine and other humans to be seen out of any window. But in this monstrous complex of tunnels and rooms carved out of solid stone, with uncountable millions of miles of pure emptiness without, the feeling of loneliness was incredible. He reflected wryly that a dog would be a comforting companion to have on such a journey as his.

He went down the long gallery with doors on either side. Past the room with the piled metal ingots. Past the door through which one saw hundreds of ten-foot metal globes. Up a ramp. Past the rooms where something like bunks must once have stood against the walls. A long way along this corridor. Emptiness, emptiness, emptiness. Innumerable echoings of his footsteps on the stone.

Three times he stopped at doors that had swung shut, but none was fully closed. All yielded readily. Then he came to the door Sandy had spoken about. He worked the handle repeatedly. It was firmly shut. He kicked the door and with a loud click it swung open.

There were lights inside this room, as everywhere else they had explored. But it was nearly impossible to see any distance. This was an extremely long room, and it contained racks of metal which reached from floor to ceiling. Each rack was a series of shallow metal troughs, and in each trough there was a row of crumbly black metal cubes, very systematically arranged. Each side was about three inches square, and they were dull black, not glistening at all. They filled the racks completely. There were narrow aisles between the rows of racks, through which Burke could make his way easily enough, but which a more portly man might have found inconvenient.

He stared at a trough, and was stunned. He picked up one of the cubes, and immediately recognized the object in his hand. It was a dull-black, smudgy cube exactly like the one his uncle had brought back from the Cro-Magnon cave in France. He knew that if he dropped this object — found two hundred seventy million miles from the other one — it would split into thousands of tissue-thin, shiny places.

He did drop it. Deliberately. And it shattered into layers which lay like films of mica on the floor.

For no clearly understandable reason, Burke found that his flesh crawled. He had to force himself to stay in this room with so many thousands of the enigmatic cubes. There had been a cube of this kind on Earth. The one he'd known as a child had belonged to a Cro-Magnon tribesman ten thousand, twenty thousand, how many years ago? And it could only have come from this asteroid. Which meant —

Presently he made his way back to the spaceship. He carried one of the cubes, rather gingerly. He meant to show it to Sandy. But the implications were startling.

Members of the garrison of this fortress, thousands of years gone by, had visited Earth. One of them, doubtless, had carried that other cube. Why? When the garrison abandoned the asteroid they left these cubes behind. They left behind intricate machinery to call them back. They left squat machines and ten-foot globes which must be weapons. They left nothing that would be useful in the place to which they had removed. But they'd left these cubes, hundreds of thousands of them.

The cube, then, could be anything. It could be impersonal, like equipment for the fortress that would be useless elsewhere. The fortress' equipment was designed to deal out death. Were the cubes? No. Burke had owned one without damage. When that cube split into glistening, tissue-thin plates, no one was injured. To be sure, there was his dream. But the cube wasn't a weapon. Whatever else it might be, it was not dangerous.

He went into the spaceship and for no reason whatever firmly locked both air-lock doors. Holmes and Keller were asleep. There was no sound from the lower compartment occupied by Sandy and Pam.

Burke put the black object on the control-desk. The single cube on Earth had been meaningless. The museum which joyfully accepted Cro-Magnon artifacts from his uncle had dismissed it as of no importance. It was fit only to be given to an eleven-year-old boy. But a roomful of such cubes couldn't be without meaning!

He dismissed this newest mystery with an almost violent effort of his will. It was a mystery. Yet there was no intention to have the fortress seem a mystery to whoever answered its call to space. He could guess that the signals were notification of some emergency which needed to be met. The automatic apparatus of the ship-lock was set to aid those who came in response to the call. But everything presupposed that those who came would know why they came.

Burke didn't. The thing must be simple, an explanation not yet thought of. But there was nowhere to start to think about it! His recurrent dream? No. That was as mysterious as the rest.

Burke was very, very lonely and depressed. He could look for no help in solving the mystery. Earth was mow past the point of conjunction with M-387, and moved nearly a million miles a day along its orbit, with nearly half of them away from the fortress. At the most hopeful estimate, it would be three months or later before an emergency space fleet of replicas of his own ship could lift off from Earth for here.

And Burke was reasonably sure that the red sparks would have reached the center of the disk in much less time than that. [If it were in some fashion like a radar, making a map of the surroundings of the asteroid, the observer's place would be in the middle.] In that event, whatever the red sparks represented would reach the fortress before more ships came out from Earth.

He sat with his chin on his chest, wearily debating the impossibility of meeting a situation in which all humanity might well be involved. His achievement of space travel provided no sense of triumph, and the discovery of the abandoned fortress produced no elation. Not when a desperate emergency requiring a nonexistent garrison to report for duty was so probable. Burke sat in the control-chair and could find no encouragement in any of his thoughts. . . .

He heard a trumpet-call and was on his feet, buckling familiar equipment about him. There were other figures all around in this bunk-room, similarly equipping themselves. Some grumbled. There was a rush for the doorway and he found himself one of a line of trotting figures which swung sharply out the door and went swiftly down one of the high-ceilinged corridors. The faces he saw were hard-bitten and resentful. They moved, but out of habit, not choice. There were other lines of men in motion. Some rushed in the same direction. Others ran stolidly into branching corridors and were lost to sight. Up a ramp, with the pounding of innumerable feet filling his ears with echoed sound. Suddenly there were fewer men before him. Some had darted through a doorway to the right. More vanished. He was at the head of his line. He turned into the doorway next beyond, and saw a squat and menacing object there. He swung up its side and seated himself. He dropped a helmet over his head and saw empty space with millions of unwinking stars beyond it. He waited. He was not Burke. He was someone else who happened to be the pointer, the aimer, of the weapon he sat astride. This might be a drill, but it could be action.

A voice spoke inside his helmet. The words were utterly strange, but he understood them. He tested the give of this lever and the response of that. He spoke crisply, militarily, in words that somehow meant this — a word missing — was ready for action at its highest rate of fire.

Again he waited, his eyes examining the emptiness he saw from within his helmet. A star winked. He snatched at a lever and centered it, snapping sharp, bitten-off words. The voice in his helmet said, "Flam!" He jerked the firing-lever and all space was blotted out for seconds by flaming light. Then the light faded and far, far away among the stars something burned horribly, spouting fire. It blew up.

Yet again he waited. He doggedly watched the stars, because the Enemy had some way to prevent detection by regular instruments, and only the barest flicker of one among myriad light-specks could reveal the presence of an Enemy craft.

A long time later the voice in his helmet spoke again, and he relaxed, and lifted the helmet. He nodded to the others of the crew of this weapon. Then a trumpet blew again, and he dismounted leisurely from the saddle of the ungainly thing he'd fired, and he and his companions waited while long lines of men filed stolidly past the doorway; They were on the way back to the bunk-rooms. They did not look well-fed. His turn came. His crew pled out into the corridor, now filled with men moving in a bored but disciplined fashion. He heard somebody say that it was an Enemy scout, trying some new device to get close to the fortress. Eight weapons had fired on it at the same instant, his among them. Whatever the new device was, the Enemy had found it didn't work. But he knew that it needn't have been a real Enemy, but just a drill. Nobody knew when supposed action was real. There was much suspicion that there was no real action. There was always the possibility of real action, though. Of course. The Enemy had been the Enemy for thousands of years. A century or ten or a hundred of quietude would not mean the Enemy had given up. . . .

Then Burke found himself staring at the quietly glowing monitor-lights of his own ship's control-board. He was himself again. He remembered opening his eyes. He'd dozed, and he'd dreamed, and now he was awake. And he knew with absolute certainty that what he'd dreamed came from the black cube he'd brought back from the previously locked-up room. But there was a difference between this dream and the one he'd had for so many years. He could not name the difference, but he knew it. This was not an emotion-packed, illusory experience which would haunt him forever. This was an experience like the most vivid of books. It was something he would remember, but he would need to think about it if he were to remember it fully.

He sat stiffly still, going over and over this new memory, until he heard someone moving about, in the compartment below.

"Sandy?"

"Yes," said Sandy downstairs. "What is it?"

"I opened the door that bothered Pam," said Burke. Suddenly the implications of what had just occurred began to hit him. This was the clue he'd needed. Now he knew — many things. "I found out what the fortress is for. I suspect I know what the signals were intended to do."

Silence for a moment. Then Sandy's voice. "I'm coming right up."

In minutes she ascended the stairs.

"What is it, Joe?"

He waved his hand, with some grimness, at the small black object on the control-desk.

"I found this and some thousands of others behind that creepy door. I suspect that it accounts for the absence of signs and symbols. It contains information. I got it. You get it by dozing near one of these things. I did. I dreamed."

Sandy looked at him anxiously.

"No," he told her. "No twin moons or waving foliage. I dreamed I was a member of the garrison. I went through a training drill. I know how to operate those big machines on the second level of the corridor, now. They're weapons. I know how to use them."

Sandy's uneasiness visibly increased.

"These black cubes are — lesson-givers. They're subliminal instructors. Pam is more sensitive to such stuff than the rest of us. It didn't affect me until I dozed. Then I found myself instructed by going through an experience in the form of a dream. These cubes contain records of experiences. You have those experiences. You dream them. You learn."

Then he said abruptly, "I understand my recurrent dream now, I think. When I was eleven years old I had a cube like this. Don't ask me how it got into a Cro-Magnon cave! But I had it. One day it dropped and split into a million leaves of shiny stuff. One got away under my bed, close up under my pillow. When I slept I dreamed about a place with two moons and strange trees and — all the rest."

Sandy said, groping, "Do you mean it was magnetized in some fashion, and when you slept you were affected by it so you dreamed something — predetermined?"

"Exactly," said Burke grimly. "The predetermined thing in this particular cube is the way to operate those machines Holmes said were weapons." Then he said more grimly; "I think we're going to have to accept the idea that this cube is an instruction device to teach the garrison without their having to learn to read or write or think. They'd have only to dream."

Sandy looked from him to the small black cube.

"Then we can find out —"

"I've found it out," said Burke. "I guessed before, but now I know. There is an Enemy this fortress was built to fight. There is a war that's lasted for thousands of years. The Enemy has spaceships and strange weapons and is absolutely implacable. It has to be found. And the signals from space were calls to the garrison of this fortress to come back and fight it. But there isn't any garrison any more. We answered instead. The Enemy comes from hundreds or thousands of light-years away, and he tries desperately to smash the defenses of this fortress and others, and when he succeeds there will be massacre and atrocity and death to celebrate his victory. He's on the way now. And when he comes —" Burke's voice grew harsh. "When he comes he won't stop with trying to smash this place. The people of Earth are the Enemy's enemies, too. Because the garrison was a garrison of men!"

CHAPTER 8

"I DON'T BELIEVE IT," said Holmes flatly.

Burke shrugged. He found that he was tense all over, so he took some pains to appear wholly calm.

"It isn't reasonable!" insisted Holmes. "It doesn't make sense!"

"The question," observed Burke, "isn't whether it makes sense, but whether it's fact. According to the last word from Earth, they're still insisting that the ship's drive is against all reason. But we're here. And speaking of reason, would the average person look at this place and say blandly, 'Ah, yes! A fortress in space. To be sure!' Would they? Is this place reasonable?"

Holmes grinned.

"I'll go along with you there," he agreed. "It isn't. But you say its garrison was men. Look here! Have you seen a place before where men lived without writings in its public places? They tell me the ancient Egyptians wrote their names on the Sphinx and the Pyramids. Nowadays they're scrawled in phone booths and on benches. It's the instinct of men to autograph their surroundings. But there's not a line of written matter in this place! That's not like men!"

"Again," said Burke, "the question isn't of normality, but of fact."

"Then I'll try it," said Holmes skeptically. "How does it work?"

"I don't know. But put a cube about a yard from your head, and doze off. I think you'll have an odd dream. I did. I think the information you'll get in your dream will check with what you find around you. Some of it you won't have known before, but you'll find it's true."

"This," said Holmes, "I will have to see. Which cube do I try it with, or do I use all of them?"

"There's apparently no way to tell what any of them contains," said Burke. "I went back to the storeroom and brought a dozen of them. Take any one and put the others some distance away — maybe outside the ship. I'm going to talk to Keller. He'll make a lot of use of this discovery."

Holmes picked up a cube.

"Ill try it," he said cheerfully. "I go to sleep, perchance to dream. Right! See you later."

Burke moved toward the ship's air-lock.

"Pam and I have some housekeeping to do," Sandy said.

Burke nodded abstractedly. He left the ship and headed along the mile long corridor with the turn at the end, a second level and another turn, and then the flight of steps to the instrument-room. As he walked, the sound of his footsteps echoed and reechoed.

Behind him, Holmes set a cube in a suitable position and curled up on one of the side-wall bunks in the upper compartment of the space-ship.

"We'll go downstairs," said Sandy.

Pam parted her lips to speak, and did not. They disappeared down the stair to the lower room. Then Sandy came back and picked up the extra cubes.

"Joe said to move them," she explained.

She disappeared again. Holmes settled himself comfortably. He was one of those fortunate people who are able to relax at will. Actually, in his work he normally did his thinking while on his feet, moving about his yacht-building plant or else sailing one of his own boats. He simply was not a sit-down thinker. Sitting, he could doze at almost any time he pleased, and for a yachtsman it was a useful ability. He could go for days on snatched catnaps when necessary. Conversely he could catnap practically at will.

He yawned once or twice and settled down confidently. In five minutes or less . . .

He wriggled down into an opening barely large enough to admit his body. The top clamped and sealed overhead. He fitted his feet into their proper stirrup-like holders and fixed his hands on the controls. There was violent acceleration and he shot away and ahead. Behind him the jagged shape of the fortress loomed. He swung his tiny ship. He drove fiercely for the tiny rings of red glow which centered themselves in the sighting-screen before him. He drove and drove, while the fortress dwindled to a dot and then vanished.

On either side of his ship a ten-foot steel globe clung. He checked them over, tense with the realization that he must very soon be within the practical timing-range of the new Enemy solid missiles. He made minute adjustments in the settings of the globes.

He released them together. They went swinging madly away at the end of a hair-thin wire which would sustain the tons of stress that centrifugal force gave the spheres. They spiraled toward darkness with its background of innumerable stars. The Enemy would be puzzled, this time! They'd developed missile-weapons with computing sights. In their last attack, five hundred years before, the Enemy had been defeated by the self-driving globes that had an utterly incredible acceleration. It was reported from the Cathor sector that in this current attack they had missile-weapons with a muzzle-velocity of hundreds of miles per second, which could actually anticipate a globe with a hundred-sixty-gravity drive. They could fire a solid shot to meet it and knock it down, because of some incredible computer-system which was able to calculate a globe's trajectory and meet it in space. They were smart, the Enemy!

The two globes went spinning toward the Enemy. Linked together, they spun round and round and no conceivable computer could calculate the path of either one so a projectile could hit. They did not travel in a straight line, as a trajectory in space should be. Whirling as they did around a common center of gravity, with the plane of their circling at a sharp angle to their line of fight, it was not possible to range them for gunfire. Their progress was in a series of curves, each at a different distance, which no mere calculator could solve without direction. A radar could not pick up the data a computer would need. One or the other globe might be hit, but it was far from likely.

The pilot of the one-man ship saw the blue-white flame of a hit. He flung his ship about and sped back toward the fortress. The Enemy would beat this trick, in time. Four thousand years before they'd almost won, when they invaded the Old Nation. They were getting bolder now. There was a time when a sound beating sent them back beyond the Coalsack to lick their wounds for two thousand years or better. Lately they came more often. There'd been a raid in force only five hundred years back, and only fifteen before that . . .

Holmes, obviously, had the odd dream Burke had prophesied. But Burke was up in the instrument-room by then. Keller gazed absorbedly at a vision-plate. It showed a section of the exterior surface of the asteroid — harsh, naked rock, with pitiless sunlight showing the grain and structure of the rock-crystals. Where there was shadow, the blackness was absolute. As Burke entered, Keller turned a knob. The image changed to a picture of a compartment inside the fortress. It was a part of the maze of rooms and galleries that none of the newcomers had visited. Panels and bus-bars and things which were plainly switches covered its walls. It was a power-distribution center. Keller turned the knob back, and the view of the outside of the asteroid returned.

Keller turned and blinked at Burke, and then said happily, "Look!"

He went to another vision-screen with an image of another part of the outer surface. He turned that knob, and the image dissolved into another. This was a gigantic room, lighted like more familiar places. In its center there was an enormous, gigantic machine. There were domes of metal, with great rods of silvery stuff reaching across emptiness between them. There were stairs by which one could climb to this part and that. Judging by the steps and the size of the light-tubes, the machine was the size of a four-storey house. And on the floor there were smaller machines, all motionless and all cryptic.

Keller said with conviction, "Power!"

Burke stared. Keller recovered the original view and went to still other plates. In succession, as he turned the knobs, Burke saw compartment after compartment. There was one quite as huge as the one containing the power-generating machine. It contained hemispheres bolted ten feet above the floor on many columns. There was a network of bus-bars, it seemed, overlying everything, and there were smaller devices on the floor below it.

"Gravity!" said Keller with conviction.

"Good enough," said Burke. "We've found something too, which may be useful with those machines. If we can —"

Keller held up his hand and went to one special screen. When he changed the image, the new one was totally unlike any of the others. This was a close-up. It showed a clumsy, strictly improvised and definitely cobbled metal case against a wall. It had been made by inept hands. It was remarkable to see such indifferent workmanship here. But the really remarkable thing was that the face of the box contained an inscription, burned into the metal as if by a torch. The symbols had no meaning to Burke, of course. But this was an inscription in a written language.

Keller rubbed his hands, beaming.

"It could be a message for somebody who'd come later," said Burke. "It's hard to think of it being anything else. But it wasn't placed for us to find. It should have been set up beside the ship-lock we were expected to come in by and did come in by."

"We'll see," said Keller zestfully. "Come on!"

Burke followed him. Keller seemed somehow to know the way. They went all the way back to the ship-lock, passed it, and then Keller dived off to the right, down an unsuspected ramp. There were galleries running in every direction here, crossing each other and opening upon an indefinite number of what must have been storerooms. Presently Keller pointed.

There was the case against the wall. It faced a wide corridor. It did not belong here. It was totally unlike any other artifact they had seen, because it seemed to have been made totally without skill. Yet there was an inscription — and the making of written records had appeared to be a skill the former occupants of the asteroid had not possessed. Keller very zestfully essayed to open it. He failed.

Burke said, "We'll have to use tools to get it open."

"Somebody made it," said Keller, "just before the garrison went away. They made it here!"

"Quite likely," agreed Burke. "We'll get at it presently. Now listen, Keller! I came along because a message might be useful. I think Holmes has found out something, though what it may be I can't guess. Come along with me. There've been developments and I want to hold a council of war. And I think I do mean war!"

He led the way back toward the ship. When they arrived, Holmes was awake and growling because of Burke's absence.

"You win," he told Burke. "I had a dream, and it wasn't a dream. I know something about those metal globes. They've got drives in them, and they can accelerate to a hundred and sixty gees, and I don't think I'll ride one."

Wryly, he told Burke what he'd experienced.

"I'm not too much surprised," said Burke. "I've managed two cube-experiences myself. I figure that these cubes trained men to operate things, without training their brains in anything else. They'd make illiterates into skilled men in a particular line, so anybody could do the work a highly trained man would otherwise be needed for. In one of my two cube-dreams I was a gun-pointer on one of those machines up on the third level. In the second cube-dream I was a rocket-pilot."

"No rockets in my cube," protested Holmes.

"Different period," said Burke. "Maybe, anyhow. In my dream we were using rockets to fight with, and the war was close. The enemy had taken some planets off Kandu — wherever that is! — and the situation was bad. We went out of here in rockets and fought all over the sky. But then there were supplies coming from home, and fresh fighting men turning up." He stopped abruptly. "How'd they come? I don't know. But I know they didn't come in spaceships. They just came, and they were new men and we veterans patronized them. The devil! Holmes, you say the globes have a hundred-sixty-gee drive! Nobody'd use rockets if drives like that were known!"

"To stay in the party," Sandy said suddenly, with something like defiance, "I tried a cube, too. And I was a sort of supply-officer. I had the experience of being responsible for supply and being short of every-thing and improvising this and that and the other to keep things up to fighting standard. It wasn't easy. The men grumbled, and we lacked everything. There was no fighting in my time, and there hadn't been for centuries. But we knew the Enemy hadn't given up and we had to be ready, generation after generation, even when nothing happened. And we knew that any minute the Enemy might throw something unex-pected, some new weapon, at us."

"History-cubes," said Keller interestedly. "Different periods. Right?"

"Dammit, yes!" said Burke. "We've got accounts of past times and finished battles, but we need to know who's coming and what to do about it! Maybe the rocket-dream was earliest in time. But how could a race with nothing better than rockets ever get here? And how could they supply the building of a place like this?"

There was no answer. Facts ought to fit together. When they don't, they are useless.

"We've got snatches of information," said Burke. "But we don't know who built this fort, or why, except that there was a war that lasted thousands of years, with pauses for centuries between battles." He waved a hand irritably. "The Enemy tries to think up new weapons. They do. They try them. So far, they've been countered. But we're not prepared to fight a new weapon. Maybe the fort is set to battle old ones, but we don't know how to use it even for that! We've got to —"

"I think —" began Keller.

"I'd give plenty for a service manual on the probably useless wea-pons we do have," said Burke angrily. "Incidentally, Keller just found what may be an explanation of how and why this place was aban-doned."

Keller said suddenly, "Where would service manuals be?"

He moved, almost running, toward the air-lock. Burke started to swear, and stopped.

"A service-and-repair manual," he snapped, "would be near the equipment it described. How many little shelves with boxes on them have we seen? They're just the right size to hold cubes! And where are they? Next to those fighting machines next to the door of the room where the ten-foot globes are! There's a shelf of them in the instrument-room! Let's find out how to fight with this misbegotten shell of a space-fort! There'll be no help coming to us, but if the Enemy's held off for thousands of years while this civilization fell apart, we might as well try to hold it together for a few minutes or seconds longer! Let's go get some real instruction-cubes!"

Keller was already gone. The others followed. Once they saw Keller in the far, far distance, hastening toward the instrument-room. Behind him, after almost running down the long corridor, Burke swung into the room where hundreds of ten-foot metal globes waited for the fortress to be re-manned and to go into action again. Inside the door he found the remembered shelf, with two small boxes fastened to it. He pulled down one box and opened it. There was a black cube inside it. He thrust it upon Holmes.

"Here!" he said feverishly. "Find out how those globes work! Find out what's in them, how they drive!"

He ran. To the end of the corridor and up the ramp and past the supposed bunk-rooms and mess-halls. Up to the level where the ugly metal machines stood, each in its separate cubicle. There were little shelves inside each door. Each shelf contained a single box. Burke took one, two, and then stopped short.

"They'll be practically alike," he muttered. "No need."

He put one back. And then he felt almost insanely angry. One would need at least to be able to doze, to make use of the detailed, vivid, and utterly convincing material contained in the black cubes. And how could any man doze or sleep for the purpose of learning such desperately needed data? He'd need almost not to want the information to be able to sleep to get it!

Sandy and Pam overtook him as he stood in harried frustration with a black cube in his hands.

"Listen to me, Joe," said Sandy. "We've all taken chances, but if you get recurrent dreams from every cube you doze near —"

"When that happened to me," snapped Burke, "I was eleven years old and had one moment only. And that dream wasn't affected by the others in the cubes that came after it. And anyhow, no matter what happens to Holmes and me, we have to get these things ready for use! I don't know what we'll use them against. I don't know whether they'll be any use at all. But I've got to try to use them, so I've got to try to find out how!"

Sandy opened her mouth to speak again.

"I'm going off to fret myself to sleep," added Burke. "Holmes will be trying it too. And Keller."

"I don't think it's necessary," said Sandy.

"Why?"

"You found a sort of library of cubes. How useful would they be if one had to doze off to read them? How handy would a manual about repairing a weapon be, if somebody had to take a nap to get instructions? It wouldn't make sense!"

"Go on!" said Burke impatiently.

"Why not look in the library?" asked Sandy. "As a quartermaster officer, I think I knew that there was a reading-device for the cubes, like a projector for microfilm. It might have been taken away, but also —"

"Come along!" snapped Burke. "If that's so, it's everything! And it ought to be so!"

They hastened to the vast, low-ceilinged room which was filled with racks of black cubes. They were stacked in their places. At the far corner they found a desk and a cabinet. In the cabinet they found two objects like metal skull-caps, with clamps atop them. A cube would fit between the clamps. Burke feverishly sat a cube in position and put the skull-cap on his head. His expression was strange. After an instant he took it off and reversed the cube. He put it on. His face cleared. He lifted it off.

"I had it on backwards the first time," he said curtly. "This is better than dreaming the stuff. This lets you examine things in detail. You know you're receiving something. You don't think you're actually experiencing. We'll get this other reading-machine to Keller, so he can understand the equipment in the instrument-room. Holmes will have to wait."

Sandy said, "I can use him. Doesn't it occur to you, Joe, that we've only partly explored the top half of the fortress? We've only looked at what's between us and the instrument-room. There are all the stores — there were stores! And the generators down below. I can lead the way there now!"

"What do you know about the weapons?" demanded Burke.

"Nothing," said Sandy. "But I know something about the morale of the garrison. When grumbling began, discipline tightened up. And that worked for the men, but the women —"

"Women!" said Pam incredulously.

"They were an experiment," Sandy told her, "to see if they would content men on duty in an outpost. It'd been going on for only a few hundred years. It didn't seem to work too well. They wanted supplies that weren't exactly military, and at the time the cube I used was made, there was trouble getting even military things!"

Burke said impatiently, "I'll get one of these things to Keller. That's the most important thing. Tell Holmes not to try to sleep. Take him down to look over the supplies, if there are any. I'd guess that the garrison took most of them along. I doubt there's much left that we could use."

He made his way out of the cube-library and vanished.

Pam said uncomfortably, "Joe dreamed about a woman and is no good to you, in consequence. If there were women in this garrison, using the cubes might make anybody —"

Sandy tensed her lips.

"I don't think Joe is thinking about his old dream. Something deadly's on the way here. His mind's on that. I suspect all three of the men are concentrating on it. They're in no mood for romance."

"Don't you think I've noticed?" Pam said gloomily. "But I'm coming with you when you show him the storerooms!"

The "him" was obviously Holmes, whose attention had been so much taken up by the problems the fortress presented that Pam felt pushed much farther on the side lines than she liked. It was one thing to be present to watch and help and cheer on a man who planned to do something remarkable. But it was less satisfying when he became so absorbed that he didn't notice being watched, and couldn't be helped, and didn't need to be cheered on. Pam was disgruntled.

Then, for a considerable number of hours, absurdly trivial activities seemed to occupy all the people in the asteroid. Burke and Keller sat in the thirty by thirty-foot instrument-room, each wearing a small metal half-cap with a black cube held atop it between a pair of clamps. Their expressions were absorbed and intent, while they seemed attired for a children's halloween party. Now and again one of them exchanged one cube for another. About them there was a multiplicity of television screens, each screen presenting a picture of infinitely perfect quality. Every square foot of the outside of the asteroid could be seen on one or another of the screens. Then, besides, there were banks of screens which showed every square degree of the sky, with every star of every magnitude represented so that one could use a magnifying glass upon the screen to discover finer detail.

Once, during the hours when Burke and Keller were sitting quite still, Keller reached over and threw a switch. Nothing happened. Everything went on exactly as it had done before. He shook his head. And much later he went to one of the star-image screens. He moved an inconspicuous knob in a special fashion, and the star-image expanded and expanded until what had been a second of arc or less filled all the screen's surface. The effect of an incredibly powerful telescope was obtained by the movement of one control. Keller restored the knob to its original place and the image returned to its former scale. These were the only actions which took place in the instrument-room.

In the lower part of the asteroid, not much more occurred. The entrance to the power and storage areas was not hidden. It simply had not been entered. Sandy and Holmes and Pam went gingerly down a corridor with doors on either side, and then down a ramp, and then into huge caverns filled with monstrous metal things. There was no sign of any motion anywhere, but gigantic power-leads led from the machines to massive switchboards, whose switches were thrown by relays operated from somewhere else.

Then there were other caverns which must have contained many varieties of stores. There were great cases, broken open and emptied. There were bins with only dust at their bottoms. There were shelves containing things which might have been textiles, but which crumbled at a touch. Some thousands of years in an absolute vacuum would have evaporated any substance giving any degree of flexibility. These objects were useless. There was a great room with a singular hundred-foot-high machine in it, but there was no vibration or sound to indicate that it was in operation. This, Sandy said decisively, was the artificial-gravity generator. She did not know how it worked. It would have been indiscreet to experiment.

She led the way through relatively small corridors to areas in which there were very many small compartments. These had been for food-stuffs. But they were empty. They had been emptied when the asteroid was abandoned.

Then they came to the crudely fashioned case with the cryptic symbols on its front.

"This is the thing Joe mentioned," said Sandy. "They had writing. They'd have to, to be civilized. But this is the only writing we've seen. Why'd they write it?"

"To tell somebody something they'd miss, otherwise," Pam said.

"Who'd come down here? Why not put it at the ship-lock where people could be expected to come?"

Holmes grunted. "Asking questions like that gets nowhere. It's like asking how the garrison was supplied. There's no answer. Or how it left."

Sandy said in a surprised voice, as if saying something she hadn't realized she knew. "There were service ships. They serviced the television eyes on the outside, and they drilled at launching missiles, and so on. They were modified fighting ships, made over after ships didn't fight any more."

She hesitated, then went on.

"It's odd that I didn't think of telling Joe this! Some of the food supply came from Earth at the time my cube was made. As a quarter-master officer, I was authorized to allow hunting on Earth in case of need. So the service-ships went to Earth and came back with mammoths tied to the outside of their hulls. They had to be re-hydrated, though. Frozen though they were, they dried out in the long trip through vacuum from Earth."

Then she shivered a little.

Pam looked at her strangely. Holmes raised his eyebrows. He'd had one experience of training-cubes. Sandy'd had quite another. Holmes felt that instinctive slight resentment a man feels when he lacks a position of authority in the presence of a woman.

"In my time — in the cube's time — there was even a hunting camp on Earth. Otherwise there simply wouldn't be enough to eat! Women were clamoring to be sent to Earth to help with the food supply. To be sent to hunt for food was a reward for exemplary service."

"Which is interesting," observed Holmes, "but irrelevant. How was the asteroid normally supplied? How did the garrison leave? Where did it come from? Where did it go? Maybe the answer's in this box. If it is," he added, "it'll be in the same language as the inscription, and we can't read it."

Archaeologists on Earth would have been enraptured by any part of the fortress, but anything which promised to explain as much as Holmes had guessed the case could, would be a treasure past any price.

But the five people in the asteroid had much more immediate and much more urgent problems to think of. They went on a little farther and came to a storeroom which had been filled with something, but now held only the remains of packing-cases. They looked ready to crumble if touched.

"There used to be weapons stored here," Sandy said. "Hand-weapons. Not for the defense of the fortress, but for the — discipline police. For the men who kept the others obedient to orders."

"I'd be glad to have one operating pea-shooter," said Holmes.

Pam wrinkled her nose suddenly. She'd noticed something.

"I think —" she began, "I think —"

Holmes kicked at a shape which once was probably a case of wood or something similar. It collapsed into impalpable dust. It had dried out to absolute desiccation. It was stripped of every molecule which could be extracted by a total vacuum in thousands of years. It was brittle past imagining.

The collapse did not end with the object kicked. It spread. One case bulged as the support of another failed. The bulged case disintegrated. Its particles pressed on another. The dissolution spread fanwise until nothing remained but a carpeting of infinitely fine brown stuff. In one place, however, solid objects remained under the covering.

Holmes waded through the powder to the solid things. He brought them up. A case of hand-weapons had collapsed, but the weapons themselves kept their shape. They had transparent plastic barrels with curiously formed metal parts inside them.

"These might be looked into," said Holmes.

He stuffed his pockets. The hand-weapons had barrels and hand-grips and triggers. They were made to shoot, somehow.

"I think —" began Pam again.

"Don't," growled Holmes. "Maybe Sandy remembers when this place was different, but I've had enough of it as it is. Let's go back to the ship and some fresh air."

"But that's what —"

Holmes turned away. Like the rest, he'd accepted great age, mentally, as a part of the nature of the fortress. But the collapse of emptied shipping-cases because they were touched was a shock. Where such decay existed, one could not hope to find anything useful for a modern emergency. He vanished.

Pam was indignant. She turned to Sandy.

"I wanted to say that I smelled fresh air," she protested. "And he acts like that!"

Sandy was not listening. She frowned.

"He could lose his way down here," she said shortly. "We'd better keep him in sight. I remember the way from my dream,"

They followed Holmes, who did make his way back to the upper levels and ultimately to the ship without guidance. But Pam was intensely indignant.

"We could have gotten lost down there!" she said angrily when they were back in familiar territory. "And he wouldn't have cared! And I did smell fresh air! Not very fresh, but fresher than the aged and dried-out stuff we're breathing now!"

"You couldn't," said Sandy practically. "There simply couldn't be any, except in the ship where the hydroponic wall-gardens keep it fresh."

"But I did!" insisted Pam.

Sandy shrugged. They went into the ship, which Holmes had already reached and where he sat gloomily beside a black cube. He would have to sleep to get anything from it. There were only two of the freakish-seeming metal caps which made the cubes intelligible to a man awake, and Burke and Keller were using them. Holmes felt offended.

Sandy looked at a clock and began to prepare a meal. Pam, brooding, helped her.

Burke and Keller came back to the ship together. Keller looked pale. Burke seemed utterly grim.

"There's some stuff to be coded and sent back to Earth," he told Sandy. "Keller's got it written out. We know how to work the instruments up above, now. My brain's reeling a little, but I think I'll stay sane. Keller takes it in stride. And we know the trick the Enemy has."

Sandy put out plates for five.

"What is it?"

"Gravity," said Burke, evenly. "Artificial gravity. We don't know how to make it, but the people who built this fortress did, and the Enemy does. So they've made artificial-gravity fields to give their ships the seeming mass of suns, and they've set them in close omits around each other. They'll come spinning into this solar system. What will happen when objects with the mass of suns — artificial or otherwise — come riding through between our sun and its planets? There'll be tidal stresses to crack the planets and let out their internal fires. There'll be no stability left in the sun. Maybe it'll be a low-grade nova when they've gone, surrounded by trash that once was worlds. Anyhow there'll be no humans left! And then the Enemy will go driving on toward the other solar systems that the builders of this fortress own. They can't conquer anything with a weapon like that, but they can surely destroy!"

Keller nodded distressedly. He gave Pam a number of sheets of paper, filled with his neat handwriting.

He said sorrowfully, "For Earth. In code."

Sandy served the meal she had prepared.

"It's a matter of days," said Burke curtly. "Not weeks. Just days."

He picked up a fork and began his meal.

"So," he said after a moment, with a sort of unnatural calm, "we've got to get the thing licked fast. Up in the instrument-room there are some theory-cubes — lectures on theories with which the operators of the room were probably required to be familiar. They were intended to figure out what the Enemy might come up with, so it could at least he reported before the fortress was destroyed. The trick of sun-gravity fields was suggested as possible, but it seemed preposterously difficult. Apparently, it was. It took the Enemy some thousands of years to get it. But they've got it, all right!"

"How do you know?" demanded Holmes.

"The disk with the red sparks in it," said Burke, "is a detector of gravity-fields. It sees by gravity, which is not radiation. Keller's sending instructions back to Earth telling how to make such detectors."

He busied himself with his food once more. After a moment he spoke again,

"We're going to try to get some help," he observed. "At least we'll try to find out if there's any help to be had. I think there's a chance. There was a civilization which built this fortress. Something happened to it. Perhaps it simply collapsed, like Rome and Greece and Egypt and Babylonia back on Earth. But on Earth when an old civilization died a new, young one rose in its place. If the one that built this fort collapsed, maybe a new one has risen in its stead. If so, it will need to defend itself against the Enemy just like the old culture did. It might prefer to do its fighting here, instead of in its own land. I think we may be able to contact it."

"How'll you look for them?"

Burke shrugged.

"I've some faint hope of a few directions in that sealed-up metal case with the inscription on it. I'm going to take some tools and break into it. It's a gamble, but there's nothing to lose."

He ate briskly, with a good appetite. Sandy was very silent.

Pam said abruptly, "We saw that case. And I smelled fresh air there. Not pure air like here in the ship, but not dead air like the air everywhere else."

"Near a power generator, Pam, there'd be some ozone," Holmes said patiently. "It makes a lot of difference."

"It wasn't ozone," said Pam firmly. "It was fresh air. Not canned air. Fresh!"

Holmes looked at Burke.

"Did you or Keller find out how the air's refreshed here? Did anybody throw a switch for air apparatus?"

Keller said mildly, "Apparatus, no. Air exchange, yes. I threw switches also for communication with base. Also emergency communication. Also dire emergency. Nothing happened."

"You see, Pam?" said Holmes. "It was ozone that made the air smell fresh."

Sandy was wholly silent until the meal was over. Then Holmes went moodily off with Keller, to use the cube-reading devices in the instrument-room and try to find, against all apparent probability, some clue or some communication which would enable something useful to be done. Holmes was trying hard to believe that things were not as bad as Burke announced, and not nearly so desperate that they had to try to find the descendants of a long-vanished civilization for a chance to offer resistance to the Enemy.

Keller said confidentially, just before they reached the instrument-room, "Burke's an optimist."

And at that moment, back in the little plastic spaceship, Burke was saying to Sandy, "You can come along if you like. There are a couple of things to be looked into. And if you want to come, Pam —"

But Pam touched the papers Keller had given her and said reservedly, "I'll code and send this stuff. Go ahead, Sandy."

Sandy rose. She followed Burke out of the ship. She was acutely aware that this was the first time since they had entered the ship that she and Burke could speak to each other when nobody could overhear. They'd spoken twice when the others were presumably asleep. But this was the first time they'd been alone.

When they'd passed through the door with the rounded corners, they were completely isolated. Overhead, brilliant light-tubes reached a full mile down the gallery in one direction, and half as far in the other. The vast corridor contained nothing to make a sound but themselves.

"It's this way," said Burke.

Sandy knew the way as well as he did, or better, but she accepted his direction. Their footsteps echoed and reechoed, so that they were accompanied by countless reflections of heel-clicks along with the normal rustling and whispering sounds of walking.

They went a full quarter-mile from the ship-lock door, and came to a very large arched opening which gave entrance to a corridor slanting downward.

"Supplies came up this ramp," said Sandy.

It was a statement which should have been startling, but Burke nodded.

Sandy went on, carefully, "That cube about a supply-officer's duties was pretty explicit. Things were getting difficult."

Burke did not seem to hear. They went on and on. They came to the place where Keller had turned aside. Burke silently indicated the turning. They moved along this other gallery.

"Joe," said Sandy pleadingly. "Is it really so bad?"

"Strictly speaking, I don't see a chance. But that's just the way it looks now. There must be something that can be done. The trick is to find it. Meantime, why panic?"

"You — act queer," protested Sandy.

"I feel queer," he said. "I know various ways to approach problems. None of them apply to this one. You see, it isn't really our problem. We're innocent bystanders, without information about the situation that apparently will kill us and everybody back on Earth. If we knew more about the situation, we might find some part of it that could be tackled, changed. There may be something in this case — perhaps a message left by the garrison for the people who sent them here. I can't see why it'd be placed here, though."

He slowed, looking down one cross-gallery after another.

"Here it is."

They'd come to the clumsily-made case with the inscription on it. It was placed against the wall of a corridor, facing the length of another gallery which came from the side at this point. A little distance down the other passage, the line of doors was broken by an archway which gave upon a hewed-out compartment. The opening was wide enough to show a fragment of a metal floor. There was no sign of any contents. Other compartments nearby were empty. The placing of the inscribed box was inexplicable. But the inscription was sharply clear.

"Maybe," suggested Sandy forlornly, "it says something like 'Explosives! Danger!'"

"Not likely," said Burke.

He'd examined the box before. He'd brought along a tool suited to the job of opening it. He set to work, then stopped.

"Sandy," he said abruptly, "I think the gravity-generator's a couple of corridors in that direction. Will you look and see if there are any tools there that might be better than this? Just look for a place where tools might be stored. If you find something, call me."

She went obediently down the lighted, excavated corridor, She reached the vast cavern. Here there were myriad tube-lights glowing in the ceiling — and the gravity machine. It was gigantic. It was six storeys high and completely mysterious.

She looked with careful intentness for a place where tools might have been kept by the machine's attendants.

She saw movement out of the corner of her eye, but when she turned there was nothing. There could be no movement in the fortress unless by machinery or one of the five humans who'd come so recently. The asteroid had been airless for ten thousand years. It was unthinkable that anything alive, even a microbe, could have survived. So Sandy did not think of a living thing as having made the movement. But movement there had been.

She stared. There were totally motionless machines all about. None of them showed any sign of stirring. Sandy swallowed the ache in her throat and it returned instantly. She moved, to look where the movement had been. She glanced at each machine in turn. One might have made some automatic adjustment. She'd tell Burke.

She passed a fifteen-foot-high assembly of insulators and bright metal, connected overhead to other cryptic things by heavy silvery bars. She passed a cylinder with dials in its sides.

She saw movement again. In a different place. She spun around to look.

Something half the height of a man, with bird-legs and feet and swollen plumage and a head with an oversized beak which was pure caricature — something alive and frightened fled from her. It waddled in ridiculous, panicky haste. It flapped useless stumps of wings. It fled in terrified silence. It vanished.

The first thing that occurred to Sandy was that Burke wouldn't believe her if she told him.

CHAPTER 9

BURKE FOUND HER, rooted to the spot. He had a small metal box in his hand. He didn't notice her pallor nor that she trembled.

"I may have something," he said with careful calm. "The case had this in it. There's a black cube in the box. The case seems to have been made to hold and call attention to this cube. I'll take it up to the instrument-room and use a reader on it."

He led the way. Sandy followed, her throat dry. She knew, of course, that he was under almost intolerable emotional strain. He'd brought her along to be with her for a few moments, but he was so tense that he could think of nothing personal to say. Now it was not possible for him to talk of anything at all.

Yet Sandy realized that even under the stress that pressed upon him, he'd asked her to go look for tools in the gravity-machine room because she'd spoken of possible danger in the opening of the case. He'd gotten her away while he opened it.

When they reached the ship-lock he said briefly, "I want to hurry, Sandy. Wait for me in the ship?"

She nodded, and went to the small spacecraft which had brought them all from Earth.

When she saw Pam, inside, she said shakily, "Is — anybody else here?"

"No," said Pam. "Why?"

Sandy sat down and shivered.

"I think," she said through chattering teeth, "I think I'm going to have hysterics. L-listen, Pam! I — I saw something alive! It was like a bird this high and big as a — There aren't any birds like that! There can't be anything alive here but us! But I saw it! And it saw me and ran away!"

Pam stared and asked questions, at first soothing ones. But presently she was saying indignantly, "I do believe it! That's near the place where I smelled fresh air!"

Of course, fresh air in the asteroid, two hundred and seventy million miles from Earth, was as impossible as what Sandy had seen.

Holmes came in presently, depressed and tired. He'd been filling his mind with the contents of black cubes. He knew how cooking was done in the kitchens of the fortress, some eons since. He knew how to prepare for inspection of the asteroid by a high-ranking officer. He was fully conversant with the bugle-calls once used in the fortress in the place of a public-address loud-speaker system. But he'd found no hint of how the fortress received its supplies, nor how the air was freshened, nor how reinforcements of men used to reach the asteroid. He was discouraged and vexed and weary.

"Sandy," said Pam challengingly, "saw a live bird, bigger than a goose, in the gravity-machine room."

Holmes shrugged.

"Keller's fidgeting," he observed, "because he thinks he's seen movements in the vision-plates that show different inside views of this thing. But he isn't sure that he's seen anything move. Maybe we're all going out of our minds."

"Then Joe's closest," said Pam darkly. "He worries about Sandy!"

"And very reasonably," said Holmes tiredly. "Pam, this business of figuring that there's something deadly on the way and nothing to do about it — it's got me down!"

He slumped in a chair. Pam frowned at him. Sandy sat perfectly still, her hands clenched.

Burke came back twenty minutes later. His expression was studiedly calm.

"I've found out where the garrison went," he said matter-of-factly. "I'm afraid we can't get any help from them. Or anybody else."

Sandy looked at him mutely, He was completely self-controlled, and he did not look like a man resolutely refusing to despair, but Sandy knew him. To her it seemed that his eyes had sunk a little in his head.

"Apparently there's nobody left on the world the garrison came from," said Burke in the tone of someone saying perfectly commonplace things, "so they didn't go back there and there's no use in our trying to make a contact with that world. This was an outpost fortress, you know. It was reached from somewhere far away, and carved out and armed to fight an enemy that didn't attack it for itself, but to get at the world or worlds that made it."

He continued with immoderate calm, "I believe the home world of that civilization has two moons in its sky and something off at the horizon that looks like a hill, but isn't."

"But —"

"The garrison left," explained Burke, "because it was abandoned. It was left behind to stand off the Enemy, and the civilization it belonged to moved away. It was left without supplies, without equipment, without hope. It was left behind even without training to face abandonment, because its members had been trained by black cubes and only knew how to do their own highly special jobs by rote. They were just ordinary soldiers, like the Roman detachments left behind when the legions marched south from Hadrian's Wall and sailed for Gaul. So when there was nothing left for them to do but leave their post or starve — because they couldn't follow the civilization that had abandoned them — they left. The cube in the box was a message they set up for their former rulers and fellow-citizens if they ever returned. It's not a pretty message!"

Sandy swallowed.

"Where'd they go? What happened to them?"

"They went to Earth," said Burke tonelessly. "By twos and fives and dozens, in the service ships that came out with meat, and took back passengers. The service ships had been assigned to bring out what meat the hunting-parties could kill. They took back men who were fighters and ready to face mammoths or sabre tooth tigers or anything else. Just the same, they left a transmitter to call them back if the Enemy over came again. But it didn't come in their lifetimes, and their descendants forgot. But the transmitter remembered. It called to them. And — we were the ones to answer!"

Sandy hesitated a moment.

"But if the garrison went to Earth," she said dubiously, "what became of them? There aren't any traces —"

"We're traces," said Burke. "They were our ancestors of ten or twenty thousand years ago. They couldn't build a civilization. They were fighting men! Could the Romans left behind at Hadrian's Wall keep up the culture of Rome? Of course not! The garrison went to Earth and turned savage, and their children's children's children built up a new civilization. And for here and for now, we're it. We've got to face the Enemy and drive him back."

He stopped, and said in a tone that was almost completely steady and held no hint of despair, "It's going to be quite a job. But it's an emergency. We've got to manage it somehow."

There was also an emergency on Earth, not simplified as in space by having somebody like Burke accept the burden of meeting it. The emergency stemmed from the fact that despite the best efforts of the air arm of the United States, Burke and the others had gotten out to space. They'd reached the asteroid M-387. Naturally. The United States thereupon took credit for this most creditable achievement. Inevitably. And it was instantly and frantically denounced for suspected space-imperialism, space-monopoly, and intended space-exploitation.

But when Keller's painstaking instructions for the building of gravity-field detectors reached Earth, these suspicions seemed less plausible. The United States passed on the instructions. The basic principle was so new that nobody could claim it, but it was so simple that many men felt a wholesome shame that they had not thought of it before. Nobody could question a natural law which was so obvious once it was stated. And the building of the device required next to no time at all.

Within days then, where the asteroid had a single ten-foot instrument, the United States had a ten-foot, a thirty-foot and a sixty-foot gravity-field detector available to qualified researchers. The new instruments gave data such as no astronomer had ever hoped for before. The thirty-foot disk, tuned for short range, pictured every gravitational field in the solar system. A previously unguessed-at Saturnian moon, hidden in the outer ring, turned up. All the asteroids could be located at one instant. The mystery of the inadequate mass of Pluto was solved within hours of turning on the thirty-foot device.

When the sixty-foot instrument went on, scaled to take in half a hundred light-years of space, the solar system was a dot on it. But four dark stars, one with planets, and twenty-odd planetary systems were mapped within a day. On that same day, though, a query went back to Keller. What, said the query, was the meaning of certain crawling, bright-red specks in mathematically exact relationship to each other, which were visibly in motion and much closer to Earth than Alpha Centaurus? Alpha Centaurus had always been considered the closest of all stars to Earth. Under magnification the bright-red sparks wove and interwove their paths as if about a common center of gravity. If such a thing were not impossible, it would be guessed that they were suns so close together as to revolve about one another within hours. Even more preposterously, they moved through space at a rate which was a multiple of the speed of light. Thirty light-speeds, of course, could not be. And the direction of their motion seemed to be directly toward the glowings which represented the solar system containing Earth. All this was plainly absurd. But what was the cause of this erroneous report from the new device?

Keller wrote out very neatly, "The instrument here shows the same phenomenon. Its appearance much farther away triggered the transmitter here to send the first signals to Earth. Data suggests red dots represent artificial gravity-fields Wrong enough to warp space and produce new spatial constants including higher speed for light, hence possible higher speed for spacecraft carrying artificial gravity generators. Request evaluation this possibility."

Pam coded it and sent it to Earth. And presently, on Earth, astronomers looked at each other helplessly. Because Keller had stated the only possible explanation. Objects like real suns, if so close together, would tear each other to bits and fuse in flaming novas. Moreover, the pattern of motion of the red-spark-producing objects could not have come into being of itself. It was artificial. There was a group of Things in motion toward Earth's solar system. They would arrive within so many days. They were millions of miles apart, but their gravity-fields were so strong that they orbited each other within hours. If they had gravity-fields, they had mass, which could be as artificial as their gravity. And, whirling about each other in the maddest of dances, ten suns passing through the human solar system could leave nothing but debris behind them.

Oddly enough, the ships that made those gravity-fields might be so small as to be beyond the power of a telescope to detect at a few thousand miles. The destruction of all the solar planets and the sun itself might be accomplished by motes. They would not need to use power for destruction. Gravitation is not expended any more than magnetism, when something is attracted by it. The artificial gravity-fields would only need to be built up. They had been. Once created, they could exist forever without need for added power, just as the san and planets do not expend power for their mutual attraction, and as the Earth parts with no energy to keep its moon a captive.

The newspapers did not publish this news. But, very quietly, every civilized government on Earth got instructions for the making of a gravity-field detector. Most had them built. And then for the first time in human history there was an actual and desperately honest attempt to pool all human knowledge and all human resources for a common human end. For once, no eminent figure assumed the undignified pose involved in standing on one's dignity. For once, the public remained unworried and undisturbed while the heads of states aged visibly.

Naturally some of the people in the secret frantically demanded that the five in the fortress solve the problem all the science of Earth could not even attack. Incredible lists of required information items went out to Burke and Keller and Holmes. Keller read the lists calmly and tried to answer the questions that seemed to make sense. Holmes doggedly spent all his time experiencing cubes in the hope that by sheer accident he might come upon something useful. Pam, scowling, coded and decoded without pause. And Sandy looked anxiously at Burke.

"I'm going to ask you to do something for me," she said. "When we went down to the Lower Levels, I thought I saw something moving. Something alive."

"Nerves," said Burke. "There couldn't be anything alive in this place. Not after so many years without air."

"I know," acknowledged Sandy. "I know it's ridiculous. But Pam's felt creepy, too, as if there were something deadly somewhere in the rooms we've never been in."

Burke moved his head impatiently. "Well?"

"Holmes found some hand-weapons," said Sandy. "They don't work, of course. Will you fix one for Pam and one for me so that they do?" She paused and added, "Of course it doesn't matter whether we're frightened or not, considering. It doesn't even matter whether there is something alive. It doesn't matter if we're killed. But it would be pleasant not to feel defenseless,"

Burke shrugged. "I'll fix them."

She put three of the transparent-barreled weapons before him and said, "I'm going up to the instrument-room and help Pam with her coding."

She went out. Burke took the three hand-weapons and looked at them without interest. But in a technician of any sort there is always some response to a technical problem. A trivial thing like a hand-weapon out of order could hold Burke's attention simply because it did not refer to the coming disaster.

He loosened the hand-grip plates and looked at the completely simple devices inside the weapons. There was a tiny battery, of course. In thousands of years its electrolyte had evaporated. Burke replaced it from the water stores of the ship. He did the same to the other two weapons. Then, curious, he stepped out of the ship's air-lock and aimed at the ship-lock wall. He pressed the trigger. There was a snapping sound and a fragment of rock fell. He tried the others. They fired something, It was not a bullet. The barrels of the weapons, on inspection, were not hollow. They were solid. The weapons fired a thrust, a push, an immaterial blow which was concentrated on a tiny spot. They punched, with nothing solid to do the punching.

"Probably punch a hale right through a man," said Burke, reflectively.

He took the three weapons and went toward the instrument-room. On the way, his mind went automatically back to the coming destruction. It was completely arbitrary. The Enemy had no reason to destroy the human race in this solar system. Men, here, had lost all recollection of their origin and assuredly all memory of enmities known before memory began. If any tradition remained of the fortress, even, it would be hidden in tales of a Golden Age before Pandora was, or of an Age of Innocence when all things came without effort. Those stories wore changed out of all semblance to their foundations, of course, as ever-more-ignorant and ever-more-unsophisticated generations retold them. Perhaps the Golden Age was a garbled memory of a time when machines performed tasks for men — before the machines wore out and could not be replaced without other machines to make them. Perhaps the slow development of tools, with which men did things that machines formerly did for them, blurred the accounts of times when men did not need to use tools. Even the everywhere-present traditions of a long, long journey in a boat — the flood legends — might be the last trace of grand-sires' yarns about a journey to Earth. It would have been modified by successive generations who could not imagine a journey through emptiness, and therefore devised a flood as a more scientific and reasonable explanation for myths plainly overlaid with fantasy and superstition.

Burke went into the instrument room as Sandy was asking, "But how did they? We haven't found any ship-lock except the one we came in by! And if a ship can't travel faster than light without wrapping artificial mass about itself . . ."

Holmes had taken off his helmet. He said doggedly, "There's nothing about ships in the cubes. Anyhow, the nearest other sun is four light-years away. Nobody'd try to carry all the food a whole colony would need from as far away as that! If they'd used ships for supply, there'd have been hydroponic gardens all over the place to ease the load the ships had to carry! There was some other way to get stuff here!"

"Whatever it was, it didn't bring meat from Earth. That was hauled out, fastened to the outside of service-boats."

"Another thing," Holmes said. "There were thousands of people in the garrison, here. How did the air get renewed? Nobody's found any mention of air-purifying apparatus in the cubes. There's been no sign of any! An emergency air-supply, yes. It was let loose when we came into the ship-lock. But there's no regular provision for purifying the air and putting oxygen into it and breaking down the CO2!"

"Won't anyone believe I smelled fresh air yesterday?" Pam asked plaintively.

No one commented. It could not be believed. Burke handed Sandy one of the weapons. He gave Pam a second.

"They work very much like the ship-drive, which was developed from them. A battery in the handle energizes them so they use the heat they contain to make a lethal punch without a kick-back. They'll get pretty cold after a dozen or so shots."

He sat down and Holmes went on almost angrily, "The garrison had to get food here. It didn't come in ships. They had to purify the air. They've nothing to do it with! How did they manage?"

Keller smiled faintly. He pointed to a control on the wall.

"If that worked, we could ask. It is supposed to be communication with base. It is turned on. Nothing happens."

"Do you know what I'm thinking?" demanded Holmes. "I'm thinking of a matter-transmitter! It's been pointed out before that we'll never reach the stars in spaceships limited to one light-speed. What good would be voyages that lasted ten, twenty, or fifty years each way? But if there could be matter-transmitters —"

Keller said gently, "Transmitters, no. Transposers, yes."

It was a familiar enough distinction. To break down an object into electric charges and reconstitute it at some distant place would be a self-defeating operation. It could have no actual value. To transmit a hundred and fifty pounds of electric energy — the weight of a man converted into current — would require the mightiest of bus-bars for a conductor, and months of time if it was not to burn out from overload. The actual transmission of mass as electric energy would be absurd. But if an object could simply be transposed from one place to another; if it could be translated from place to place; if it could undergo substitution of surroundings . . . That would be a different matter! Transposition would be instantaneous. Translation would require no time. Substitution of position — a man who was here this instant would be there the next — would have no temporal aspect. Such a development would make anything possible. A ship might undertake a voyage to last a century. If a matter-transposer were a part of it, it could be supplied with fuel and air and foodstuffs on its voyage. Its crew could be relieved and exchanged whenever it was desired. And when it made a planet-fall a hundred years and more from home, why, home would still be just around the transposer. With matter-transposition an interstellar civilization could arise and thrive, even though limited to the speed of light for its ships. But a culture spread over hundreds of light-years would be unthinkable without something permitting instant communication between its parts.

"All right!" said Holmes doggedly. "Call them transposers! This fortress had to be supplied. We've found no sign that ships were used to supply it. It needed to have its air renewed and refreshed. We've found no sign of anything but emergency stores of air in case some unknown air-supply system failed. What's the matter with looking for a matter-transposer?"

Burke said, "In a way, a telephone system transposes sound-waves from one place to another. Sound-waves aren't carried along wires. They're here, and then suddenly they're there. But there has to be a sending and receiving station at each end. When the fortress here was 'cut off' from home it could be that its supply-system broke down."

"Its air-system didn't," said Holmes. "It hadn't used up its emergency air-supply. We're breathing it!"

"Anyhow we could try to find even a broken-down transposer," said Sandy.

"You try," said Burke. "Keller's been looking for something for me in the cubes. I'll stay here and help him look."

Sandy examined the weapon he'd given her.

"Pam says she's smelled fresh air, down below where there can't be any. Mr. Keller thought he saw movements in the inside vision-plates, where there can't be any. I still believe I saw something alive in the gravity-machine room, where such a thing is impossible. We're going to look, Pam and I."

Holmes lumbered to his feet.

"I'll come, too. And I'll guarantee to defend you against anything that has survived the ten thousand years or so that this place was without air. My head's tired, after all those cubes."

He led the way. Burke watched as the two girls followed him and closed the door behind them.

"What have you found, Keller?"

"A cube about globes," said Keller. "Very interesting."

"Nothing on communication with base?"

Keller shook his head.

Burke said evenly, "I figured out three chances for us — all slim ones. The first was to find the garrison when the radio summons didn't and get it or its descendants to help. I found the garrison — on Earth. No help there. The second chance was finding the civilization that had built this fortress. It looks like it's collapsed. There's been time for a new civilization to get started, but it's run away. The third chance is the slimmest of all. It's hooking together something to fight with."

Keller reached out over the array of cubes that had been experienced by Holmes and himself while using the helmets from the cube-library. One cube had been set aside. Keller put it in place on the extra helmet and handed it to Burke.

"Try it," said Keller.

Burke put the helmet on his head.

He was in this same instrument-room, but he wore a uniform and he sat at an instrument-board. He knew that there were drone service-boats perhaps ten thousand miles out, perhaps a hundred. They'd been fitted out to make a mock attack on the fortress. Counter-tactics men devised them. There was reason for worry. Three times, now, drones pretending to be Enemy ships had dodged past the screen of globes set out to prevent just such an evasion. Once, one of the drones had gloatingly touched the stone of the fortress' outer surface. This was triumph for the counter-tactics crew, but it was proof that an Enemy ship could have wiped out the fortress and all its garrison a hundred times over.

Burke sweated. There was a speck with a yellow ring about it. It was a globe, poised and ready to dart in any conceivable direction if an Enemy detection-device ranged it. The globes did not go seeking an Enemy. They placed themselves where they would be sought. They set themselves up as targets. But when a radar-pulse touched them, they flung themselves at its source, their reflex chooser-circuits pouring incredible power into a beam of the same characteristics as the radar-touch. That beam, of course, paralyzed or burned out the Enemy device necessarily tuned to it. And the globes plunged at the thing which had found them. They accelerated at a hundred and sixty gravities and mere high explosive would be wasted if they carried it. Nothing could stand their impact. Nothing!

But in drills three drones had dodged them. The counter-tactics men understood the drones, of course, as it was hoped the Enemy did not. But it should not be possible to get to the fortress! If the fortress was vulnerable, so was the Empire. If the Empire was vulnerable, the Enemy would wreck its worlds, blast its cities, exterminate its population and only foulness would remain in the Galaxy.

On the monitor-board a light flashed. A line of green light darted across the screen. It was the path of a globe hurtling toward something that had touched it with a radar-frequency signal. The acceleration of the globe was breathtaking. It seemed to explode toward its target.

But this globe hit nothing. It went on and on. . . . A second globe sprang. It also struck nothing. It went away to illimitable emptiness. Its path exactly crossed that of the first. A third and fourth and fifth. . . . Each one flung itself ferociously at the source of some trickle of radiation. Their trails crossed at exactly the same spot. But there was nothing there. . . .

Burke suddenly flung up a row of switches, inactivating the remaining globes under his control. Five had flung themselves away, darting at something which radiated but did not exist. Something which was not solid. Which was not a drone ship impersonating an Enemy. They'd attacked an illusion. . . .

At the control-board, Burke clenched his fist and struck angrily at the flat surface before him. An illusion! Of course!

Cunningly, he made adjustments. He had five globes left. He chose one and changed the setting of its reflex chooser-circuit. It would ignore radar frequencies now. It would pick up only stray radiation — induction frequencies from a drone ship with its drive on.

The globe's light flashed. A train of green fire appeared. A burst of flame. A hit! The drone was destroyed. He swiftly changed the setting of the reflex circuits of the rest. Two! Three! Three drones blasted in twice as many seconds.

He mopped his forehead. This was only a drill, but when the Enemy came it would be the solution of such problems that would determine the survival of the fortress and the destruction of the Enemy.

He reported his success crisply. Burke took off the helmet.

Keller said mildly, "What did he do?"

Burke considered.

"The drone, faking to be an enemy, had dumped something out into space. Metal powder, perhaps. It made a cloud in emptiness. Then the drone drew off and threw a radar-beam on the cloud of metal particles. The beam bounced in all directions. When a globe picked it up, it shot for the phony metal-powder target. It went right through and off into space. Other globes fell for the same trick. When they were all gone, the drones could have come right up to the fort."

He was almost interested. He'd felt, at least, the sweating earnestness of an unknown member of this garrison, dead some thousands of years, as he tried to make a good showing in a battle drill.

"So he changed the reflex circuits," Burke added. "He stopped his globes from homing on radar frequencies. He made them home on frequencies that wouldn't bounce." Then he said in surprise, "But they didn't hit, at that! The drones blew up before the globes got to them! They were exploding from the burning-out of all their equipment before the globes got there!"

Keller nodded. He said sorrowfully, "So clever, our ancestors. But not clever enough!"

"Of our chances," said Burke, "or what I think are chances, the least promising seems to be the idea of trying to hook something together to fight with." He considered, and then smiled very faintly. "You saw movements you couldn't identify in the vision-plates? Sandy says she saw something alive. I wonder if something besides us answered the space-call and got info the fortress by a different way, and has been hiding out, afraid of us."

Keller shook his head.

"I don't believe it either," admitted Burke. "It seems crazy. But it might be true. It might. I'm scraping the bottom of the barrel for solutions to our problem."

Keller shook his head again. Burke shrugged and went out of the instrument-room. He went down the stairs and the first long corridor, and past the long rows of emplacements in which were set the hunkering metal monsters he'd cube-dreamed of using, but which would be of no conceivable use against speeding, whirling, artificial-gravity fields with the pull and the mass of suns.

He reached the last long gallery on which the ship-lock opened. He saw the broad white ribbon of many strands of light, reaching away seemingly without limit. And he saw a tiny figure running toward him. It was Sandy. She staggered as she ran. She had already run past endurance, but she kept desperately on, Burke broke into a run himself.

When he met her, she gasped, "Pam! She — vanished — down below! We were — looking, and Pam cried out. We ran to her. Gone! And we — heard noises! Noises! Holmes is searching now. She — screamed, Joe!"

Burke swung her behind him.

"Tell Keller," he commanded harshly. "You've got that hand-weapon? Hold on to it! Bring Keller! We'll all search! Hurry!"

He broke into a dead run.

It might have seemed ironic that he should rush to help Sandy's sister in whatever disaster had befallen her when they were facing the end of the whole solar system. In cold blood, it couldn't be considered to matter. But Burke ran.

He panted when he plunged dawn the ramp to the lower portions of the asteroid. He reached the huge cavern in which the motionless power-generator towered storeys high toward a light-laced ceiling.

"Holmes!" he shouted, and ran on. "Holmes!"

He'd been no farther than this, before, but he went on into tunnels with only double lines of light-tubes overhead, and he shouted and heard his own voice reverberating in a manner which seemed pure mockery. But as he ran be continued to shout.

And presently Holmes shouted in return. There was a process of untangling innumerable echoes, and ultimately they met. Holmes was deathly white. He carried something unbelievable in his hands.

"Here!" he growled. "I found this. I cornered it, I killed it! What is it? Did things like this catch Pam?"

Only a man beside himself could have asked such a question. Holmes carried the corpse of a bird with mottled curly feathers. He'd wrung its neck. He suddenly flung it aside.

"Where's Pam?" he demanded fiercely. "What the hell's happened to her? I'll kill anything in creation that's tried to hurt her!"

Burke snapped questions. Inane ones. Where had Pam been last? Where were Holmes and Sandy when they missed her? When she cried out?

Holmes tried to show him. But this part of the asteroid was a maze of corridors with uncountable doorways opening into innumerable compartments. Some of these compartments were not wholly empty, but neither Burke nor Holmes bothered to examine machine-parts or stacks of cases that would crumble to dust at a touch. They searched like crazy men, calling to Pam.

Keller and Sandy arrived. They'd passed the corpse of the bird Holmes had killed, and Keller was strangely white-faced. Sandy panted, "Did you find her? Have you found any sign?"

But she knew the answer. They hadn't found Pam. Holmes was haggard, desperate, filled with a murderous fury against whatever unnameable thing had taken Pam away.

"Here!" snapped Burke. "Let's get some system into this! Here's the case with the message-cube. It's our marker. We start from here! I'll follow this cross corridor and the next one. You three take the next three corridors going parallel. One each! Look in every doorway. When we reach the next cross-corridor we'll compare notes and make another marker."

He went along the way he'd chosen, looking in every door. Cryptic masses of metal in one compartment. A heap of dust in another. Empty. Empty. A pile of metal furniture. Another empty. Still another.

Holmes appeared, his hands clenching and unclenching. Sandy turned up, struggling for self-control.

"Where's Keller?"

"I heard him call out," said Sandy breathlessly. "I thought he'd found something and I hurried —"

He did not come. They shouted. They searched. Keller had disappeared. They found the mark they'd started from and retraced their steps. Burke heard Holmes swear startledly, but there were so many echoes he could not catch words.

Sandy met Burke. Holmes did not. He did not answer shouts. He was gone.

"We stay together," said Burke in an icy voice. "We've both got hand-weapons. Keep yours ready to fire. I've got mine. Whatever out of hell is loose in this place, we'll kill it or it will kill us, and then —"

He did not finish. They stayed close together, with Burke in the lead.

"We'll look in each doorway," he insisted. "Keep that pistol ready. Don't shoot the others if you see them, but shoot anything else!"

"Y-yes," said Sandy, She swallowed.

It was nerve-racking. Burke regarded each doorway as a possible ambush. He investigated each one first, making sure that the compartment inside it was wholly empty. There was one extra-large archway to an extra-large compartment, halfway between their starting point and the next cross-corridor. It was obviously empty, though there was a large metal plate on the floor. But it was lighted. Nothing could lurk in there.

Burke inspected the compartment beyond, and the one beyond that.

He thought he heard Sandy gasp. He whirled, gun ready.

Sandy was gone.

CHAPTER 10

THE STAR SOL was as bright as Sirius, but no brighter because it was nearly half a light-year away and of course could not compare in intrinsic brightness with that farther giant sun. The Milky Way glowed coldly. All the stars shone without any wavering in their light, from the brightest to the faintest tinted dot. The universe was round. There were stars above and below and before and behind and to the right and left. There was nothing which was solid, and nothing which was opaque. There were only infinitely remote, unwinking motes of light, but there were thousands of millions of them. Every where there were infinitesimal shinings of red and blue and yellow and green; of all the colors that could be imagined. Yet all the starlight from all the cosmos added up to no more than darkness. The whitest of objects would not shine except faintly, dimly, feebly. There was no warmth. This was deep space, frigid beyond imagining; desolate beyond thinking; empty. It was nothingness spread out in the light of many stars.

In such cold and darkness it would seem that nothing could be, and there was nothing to be seen. But now and again a pattern of stars quivered a little. It contracted a trace and then returned to its original appearance. The disturbance of the star-patterns moved, as a disturbance, in vast curved courses. They were like isolated ripplings in space.

There seemed no cause for these ripplings. But there were powerful gravitational fields in the void, so powerful as to warp space and bend the starlight passing through them. These gravity-fields moved with an incredible speed. There were ten of them, circling in a complex pattern which was spread out as an invisible unit which moved faster than the light their space-twisting violence distorted.

They seemed absolutely undetectable, because even such minute light-ripplings as they made were left behind them. The ten ships which created these monstrous force-fields were unbelievably small. They were no larger than cargo ships on the oceans of one planet in the solar system toward which they sped. They were less than dust particles in infinity. They would travel for only a few more days, now, and then would flash through the solar system which was their target. They should reach its outermost planet — four light-hours away — and within eight minutes more swing mockingly past and through the inner worlds and the sun. They would cross the plane of the ecliptic at nearly a right angle, and they should leave the planets and the yellow star Sol in flaming self-destruction behind them. Then they would flee onward, faster than the chaos they created could follow.

The living creatures on the world to be destroyed would have no warning. One instant everything would be as it had always been. The next, the ground would rise and froth out flames, and more than two thousand million human beings would hardly know that anything had occurred before they were destroyed.

There was no purpose to be served by notifying the world that it was to die. The rulers of the nations had decided that it was kinder to let men and women look at each other and rejoice, thinking they had all their lives before them. It was kinder that children should be let play valorously, and babies wail and instantly be tended. It was better for humanity to move unknowing under blue and sunshine-filled skies than that they should gaze despairingly up at white clouds, or in still deeper horror at the shining night stars from which devastation would presently come.

In the one place where there was foreknowledge, no attention at all was paid to the coming doom. Burke went raging about brightly lighted corridors, shouting horrible things. He cried out to Sandy to answer him, and defied whatever might have seized her to dare to face him. He challenged the cold stone walls. He raged up and down the gallery in which she had vanished, and feverishly explored beyond it, and returned to the place where she had disappeared, and pounded on solid rock to see if there could be some secret doorway through which she had been abducted. It seemed that his heart must stop for pure anguish. He knew such an agony of frustration as he had never known before.

Presently method developed in his searching. Whatever had happened, it must have been close to the tall archway with the large metal plate in its floor and the brilliant lights overhead. Sandy could not have been more than twenty feet from him when she was seized. When he heard her gasp, he was at this spot. Exactly this spot. He'd whirled, and she was gone. She could not have been farther than the door beyond the archway, or else the one facing it. He went into the most probable one. It was a perfectly commonplace storage-room. He'd seen hundreds of them. It was empty. He examined it with a desperate intentness. His hands shook. His whole body was taut. He moved jerkily.

Nothing. He crossed the corridor and examined the room opposite. There was a bit of dust in one corner. He bent stay and fingered it. Nothing. He came out, and there was the tall archway, brightly lighted. The other compartments had no light-tubes. Being for storage only, they would not need to be lighted except to be filled and emptied of whatever they should contain. But the archway was very brilliantly lighted.

He went into it, his hand-weapon shaking with the tension in him. There was the metal plate on the floor. It was huge — yards in extent. He began a circuit of the walls. Halfway around, he realized that the walls were masonry. Not native rock, like every other place in the fortress. This wall had been made! He stared about. On the opposite wall there was a small thing with a handle on it, to be moved up or down. It was a round metal disk with a handle, set in in masonry.

He flung himself across the room to examine it. He was filled with terror for Sandy, which would turn into more-than-murderous fury if he found her harmed. The metal floor-plate lay between. He stepped obliviously on the plate . . .

The universe dissolved around him. The brightly lit masonry wall became vague and misty. Simultaneously quite other things appeared mistily, then solidified.

He was abruptly in the open air, with a collapsed and ruined structure about and behind him. This was not emptiness, but the surface of a world. Over his head there was a sunset sky. Before him there was grass, and beyond that a horizon, and to his left there was collapsed stonework and far off ahead there was a hill which he knew was not a natural hill at all. There was a moon in the sky, a half-moon with markings that he remembered. There were trees, too, and they were trees with long, ribbony leaves such as never grew on Earth.

He stood frozen for long instants, and a second, smaller moon came up rapidly over the horizon and traveled swiftly across the sky. It was jagged and irregular in shape.

Then flutings came from somewhere to his rear. They were utterly familiar sounds. They had distinctive pitch, which varied from one to another, and they were of different durations like half-notes and quarter-notes in music. And they had a plaintive quality which could have been termed elfin.

All this was so completely known to him that it should have been shocking, but he was in such an agony of fear for Sandy that he could not react to it. His terror for her was breath-stopping. He held his weapon ready in his hand. He tried to call her name, but he could not speak.

The long, ribbony leaves of the trees waved to and fro in a gentle breeze. And then Burke saw a figure running behind the swaying foliage. He knew who it was. The relief was almost greater pain than his terror had been. It was such an emotion as Burke had experienced only feebly, even in his recurrent dream. He gave a great shout and bounded forward to meet Sandy, crying out again as he ran.

Then he had his arms about her, and she clung to him with that remarkable ability women have to adapt themselves to circumstances they've been hoping for, even when they come unexpectedly. He kissed her feverishly, panting incoherent things about the fear he'd felt, holding her fast.

Presently somebody tugged at his elbow. It was Holmes. He said drily, "I know how you feel, Burke. I acted the same way just now, But there are things to be looked into. It'll be dark soon and we don't know how long night lasts here. Have you a match?"

Pam regarded the two of them with a peculiar glint of humor in her eyes. Keller was there too, still shaken by an experience which for him had no emotional catharsis attached.

Burke partly released Sandy and fumbled for his cigarette lighter. He felt singularly foolish, but Sandy showed no trace of embarrassment.

"There was a matter-transposer," she said, "and we found it, and we all came through it."

Keller said awkwardly, "I turned on the communicator to base. It must have been a matter-transposer. I thought, in the instrument-room, that it was only a communicator."

Holmes moved away. He came back bearing broken sticks, which were limbs fallen from untended trees. He piled them and went back for more. In minutes he had a tiny fire and a big pile of branches to keep it up, but he went back for still more.

"It works both ways," observed Sandy. "Or something does! There must be another metal plate here to go to the fortress. That huge, crazy bird I saw in the gravity-generator room must have come from here. He probably stepped on the plate because it was brightly lighted and —"

"You've got your pistol?" demanded Burke.

The sunset sky was darkening. The larger, seemingly stationary moon floated ever-so-slightly nearer to the zenith. The small and jagged moon had gone on out of sight.

"I have," said Sandy. "Pam gave hers to Holmes. But that's all right. There won't be savages. Over there, beyond the trees, there's a metal railing, impossibly old and corroded. But no savage would leave metal alone. I don't think there's anybody here but us."

Burke stared at something far away that looked like a hill.

"There's a building, or the ruins of one. No lights. No smoke. Savages would occupy it. We're alone, all right! I wonder where? We could be anywhere within a hundred or five hundred light-years from Earth."

"Then," said Sandy comfortably, "we should be safe from the Enemy."

"No," said Burke. "If the Enemy has an unbeatable weapon, destroying one solar system won't be enough. They'd smash every one that humanity ever used. Which includes this one. They'll be here eventually. Not at once, but later. They'll come!"

He looked at the small fire. There were curious, familiar fragrances in the air. Over to the west the san sank in a completely orthodox glory of red and gold. The larger moon swam serenely in the sky.

"I'm afraid," said Pam, "that we won't eat tonight unless we can get back to the fortress and the ship. I guess we're farther from our dinners than most people ever get. Did you say five hundred light-years?"

"Ask Keller," grunted Burke. "I've got to think."

Far off in the new night there was something like a bird-song, though it might come from anything at all. Much nearer there were peculiarly maternal clucking noises. They sounded as if they might come from a bird with a caricature of a bill and stumpy, useless wings. There was a baying noise, very far away indeed, and Burke remembered that the ancestry of dogs on Earth was as much a mystery as the first appearance of mankind. There were no wild ancestors of either race. Perhaps there had been dogs with the garrison of the fortress, which might be five hundred light-years away, in one sense, but could not be more than a few yards, in another.

Holmes squatted by the fire and built it up to brightness. Keller came back to the circle of flickering light. His forehead was creased.

"The constellations," he said unhappily. "They're gone!"

"Which would mean," Burke told him absently, "that we're more than forty light-years from home. They'd all be changed at that distance."

Holmes seated himself beside Pam. They had reached an obvious understanding. Burke's eyes wandered in their direction. Holmes began to speak in a low tone, and Pam smiled at him. Burke jerked his head to stare at Sandy.

"I think I forgot something. Should I ask you again to marry me? Or do I take it for granted that you will? — if we live through this?" He didn't wait for her answer. "Things have changed, Sandy," he said gruffly. "Mostly me. I've gotten rid of an obsession and acquired a fixation — on you."

"There," said Sandy warmly, "there speaks my Joseph! Yes, I'll marry you. And we will live through this! You'll figure something out, Joe. I don't know how, but you will!"

"Yes-s-s," said Burke slowly. "Somehow I feel that I've got something tucked away in my head that should apply. I need to get it out and look it over. I don't know what it is or where it came from, but I've got something . . ."

He stared into the fire, Sandy nestled confidently against him. She put her hand in his. The wind blew warm and softly through the trees. Presently Holmes replenished the fire.

Burke looked up with a start as Sandy said, "I've thought of something, Joe! Do you remember that dream of yours? I know what it was!"

"What?"

"It came from a black cube," said Sandy, "which was a cube that somebody from the garrison took to Earth. And what kind of cube would they take? They wouldn't take drill-instruction cubes! They wouldn't take cubes telling them how to service the weapons or operate the globes or whatever else the fortress has! Do you know what they'd take?"

He shook his head.

"Novels," said Sandy. "Fiction stories. Adventure tales. To — experience on long winter evenings or even asleep by a campfire. They were fighting men, Joe, those ancestors of ours. They wouldn't care about science, but they'd like a good, lusty love story or a mystery or whatever was the equivalent of a Western twenty thousand years ago. You got hold of a page in a love story, Joe!"

"Probably," he growled. "But if I ever dream it again I'll know who's behind those waving branches. You." Then, surprised, he said, "There were flutings when I came through the matter-transposer. They've stopped."

"They sounded when I came through, too. And when Pam and Holmes and Keller came. Do you know what I think they are?" Sandy smiled up at him. "'You have arrived on the planet Sandu. Surface-travel facilities to the left, banking service and baggage to the right, tourist accommodations and information straight ahead.' We may never know, Joe, but it could be that!"

He made an inarticulate sound and stared at the fire again. She fell silent. Soon Keller was dozing. Holmes strode away and came back dragging leafy branches. He made a crude lean-to for Pam, to reflect back the warmth of the fire upon her. She curled up, smiled at him, and went confidently to sleep. A long time later Sandy found herself yawning. She slipped her fingers from Burke's hand and settled down beside Pam.

Burke seemed not to notice. He was busy. He thought very carefully, running through the information he'd received from the black cubes. He carefully refrained from thinking of the desperate necessity for a solution to the problem of the Enemy. If it was to be solved, it would be by a mind working without strain, just as a word that eludes the memory is best recalled when one no longer struggles to remember it.

Twice during the darkness Holmes regarded the blackness about them with suspicion, his hand on the small weapon Pam had passed to him. But nothing happened. There were sounds like bird calls, and songs like those of insects, and wind in the trees. But there was nothing else.

When gray first showed in the east, Burke shook himself. The jagged small moon rose hurriedly and floated across the sky.

"Holmes," said Burke reflectively. "I think I've got what we want. You know how artificial gravity's made, what the circuit is like."

To anybody but Holmes and Keller, the comment would have seemed idiotic. It would have seemed insane even to them, not too long before. But Holmes nodded.

"Yes. Of course. Why?"

"There's a chooser-circuit in the globes," said Burke carefully, "that picks up radiation from an Enemy ship, and multiplies it enormously and beams it back. The circuit that made the radiation to begin with has to be resonant to it, as the globe burns it out while dashing down its own beam."

"Naturally," said Holmes. "What about it?"

"The point is," said Burke, "that one could treat a suddenly increasing gravity-field as radiation. Not a stationary one, of course. But one that increased, fast. Like the gravity-fields of the Enemy ships, moving faster than light toward our sun."

"Hmmmm," said Holmes. "Yes. That could be done. But hitting something that's traveling faster than light —"

"They're traveling in a straight line," said Burke, "except for orbiting around each other every few hours. There's no faster-than-light angular velocity; just straight-line velocity. And with the artificial mass they've got, they couldn't conceivably dodge. If we got some globes tricked up to throw a beam of gravity-field back at the Enemy ships, there might be resonance, and there's a chance that one might hit, too."

Holmes considered.

"It might take half an hour to change the circuit," he observed. "Maybe less. There'd be no way in the world to test them. But they might work. We'd want a lot of them on the job, though, to give the idea a fair chance."

Burke stood up, creaking a little from long immobility.

"Let's hunt for the way back to the fortress," he said. "There is a way. At least two crazy birds were marching around in the fortress' corridors."

Holmes nodded again. They began a search. Matter transposed from the fortress — specifically, the five of them — came out in a nearly three-walled alcove in the side of what had once been a magnificent building. Now it was filled with the trunks and stalks of trees and vines which grew out of every window-opening. There were other, similar alcoves, as if other matter-transposers to other outposts or other worlds had been centered here. They were looking for one that a plump, ridiculous bird might blunder into among the broken stones.

They found a metal plate partly arched-over by fallen stones in the very next alcove. They hauled at the tumbled rock. Presently the way was clear.

"Come along!" called Burke. "We've got a job to do! You girls want to fix breakfast and we want to get to work. We've a few hundred light-years to cross before we can have our coffee."

Somehow he felt no doubt whatever. The five of them walked onto the corroded metal plate together, and the sky faded and ghosts of tube-lights appeared and became brilliant, and they stepped off the plate into a corridor one section removed from the sending-transposer which had translated them all, successively, to wherever they had been.

And everything proceeded matter-of-factly. The three men went to the room where metal globes by hundreds waited for the defenders of the fortress to make use of them. They were completely practical, those globes. There were even small footholds sunk into their moving sides so a man could climb to their tops and inspect or change the apparatus within.

On the way, Burke explained to Keller. The globes were designed to be targets, and targets they would remain. They'd be set out in the path of the coming Enemy ships, which could not vary their courses. Their circuits would be changed to treat the suddenly increasing gravitational fields as radiation, so that they would first project back a monstrous field of the same energy, and then dive down it to presumed collision with the ships. There was a distinct possibility that if enough globes could be gotten out in space, that at the least they might hit one enemy ship and so wreck the closely orbited grouping. From that reasonable first possibility, the chances grew slimmer, but the results to be hoped for increased.

Keller nodded, brightly. He'd used the reading helmets more than anybody else. He understood. Moreover, his mind was trained to work in just this field.

When they reached the room of the many spheres he gestured for Burke and Holmes to wait. He climbed the footholds of one globe, deftly removed its top, and looked inside. The conductors were three-inch bars of pure silver. He reached in and did this and that. He climbed down and motioned for Burke and Holmes to look.

It took them long seconds to realize what he'd done. But with his knowledge of what could be done, once he was told what was needed, he'd made exactly three new contacts and the globe was transformed to Burke's new specifications.

Instead of days required to modify the circuits, the three of them had a hundred of the huge round weapons changed over within an hour. Then Keller went up to the instrument-room and painstakingly studied the launching system. He began the launchings while Holmes and Burke completed the change-over task. They joined him in the instrument-room when the last of the metal spheres rose a foot from the stony floor of the magazine and went lurching unsteadily over to the breech of the launching-tube they hadn't noticed before.

"Three hundred," said Keller in a pleased tone, later. "All going out at full acceleration to meet the Enemy. And there are six observer-globes in the lot."

"Observers," said Burke grimly. "That's right. We can't observe anything because the information would come back at the speed of light. But if we lose, the Enemy will arrive before we can know we've lost."

Keller shook his head reproachfully.

"Oh, no! Oh, no! I just understood. There are transposers of electric energy, too. Very tiny. In the observers."

Burke stared. But it was only logical. If matter could be transposed instead of transmitted between distant places, assuredly miniature energy-transposers were not impossible. The energy would no more travel than transposed matter would move. It would be transposed. The fortress would see what the observer-globes saw, at the instant they saw it, no matter what the distance!

Keller glanced at the ten-foot disk with its many small lights and the writhing bright-red sparks which were the Enemy gravity-ships. There was something like a scale of distances understood, now. The red sparks had been not far from the disk's edge when the first space call went out to Earth. They were nearer the center when the spaceship arrived here. They were very, very near the center now.

"Five days," said Burke in a hard voice. "Where will the globes meet them?"

"They're using full acceleration," Keller reminded him gently. "One hundred sixty gravities."

"A mile a second acceleration," said Burke. Somehow he was not astonished. "In an hour, thirty-six hundred miles per second. In ten hours, thirty-six thousand miles per second. If they hit at that speed, they'd smash a moon! They'll cover half a billion miles in ten hours — but that's not enough! It's only a fifth of the way to Pluto! They won't be halfway to Uranus!"

"They'll have fifty-six hours," said Keller. The need to communicate clearly made him almost articulate. "Not on the plane of the ecliptic. Their course is along the line of the sun's axis. Meeting, seven times Pluto's distance. Twenty billion miles. Two days and a half. If they miss we'll know."

Holmes growled, "If they miss, what then?"

"I stay here," said Keller, mildly. "I won't outlive everybody. I'd be lonely." Then he gave a quick, embarrassed smile. "Breakfast must be ready. We can do nothing but wait."

But waiting was not easy.

On the first day there came a flood of messages from Earth. Why had they cut off communication? Answer! Answer! Answer! What could be done about the Enemy ships? What could be done to save lives? If a few spaceships could be completed and take off before the solar system shattered, would the asteroid be shattered too? Could a few dozen survivors of Earth hope to make their way to the asteroid and survive there? Should the coming doom be revealed to the world?

The last question showed that the authorities of Earth were rattled. It was not a matter for Burke or Keller or Holmes to decide. They transmitted, in careful code, an exact description of the sending of the globes to try to intercept the Enemy gravity-ships. But it was not possible for people with no experiential knowledge of artificial gravity to believe that anything so massive as a sun could be destroyed by hurling a mere ten-foot missile at it!

Then there came a sudden revulsion of feeling on Earth. The truth was too horrible to believe, so it was resolved not to believe it. And therefore prominent persons broke into public print, denouncing Burke for having predicted the end of the world from his safe refuge in Asteroid M-387. They explained elaborately how he must be not only wrong but maliciously wrong.

But those denunciations were the first knowledge the public had possessed of the thing denounced. Some people instantly panicked because some people infallibly believe the worst, at all times. Some shared the indignation of the eminent characters who denounced Burke. Some were bewildered and many unstable persons vehemently urged everybody to do this or that in order to be saved. Get-rich-artists sold tickets in non-existent spacecraft they claimed had secrecy been built in anticipation of the disaster. They would accept only paper currency in small bills. What value paper money would have after the destruction of Earth was not explained, but people paid it. Astronomers swore quite truthfully that no telescope gave any sign of the alleged sun-sized masses en route to destroy Earth. Government officials heroically lied in their throats to reassure the populace because, after all, one didn't want the half-civilized part of educated nations to run mad during Earth's probable last few days.

And Burke and the others looked at the images sent back by the observer-globes traveling with the rest. The cosmos looked to the observer-globes just about the way it did from the fortress. There were innumerable specks of light of enumerable tints and colors. There was darkness. There was cold. And there was emptiness. The globe-fleet drove on away from the sun and from that flat plane near which all the planets revolve. Every second the spheres' pace increased by one mile per second. Ten hours after Keller released them, they had covered five hundred eighty-eight thousand thousand miles and the sun still showed as a perceptible disk. Twenty hours out, the globes had traveled two billion six hundred million miles and the sun was the brightest star the observers could note. Thirty hours out, and the squadron of ten-foot globes had traveled five billion eight hundred thirty-odd million miles and the sun was no longer an outstanding figure in the universe.

Holmes looked fine-drawn, now, and Pam was fidgety. Keller appeared to be wholly normal. And Sandy was conspicuously calm.

"I'll be glad when this is over," she said at dinner in the ship in the lock-tunnel. "I don't think any of you realize what this fortress and the matter-transposer and the planet it took us to — I don't believe any of you realize what such things can mean to people."

Burke waited. She smiled at him and said briskly, "There's a vacant planet for people to move to. People occupied it once. They can do it again. Once it had a terrific civilization. This fortress was just one of its outposts. There were plenty of other forts and other planets, and the people had sciences away ahead of ours. And all those worlds, tamed and ready, are waiting right now for us to come and use them."

Holmes said, "Yes? What happened to the people who lived on them?"

"If you ask me," said Sandy confidentially, "I think they went the way of Greece and Rome. I think they got so civilized that they got soft. They built forts instead of fighting fleets. They stopped thinking of conquests and begrudged even thinking of defenses, though they had to, after a fashion. But they thought of things like the Rhine forts of the Romans, and Hadrian's Wall. Like the Great Wall of China, and the Maginot Line in France. When men build forts and don't build fighting fleets, they're on the way down."

Burke said nothing. Holmes waited for more.

"It's my belief," said Sandy, "that many, many centuries ago the people who built this fort sent a spaceship off somewhere with a matter-transposer on board. They replaced its crew while it traveled on and on, and they gave it supplies, and refreshed its air, and finally it arrived somewhere at the other side of the Galaxy. And then the people here set up a matter-transposer and they all moved through it to the new, peaceful, lovely world they'd found. All except the garrison that was left behind. The Enemy would never find them there! And I think they smashed the matter-transposer that might have let the Enemy follow them — or the garrison of this fort, for that matter! And I think that away beyond the Milky Way there are the descendants of those people. They're soft, and pretty, and useless, and they've likely let their knowledge die, and there probably aren't very many of them left. And I think it's good riddance!"

Pam said, "If we beat the Enemy there'll be no excuse for wars on Earth. There'll be worlds enough to take all the surplus population anybody can imagine. There'll be riches for everybody. Joe, what do you think the human race will do for you if, on top of finding new worlds for everybody, you cap it by defeating the Enemy with the globes?"

"I think," said Burke, "that most people will dislike me very much. I'll be in the history books, but I'll be in small print. People who can realize they're obligated will resent it, and those who can't will think I got famous in a disreputable fashion. In fact, if we go back to Earth, I'll probably have to fight to keep from going bankrupt. If I manage to get enough money for a living, it'll be by having somebody ghostwrite a book for me about our journey here."

Keller interrupted mildly, "It's nearly time. We should watch."

Holmes stood up jerkily. Pam and Sandy rose almost reluctantly.

They went out of the ship and through the metal door with rounded corners. They went along the long corridor with the seeming river of light-tubes in its ceiling. They passed the doorway of the great room which had held the globes. It looked singularly empty, now.

On the next level they passed the mess-halls and bunk-rooms, and an the third the batteries of grisly weapons which could hurl enormous charges of electricity at a chosen target, if the target could be ranged. They went on up into the instrument-room by the final flight of stairs.

They settled down there. That is, they did not leave. But far too much depended on the next hour or less for anybody to be truly still in either mind or body. Holmes paced jerkily back and forth, his eyes on the vision-screens that now relayed what the observer-globes with the globe-fleet saw.

For a long time they gazed at the emptiness of deepest space. The picture was of an all-encompassing wall of tiny flecks of light. They did not move. They did not change. They did not waver. The observer-globes reported from nothingness, and they reported nothing.

Except one item. There were fewer red specks of light and more blue ones. There were some which were distinctly violet. The globes had attained a velocity so close to the speed of light that no available added power could have pushed them the last fraction of one per cent faster. But they had no monstrous mass-fields to change the constants of space and let them travel more swiftly. The Enemy ships did. But there was no sign of them. There could be none except on such a detector as the instrument-room had in its ten-foot transparent disk.

Time passed, and passed. And passed. Finally, Burke broke the silence.

"Of course the globes don't have to make direct hits. We hope! If they multiply the gravity-field that hits them and shoot it back hard enough, it ought to burn out the gravity-generators in the ships."

There was no answer. Pam watched the screens and bit nervously at her nails.

Seconds went by. Minutes. Tens of minutes. . . .

"I fear," said Keller with some difficulty, "that something is wrong. Perhaps I erred in adjusting the globes —"

If he had made a mistake, of course, the globe-fleet would be useless. It wouldn't stop the Enemy. It wouldn't do anything, and in a very short time the sun and all its planets would erupt with insensate violence, and all the solar system would shatter itself to burning bits — and the Enemy fleet would be speeding away faster than exploding matter could possibly follow it.

Then, without warning, a tiny bluish line streaked across one of the screens. A second. A third-fourth-fifth-twentieth-fiftieth — The screens came alive with flashing streaks of blue-green light.

Then something blew. A sphere of violet light appeared on one of the screens. Instantly, it was followed by others with such rapidity that it was impossible to tell which followed which. But there were ten of them.

The silence in the instrument-room was absolute. Burke tried vainly to imagine what had actually happened. The Enemy fleet had been traveling at thirty times the speed of light, which was only possible because of its artificial mass which changed the properties of space to permit it. And then the generators and maintainers of that artificial mass blew out. The ships stopped — so suddenly, so instantly, so absolutely that a millionth part of a second would have been a thousand times longer than the needed interval.

The energy of that enormous speed had to be dissipated. The ships exploded as nothing had ever exploded before. Even a super-nova would not detonate with such violence. The substance of the Enemy ships destroyed itself not merely by degenerating to raw atoms, but by the atoms destroying themselves. And not merely did the atoms fly apart, but the neutrons and protons and electrons of which they were composed ceased to exist. Nothing was left but pure energy — violet light. And it vanished.

Then there was nothing at all. What was left of the globe-fleet went hurtling uselessly onward through space. It would go on and on and on. It would reach the edge of the galaxy and go on, and perhaps in thousands of millions of years some one or two or a dozen of the surviving spheres might penetrate some star-cloud millions of millions of light-years away.

In a pleased voice, Keller said, "I think everything is all right now."

And Sandy went all to pieces. She clung to Burke, weeping uncontrollably, holding herself close to him while she sobbed.

On Earth, of course, there was no such eccentric jubilation. It was observed that crawling red sparks in the gravity-field detectors winked out. As hours and days went by, it was noticed that the solar system continued to exist, and that people stayed alive. It became evident that some part of the terror some people had felt was baseless. And naturally there was much resentment against Burke because he had caused so many people so much agitation.

Within two weeks a fleet of small plastic ships hurtled upward from the vicinity of Earth's north magnetic pole and presently steadied on course toward the fortress asteroid. Burke was informed severely that he should prepare to receive the scientists they carried. He would be expected to cooperate fully in their investigations.

He grinned when Pam handed him the written sheet.

"It's outrageous!" snapped Sandy. "It's ridiculous! They ought to get down on their knees to you, Joe, to thank you for what you've done!"

Burke shook his head.

"I don't think I'd like that. Neither would you. We'd make out, Sandy. There'll be a colony started on that world the matter-transposer links us to. It ought be fun living there. What say?"

Sandy grumbled. But she looked at him with soft eyes.

"I'd rather be mixed up with — what you might call pioneers," said Burke, "than people with reputations to defend and announced theories that are going to turn out to be all wrong. The research in this fortress and on that planet will make some red faces, on Earth. And there's another thing."

"What?" asked Sandy.

"This war we've inherited without doing anything to deserve it," said Burke. "In fact, the Enemy. We haven't the least idea what they're like or anything at all about them except that they go off somewhere and spend a few thousand years cooking up something lethal to throw at us. They tired out our ancestors. If they'd only known it, they won the war by default. Our ancestors moved away to let the Enemy have its own way about this part of the galaxy, anyhow. And judging by past performances, the Enemy will just stew somewhere until they think of something more dangerous than artificial sun-masses riding through our solar systems."

"Well?" she demanded. "What's to be done about that?"

"With the right sort of people around," said Burke meditatively, "we could do a little contriving of our own. And we could get a ship ready and think about looking them up and pinning their ears back in their own bailiwick, instead of waiting for them to take pot-shots at us."

Sandy nodded gravely. She was a woman. She hadn't the faintest idea of ever letting Burke take off into space again if she could help it —

unless, perhaps, for one occasion when she would show herself off in a veil and a train, gloating.

But it had taken the Enemy a very long time to concoct this last method of attack. When the time came to take the offensive against them, at least a few centuries would have passed. Five or six, anyhow. So Sandy did not protest against an idea that wouldn't result in action for some hundreds of years. Argument about Burke's share in such an enterprise could wait.

So Sandy kissed him.